The Steins:
Portrait of a Jewish-American Family

Milton Cohen

First published in 2025 by Blossom Spring Publishing
The Steins: Portrait of a Jewish-American Family
© 2025 Milton Cohen
ISBN 978-1-0684329-3-4
E: admin@blossomspringpublishing.com
W: www.blossomspringpublishing.com

To Florence

Part I: The Patriarch

1.

Mordecai Stein's grandchildren sometimes referred to him as 'the patriarch'. Because his own parents never made it out of Russia, he was the oldest ancestor they knew. That hadn't been the plan, of course. When Mordecai and his sister, Chava, were sent ahead in 1912, the family planned to follow soon after with his parents, two younger brothers and a younger sister. But things kept getting in the way of their departure.

First, his father, Schmuel, was reluctant to leave. The farm that the family operated was doing well; the harvests had been good these past few years, and the Steins were permitted to keep a share of the wheat they raised. Not just Jews, but peasants too came from the nearby town of Motal to grind their wheat on the Steins' mill. So why give up a prosperous farm, even if you didn't own it, for the uncertain future of emigrating, with its difficult journey to a port, probably Danzig, the long boat trip in steerage and an unknown future in America? Schmuel's brother Yitzhak had made the journey in 1907, and his letters raved about the freedom and opportunity that he and his young family enjoyed in America. He never mentioned his sweatshop work or the squalid living conditions on the Lower East Side of New York. Yitzhak urged his brother to make the leap he would never regret. And why risk another pogrom at the Czar's whim? The last one had burned down the homes of many Motal Jews. Schmuel had his doubts, however. His brother had always been optimistic and tended to exaggerate — a sunny disposition contrasting Schmuel's gloomy pessimism, which his exasperated wife, Rachel, had called typically Russian.

When the Great War broke out in 1914, it also held them back. Crossing enemy borders was out of the question. They would have to ride out that storm where they were: in the southwestern corner of what is now Belarus. Fortunately, Schmuel's bad leg kept him out of the Russian Army, and his sons were too young. The influenza outbreak also took its toll, killing one of Mordecai's brothers and leaving his mother permanently weakened. Then, the Bolsheviks' war with Poland in 1919 again closed the borders. By the time they reopened, the family's enthusiasm for the big journey to America had faded. Despite his ingrained pessimism, Schmuel had hopes that the Bolsheviks would keep their promise of giving the peasants land of their own. After all, the Reds had pulled out of the Great War, as they had promised. And if the peasants received land, then why not the Jews, who made up a big part of the Bolshevik government under Lenin? Sit tight and wait was Schmuel's view.

Meanwhile, Mordecai and Chava had made the journey and slowly adjusted to America. After what seemed an endlessly miserable boat trip in steerage, during which they were seasick much of the time, they were finally allowed to go up on deck as the ship pulled into Ambrose Channel. People were all on one side of the ship, pointing to and talking about a large statue on its own little island.

"What is that?" Chava asked her older brother.

"I don't know. I overheard a man saying it represents liberty. American liberty."

"What's 'liberty'?"

"I'm not sure. It means freedom, I think. Freedom to do what you want, maybe. Without having to fear a pogrom."

"That would be wonderful," Chava breathed. "She's holding a book of some sort. What does that mean?"

"It has the names of little girls who ask so many questions that they'll be sent back. Come. Let's get our belongings. We'll be leaving the ship soon."

They were met at Ellis Island by Uncle Yitzhak, a big bear of a man with black curly hair and a bushy black beard. He vouched for them to the authorities, showed enough money to get them through Immigration and told them what a wonderful future they had in store. America was truly a land of wonders, he said, as they would soon see in the towering buildings that their horse-drawn trolley would pass en route to Mott Street. He was right, and their necks hurt from craning them left and right to take in these endless buildings. Arriving at Mott Street was a letdown, however. Yitzhak's wife, Minna, and their three children were notably cooler in greeting their relations. Their railroad flat on the fifth floor of a shabby tenement was already crowded. Now, the daughter would have to share her bed with Chava, while Mordecai would sleep on a skinny mattress on the parlor floor.

Getting used to the crowded Lower East Side took time. The farm they had left had fresh air and open space; in fact, the woodland was so thinly populated that wolves felt free to show themselves in the distance. Mordecai had even shot at some from the back porch of the farmhouse. Mott Street, by contrast, was teeming with food stalls, horse-drawn carts, and hawking, bartering, bickering, noisy people. Noise was a constant; so was horseshit in the street, and dark stairways of tenement buildings smelling of cabbage and sometimes urine. And people — nearly all Jews — were everywhere, sitting on tenement steps, arguing in groups, shopping; boys Mordecai's age playing stoopball and (in alleys) stickball; girls like Chava playing jacks or hopscotch. Altogether, another world from slow, quiet, sparse, rural Motal.

When Mordecai's family didn't follow in the next few months, his homesickness intensified, and he especially missed his mother. His Aunt Minna had her own family to worry about. The cool reception he and Chava had received from their aunt and cousins grew noticeably colder, except for the ebullient Yitzhak. Five months after his relatives' arrival, he came home with exciting news: the family was moving to Detroit! He had never liked stooping over the patterns he had to cut in a Third Avenue sweatshop — he could barely straighten his back after a ten-hour day. And he had heard that Detroit was thriving with new automobile factories and much higher-paying jobs. Although Mordecai, at fourteen, was already enrolled in elementary school and was learning English quickly (Chava even quicker), he was eager for this new adventure. Perhaps they would find a nicer place on a quieter street. He gladly gave up his job selling newspapers on a street corner at 6 a.m. — doubtless, he could find the same job in Detroit. With varying degrees of eagerness, the family packed for its move. Even the train ride would be an adventure and show them much more of America. Fortunately, Yitzhak had set aside enough money to help them get settled before he found that better job. America was all about better jobs.

Detroit lived up to its reputation. It was indeed thriving in the fall of 1912. Ford's was selling Model-Ts hand over fist, and a dozen other Detroit auto makers were also doing well. The city was expanding rapidly with tax dollars providing new parks, new schools, a stately art museum and central library, and wide boulevards fanning out from the downtown like spokes from a hub. New neighborhoods of all sorts were springing up, some quite posh like Indian Village on the East Side and Chicago and Boston Boulevards on the West. More common were working-class neighborhoods like Delray and Hamtramck with their small, look-alike clapboard homes to house the workers of the car factories and their numerous subsidiaries. The Steins, however, settled on Hastings Street, where many Jewish immigrants lived. And much to the family's disappointment, Hastings Steet wasn't so very different from Mott Street: crowded, noisy, dirty. Still, the family flat was larger. Chava and Katya Stein now shared a room not a bed, as did Mordecai and the two Stein boys, neither of whom he particularly liked. But at least he was no longer sleeping on the floor and feeling mice running over his toes.

As he'd expected, he found another job selling newspapers. But this time, instead of standing on freezing street corners in the Detroit winter, he had a news route of some sixty customers, which kept him moving and thus fairly warm. Since the customers were bunched in the various apartment buildings on Hastings, it took little time to deliver his papers each morning. And he made a dollar and a half a week, which he could contribute to his room and board. The only drawback was that some of the other newsboys were rough, and while waiting for the papers to come in, they liked to pick fights with foreigners, especially Jewish foreigners. There was no ducking it — Mordecai had to learn how to use his fists and exulted the morning he gave a Polish bully a bloody nose. Gradually,

5

they learned to leave him alone.

His elementary school was a short walk. He was put in the eighth grade, appropriate for his age of fourteen, but not for his poor English. That required an additional class in the afternoon. But he liked school, did well and even made a few friends. Chava, at twelve, had started playing a third-hand violin that Uncle Yitzhak had bought for his own indifferent children; resignedly, he soon paid for lessons that he had intended for them. At least he could afford them because his assembly-line job at the Maxwell auto plant was paying him more than double what he'd made as a pattern cutter in New York. He was already planning to move the family to a better location on Twelfth Street, where the more prosperous Jews lived.

Mordecai had his own plans. Next fall, when he was fifteen, he would have gone on to Eastern High School, but he was determined to follow Uncle Yitzhak's example and get a good-paying factory job. Ford Motor had announced it would begin paying the unheard of sum of five dollars *a day* for eight hours work, about twice the going rate. Since Mordecai was big for his age, he could easily pass for sixteen, the minimum age for employment. But before he left Balch Elementary, he needed to speak with his favorite teacher, Miss Ryan.

Cornelia Ryan seemed to take a special interest in Mordecai Stein's progress. Not that he was the only recent immigrant she taught — her enrollment lists at Balch Elementary were a conglomeration of Eastern European, Irish and Italian names. But something about Mordecai's eagerness to learn appealed to her. (His wavy dark hair and dark eyes didn't hurt either, but she refused to admit that to herself.) He was rapidly progressing in his English and would soon no longer need the remedial class she taught after school. It was at the end of this class in March that he shyly approached her desk.

"Hello, Mordecai," she said, in her professionally chipper voice, putting away her instructional pamphlet. "Did you want to see me about something? You're making excellent progress. Next year at Eastern, you won't need any extra classes in English."

"That's what I wanted to talk with you about, Miss Ryan, if you have a moment."

"Why, of course," she said, turning toward him. "What can I help you with?"

"Well, I don't plan to go on to high school." He knew she would be disappointed, but it couldn't be helped. "I need to start working and earning money. To help out at home." He would have explained about his and Chava's burden for Uncle Yitzhak's family, but it seemed too complicated.

"Well, I certainly understand that need. Unfortunately, many of our students have to drop out and never go on to high school. But I won't say I'm not disappointed in your case. You show a special knack for learning, and I think you could go far with the right education."

"That's what I wanted to talk with you about, Miss Ryan," he said eagerly. "You see, I want to keep learning on my own, maybe at night if I'm not too tired. I could check books out of the library and read on my own. Educate myself, sort of. But I don't know which books or what writers to read. There are so many, so much to know."

"You could also enroll in night classes," Miss Ryan added. "If you stayed with it long enough, you could still get your high school diploma."

"Yes, I could do that," Mordecai agreed. "But I would

like to ask a very big favor — is it 'of you'?"

"Yes, that's correct. 'Of you'."

"Well, I would like you to write down a list of authors and books you think I should read to be an educated man. Just because I'm going to work, I don't want to be — what's the right word? — ignorant all my life. Or, we'd say at home, a *dummkopf*, a dummy."

"That's quite a task, to write such a list," Miss Ryan laughed. "But I must say I'm impressed with your ambition — and goal. Yes, of course, I'll write one. It will take me a while, though, perhaps a week. So, let's plan to discuss it a week from today after this class."

"Yes, that would be fine," Mordecai said. His heart was racing; he felt he was beginning to take control of his life. Perhaps Miss Ryan's Irish good looks also had something to do with that racing. She had red hair, something Mordecai wasn't used to seeing, and milky white skin. He thought he saw some light freckles on her face.

A week later, she handed him a list two pages long. "This is the best I could come up with on such short notice," she said. "Let me go over it with you." She pulled up her chair next to his desk.

"I've divided it into categories, and I asked myself the same question you asked me: what should an educated man know? What does it mean to be educated? I think it means that you should know something about a lot of subjects. You'll note that the categories name different subjects: history, religion, literature, philosophy and science. I could have also added the arts, but that would have required a separate list — there are so many great artists and composers you should know about. Under each subject, I've listed just one or two titles. They're mostly introductory works — for beginners who want to know about the subject."

"Like me," Mordecai added helpfully.

"Yes, like you. For example, under history I've listed a fine book that came out a few years ago, C. R. Nevins's *A History of the World*. I have a copy myself, and I can tell you he writes very well; it's easy to read. He goes back to prehistoric man and covers various civilizations — groups of people — all the way to the present."

"That sounds like a lot to read," Mordecai said, uneasily.

"Now, for literature," Miss Ryan continued, ignoring the boy's hesitancy, "I subdivided the list into fiction, poetry and drama."

"What is fiction?" Mordecai was ashamed to admit he didn't know the word.

"Stories and novels."

"Oh, like Zane Grey," the boy perked up. I really liked that *Riders of the Purple Sage* that you recommended."

"I'm glad," his teacher replied. "The drama is limited to the plays of William Shakespeare because he is, without question, our finest writer in English. He wrote about thirty plays, but I've listed just a few of his tragedies because they're considered his finest and most profound. His language is magnificent. You can find all his plays in a big, single book, *Complete Works of William Shakespeare*. Your library will have it. It will also probably contain his poetry. His sonnets are very beautiful. No," she shook her pretty head, "don't ask me what a sonnet is — we don't have time for that now. Maybe some other time. For poetry, I've selected a book we used in college, *A Treasury of Great Poems*. Fiction

9

we'll talk about later.

"All right," she continued, "under religion, I've listed Dawson's *An Introduction to the World's Great Religions.* Am I going too fast for you?"

Mordecai shook his head. In truth, his head was spinning, and he felt thoroughly overwhelmed but didn't want to disappoint Miss Ryan. He also thought he detected a faint scent of cologne, she was sitting that close to him. But he tried to keep his mind on what she was saying.

"I've also listed under religions, the *Bible*, Old and New Testaments. You're probably already familiar with the Old Testament — you're Jewish, aren't you? — but you should also know the New Testament because that's the book about Jesus Christ which Christians are most familiar with and refer to all the time. So, you should know it too. For that matter, it wouldn't hurt to read the *Koran* in English translation since that's the holy book of Mohammedans, and they make up a big part of the world's population. Unfortunately, I don't know the name of the holy books for the Hindus and Buddhists. Probably, Dawson discusses them."

Mordecai held up his hand. "Miss Ryan, could we please stop talking about the list now. I'm feeling a little too — I don't know the right word."

"Overwhelmed?"

"I guess so. I don't know that word."

"It's okay, Mordecai," she touched his arm gently to reassure him. "I realize that it's a lot to take in in one afternoon. We'll talk about the sciences and fiction some other time, maybe next week."

"That would be fine," Mordecai said rising. "Thank you, so much, Miss Ryan, for taking so much trouble, no, 'effort', to write this list. I'll be careful with it and use it to check out books from the library."

"There's no need to thank me, Mordecai. I enjoyed writing it. It was sort of a challenge. And I like mental challenges," she said, rising from her chair.

He had never thought of her as a woman before, but he couldn't help noticing her trim features. Still, he blocked his thoughts in that direction. She was his teacher, and that's that.

"So, where should I start?" he said jovially, heading toward the door.

"Start with the Nevins," Miss Ryan replied. "And you might start reading Shakespeare if you get tired of history. By the way, the Shakespeare edition explains a lot of the unfamiliar words at the bottom of each page."

"That's good," Mordecai laughed. "I'll need all the help I can get. Maybe, I'll bring the book to class and ask you about difficult words, if you don't mind too much. I don't want to be a bother."

"No, I don't mind, Mordecai. Please do."

The job at Ford's never materialized. First, there was a long line of job seekers at the employee entrance to the Highland Park factory. When Mordecai finally approached the hiring window, he feared they would tell him they'd hired all the people they needed today. But the man at the window with a narrow face — a face like a hatchet — said no such thing.

"Last name?" The man was looking down, writing.

"Stein. S-T-E-I-N."

"Age?"

"Sixteen."

"Stein," the man repeated to himself, as if trying to

remember something. Then he asked, "What's your first name?"

"Mordecai." He was about to help the man spell it, but it wasn't necessary.

"Oh," the man said with certainty. Sorry, there's no work for you here. Next!"

Mordecai walked slowly away, overwhelmed with disappointment — it had been a long streetcar ride with transfers just to get to the Ford factory. An older man sidled up next to him. "It's because you're a Jew," he said. "I was turned down too for the same reason. I didn't know before that they don't hire Jews here. Someone told me in line that Ford himself hates Jews. If I'd known that before, I could have saved myself the carfare."

"Thanks for letting me know," Mordecai said through his disappointment.

"Don't let it bother you, kid," the man reassured him. He had on a flat cap and had a deeply lined face. "There are plenty of other factories and plenty of other jobs. They don't all think like Ford. You'll find something, a big strong boy like you."

"Thank you for the..." *what was the right word?* "...encouragement."

"It's nothing, kid. So, *mazel tov.* Good luck to you. Maybe I'll see you at one of the other factories — working." And with that he left.

When Uncle Yitzhak learned of Mordecai's rejection, he had an immediate solution. "Don't be downhearted. You come with me tomorrow. I'm sure I can get you into Maxwell's. I know the hiring boss. I ought to know him, I've paid him off enough." When Mordecai gave him a puzzled look, Yitzhak explained. "You see, sometimes they tell you 'We don't need you anymore. We've made enough of this kind of car for now. So go get your pay.' But what you do is, you come back in the afternoon and put a couple of dollars in front of the hiring guy, and boom! You're hired back on the line, maybe for a different model, but you're doing pretty much the same thing you were doing before, working on the assembly line. It's called 'paying him off.'"

"I think I understand," Mordecai said with disgust.

"Don't make a face, Mordecai." Uncle Yitzhak's bushy eyebrows closed in a frown. "That's how things are done in America. And tomorrow, if he says they don't have an opening, I'll give him a few bucks, and then we'll see. He knows me already."

It worked exactly as Uncle Yitzhak had predicted, except the payoff wasn't necessary. They needed someone on the line right away — at two dollars a day.

His job was to place four large nuts on the four bolts sticking out of the right front wheel and tighten the nuts with two quick turns of the wrench. Then repeat the same thing for the next car coming down the line. And the next. And the next. If he fell behind, the line would not slow down for him. He'd have to keep up with the moving car and tighten the nuts on the run. The next man did the same job with the right rear wheel, and two men across from them did likewise with the left wheels. His uncle worked further up the line and used his considerable size and strength as part of a team to pull down a hood from an overhead conveyor belt and fit it over the engine block.

They had come in at 7:30 a.m., and as they walked to their positions on the main line at the far end of the floor near the outside doors, Uncle Yitzhak explained, "You get a five-minute break at 10 a.m. and a half-hour for lunch. You've got your lunch bag, right?" (Mordecai silently thanked his Aunt Minna for making the lunch without being asked). "You eat lunch right at your work station, and if you're lucky, some guy nearby is selling coffee and doughnuts. Otherwise, you'll need to get water from a pail and ladle — I'll show you where. Another five-minute break at 2 p.m. Quitting time is five, so eight and a half hours, not counting lunch." As they walked, careful to dodge moving men, machines, trolleys and conveyor belts, Mordecai was struck by the noise of the place; loud banging, clanking and harsh squeaks and squeals were a regular part of the din. *I'll need to put something in my ears*, he thought, *or I'll go deaf.*

The foreman, a big man named Kowalski, took him to his work station, pointed out the deep pan where Mordecai was to keep his supply of nuts, enough for fifty cars and the wrench when he wasn't using it. He was to refill the pan with nuts from the supply shop during his lunch hour. *On my own time of course*, Mordecai thought grimly. The foreman then repeated what Uncle Yitzhak had told him about breaks and lunch.

"There are no extra bathroom breaks," he said harshly. "You got to crap or piss, you do it on your break time or not at all. You got it?"

"Yeah," Mordecai said grimly, "I got it." He noticed there was already a man doing his job.

"Donovan, here, will show you how to do your job, so you can get the hang of it. He's our sub for this part of the line. Knows how to do all the separate jobs."

"You bet I do," Donovan crowed.

"Thanks," Mordecai said, only because he knew it was expected of him.

The job was simple. The hard part was keeping his mind focused when it wanted to wander and daydream. That's when he could fall behind, he quickly learned. And the guy at the next station was not pleased to see him when that happened. "Stay out of my way, rookie!" he had barked once.

So, there were essentially two problems with the job. The first was physical. Repeating the same motions over and over, especially those twists of the wrench, his body soon began to protest in muscle aches and stiffness, especially in his lower back.

"How do people get used to this?" he asked Uncle Yitzhak on the way home. "My back hurts all over!"

"You'll see. The first day is the worst," Yitzhak replied.

"Your back doesn't hurt?"

"Of course it does."

The harder part was mental: the mind-numbing repetition of doing the same thing over and over for eight hours. *Eight? The first day seemed like eighty!* Gradually, though, he learned that he could separate his physical actions from his thoughts. He could make his body do the same motions mechanically while his thoughts were somewhere else. As he had begun to read Nevins's history — the local library had acquired a brand-new copy — he reviewed in his mind what he had read the night before, the key points, as if preparing for an exam. With literature, however, it was more difficult. He couldn't remember Shakespeare's lines unless he reviewed them several times. And only some of the lines in the longer speeches, such as when the person thought he was alone, were worth remembering. Otherwise, Mordecai recalled the play's evolving action and tried to keep straight which person was which. In this division of mind and body, he could do his job and not go insane.

At the end of the week, he turned over his twelve dollars to Uncle Yitzhak, who promptly gave him back a dollar for spending money, even though Mordecai really had nothing to spend it on nor much time to do so. Uncle Yitzhak's own children stayed in school — the older boy had gone on to Eastern High — but none of the three seemed especially interested in learning. Their English was better than Mordecai's, but essentially, they just did what was expected of them. Since he had dropped out, Mordecai envied them their free education, especially the time to study, and scorned their taking it for granted. Meanwhile, he worked at educating himself according to Miss Ryan's plan. He had checked out the Nevins and Shakespeare books from the Beaubien Street Library, accepting the librarian's quizzical looks as she handed him the large volumes.

Both books proved a considerable challenge. The Nevins history started so far back, with prehistoric tribes, that Mordecai knew it would take a long time and a lot of reading before he came to the chapters he was particularly interested in: the history of the ancient Jews and Israel. And the Shakespeare was much more difficult than he'd expected. The word order was often puzzling at first. Instead of *Words without thoughts never go to heaven*, it was *Words without thoughts never to heaven go*. The poems (sonnets, he remembered Miss Ryan calling them) used even more of these reversals: *Thou mayst in me behold* instead of *Thou mayest behold in me* (The *thou*'s and the *est* at the end of some verbs also took some getting used to). Miss Ryan explained — fortunately, he had started reading the plays and poems before leaving Balch Elementary, so he could draw on her knowledge — that the inversions, as she called them, were often done to make the lines rhyme — in the *Hamlet* passage, *go* rhymes with *below* in the preceding line. And in the sonnet, *behold* rhymes with *cold* two lines further on. In the plays, she continued, the inversions often enable the ten-syllable lines to alternate the stresses into a regular pattern called 'blank verse'. So, these lines, too, were a kind of poetry. Mordecai was deeply impressed with the achievement, but it didn't make the lines any easier to read. Having a glossary of unfamiliar words at the bottom of each page helped somewhat, but there were many more unfamiliar words. He copied them down on paper, hoping to look them up sometime. The real challenge was staying awake. Each night, he came home dog-tired from the factory work, and after dinner, it was all too easy to fall asleep over the books. But as he made his way through *Hamlet* — with painful slowness — he was struck by the all-too-human qualities the characters showed: lust and desire for power (Claudius), self-importance and nosiness (Polonius), rashness (Laertes), uncertainty (Hamlet), and hesitant, unfulfilled love (Hamlet and Ophelia). Those traits and the way they made the characters act required no explanation; Mordecai had seen them in action every day — and so, he realized, had Shakespeare.

What he didn't understand, he admitted to Miss Ryan, was why Hamlet didn't obey his ghost-father's urging right away and take revenge on Claudius — kill him immediately.

"Why did he talk about it so much — for almost the entire play — and wait so long until he was almost forced to act in Act Five?"

Miss Ryan smiled. "Well, that's one of the play's great mysteries, and a lot of scholars have tried to answer that question. You know, there are people who *do* things easily, without thinking too much about them, and people who don't, who think maybe too much about everything. Hamlet's in the second category. *Why* he's that way you'll have to figure out for yourself."

"I think he's a mama's boy," Mordecai said bluntly. "He's afraid."

"Hmm. That may be true," Miss Ryan conceded, "but I don't see why that would make him hesitate so long. After all, he resents Claudius marrying his mother and, um, sharing her bed. That would be another reason to take revenge."

"I guess I'll have to think about that more," the boy said. "I wish I could talk about all the plays with you like this. But I've already graduated from Balch. I'm not even supposed to be here now, am I? I wouldn't have been, but they told us not to come in today because they're changing the production line."

"That's all right, Mordecai. I enjoy talking about them with you. But I don't see how we can with you working every day. Unless..."

"Unless what?"

"Unless we met sometime after you got off work and before you go home."

"That wouldn't be easy," Mordecai said, "My uncle would wonder why I'm not going home with him. And I wouldn't have much time before I'd have to be home for dinner."

"Well, you're probably right," Cornelia Ryan sounded relieved. "It probably wouldn't work out."

As he walked home from Balch Elementary, Mordecai

was not thinking about Hamlet's indecision. He was thinking about Miss Ryan's and his own. 'Meeting sometime' — that didn't sound like the way he was used to thinking of Miss Ryan. It sounded... exciting. It sounded like something his friend, David Riskin, had said at work about seeing neighborhood girls in his free time. He called it a 'date'. *He wanted to take them out on a 'date'. To a moving picture show or for a soda. Would his meeting Miss Ryan away from school also be a 'date'? Would she think of it that way? And if dates were romantic, as David's clearly were, would that make his 'date' with Miss Ryan romantic? Was that why she sounded relieved when they realized it wouldn't work? But she had been his teacher! And she was several years older than he was! I'm fifteen*, he thought; *she must be in her twenties*. Still, she was very attractive and gave him the same feeling — a warm feeling, a desiring feeling — that other attractive girls gave him when he saw them sashaying down the street. He admitted that much to himself. The whole situation was confusing, and Mordecai didn't know how he really felt about it. *Better to put it out of my mind*, he thought, turning into his shabby apartment building. *Just like Hamlet.*

"*Nu*, where were you? How did you spend your unpaid day off?" Uncle Yitzhak inquired before Mordecai could even hang up his coat. His kindness was mingled with nosiness; both came from a genuine concern for the boy's welfare, from thinking of him as the son he wished his sons were like. Before Mordecai could answer, his uncle steered him back outside onto the landing — it was the only place they could talk in private. Mordecai had already described to Yitzhak his self-education project and Miss Ryan's contribution to it.

"I went over to talk with Miss Ryan after her last class," he explained. "I had some questions about the play I'm reading, *Hamlet.*"

"She must be very nice to take such an interest in you," his uncle reflected. "And it's a compliment to you. She must think highly of you. Did she answer your questions?"

"Pretty much. We talked about it. It's easier to understand the play if you have someone to talk to who knows it. It makes it more enjoyable."

"Yes, I suppose it does. It's certainly not something *we* could talk about." Then, a wrinkle creased his uncle's brow. His tone lowered as he became inquisitive.

"This Miss Ryan. She's young?"

"I don't know. I guess so, for a teacher."

"I see." Uncle Yitzhak paused. "Is she pretty?"

"Uncle," Mordecai protested, "really, I don't think that has anything to do with—"

"So, she *is* pretty," Uncle Yitzhak chuckled. "Do you think, Mordecai," he hesitated, groping for the right words, "that she may be interested in you for other reasons, besides just wanting to help you learn? You're a good-looking boy. And you said she is a young, unmarried woman."

"I don't think it's that way at all, Uncle," Mordecai said, wondering if it was.

"Well, I don't want to butt into your private life," Yitzhak said. But I think you should be careful. She is much older than you. And she's Gentile."

"I know that," Mordecai was beginning to lose patience. "Don't worry, Uncle. It's just for my education."

"All right," Yitzhak said. "That's good. Keep it like that. Now let's see what Minna made for dinner. Not cabbage again, I hope."

Two weeks later, his relationship with Cornelia Ryan came to a sudden end. They had met one time away from school. Mordecai had set it up. He found a restaurant not far from the school and arranged to meet her there after work. She would stay late at Balch Elementary, correcting papers. By the time he got there from Maxwell's, they would have a half hour at most before he had to be home for dinner. He let her know through a sealed note he left for her in the office, never thinking that the office staff would find this note-leaving odd. Since she had no way of contacting him, he just gambled that she would be there. She was.

His heart turned over, seeing her at the table. She wasn't just pretty, she was beautiful, her red hair more striking than ever. She signaled him over, smiling. As he sat, he felt he needed to explain, as if he were a referee laying out the rules.

"I can only stay a half hour. Then I must get home for dinner."

"That's quite all right, Mordecai," she smiled. "I'm expected home, too."

"After I came home the last time I saw you, my uncle asked me where I was. He already knew about your helping me with my learning. But this time he warned me not to get — I don't know what the right word is."

"Romantic?" she asked. Her smile was gone.

"I don't know. I guess so."

"Well, your uncle needn't worry." She was frowning now. "I had no such intention when I decided to meet you. We'd better order something, by the way. They're staring at us from the counter. Is coffee all right?"

"Yes, that's fine," he said, taking out his wallet.

"She stopped him by putting her hand on his arm. "That's all right, Mordecai. I'll get this. It's only ten cents, anyway. We don't have time for a meal." She went to the counter to order.

This didn't seem right to Mordecai. The man is supposed to pay, he was sure. Now he felt like a boy. But perhaps that was how she wanted him to feel.

When she returned, her frown had returned. "We simply cannot meet outside of school anymore. No matter how innocent it really is, people will see us, and people will talk. I already got a nosy question from one of the office secretaries who recognized you when you left the note. One of those secretaries might see us here, or someone who knows you. Or your uncle!"

"No, he goes straight home from Maxwell's. He means well, Miss Ryan; really, he does."

"Well," she continued, "It's just not a good idea." Their coffee came, and they both sipped it, Mordecai after adding cream and several sugars. "After all," Cornelia continued, "I'm twenty-two and you're just, what, fifteen or sixteen?"

"Fifteen."

"I'm still 'Miss Ryan' to you. And that's how I'll stay. Listen, Mordecai," her hand was on his arm again. "You know I think you're a fine boy. But you *are* a boy. I was happy to help you educate yourself. I think it's a fine and worthy ambition. But that's where we'll have to leave it. Since you can't really come back to Balch Elementary anymore, I guess we really won't be able to meet anywhere to discuss the plays or the other readings. That's too bad. I would have liked to discuss them with you."

"And I would, too," Mordecai put in. "Very much so. It made understanding *Hamlet* much easier. It's nice to be able to *talk* with someone about these things."

"Yes, it is. I agree wholeheartedly. But it's just not possible. It's a shame, really a shame, that we can't, that people always get the wrong idea and think the worst about such things, such innocent meetings. But that's the way things are. I could get into a lot of trouble if anyone knew I was meeting you like this. I could lose my job."

Mordecai put down his cup. "I didn't know that. I don't want that to happen."

"Nor do I. My first job out of teacher's college," she laughed without humor.

"Well, then, I guess this is goodbye," he said, trying to sound forthright. He put his hand across the table to shake hands. Reluctantly, seeing the absurdity of the gesture, she took it.

"Yes, goodbye, dear Mordecai. Perhaps I'll read about you one day in the newspaper. Perhaps, after you've educated yourself, you'll become a great man."

"If I do, I'll have you to thank for it," he said, reluctantly rising. "Thank you for everything you've done for me, Miss Ryan. You don't know how much you've helped me already."

"I was happy to do it," she said, looking up at him. Now she looked as if she were going to cry. *I'd better leave quickly*, he thought, turning toward the door. *I don't know what I would do if she started crying.*

2.

Toward the end of June 1914, the newspapers were full of a story coming out of Eastern Europe. Archduke Ferdinand, the son of the Austro-Hungarian Emperor, had been shot and killed by a Serbian nationalist. Mordecai had no understanding of the political situation. He didn't know Serbia even existed much less where it was. He had heard of the Austro-Hungarian Empire, of course. Many Jews came from there, especially from its northern-most province, Galicia, which bordered Poland. As he and Uncle Yitzhak rode the streetcar up Oakland Avenue to the Maxwell plant, he discovered that Yitzhak knew as little about the situation as he did.

"Some crazy nationalist," Yitzhak surmised. "Or maybe an anarchist. Vicious. He killed the Archduke's wife too. Too bad it didn't happen to the Czar."

"What's an anarchist?"

"I don't know. But it must be bad. I've heard people talk about them."

"But why did he do it?" Mordecai asked. Just as with his history book, he wanted to understand, to comprehend the larger picture. This was history happening *now*. A big event in his own lifetime.

"Who knows? Maybe he was *meshuga*, crazy."

"Where is Serbia?"

"I don't know. But the Archduke and his wife were visiting there, the newspaper says. So, maybe it's part of that Austria-Hungary Empire."

"Will there be a war?"

"You're asking the wrong person, Mordecai. I know as little about it as you do. Less maybe, now that you're reading these history books."

"I haven't gotten that far yet. I'm only up to the Greeks. Five hundred years B.C."

"What is 'B.C.'?"

"Before Christ."

"Oh. Well, I can tell you one thing," Uncle Yitzhak said sadly. "Whoever fights, the Jews will get it in the neck. It always happens. From one side or the other — the Russians, the Germans, the Poles, the Austrians.

Maybe even from the Serbians, whoever they are. They all hate us."

"Why is that, Uncle? Why do they hate the Jews so much?"

"Who knows? I'm not a wise man, just a factory worker. But I have my own idea."

"Yes? What is it?" Mordecai was curious.

"Because wherever they go, the Jews do well. Not where we live right now, of course. But you wait. We'll be moving to a better neighborhood pretty soon. A lot of Jews here already have. They learn how to do well for themselves. To make money. They go into business and work hard. Or go into professions that people respect: doctors, lawyers. And people, the *goyim*, see Jews getting ahead, and they're jealous of them. They want to slap us down. Well, that's what I think, anyway."

"There's also the difference of religions," Mordecai said, thinking of Nevins and his contempt for religious persecutions throughout history. He had read ahead on the subject.

"Yes, I forgot about that," Yitzhak agreed. "They call us Christ-killers. Especially the Catholics. Another reason for killing Jews. One of the men I work with on the line calls me that all the time. 'Christ-killer.' He hates my guts, I know that. But we have to work together to get that hood cover in place. It's a two-man job."

"But it was the Romans who killed Christ, wasn't it?" Mordecai asked. Uncle Yitzhak suddenly became self-conscious. People nearby seemed to be listening in. "Hush," he told Mordecai, "We'll talk about it some other time."

Meanwhile, their streetcar had arrived at the Maxwell plant, and the two, along with many others, stepped off.

Mordecai had acclimated to his job on the line. His back ached less at the end of work. But now the company introduced something new: speedups.

"It's when they're behind on their orders," David Riskin said. He always seemed a step ahead of Mordecai in understanding how things worked, not just technical things at the factory but social ones, like dating. He was two years older; perhaps that explained it. Over the months, they had become close friends, and David usually shared the streetcar ride home with Mordecai and Uncle Yitzhak. There was lots to talk about. The speedups, of course, forced everyone on the line to work faster. But often they couldn't finish their job in time and had to run along the line to keep up. This time, Mordecai's neighbor didn't complain because he was running too. And no sooner had Mordecai finished wrenching those nuts on the run, he had to run back to put on more for the next car. It was awful. Fortunately, the speedups didn't last long — they nearly always produced jam-ups that had to be disentangled. So, in the end, they didn't really create more production, and the company gradually stopped them, to everyone's relief.

Barely a month after the assassination of Archduke Ferdinand and his wife, Europe was at war. To Mordecai, it seemed like a string of interlocking firecrackers exploding. First Austria declared war on Serbia; then Russia declared war on Austria; Germany then declared war on Russia *and* France. *Why France?* Mordecai wondered. He later discovered that France and Russia were allied, so if one went to war, the other would too. In fact, all of these declarations, he learned, came from previous alliances — 'If you fight, I'll fight too'. It seemed to him a stupid promise and shocking that a whole country could be dragged into a war on that basis. *If Austria-Hungary got into it with Russia, why is that Germany's business? Or France's?* Nonetheless, they had all mobilized their armies, the newspapers reported, and were sending them to the 'front' to do battle as quickly as they could. Several days later, Great Britain declared war on Germany for invading neutral Belgium. Again, Mordecai wondered why. The news articles explained: Great Britain had signed a treaty with Belgium 'guaranteeing' their borders. *Like a big brother protecting his defenseless kid brother,* he thought. *If someone (like Germany) punches you, I'll punch him. Shouldn't nations be beyond behaving as if they were in a schoolyard fight? At least America had sense enough to stay out of it. That was what President Wilson declared. And hurrah for that! What business is it of ours?* He worried, though, about his family, still stuck in Motal, Russia. *How would they ever get out with this war going on?*

3.

Almost three years later, April 1917, the presidential wisdom that Mordecai had admired seemed to vanish. Now, President Wilson was leading America into this same war that had already killed so many people — millions, he had read — for so little purpose. Wilson's reasons for this dramatic reversal weren't clear to Mordecai, but the President made America's entering the war seem a noble undertaking: 'To make the world safe for democracy'. *It sounded good, but what did it mean?* Newspapers called it 'the war to end war'. That, too, made no sense to him. *How does a bloody war do that when wars have always existed? They seemed part of human nature.* Nonetheless, the streets were crowded with people listening to pro-war speakers. Anyone who dared to voice an opposing view in public was called a Heinie-lover or a damn pacifist and knocked off his soapbox. Or hers — some of the anti-war speakers were women, and Mordecai admired them for their courage. It was astonishing to see the same people who were once for neutrality and peace now so bloodthirsty and eager for war. Besides the pro-war speeches, there were rallies, parades and bond drives to raise money for the war. Once war was declared, overnight, Germany was vilified as the enemy. Stores run by German-Americans (there were several on Hastings Street) had their windows broken or smeared with paint. German street names and food names were changed to 'American' ones. People with German last names were attacked or fired from their jobs, or both. At Maxwell's, the employment manager was going around talking to anyone with a German-sounding name. Mordecai and Uncle Yitzhak were at pains to explain that they had come from Russia. To Mordecai, this persecution of German-Americans was like a fever that infected people and made them behave in ways they never would have earlier.

Meanwhile, the war now affected him — and all young men — directly. Those twenty-one and older who didn't volunteer would be subject to a draft, it was said, and forced to serve. Only those with jobs considered essential to the war effort or with some disqualifying ailment would be exempt.

Mordecai would be nineteen in June, old enough to volunteer for the Army. He discussed it with both Uncle Yitzhak and David. Both were astonished that he was even considering enlisting, but, predictably, their attitudes and advice sharply contrasted.

Uncle Yitzhak took him seriously and gave practical advice. "You are being idealistic, Mordecai. You don't know what war really is, and I don't want to see you get hurt or killed needlessly. Why not wait until you're drafted? From what I've heard about this new law, that would be when you're twenty-one. Two years from now. The war will probably be over by then."

"Yes," Mordecai replied sourly, "and I will have missed my chance to participate, to help my country."

All Yitzhak could do was sigh.

David's response was blunter, even insulting. "Enlist? Are you crazy? You're still wet behind the ears. You want to become cannon fodder? Because that's what you'll be, chum, depend on it!" They were sitting by the line, bolting down their lunches, and David continued, "Listen, I'm no Bolshevik, but this is a sucker's game." (He was always picking up current expressions.) "Who will be doing the fighting? You can bet your ass it won't be Maxwell's kids or any other rich guy's kids. It will be people like us, poor people. People who don't know any better. And when it's all over, what'll we have — *if* we survive? Nothing more than we had before. A rich man's war and a poor man's fight. You don't know how lucky you are, Mordecai, to be safe from the Draft. Now me, on the other hand, I'm liable to be drafted at any time, since I'm twenty-one."

"What will you do if you're drafted?"

"You mean 'when', pal, not 'if.' I don't know." His confident tone had vanished. "They'll throw you in jail if you refuse to serve, and then you won't be able to find work when you get out. I've heard they're building a tank factory in Detroit, and everyone who works there will be exempt from the Draft. I may try to get in there."

"What's a tank?" Mordecai hated to reveal his ignorance.

"It's like a big truck with heavy steel sides to protect it and lots of guns. And it has big treads over the wheels so it can go in the mud and snow. But with my luck, I won't get in there — probably hundreds of guys will want those jobs. So, there it is —draft bait and cannon fodder. What a future! You're lucky to be free of it, Mordecai. Just sit tight. Besides, think of all those available girls here with their boyfriends off in the Army. Easy pickings!"

But as Mordecai mulled it over in the days following, he realized he felt something that David didn't. He already knew the word 'patriotism' — it was much used in speeches these days. 'Do your patriotic duty!' 'Show your patriotism!' Posters showed 'Uncle Sam' (who stood for the whole country, Mordecai knew) pointing directly at the viewer, calling on him to volunteer: 'I WANT **YOU** FOR U.S. ARMY'. Mordecai felt the pull; he lacked David Riskin's cynicism. *This is my country now*, he said to himself. *A country that has welcomed me, provided me a home and a job and, much more important, a future. Should I spit in its eye when it says it wants me, needs me, to serve? Don't I have an obligation to help my country when it needs me? I don't really understand why we are fighting Germany, but we are.* He remembered lines from a poem he had read recently in the *Treasury of Great Poems*,

> *Theirs not to reason why,*
> *Theirs but to do and die.*

Well, I certainly don't want to die. But perhaps sometimes you have to risk that to help your country in a war when it is fighting for its life. But was *America fighting for its life? The war was across the ocean, after all, in France and Belgium. Why is it our war?*

He couldn't answer that, and the newspapers were no help with their sensationalist stories of big battles. But the fact remained: his country was at war and said it needed him. He would answer the call and enlist.

After he signed the papers, he was told to report to Fort Wayne for a physical exam.

Finding where Fort Wayne was and getting there were difficult enough. Then he had to find the building where they gave the physicals. Eventually, he did. He was instructed to strip to his underwear and shoes, check his clothing in a basket at a counter and carry his valuables in a bag. Mordecai was glad about the bag — he couldn't afford to lose the $10 in his wallet.

The physical was embarrassing, even humiliating at times. Once, he and everyone else in line were required to pull down their shorts and bend over while someone, walking behind them called out, "Spread 'em!" *He means my ass*, the boy realized. The man walked down the row, inspecting them. *What a horrible job*, Mordecai thought, *looking at assholes all day! What is he checking for?* In any case, Mordecai passed the test and, self-conscious, quickly pulled up his shorts, only to have to lower them again further on, when another man — *a doctor?* — checked him for hernia.

"Turn your head and cough!" the man barked, partially protected by a shield and feeling the boy's testicles. Mordecai almost jumped back but endured it. *The poor man*, he thought. *How many germs he must be getting with all those coughs! Is this where they send the students who don't make it through medical school?*

A real doctor, or at least someone in a white lab coat wearing a stethoscope, was present further on. He placed the stethoscope on Mordecai's chest and listened perfunctorily. Then he frowned and listened again more carefully.

"Step to the side." He gestured to a place away from the main line where a few men stood. When another doctor had relieved this one a few minutes later, he came over to the waiting men. "All of you were singled out because you have heart murmurs. You'll be exempted from the Draft. Go back to the counter and get your clothes." He took the physical inspection card that each carried and scribbled the finding on it under the category 'Class V.'

The other men were obviously relieved and smiling. They were free! Mordecai was puzzled and disturbed. He asked the doctor, now hurrying to his coffee break, "What is a heart murmur?"

"It means an irregular heartbeat," the doctor said, not slowing down.

"Is it serious?"

"I don't know. Can be. But often it's not, and you can live your whole life with one." He turned into a small room with a coffee urn and a box of doughnuts on the table. "In any case," he turned back to Mordecai, "it got you out of the Army. You should be happy."

"Yes," said Mordecai, now standing alone in his underwear, still shocked by the finding. "I guess I should be."

The responses to Mordecai's medical condition varied predictably. His Aunt Minna was worried, as she was about every new development, good or bad. Uncle Yitzhak had mixed feelings, as always. He was happy his nephew was safe from the war but concerned about the diagnosis. "So, what is this heart murmur? Something serious?"

"How should I know?" Mordecai was becoming irritated, not so much with the repeated question but with not having an answer. "I'm going to the library today to look it up. The next time you see me, I should be an expert on heart murmurs."

Unfortunately, the library had little information. The encyclopedias defined it just as the doctor had at his physical, as an irregular heartbeat, sometimes serious, sometimes not.

David Riskin was jubilant for Mordecai and envious. "You lucky stiff! You're free! Just don't lose that 'Class V' card. Always carry it with you because the police'll stop you on the street and demand to see it. They're on the lookout for slackers, that's what I've heard."

"Do you know anything about this murmur business? Is it serious?"

"I don't know anything about it," David replied. "Just be glad it kept you out of the service. Hah! Your body was smarter than you were."

"What about you? What are you going to do?"

"I'm still not sure. I was thinking about enlisting in the Navy. It's a lot safer, for sure, but the problem is the enlistment is for four years. I can't waste four years of my life swabbing decks and getting seasick! If I enlist in the Army, it's for three years, so that's only a little better. If I wait to be drafted, it's for the duration of the war — six months? Six years? — And you can guess where they'll send the draftees. It would really be a gamble."

"What about working in the tank factory?"

"That's pretty much out. Maxwell didn't get the contract. And the company that did is way across town on the far West Side. It would take most of an hour just to get there on the streetcar. And I'm sure it'll be tough to get a job there, since it would keep you out of the Draft."

"I'm sorry to hear that."

"Don't be. I'll figure out something."

But as it turned out, David Riskin didn't figure out anything. He dutifully reported for and passed his draft physical, even though he'd gone to bed the night before with a bar of soap under each arm. He'd heard that was a sure-fire way to be disqualified, but it didn't work. He was assigned to an Army division training at Camp Custer near Battle Creek. Before he went off, he offered his friend some advice. "Listen, Mordecai, save your money." (Mordecai was struck by how similar his advice was to Iago's in *Othello*, who keeps telling the stupid Roderigo, *Put money in thy purse*.)

David continued, "Get your uncle to let you keep more of your paycheck and save it! When I get out — and I'm going to get out, count on it — we're not just going back to the factory line. Sure, we may have to do it for a few more years to build up some capital. But we're not going to waste our whole lives just putting nuts on bolts for $3 a day. I've got bigger plans for us, but it will take money to get us started."

"What plans are those?" Mordecai asked, skeptical, because David always had big plans.

"Filling stations. Look, almost every car runs on gasoline, right? They have to have it. And more and more people are driving cars. Pretty soon everyone will be able to afford at least a Model-T. So, there'll be a *huge* demand for gasoline. What we'll need to do is to buy or lease a station and sell that gas. We won't need to look for customers — they'll come to us!"

"But what do we know about selling gas? I don't know how to repair a car. Do you?"

"No, but we can learn. And anyway, we can always hire a mechanic for that. That's why we need to save as much money as we can to get that first station."

"First?"

"Hey, if we can be successful with the first station, then why not get a second and a third?"

"Slow down, David. We don't even have the first one yet."

"But we will. Just you wait. And save your money. Unfortunately, I won't be able to save diddly squat from what they pay buckass privates. But I've already saved a bunch from working on the line these years, and I'll save a bunch more when I come back."

If you come back, Mordecai couldn't help thinking, but of course, said nothing.

"We'll be *partners* one day," David predicted with confidence.

"Partners," Mordecai repeated. He liked the sound of that word.

4.

Occasionally, he got postcards and brief letters from David from his training camp.

They're teaching us to use a bayonet, he wrote.
The sarge says, I want to see guts at both ends.

Mordecai didn't quite understand this, but he guessed it meant something violent — stabbing Germans in their bellies.

I'm also becoming a good shot with my rifle, David boasted. *Maybe I'll get a Heinie with it.*

He didn't mention their sailing for France, but Mordecai realized that he couldn't. If he'd written anything, it would have been crossed out by a censor. In the late spring of 1918, America was now sending boatloads of soldiers, tens of thousands, to France and just in time. The Germans, knowing the Americans were coming in force, had launched a desperate offensive that spring and had pushed the Allies back several miles. American troops, commanded by General Pershing, were rushed to the front lines to plug gaps. Mordecai had read that Pershing refused to simply give the troops to the French or British but insisted they be used in *American* divisions and regiments.

He didn't hear from David for several weeks. Then, a muddy card came in the summer.

Bon jour, Mordecai!" it began jauntily. *We've been in France a few weeks, getting some final training before they send us to the front. Wish me luck! And the French girls — Ooh-la-la! There I don't need luck! Yours, David*

Mordecai was torn by conflicting emotions. He had to admit he was glad to be safely away from the fighting. But he also felt guilty. Why should the Davids have to serve, while he was safe and comfortable? He also received a lot of dirty looks from people on the street for not being in uniform.

"Slacker!" someone muttered, loud enough for him to

hear.

It used to be 'dirty Jew', he thought; *now it's 'slacker'.*

At work, his years of experience, along with the manpower shortage, led to his promotion to foreman. That meant a raise to $3.75 a day from $3. And not having to do the same thing hour after hour, day after day, was a great relief. Now he could move along the line checking the work of others, showing the greenhorns how to do their job — he had done several jobs in the intervening time. Every so often, he'd get a letter from his draft board instructing him to report, as if they'd forgotten why they classified him 'Class V' or believed his heart had miraculously healed itself. *A complete waste of time,* he thought, *but at least it gives me most of the day off.*

After one of these draft board visits, he even managed to squeeze in a baseball game. He went with a friend from his apartment building to Navin Field to see the Detroit Tigers play. The great Ty Cobb was the star, and Mordecai marveled at how aggressively he played, sliding 'spikes high' into second base. His friend had already explained the fundamentals, such as stealing bases. The Boston team they played against featured a remarkable pitcher named Ruth, who was also a powerful hitter. In fact, he hit a towering home run that day. It made Mordecai feel more like a real American to understand this most popular of American sports. While he was there, he saw others drinking beer. He drank one too, his first. It tasted awful.

At the end of September, he got another muddy card from David. It was maddeningly brief.

Was just in a huge battle. Looks like we caught the Heinies by surprise. What I most hate about this war

— mud lice and gas! What I like — NOTHING! Save your money, buddy!
David

Mordecai was doing just that. Uncle Yitzhak had also been promoted, and, just as he'd promised, he had moved the family to Twelfth Street, where they now had a comfortable flat. Since he needed less of Mordecai's weekly contribution and Mordecai was now earning more, the boy's savings mounted steadily. When David came back, there would be a nice nest egg to start their business.

For almost six weeks, he heard nothing from David, an ominous silence heightened by the newspaper headlines proclaiming a new and sweeping American offensive in the Argonne Forest near the Meuse River (Mordecai looked up the location on a library atlas, since the maps in the newspaper were too localized). The battle lasted for many weeks, and there were heavy casualties. But this offensive did the trick and seemed to break the Germans' back. They asked for an armistice, which took effect November 11. The newspapers proclaimed a German 'surrender', and the streets were filled with delirious crowds celebrating it. Mordecai tried to discover if there was a difference between 'armistice' and 'surrender', but it didn't seem to matter. The war was over, and the Allies had won. He even got the day off to celebrate. Uncle Yitzhak took the whole family to Woodward Avenue where a large impromptu parade was being held. He bought several small American flags from a vendor so that all his family could wave them.

Best of all, another postcard from David arrived in mid-November.

Well, I made it through the Argonne with only a little gassing. Be home soon!

Meanwhile, Mordecai's life had also changed. After the family moved to Twelfth Street, he began going to the nearby Jewish Community Center in his free time. A single membership for a young person was inexpensive. On Sundays there was usually a lecture of some sort scheduled, mostly on Jewish culture but sometimes on history or current events. The Center also had a library, which Mordecai eagerly perused, looking for some of the books Miss Ryan had listed. Miss Ryan. He hadn't thought of her in a long time. She was so sweet to have taken an interest in him and encouraged him. It was too bad that they couldn't keep meeting to discuss his reading. But Mordecai remembered that more was at stake besides discussing books, and he was glad that it had ended when it did. He was twenty now, still big for his age — a man. And he thought it was time he started meeting some girls and, to use David's strange word, 'dating'.

The Jewish Center sponsored dances on some Saturday nights for its members, attended as well by young peoples' clubs that were part of the Center. Though he knew next to no one at the Center, Mordecai began attending the dances as a 'stag' — another new word — and asked unescorted girls to dance. Before going the first time, he had prepared, of course, by asking Chava and his cousin, Katya, to teach him to dance. The family already owned a windup phonograph, and to the singing of John McCormick, the girls taught him the box-step waltz.

At his second dance, something surprising happened. From the line of unattached girls hugging the wall, one came forward and boldly asked *him* to dance. Stifling his surprise, he accepted and managed to keep from stepping on her toes. *Is this how they do things in America, the girls asking the boys?* he wondered. *At least, that lets you know who's interested in you.*

He found her dark features, her eyes especially, very attractive, and they seemed to dance well together. Her name was Miriam Reubner, and she lived several blocks away on Clairmount Avenue.

After several dances with her, Mordecai screwed up his courage and asked if he could escort her home. Miriam had come to the dance with her girlfriend, she explained, and she couldn't just leave her. So, Mordecai escorted both girls. Before Miriam walked up to her family's apartment building, though, he asked her if he might call on her next Saturday night. She nodded and wrote out the family's apartment number. He had made his first date.

Miriam Reubner considered herself a 'New Woman'. In a few years, she would be able to vote, as any man could in Detroit. and she was determined not simply to be someone else's 'wife', but independent and self-supporting. To that end, she bypassed Central High, the closest high school to Clairmount Avenue, for the recently completed Cass Technical High School, which offered a business as well as science curriculum. Miriam's parents were none too happy about her ambitions. Though they were well off and thought themselves modern, they still held traditional views about the role of women. Business courses? A woman working outside the home? Never in the old country! But this was America, Miriam kept reminding them. *If a man was expected to support himself, why not a woman? Did they expect her to sit home doing nothing after getting her diploma?* Since the Reubners had always indulged Miriam, their oldest, they acquiesced with a few grumbles. Miriam took business and secretarial courses at Cass: typing, shorthand and bookkeeping. With her proficient skills, she had no trouble finding a secretarial position. Her Jewish last name was not a problem, since the law firm that hired her had Jewish partners.

Determined to be up to date, Miriam regularly read H. L. Mencken's *Smart Set* magazine to absorb The Baltimore Sage's irreverent opinions, study the latest fashions and read modern writers like Edna St. Vincent Millay and Theodore Dreiser. With their daring plots and characters, Dreiser's novels were hard to find in libraries, forcing Miriam to splurge occasionally and buy one. At the Jewish Center dances, she saw no reason to wait for a boy to come by and ask her to dance. When she saw a good-looking boy with dark, wavy hair standing unattached, she strode right up to him and asked him to dance. Mordecai was taken aback but took her hand and was soon following her lead on the dance floor.

5.

By the time David came back in late January 1919, Mordecai had gone out with Miriam several times. Their dates were simple: going to a 'movie', usually to see Charlie Chaplin or Fatty Arbuckle, then to a nearby sweet shop for an ice cream soda. Once they went to a Sunday lecture at the Jewish Center and seriously discussed the topic on their walk home. Miriam was as intelligent as she was pretty and bolder than him (he didn't know how he felt about that). But she seemed to care for him as much as he did for her. After a few dates, he was trying to work up the courage to kiss her good night, when she surprised him again. She simply skipped ahead of him on the walkway to her family's apartment building, turned and blocked his path, putting her arms up to be kissed. It freed Mordecai of making the first move, and he was grateful. After that, it was easy.

When David returned, he looked as if he had lost several pounds — his uniform, now with corporal stripes, seemed too big for him. He seemed to be his old self, confident and jovial, but Mordecai noticed small differences. His hand had a tremor sometimes, which he tried to conceal. And he coughed frequently.

"From gassing," he explained. "I caught a whiff before I could get my mask on. It put me in the hospital for a week. I guess I should be glad about that. I missed some heavy fighting in the Argonne. But that gas does bad things to your lungs. Be glad you weren't there, Mordecai."

They were sitting in a speakeasy which David knew about, drinking beer.

"When did Michigan pass this stupid Prohibition law — 1917 or thereabouts?" he complained. "It's quite a shock to leave the land of wine and come back to this mecca of bluenoses. Booze was one of the few good things about being over there," he reflected. "The frogs don't care how old you are so long as you can pay for your wine. And some of their wine is damn good. I see you're not a drinker. You haven't even touched your beer."

Mordecai shrugged self-consciously. "I'm sorry, I can't get used to the taste."

"You get used to it quick enough when you need it,"

David muttered. "Guys would get high on anything they could get their hands on, even ether, if they knew they were going over the top. I was tight myself more times than I can count."

"It must have been terrible," Mordecai tried to sympathize.

David frowned. "I can't even *begin* to tell you how bad it was. No one who wasn't there can understand. That's why all this patriotic hoopla here about 'We won! We won!' just turns my stomach. Won what? Beat who? The Heinies were just as miserable as we were. They gassed us. We gassed them. So, who really won? They quit because they were exhausted. Ran out of money and men and supplies too, I'm guessing. Their people back home were starving, that's what I heard. And here come a whole bunch of fresh-faced Americans, a million of them or more, just eager to bayonet them, and who hadn't spent that last four years in muddy trenches under artillery fire. It was just like I said before I left — a rich man's war, a poor man's fight. Well, let's talk about happier things," he said, draining his beer and ordering another. "You tell me you're dating a girl. Congratulations! So, tell me about her."

Mordecai did, briefly. David was amused at Miriam's boldness.

"Just like the girls in France," he remarked. But his attention wandered. He seemed restless, even with the beer. "And did you save up a bundle, like I told you? I still want to try that gasoline business if you're game."

Mordecai nodded. "I've saved up about $300."

David frowned. "That's not enough by itself to get us started. I didn't get paid diddly shit, but I made a few bucks on the boat coming home playing poker. Ever

43

play? It's a great game. Anyhow, I've got about a hundred bucks. So, I guess it's back to the assembly line for us, *if* I can still get my job back. Things aren't so good, I've heard, I mean with jobs."

"No," Mordecai agreed, relying on his newspaper knowledge. "There's a lot of unemployment, what with all the soldiers coming back looking for work. Still, I think I can get you back into Maxwell. I'm a foreman now."

"That's great. You didn't just stand still. I'm proud of you, Mordecai."

"You'd have been one too if you didn't have to go over."

"Yeah, well..." David let it die. "Well, we've got some time. I don't plan to look for work right away. I want to enjoy a little freedom before I become a wage slave again. Either an Army slave or a wage slave. Not much freedom, is there? That's why we've got to get out on our own where there's no boss telling us what to do and when to do it. I wonder how much it will take to lease our first station. I'm assuming we won't have nearly enough to buy one."

"I don't know," Mordecai said. "To be honest, I haven't looked into it. I was waiting for you to return. But now I think we should, so that we have a definite amount we're aiming for."

"Agreed," David said, closing the subject.

The following Saturday night, Miriam wasn't free to go out with Mordecai. Instead, he called David (both families now had telephones), and the two met at the same speakeasy.

"So, your girl let you down tonight?" David gibed. "Probably got a heavy date with some mucker with money."

The possibility hadn't even occurred to Mordecai.

"God, I hope not," he said.

"Relax, kid. I was just joshing you. I'm sure she's true blue to you. Hey, that rhymes. Meantime, I've got a personal question for you."

"Yes?" Mordecai braced for it.

"You're still a virgin, aren't you?"

Mordecai felt himself blushing, which made him even more self-conscious.

"Well, yes."

"Hey, don't be ashamed of it, buddy," David reassured him. "I was too until I got over to France. Boy, those French girls. Even the ones you pay for are hot. Well, I think our first order of business is to get you laid good and proper."

Mordecai didn't know what to say. He had often wondered about it, of course. But he would never dream of trying anything with Miriam. There were nice girls and not-so-nice ones. Miriam was definitely a nice girl, a little bold but nice. 'Sex', as he heard it called, was something you did with a 'not-so-nice' girl. But David had something else in mind.

"Look, I know of this house on Brush Street. I've been there myself. The madam is all right — she won't make you feel funny about it being your first time. We won't even tell her. And the girls there are pretty. They'll show you what you need to know."

"How much will it cost?" Mordecai asked trying to sound practical.

"Cost me two bucks. They stay with you about ten minutes, fifteen if you can stretch it out. But that should be more than enough time, especially the first time."

"Is there anything else I should know?" Mordecai asked. "This isn't something I can look up in the encyclopedia."

David laughed. It was good to see that laugh, but also rare. "No, nothing else. C'mon, let's walk over. It's better to get there early before the drunks roll in and the girls aren't too sweaty from all the work."

"You don't make it sound very…" *what was the right word?* "attractive."

"Just being practical, pal. Anyway, it's just for this one time. If you don't like it, you don't have to go back."

"Okay, I'll try it," Mordecai said. "What can I lose, besides the two dollars, right?"

"Just your cherry," David replied. "And that's best lost."

Mordecai was dreading it (though more than a little curious), but the evening at Miss Sophie's wasn't nearly as harrowing as he'd feared. As soon as they walked in, admitted by a massive Black doorman, he was impressed by the ornate living room, stuffed with sofas and easy chairs, a real fireplace topped by a gilt-framed mirror and nearby a polished wooden staircase. In the corner, a Black pianist was playing ragtime on a polished upright piano. Even though it was only 8 p.m., the living room was fairly full, with men of all descriptions comfortably seated, some talking with scantily clad young women. There was a constant hubbub of conversations and constant movement of couples going up the stairs and mostly singles coming down.

David was comfortable and offhand in introducing Mordecai to Miss Sophie. Mordecai could see she had once been a beauty and, though aging, still retained her good looks. Her greeting was professionally friendly but also coolly appraising.

As they approached a small group of girls who had

just come down, David said to Sophie in a stage whisper, "He's a newcomer, if you know what I mean." Mordecai felt a surge of anger. *He had broken his promise!*

"Nothing to worry about," Sophie said, taking Mordecai's hand. Her own hand was soft and warm, inviting. "I think I have just the right girl for you. Estelle," she called to one of the girls. "I'd like you to meet — what did you say his name was?"

"Mordecai."

"Mordecai," Sophie finished, turning away from the group to resume her easy chair near the front door. Not for the first time, Mordecai felt intensely self-conscious about his name, as if it called out, 'Jew! Here's a Jew!'

A girl with blonde curls approached him. "Hi there, cutie. Where did you get such wavy dark hair? Did you perm it?"

The other girls laughed. David, meanwhile, was chatting with a redhead.

Mordecai knew she was kidding, but also knew he had to say something. "No, it's just natural."

"I knew that, sweetie," Estelle said. "Just making conversation. Part of the job, you know. Sophie usually gives me the first-timers, so that must be you."

Before Mordecai had a chance to respond, she had taken his hand and was leading him to the staircase. She was wearing a nightgown that was almost transparent, and Mordecai admired her curvy figure moving freely beneath it. She led him up the thickly carpeted staircase and to a hallway with many doors. Unlike the living room below, the hallway was plain and drab, the floor uncarpeted.

"This way," Estelle guided him firmly to an open doorway. Once inside, she held out her hand. "Two dollars."

Mordecai paid her and watched her put the money in a small, locked compartment in the dresser. "Thanks, dearie," she said, hiding the key and slipping off her nightgown. "Well, c'mon. Let's get your clothes off."

Mordecai realized he'd been staring at her like a greenhorn and rapidly started undressing. His chest felt tight with excitement. He had never seen a young woman naked and was astonished at how beautiful she was.

She was appraising him frankly. "Well, the equipment works okay." She gestured for him to join her in bed. "Okay, let's go slow, dearie. Here, I'll help you," she said, reaching for him.

After that, Mordecai's only regret was that it didn't last longer. Afterwards, he had barely started to lay back and relax when Estelle popped out of bed and threw on her nightie.

"You were fine, honey, just fine." she said. "I really hate to rush you, honey, but you see there are others waiting to use the room. So..."

Mordecai got up and forced himself to dress quickly.

Going downstairs, he could see the living room was more crowded, smokier, noisier. David was nowhere to be seen. All the easy chairs were occupied, so Mordecai wandered over to watch the pianist bang out the ragtime tunes. The man looked to be about fifty or so, very dark, with a creased face topped by a derby, tipped back. He was smoking a stubby cigar and had a half-drunk beer on the keyboard.

"How ya doin', boss? he muttered out of the side of his mouth.

"Fine, just fine," Mordecai said, relaxed. "I was admiring your playing."

"Well, thanks, boss. I picked up this tune in Kansas

City. I met the guy who wrote it, Scott Joplin. He called it *Maple Leaf Rag*."

"It's very catchy," Mordecai used a word he'd heard David use.

"It is," the pianist agreed. "But you usually hear it played half again as fast as I'm playing it. Most people don't know this, ragtime players, I mean, but Joplin didn't want his music played fast. Told me so himself. I heard he died a few years ago. Too bad."

"Yes," Mordecai agreed. He noticed how the rhythm of this ragtime was different — looser — than the regular beats of a waltz or a four-beat song.

"Learning to play ragtime?" a voice inquired. Mordecai turned as David approached him, smiling.

"I was admiring this man's playing," Mordecai explained. "I'm sorry you didn't tell me your name."

"Josh."

"Short for Joshua. Well, I'm Mordecai" he said, putting out his hand and getting a quick shake since Josh was still playing.

"Both Old Testament names," Josh observed. "Both leaders and protectors of the Jews. Well, let's hope the Good Lord don't consider this place Sodom and send down his thunderbolts. Pleased t'meet you, Mr. Mordecai."

"Same here, Josh," Mordecai said as he felt David's arm firmly steering him away toward the front door.

"Sophie doesn't like the customers hanging around after they've finished," he explained. She needs the space. Besides, she might not like you talking to the hired help, especially the colored help."

"I was just waiting for you," Mordecai explained. He knew it sounded lame.

"I know. But still..."

The doorman opened the door for them, and the street air felt cool and fresh.

"So, how did it go? Did you enjoy it?"

"I did," Mordecai was emphatic. "Only, it was over too quickly."

David laughed. "It was for me too. Well, at least you've lost your cherry."

What a strange word for virginity, Mordecai thought. He liked cherries.

A week or so later, he discovered that Estelle had given him a souvenir of their coupling. A painful souvenir every time he urinated.

"You've got the clap," David said, authoritatively. "Or worse, syph."

"What are those?" Mordecai asked with dread.

"Clap is gonorrhea. Syph is syphilis. Syphilis is the more serious of the two. Tell me your symptoms. I knew a lot of guys in the Army who had one or the other, or both."

"Well..." Mordecai was intensely embarrassed.

"C'mon, out with it. Don't be embarrassed. But answer me one question first. Did you wear a rubber?"

"A rubber?"

"I should have explained before we went. A rubber is a little rubber bag you put over your cock when you have a hard-on. You roll it on to prevent disease. Also to prevent pregnancy, though it doesn't always work for that."

"No, I wore nothing."

"I'm sorry I didn't think to warn you. I thought Sophie would take better care of her girls than that."

"Did you wear one?"

"Yes. I always do. I could kick myself for not warning you. So, what are your symptoms?"

"It hurts when I pee. A lot. It's a burning feeling."

"Yep, that's the giveaway. And do you have a yellowish stain in your underwear?"

"Well, yes, now that you mention it."

"Yeah, you've got it all right. Any new pimples or open sores nearby?"

"Not that I've noticed."

"That's good. That's a sign of syph. So, you've probably got clap. We'll have to get you to a doctor right away before it gets worse."

It wasn't easy getting time off to see a doctor, but Mordecai relied on his good attendance record. David picked out the doctor, someone he knew who handled these cases, but he couldn't get time off. Mordecai would have to go through this alone.

Up a flight of shabby stairs in a decrepit building on a side street. The waiting room was surprisingly crowded with men. When it was finally Mordecai's turn an hour later, the doctor took him into the adjoining room and closed the door. He was middle-aged and fat with a pointed, dark beard and a large nose.

"So," he said brusquely, washing his hands, "what are your symptoms?" No introductions, Mordecai noted, gets right down to business. Probably all the men waiting in the outer room had the same problem or worse. He explained his symptoms.

"Yep. Sounds like gonorrhea, all right. Let's have a look. Take down your pants." After going through the Army physical, Mordecai was no longer embarrassed to comply.

"Uh-huh," the doctor said, examining him closely.

Good, no sores or pimples. That would be syphilis. Well, Mr. Stein," he said, straightening up, "there's two ways to treat this, and I recommend doing both. That way, if one method doesn't fully get it, the other one should."

"What are these ways?"

"The first is an injection of mercurochrome mixed with some other chemicals. The other is a heat treatment that takes about two hours. You sit in a hot box around your pelvis, and the heat should kill the little buggers. For that, though, you'll need to see my partner, up another flight."

"How much will it all cost?" Mordecai dreaded asking.

"Twenty bucks for the two treatments, plus two dollars for this office visit."

"How soon can we start?"

"Right now, if you've got the money."

Mordecai took out his wallet and counted out twenty-two dollars. The doctor pocketed it carefully and went to a sink to wash his hands again. Then he opened a drawer and took out a hypodermic already prepared and set it on a clean cloth. Mordecai could see several more sitting side by side in the drawer. He also noticed that this doctor, if he was a doctor, didn't use a nurse.

"I can inject you anywhere with this, but I think that the closer to the source of the infection the better. That means your penis. I'm going to put on something to numb the pain," he said, swabbing it. Mordecai immediately felt the cold numbing sensation. After half a minute passed, the doctor took up the hypodermic. Mordecai looked away. The injection was still painful with the numbing but not excruciating.

"There, that gets it," the doctor said, putting the used hypodermic in a different drawer crowded with them.

"That wasn't too bad, was it?"

"No."

"Okay, pull up your pants. Now you'll need to get the heat treatment. Dr. Macy's office is another flight up and to the right, room 303. These treatments should be working in a day or two at most. If it still hurts to piss after that, come back and we'll do a second round."

He opened the examining room door to let Mordecai out and to call in the next man.

The heat treatments involved sitting in a wooden box with electric heating coils. Once seated in the box, one had to avoid moving around lest he burn himself on the coils. An adjustable top was fitted to trap the heat, which reached about 130 degrees Fahrenheit. The hard part was not moving for two hours. Several of these heating boxes were placed in one large room, electric cords going every which way. Dr. Macy had thoughtfully placed a reader in the room to read aloud newspaper stories to distract the sitters and make the time pass. When it ended an eternity later, Mordecai had to wait for the coils to cool before lifting himself out of the box. His underwear was soaked with sweat.

"Well, how did it go?" David asked at work next day as they ate their lunch. Mordecai explained the procedure.

"Pretty rough," David said. "The Army didn't bother with those heat treatments. Just used injections. Poor Mordecai, your first time and look what happens."

"Yes, I paid two dollars for the disease and twenty-two to cure it."

"You'll know better next time."

"There won't be a next time. I'm never going to a whorehouse again."

"Well, that's a little extreme, but I can see how you feel."

"You don't know how I felt while I was there getting that heat treatment."

"But did it work? That's the important thing."

"It seems to have. The last time I peed, I felt much less pain."

"That's good. Let's hope it'll be all gone in a few days."

"Yes, I wouldn't want to go through that again. Besides, it's expensive."

He never told anyone else about his infection or the treatment. It was not only embarrassing, it made him feel dirty, soiled. And he didn't want to reveal his trip to the brothel. Going out with Miriam was difficult the next time. She sensed something was troubling him, but he denied it and just said he was tired. That was true. His body needed time to recover, he assumed. David was right — he'd know better in future.

6.

That future — the future they had planned together in the gasoline business — seemed as far away as ever. Mordecai had investigated a few filling stations that were for rent. They varied, depending on whether they had a garage and stalls for repairs and oil changes or were just a single building with one or two forlorn pumps. For a station with garage, two gas pumps and two large underground tanks, the rent was about $80 a month; for a station without the garage, about $40. By January 1920, their combined savings were about $450, nearly all of it Mordecai's. Especially since coming back from the war, David seemed incapable of saving money. He bought new clothes — 'snazzy' suits, shirts, collars, ties, shoes, a straw hat — and often went out at night, while Mordecai stayed home and read his library books. He was learning a lot of world history and had come to deeply admire Shakespeare, though he still had trouble understanding some of the sonnets, which seemed to be addressed to a young man, 'the master-mistress of my passion'. *Was Shakespeare a 'queer'?* (another new word for Mordecai). He wished he could discuss it with Miss Ryan.

"This saving plan isn't working," David concluded one Sunday afternoon at their favorite speakeasy. "I guess I'm just no good at saving. The war taught me to live for today."

"*Carpe diem.*"

"What? Where did you learn that? What's it mean?"

"It means," Mordecai explained patiently, "'seize the day'. Live for today. It's Latin. I read it in an explanation of a poem by Andrew Marvell, an English poet."

"Oh."

"Well, do you think we should just drop our plans?"

"No. I have a different idea," David said, pulling his chair closer and speaking in a low voice. "Look, Mordecai, since Prohibition came in, there's a lot of money to be made by providing people beer and hard stuff. It's called 'bootlegging.'"

"I've read about it in the papers."

"It's new in other parts of the country, but they've been doing it for a few years already here in Michigan. I've been talking with some friends of mine from the Army. They're already into it in a big way, and they're making tons of money. They could use me as a driver or delivery man. I'd make more money in a week than I'd make in a month at Maxwell's."

"Couldn't you get arrested? It's illegal, isn't it?"

"Well, sure, there's always that risk. That's why it pays so well. But these guys have already thought of that, and they pay off the cops on the beat where we pick up the stuff to look the other way. Also, they pay off those who are most likely to make the raids. Even some of the big bugs above them, I've heard, the politicians. It's a big money operation. I could make enough money doing this to quit my job at Maxwell's and have enough saved in six months to match your $350. The way I figure it, once our gas business gets going, I won't have to keep bootlegging and could join you full time."

"It sounds pretty risky to me," Mordecai said, knowing he was throwing cold water on David's enthusiasm.

David shook his head.

"Mordecai, you're just not a gambler, are you? 'Play it safe' is your motto. Well, I can understand that, but you're never going to get very far if you never take a chance. Look how long it took you to save $350. I still think the filling stations are a good idea, especially if we can run a string of them where we wouldn't just be doing the drudge work. But bootlegging is our shortcut to get there. And anyhow, I'll be taking the risk, not you."

That was how they left the matter, until Mordecai noticed a few days later that David wasn't at his place on the line.

"He just up and quit," his foreman explained. "Guess he must have found a better job somewhere."

In the meantime, a letter arrived from Mordecai's family in Motal. It was in Yiddish, written in neat cursive, apparently by his sister Anna. Though he was losing his fluency, Mordecai could still understand his native language. He read it aloud to his uncle.

Dear family,
We couldn't leave during the war and now Russia is at
war with Poland. Father hopes to receive land from
the Bolsheviks and doesn't want to leave. You should
also know that the influenza killed your brother Sasha
and has left Mother very weak. So, it looks like we're
staying for a while longer. The farm is doing all right,
but father needs more help in running it. Saul says
hello. We miss you and Chava terribly. How is life in
America? Are the streets really paved with gold?

Love, Anna

"So, I guess we're stuck with you and Chava forever,"
Uncle Yitzhak said, jabbing him in the ribs to let
Mordecai know he was teasing. "No, I am happy to have
you both. You have been as close to my heart as my own
children, closer in some ways (I tell you this in
confidence). You both have ambition which my children
seem to lack — you with working, Chava with learning
the violin."

"Thank you, Uncle. You're my real father. Chava's
too. Someday soon we won't be a burden to you — we'll
be able to support ourselves."

"Hush! What do you mean 'burden'? You're not a
burden; you're a joy, both of you."

Mordecai hugged him, his eyes wet.

He didn't see David for a few weeks. Then he got a
telephone call one evening.

"Hey, buddy. Haven't seen you in a while. You know I
left Maxwell's. How 'bout we meet at Ricky's for a beer
Saturday night? You can bring your girl if you want."

Ricky's used to be a thriving night club. Now, it was a

speakeasy. On the ground level windows were large signs declaring 'Closed'. And the ground floor was indeed empty. But a door below ground level admitted anyone with the right password, which David had provided. Mordecai had decided not to bring Miriam.

The large room on this Saturday night was crowded with drinkers, a full bar and waiters hurrying back and forth carrying drinks. The place was smoky, noisy and jovial. People were having a good time — it was fun to defy the law, especially such a silly law as Prohibition. As Mordecai's eyes adjusted to the dim lighting, he finally saw David waving at him. He was sitting at a table with two other men about his age. All were dressed in new suits of the latest fashion.

As Mordecai approached, David rose and introduced him; the other two just reached up to shake hands. One had a large gold ring on his index finger. Once again, Mordecai felt self-conscious about his name. *I'll have to change it to something more American*, he thought. *Mort or Mike, maybe.*

David was explaining, "Sam and me were in the same platoon. Abie here was in a different one, same company. We all three went through Saint-Mihiel together and the Argonne Forest." The other two grunted. Even though they both had Jewish names, they looked tough to Mordecai. He wasn't used to thinking of Jews that way.

"We were just talking shop," David explained a little nervously. "But we're just about through, right?" The other two nodded. "So, if you guys'll excuse us," David said rising, "Mordecai and me have some catching up to do. We're old friends from the assembly line at Maxwell's."

"Hey, I used to work there too," Sam said.

"Don't forget what we told you about the pickup at the pier," Abie said. The menace in his voice was obvious.

As they found a new table, Mordecai couldn't resist saying, "Nice friends you've got there."

"Oh, they're all right," David replied. "They were the ones who hired me on. We get along fine." The waiter came up. "I know you don't like beer, Mordecai, but have you ever tried an Old Fashioned? They're good. Whiskey, fruit, a little sugar and bitters. Why don't we order two?"

"That's fine. So, how do you like bootlegging?"

"Hey, go easy on the word," David cautioned. "You don't know who's at the next table listening."

"Sorry, I'll be more careful."

"I like the work fine," David said. "I'm driving a truck, a covered one. I pick up cases and deliver them to addresses I'm given. That's it. And collect the money. You want to know what I'm making a week? Sixty dollars! About three times what I was earning at Maxwell's for less work. The hours are a little difficult — I work mostly at night, but overall, a lot fewer hours than at Maxwell's. And it's not nearly as monotonous. Kind of interesting, really. You'd be surprised who's buying this stuff — lawyers and judges and the like. But that's all I can say about it. I mostly deal with their servants."

"Sounds nice," Mordecai said. He was determined not to be — *what was the expression?* — a wet blanket.

"It is nice. And I get a lot of free booze too. Sometimes a potential customer wants to sample our hooch, so I keep a bottle under the seat. At the end of the day, *I* take it home."

"Nice."

"Mostly, we're importing the stuff from Canada," David said in a low voice. "Detroit's a great place for that. They bring it across the river at night in speed boats. But they also make some of the stuff here, like gin and vodka. You should see how they mass produce the stuff. Ford wasn't the only guy who had that idea."

Mordecai couldn't hold back. "What if the cops show up when you're at the pier?"

"I told you before," David said, irritated. "They've already taken care of that. Anyway, it hasn't happened once."

"That's good. I'm happy for you, David."

"Thanks. Don't be such a worry-wort. I know what I'm doing. And it won't be for that long. Once I've built up my savings and we get that station going, my bootlegging days will be over."

"I'm really looking forward to that. Do you know how to repair cars?"

"Not really," David replied. "But we can hire a good mechanic for that. They're plenty of guys who did that in the war and need work."

"Good."

Meanwhile, Mordecai continued going out with Miriam when he could. That meant sacrificing some of his nighttime reading, but an evening with the exciting Miriam far outshined struggling with Shakespeare. Her boldness expressed itself in several ways; holding advanced views was one. She was all in sympathy with the 'New Woman' movement and talked about 'bobbing' her hair. But her parents were apoplectic at the idea — a good Jewish girl should look like a fast woman? Never! They were intensely protective of her; an old-world vigilance Miriam could have done without. But she admitted she wasn't quite ready to defy them, so her dark auburn hair stayed long (for which Mordecai was secretly grateful). Her parents still hadn't gotten over her marching in a women's suffrage parade down Woodward Avenue, Miriam laughed. But they had come around about her working and now took pride in her job at the law firm. It wasn't exciting work, she admitted, but it gave her an income. She also confided to Mordecai that she was a strong supporter of Margaret Sanger's campaign to disseminate 'birth control' information.

That confidence brought them inevitably to talking about sex. Just to hear a woman discussing it freely was exciting — advocating the idea of free love, for example, though Miriam wasn't entirely sure what that meant. Her views, however, were in advance of her behavior. She was still a virgin, she admitted, and Mordecai doubted that would change during their courtship. Nonetheless, that courtship was progressing steadily with a new vocabulary in vogue to describe its successive stages. They had moved from 'necking' to what was soon to be called 'petting'. And just as in the earlier stages of their relationship, Miriam often initiated things. Those dark eyes were as passionate as they were lovely.

The problem was privacy. When the two came back from a date, Miriam's parents never abandoned the parlor to give them some time alone. Unless Mr. and Mrs. Reubner went out for the evening, leaving Miriam to babysit her younger siblings, she and Mordecai had no way of being together in private. At Miriam's suggestion, they determined to take advantage of those opportunities. Mordecai would time his arrival to the narrow window between the kids falling asleep and the parents returning.

He didn't like sneaking over, but what alternative did they have? David had joked with him that they could rent a room in some sleazy hotel for a few hours, but none of them took that suggestion seriously. So, as the Marvell poem that Mordecai admired put it, they made the most of time. At the end of their brief interludes, both were excited and breathing hard. Both were physically frustrated that they couldn't go 'all the way'. But secretly, neither was quite ready to take that momentous step. That would have to wait until marriage.

7.

It was another three months, mid-June, before David decided they had saved enough to take the plunge. "I've saved up about $350," he announced. "With your $375 — that's what you told me, right? — we'd have about $725 altogether. We could easily hire a mechanic if we needed to and pay him about $25 a week."

"Makes sense," Mordecai said.

"Now, here's the thing," David continued. "I made a delivery to a gas station that's for rent on Grand River at Trumbull. I think the guy sells the booze from the back of the station. Anyhow, he pays eighty a month rent. It's got one stall for oil changes, lubes and repairs. Good location, lots of traffic and visibility. We'll probably need our own sign when we can afford it. By the way, that reminds me, what are we going to call our company?"

"I don't know," Mordecai said, his head swimming. "I never gave it any thought."

"Well, the sign there now is 'Sinclair'. That's good enough for now. Say, listen, I've been thinking. Maybe we need a gimmick to attract business. You know, like becoming a discount station and selling the gas for a penny or two less a gallon."

"Would we still make money?"

"Well, the discount stations seem to. They sure do plenty of business. You see more cars there than at the full-price stations. People always like a bargain. Let's drive out and take a look at it."

They did the same day in David's new Chevrolet. The station seemed in good repair, with a colorful 'Sinclair' sign, but just to be sure, David had the stall and lift checked a few days later by the mechanic he was thinking of hiring. They were fine. The lease had already expired, and the owner was eager to sign a new one. He wanted a year, but David insisted on six months with an option for a one-year renewal. The owner agreed, and the boys promised to come back later that day with their decision.

At a nearby café, while Mort watched, fascinated, David figured their costs and expected profit on a note pad.

"The guy said he refills his tanks about twice a week. So, that's 250 gallons per tank times two tanks, times twice a week is 1,000 gallons max a week. Okay, now at the current wholesale price — 24 cents per gallon — it would cost us about $240 a week to fill those tanks all the way. If we sell it at 27 cents a gallon, two cents below the market, we'd get $270, about $30 profit each week."

"Minus rent and upkeep and what we'd pay someone to operate the station and do the repairs," Mordecai put in. "That cuts it down a lot."

"But the repairs should bring in money," David protested. "And we can pump the gas — that doesn't take any skill. Artie can do the oil changes, lube jobs and repairs. We'll see if there's enough work for him to be full-time. I still think it sounds good."

"So do I," Mordecai said decisively. "Let's do it."

They returned to the station and signed the lease. They would take possession beginning next month.

"We'll figure out the partnership later," David said, "after we see if this is going to work out."

"Of course, it's going to work. Where's your optimism?" Mort teased him. He had never seen David so serious.

"Oh, by the way," David added. "I think it would be a good idea if you got your citizenship right away. I got mine in the Army. That way, you'd have legal rights you don't have as an immigrant. Remember how they deported all those immigrants last year without even a trial? And if we become legal partners, it might be more convenient."

"Suddenly, everything is 'legal.'"

"Well, them's the rules. We might as well play by them."

"At least for this," Mordecai smiled. David caught the allusion and just shrugged.

Mordecai gave his notice and waited for July 1st. It was a big gamble. If it didn't work out, he would lose not only his savings, but his foreman's job. At best, he'd have to start on the line again. *Be optimistic*, he thought. *This thing ought to work. Other people do it and make money. Why shouldn't we?* And Miriam was all for it.

David told his bosses too. "They weren't too happy about it," he explained. "Once you start working in their organization, they expect you to stay in. I made it better by saying that, for now, I just wanted to cut back on my deliveries, do only the night ones. That would keep my days open. And if this doesn't work out, I'd go back to full-time."

"What did they say to that?"

"Like I said, they weren't too pleased. But they agreed to let me just do nights for now, so long as I train my daytime replacement."

"When will you sleep?"

"That's a good question. I suppose in the first few months very little, where I can catch naps. By the way, I wanted to talk with you about sharing an apartment, but we'll discuss that later, after we see if this thing is going to work."

It did work. In the first two weeks of their taking over, business was good. Drivers were attracted by the discounted price and even lined up at times, especially after the bigger price signs went up. David and Mordecai quickly became adept at pumping gas; it required cranking the right amount to the top of the Gilbarco pump, like pumping a well, and letting gravity do the rest. Checking oil and water was also routine for each customer, as well as cleaning the windscreen. Occasionally, they had to check tire pressures. David came to work exhausted in those weeks, since he was still making night deliveries. They bought a cot and put it in the back room for him to nap when business was slack. Once, Mordecai forgot to use a rag to open a radiator cap and burned his hand. *I'll never make that mistake again*, he thought, looking at his Vaselined palm.

They also did a steady business in oil changes, lube jobs and repairs. Artie easily adapted his Army experience repairing trucks to cars. They paid him $25 a week with an

65

agreement to raise it to $30 in six months if business permitted. The repair business easily brought in $40-$50 more a week. Just as the former proprietor had described, the Sinclair delivery truck came twice a week, and the filling went smoothly.

At the end of the first week, after deducting expenses, they had cleared $47 and were jubilant. "We did it!" David exulted over beer that Sunday. This time, Mordecai brought Miriam with him. She was polite to David, taken aback somewhat by his impetuous nature, but seemed a bit bored by their wanting only to talk shop. "If this keeps up," David crowed, "we could get another station in a few months."

"Who would run it?"

"I would. I'd quit the nighttime deliveries and start sleeping regularly. We might need to hire a second mechanic, depending."

"Well, let's not go too fast," Mordecai cautioned, glancing at Miriam. "We've only been at this a week. Let's make sure it's really working for the next few months."

"Okay, Mr. Cautious. Miriam, you probably already know how conservative your boyfriend is. He doesn't like to take chances."

"He took one by quitting his job and going in with you," she said sharply. Then, as if to soften her response, she added, "Yes, I've noticed that he's cautious. I like that." She took his hand.

"Oh, I forgot to tell you both," Mordecai said. "I checked on the citizenship, which I agree is a good idea. But it can't happen for two years. First, you sign a 'Declaration of Intent', and then you have to wait at least two years to petition for citizenship. Meanwhile, you acquire a few letters saying that you're of good character.

And apparently, they send someone out to investigate you. Good thing you got your citizenship in the Army, David. I don't think letters from Abie and that other fellow I met would be too impressive."

"Yeah, good thing. Well, my time with them should be over pretty soon," David said, not wanting to identify them to Miriam.

At home, Uncle Yitzhak's family was also excited by Mordecai's new business, at least Uncle Yitzhak was.

"So, now you are a real American businessman!" he exulted. "I promise you that when I buy an automobile, I shall buy my gasoline only at your station."

"You should live so long," Minna muttered. *A true pessimist*, Mordecai thought. *Do opposites attract?*

The children had become almost fully Americanized and talked about the best kind of car to get, knowing that their father would keep taking the streetcar.

"A Pierce-Arrow is what I want," Jascha, the eldest, said.

"Yeah," his brother replied. "And you'll only need about five thousand to buy one."

"Well, I can dream, can't I? I saw one on Woodward yesterday. It's the bee's knees."

"So, you'll be making more money than you did at Maxwell's?" Uncle Yitzhak asked.

"It looks that way. Of course, we've only been doing it a few weeks. But business has been good. David's idea of selling the gas for less seems to be working very well."

"Why shouldn't it?" Jascha put in. "It's all the same gas, isn't it?"

"Yes, Sinclair gas."

"So why not save two bits on a fill-up? Plus, you've

got a good location, sounds like."

"Yes," Mordecai agreed. You can drive in from Grand River or from Trumbull, and both have a lot of traffic."

"Well, I'm proud of you, *boychik*," Uncle Yitzhak said. "I knew you wanted to get ahead when you started working at Maxwell's. You've shown real — I don't know what the right word in English is. In Yiddish, we'd call you a *macher*. A do-er."

"The word you wanted was 'initiative.'" Katya said, without interest. Everything seemed to bore her except the stars of the picture shows whose pictures she pinned to her walls.

"Yes, that's it," Uncle Yitzhak agreed. "He is, no, he *has i*nitiative."

"Moxie," his younger son put in.

Mordecai was pleased but also sensed, as always, the jealousy of his cousins over Uncle Yitzhak's admiration. At least, Chava was genuinely pleased.

"You're going to be a big man one day, Mordecai. A capitalist," she chaffed, poking him in the ribs. "Then I would have to oppose you."

"The only thing I regret," Yitzhak concluded, "is that now I have to ride the streetcar to and from Maxwell's alone. Oh well. *Mazel tov* on your success! We should have a party to celebrate it. And of course, David and Miriam should come," he said, eyeing Minna. She pretended not to have heard.

"That would be very nice," Mordecai said. "But let's wait a while to make sure things work out."

8.

68

1920 proved to be a momentous year for several reasons. The filling station was successful enough for the unofficial partners to open a second station about a mile away on Warren Avenue and Brooklyn Street. David operated this one, which lacked a stall for repairs. The two partners decided to give their enterprise a new name: *$AVON GAS!*

"It's short and gets the message across," David said. They had the 'Sinclair' and 'Standard Oil' signs removed and their own large signs put up along with the daily gas price. Though it brought in less business than the first station, the Warren Avenue station was still profitable.

"We should make our partnership official," David said.

"That would require seeing a lawyer,' Mordecai replied. "And they charge an arm and a leg for drawing up the papers."

"Still, I'd like to see it done. Just as soon as we're sure of what we're doing by expanding. My idea is for us to run four or five stations, where we would hire people to operate them. Our job would be to go from one to another each day, collect the receipts, pay the bills, hire and fire, check on how it's going."

"Administer them," Mordecai offered.

"Why not just say 'run them'? I'd like to go home each day without grease on my shirt. Wear a coat and tie. I won't miss working for Sam and Abie so long as I'm making more than the $60 a week I made as a driver. By the way, I didn't tell you," he added quietly, "they've branched out into other rackets — prostitution, extortion, protection, even kidnapping. And they've got a name, The Purple Gang."

"I've heard of it," Mordecai said. "How does protection work?"

"Simple. You pay them a buck or two a week, and they don't blow up your store. I can tell you, I'm glad to be out of it," David continued. "Running booze is one thing. That's harmless, even provides a useful service. But kidnapping..."

"I'm glad you're out, too."

A second event of 1920 was Mordecai's new name. He had long wanted to Americanize it. "When I filled out the Petition for Citizenship, I put down 'Morton. Morton M. Stein'," he announced proudly to Miriam and David over drinks. "Morton is close to Mordecai but American."

"What does the 'M' stand for?" David asked.

"Nothing, I made it up. It's alliterative." (He knew Miss Ryan would be proud of his poetry vocabulary even though the word made David frown.)

"Okay, Mort."

"Morton," Miriam said, "I like the sound of it. It sounds dignified."

"It's a good thing you decided this before we drew up any partnership documents," David pointed out. "Anyhow, I've been telling you to do this ever since I got back from Europe. An American company should be run by Americans."

"It still feels funny to me. But I guess I'll get used to it if I sign enough papers and checks."

"I'm sure you will... Morton," Miriam agreed.

"Just call me Mort," he said, picking up David's cue.

"I hope you don't expect me to change my name to Mary or something."

"No, of course not. I like Miriam."

He liked it so much that he proposed marriage a few weeks later. Miriam promptly accepted. The two set the wedding date for December 1920. Mort had no trouble gaining her family's approval — an ambitious Jewish businessman with an expanding business? Why not? Like Mordecai's name change, the couple was determined to shed old-world trappings. Just as they hadn't relied on a matchmaker to bring them together — few Jewish couples did these days — they rejected any notion of an old-world dowry, with its insulting implications for women. This was America, after all. They resolved to enter the marriage as equals, and that's how they'd remain. Miriam would continue working at the law firm for the time being. But they wanted to start a family right away.

Their wedding in late December was both a delight and a disaster. Since their circle of friends was small, Miriam's family held it at their home. David used his contacts to provide wine and whiskey, and all seemed to go well until Uncle Yitzhak got drunk. He'd made the mistake of drinking whiskey for the many toasts to the health and good fortune of the newlyweds. By the third whiskey, his head was spinning. His own toast to the newlyweds was rambling and incoherent. Shortly after, he stumbled and fell squarely into the wedding cake. Amid the uproar, Morton quietly escorted him out of the apartment and into the alley, where, as he had expected, Uncle Yitzhak unceremoniously vomited.

"Feel better?" Mort tried to hide his irritation.

"I feel terrible," Yitzhak replied, "Why in God's name did I let myself do this? I'm not a *schicker*."

"That's obvious. But it can happen to anyone," Mort said, thinking of his own disaster with — what was her name? — Estelle? "Here," he said, handing Yitzhak a clean handkerchief. "Clean yourself up."

When they returned to the Reubners' apartment, Mort ignored their angry looks and steered his uncle directly to the bathroom to wash up. Meanwhile, the wedding cake had been repaired as much as possible, and the wedding party continued, albeit a bit subdued.

For their honeymoon, Mort and Miriam decided to see New York again, not as the immigrants they'd been (or in Miriam's case, a child of immigrants) but now as American tourists. They went to see the Statue of Liberty, the Woolworth Building (the tallest skyscraper) and Ellis Island, which was still doing a thriving business with immigrants of all nationalities crowding the Great Hall. They also went to 'cultural' places: to hear the New York Philharmonic-Symphony (Miriam loved classical music, Mort was learning to like it), to the Museum of Art with its cavernous rooms, and the Museum of Natural History. They saw Broadway plays, such as the musical *Sally*. Mort wanted very much to see a Shakespeare play and persuaded Miriam to see *A Midsummer Night's Dream*, a lighthearted change from the dark tragedies he'd already read. They also saw a drama by a newcomer named O'Neill, *Beyond the Horizon*, which won the Pulitzer Prize for drama that year. Miriam considered it quite poetic; Mort was a bit bored by it. Nostalgia took them back to the Lower East Side, and Mort reflected on how far they'd already come from Mott and Hester Streets. He'd almost forgotten the noisy, dirty, pushcart-filled streets, but they were still there. They also sampled many kinds of restaurants: Chinese, Italian, and of course Jewish delicatessens. David had recommended a wonderful Romanian steak house on Second Avenue. The whole trip was a culinary delight, even the overnight train back to Detroit. Six weeks later, Miriam discovered she was pregnant.

In Detroit, they found a nice two-bedroom apartment in a fairly new building on Richton Street. It was close to Dexter Avenue, where many Jewish families were moving from Twelfth Street. Miriam immediately began decorating the second bedroom as the baby's room, while Mort abandoned his wistful notion of making it an office with a desk and a bookcase for his future library. In no time at all, they settled into a comfortable domesticity. With help from Miriam's parents, they furnished the apartment and bought a Victrola and some classical recordings. Mort even assembled a crystal set to pick up the first radio station broadcasting in Detroit, WWJ. Its headphones, however, permitted only one person at a time to listen. In the evenings, they read, sometimes discussed current events or listened — quietly — to the recordings Miriam was eagerly acquiring. Mort dreamed of the day when they owned their own home and could play their recordings as loud as they wanted. The neighborhood was predominantly brick two-flats, one flat atop the other. If they could buy one, they'd live in one flat and have a steady income from renting the other. Each flat typically had three small bedrooms, a dining room, living room and a spacious front porch, plus a basement, attic and front and back yards for the building — considerably more space than their apartment.

In his reading, Mort had long since finished the Nevins history and was now reading the religious books that Miss Ryan had recommended. He was struck more by similarities and parallels between the Old and New Testaments and the *Koran* than by their differences. *Yet these are the books*, he mused, *which led hordes to murder their countrymen in religious wars and to persecutions through the centuries.* Just as when he was dating Miriam, he was impressed by her interest in ideas. Her devotion to Mencken's *Smart Set* led her to recommend other books in other subjects, but his appetite for learning was never sated. Equally pleasing was Miriam's passion in bed, which their restricted courtship had only hinted at.

The arts continued to be important for the couple. Just two years earlier, the Detroit Symphony had appointed a new music director, Ossip Gabrilowitsch, who had already made a name for himself in Europe. Before accepting the post, 'Gabby', as he became affectionately known to Detroiters, insisted that the city build a music hall befitting its orchestra. Flush with tax receipts, the city complied and created Orchestra Hall on Woodward Avenue, which proved to have superb acoustics. Mort and Miriam became patrons. Similar largesse was granted to the young director of the imposing Art Institute, William Valentiner, who traveled after the war to his native Germany, where he bought the paintings of several German Expressionist artists. These purchases not only enabled these hungry artists to survive the dire post-war conditions in Germany but also gave Detroit a world-class collection of Expressionist art. Many patrons, including some of the Institute's board members, were skeptical of this 'crazy, modern art', notably the paintings of Franz Marc and Paul Klee (not to mention the Cubist works of Picasso and Braque, which Valentiner had also bought). But the intrepid director maintained his tenure at the Institute. He also improved its general collection. With Europe still recovering from the Great War and in an economic recession, there were bargains to be found in the old masters. The Steins went to the Art Institute several times; Miriam was much impressed by the new

German art; Mort was confused by it and preferred the old masters.

9.

Miriam's first pregnancy was uncomplicated, though the last few months were uncomfortable. The baby was born in October 1921, a healthy boy, and weighed eight pounds. Since it was a boy, Uncle Yitzhak had urged them to name it Rueben or Rueven, the name of the biblical Jacob's first-born son. The name meant 'Behold, a son!'

"I bet he'd have no such suggestion if it had been a girl," Miriam said, with an edge in her voice. She could be quite biting at times, and Mort had felt the lash of her tongue.

"Well, it wasn't, as it turned out."

"That's fine. But I'm not naming him Rueben."

"Do I have a say in this?"

"Of course. You're free to agree with me."

They settled on Edward, which both considered a good Anglo-American name.

"Edward Avram, after my grandfather," Miriam said.

"Fine. If he doesn't like the Avram, he can just be Edward A. Edward A. Stein."

"You think he'll be self-conscious about a Jewish middle name? Really, Mort."

"Well, I was about Mordecai. I'm not ashamed of being Jewish, you know that. But I saw no reason to declare it in my name, which is the first thing people encounter about you, besides your looks."

"And are we going to raise him Jewish?" Miriam asked.

"That depends on what you mean by Jewish. We don't keep kosher."

"I said Jewish, not Orthodox. He's *not* going to wear a skullcap and a *tallit* all the time."

"I'd like him to grow up feeling Jewish," Mort said. "Might as well, since the rest of the world will treat him that way."

"But what does that mean? What does it entail?"

"It means that we celebrate the Jewish holidays, the major ones anyway, and that he learns Hebrew so he can *daven* in the *shul* and have a Bar Mitzvah."

"But you didn't have one."

"That was different. My father had no interest in religion. And he would have been too cheap to host a Bar Mitzvah party."

"You don't like him very much, do you?"

"No, not very much. The more I think back on my childhood with him, the more I think he was one selfish bastard. But back to Edward., do you agree with me?"

"I suppose so, if that's what you really want. I had hoped we could put all that superstition behind us and be a modern couple."

"It isn't just superstition, Miriam. It's the history of our people. History is important."

"Don't I know it. After two weeks of dating you, I realized how important it is to you."

"He should know about our people. Our history. Our holidays. Then, after he's grown, if he wants to reject it, that will be his decision."

"I'm glad you've worked this all out, just surprised we didn't discuss it earlier."

"I don't know why we didn't. It just never came up."

"Well, I suppose you want him circumcised."

"Of course. If he's a Jew, he must be circumcised."

"It seems barbaric to me. Like something out of the Dark Ages."

"Nonetheless, we have to do it if we're going to raise him Jewish. We'll need to find a *moyle*. There should be a little celebration after the ceremony — we'll invite our Jewish friends. Maybe your folks can host it. I promise to keep Uncle Yitzhak away from the cake."

"At least keep him away from the *schnapps*," Miriam smiled, remembering.

"I think David better leave his flapper girlfriends home for this one," Mort laughed. "They might faint."

Miriam looked at the baby. "I hope Edward forgives us some day for messing with him this way."

"He'll never know. It will seem normal afterwards."

Mort wrote his family in Russia about the birth, and their reply, written by Anna, came as a surprise. After congratulating Mort and Miriam on the birth, she informed him,

We, that is Motal, are no longer part of Russia. We are now part of Poland. We think it was because of the recent war between Russia and Poland. They have changed the borders. Even Pinsk, which is several miles to the East, is now part of Poland. Our village's commissioner is Polish, and no one is permitted to speak Russian. It makes little difference to us living out on a farm so long as they don't bother us.

The letter went on to talk about the family. In short, everyone was okay except Mother, who was still weak from her influenza. Father was as cantankerous as ever.

Two more children followed Edward in close succession:

Sarah in 1922, and Andrew two years later. Both seemed healthy, but Miriam's attitude had changed with Andrew's birth.

She had already left her secretarial job before Sarah's birth to be a full-time homemaker. Now, she declared from her hospital bed while nursing Andrew, "That's it! The end of the Stein brood. No more children for me!"

"You might have discussed it with me first," Mort said, hurt.

"And if you objected? No, this is my decision, dear husband. I'm the one who has to go through this burden each time, and let me tell you, it *is* a burden. Besides, it's not the fashion to have large families anymore, if you care about that sort of thing. These days, you're not likely to lose half of them to disease."

"Thank God!" Mort said automatically.

"I thought you were agnostic," Miriam taunted him.

"I am. But why tempt fate?"

When Miriam had recovered after Andrew's birth, their sex life changed and not for the better. It was much less relaxed and spontaneous. Now, Miriam demanded that Mort wear a condom. Stopping to put it on cooled their passion temporarily, made their couplings more deliberate. *And fewer*, Mort noted sadly. *But at least it reduced Miriam's fear of getting pregnant again.*

Meanwhile, his partnership with David, still unofficial, continued without mishap. The two filling stations they leased continued to show a profit of about $50 a week for the bigger station, $30-35 for the smaller one. David's dream of driving from station to station in his business suit to collect receipts was still a long way off, and the two still put in long hours pumping gas, checking oil and water, and wiping windows. But Mort agreed with David's plan to rent a third station with repair stalls as soon as they could afford to. This would require hiring someone to manage it and someone else to do the repairs. They went with recommended people; Art, the mechanic at the Grand River station, knew several men with experience. To prevent skimming, the partners kept close tabs on gallons sold versus the receipts and asked questions if the two didn't jibe. By late 1923, they had their third station, this one on the near East Side on John R, and the two alternated in checking on its operations each day. Their stations' name, *$AVON GAS!* was becoming known and attracting regular customers. The partners met twice a week at David's apartment to go over receipts, bank deposits, purchase orders and the like. David, as usual, was forward-thinking.

"Now if we can clear $150 a week in profits — and we're almost there — we could afford to hire operators for the first two stations and expand further."

"You won't be happy until you've realized your dream," Mort remarked.

"What dream is that?"

"Being a businessman and wearing a suit, not operating a filling station in overalls."

"Well, why not? There's plenty of money to be made at this racket."

"It's not a racket, David. It's an honest business."

"You know what I meant. It's just an expression. We could also think about buying these stations outright if they're money-makers."

"That will take a lot more money than we're earning now."

"Yeah, but eventually... Speaking of making money,

have you thought about investing your money? The banks don't pay diddly squat in interest. You could get a much better return on your money in the stock market." He held up a hand. "I know what you're going to say: 'That's gambling.' Well, of course it is! But look how well the market has been doing since that last downturn in twenty-one. And the best part is, you only need to put ten percent down. It's called 'buying on margin'."

"I've heard about it," Mort said. "Always the gambler, eh?"

"Well, I'd say it's a good bet. When the market goes up and increases the value of the stock, it sort of covers the 90% you owe."

"*If* you cash in then. And what if the market goes down?'

"But it hasn't in almost three years. But if it did, you'd just have to put up more margin to cover the loss."

"And if you didn't happen to have more margin to put up?"

"Then you'd lose your investment. But the brokerage would give you more time to get it, because they want your business."

Mort reflected for a moment. "I like the idea of buying stock, but not the idea of buying it on margin. If you paid full price, then you'd own the stock outright, and they couldn't sell you out."

"Right," David agreed. "But that costs a lot more and leaves less money for investing."

"For playing the market, you mean. Still, you're gambling that the market will go up to cover what you owe."

"And it will. It has."

"Maybe. Well, it's your money."

In the end, after discussing it with Miriam, Mort

bought a few stocks but paid full price. After consulting some business friends and doing some research about investing, he decided to buy expensive 'blue chip' stocks: Ford Motor Co. and AT&T, also a utility, Detroit Edison. These seemed the most secure, even though they paid less in dividends and their price was considerably higher than the supposedly high-profit stocks. *High-profit, high risk*, Mort concluded. Once he bought them, he gradually added shares but otherwise didn't think much about them except to note with pleasure the quarterly dividend checks that arrived like clockwork.

David's collection of stocks was much bigger, and he was constantly buying and selling them, based on tips he received from friends who were 'in the know'. He must have been making money on them because his standard of living was considerably flashier than Mort and Miriam's. Though he lived alone, his apartment was bigger and had newer appliances. He had already traded in his modest Chevy for an impressive Packard.

"An eight-cylinder!" he boasted.

His nights were taken up by an active social life — flappers, night clubs and parties, where drinking and dancing were the chief entertainments. He took Mort and Miriam to some of the new jazz clubs springing up in Detroit's 'Black Bottom' or to the Graystone Ballroom on Woodward. There, they heard performers like Jean Goldkette's band and McKinney's Cotton Pickers with Don Redman. In return, the couple often invited David to Sunday dinner, along with his latest flame, typically an over-rouged flapper. Though Miriam had taught herself to be a good cook, Mort could see that David and his girlfriend would soon become restless with after-dinner conversation and were itching for something livelier — a party or a nightclub.

Mort had to admit that David's free-wheeling life was more typical of the times, which had made speakeasy drinking a national sport. Detroit alone had hundreds of 'blind pigs'. By contrast, Mort and Miriam's quiet domesticity seemed rather stuffy — old-fashioned and conservative. But 'conservative', Mort gradually came to understand, was his true self. He was careful and cautious, where David was bold, sometimes reckless. Mort even voted conservative, now that he was a citizen. In 1924 he voted for Coolidge, believing that the Republican Party favored businessmen like himself and was less likely to impose new taxes. He liked Coolidge's expression, 'The business of this country is business'.

Besides Andrew's birth and Coolidge's election, 1924 had another significance. That year, Congress passed a new restrictive immigration bill that virtually closed American shores to Eastern European immigrants. The backlash that had been building for years against the hordes flooding Ellis Island had finally come to a head. In fact, intolerance was growing in all sorts of ways. The Ku Klux Klan would soon feel bold enough to march down Washington's Pennsylvania Avenue in their white robes and hoods. The new immigration restrictions were aimed not just at Jews, but also Italians, Slavs and other groups. The Klan harassed Blacks, of course, but also hated Catholics and Jews. Aligning with these actions, a supposed 'science' was growing in popularity. Called 'eugenics', it described the allegedly negative effects of race mixing for Nordic Whites, whose putatively superior genetic stock was being diluted by the influx of 'inferior' races. Though many scientists debunked the theory, it gave bigots in Congress a pseudo-scientific rationale for their immigration restrictions.

Mort considered the eugenics argument for the new law stupid. Would Einstein have 'diluted' the racial stock? But the law's consequences hit home. His family in Motal had waited too long. Now, they weren't likely to get immigration visas to the United States even if they tried. When Mort gave them the bad news, it didn't matter a bit to Schmuel Stein, since he didn't want to leave. But the remainder of his family despaired of ever being reunited with Mort and Chava. For better or worse, they were now stuck in Motal as its national controllers oscillated between Russia and Poland, and now a new nation that had resulted from the Polish-Russian settlement in 1922, Belarus.

By 1925, the partners had finally achieved their dream of managing several stations in suits and ties, rather than operating a few as uniformed attendants. Their fourth station, a large one with a two-stall garage, was located on Fort Street at Trumbull. Though its rent was higher, its gas sales more than covered that cost, and it did a steady business in repairs, tune-ups, and the like. David thought of adding new tires for each station with a garage — the most popular brands and sizes — as well as the equipment for changing tires and fixing flats, a common problem with 1920s tires. From all four stations, the partners were clearing about $225 a week.

Much of their time was taken up in sending in orders — each station carried supplies for cars (oil, fan belts and the like), plus soft drinks and candy. They had rest rooms that needed constant cleaning and plumbing repairs. It also took time to check sales of gas and oil against cash receipts. Suspicious discrepancies — and they were unfortunately common — led to their firing operators, which meant advertising and interviewing for new ones. David suggested hiring a bookkeeper to keep track of sales, orders and receipts, but Mort felt it would cut too deeply into their profits. Miriam solved that problem by volunteering her own bookkeeping skills. The three would meet at the Steins' apartment on Sunday afternoons to go over the books. A carry-out deli meal followed, and the three adults could relax into social conversations. In this way, the Sunday dinners evolved.

Mishaps were still inevitable, of course. When an operator called in sick, one of the partners filled in and swapped his suit for overalls and a cap. On these occasions, Mort learned more about human nature than he'd previously known. Most customers were pleasant enough, provided they didn't have to wait too long for service. But Mort grew to despise the impatient horn-honkers when he was in the garage talking to a mechanic. Occasionally, women were customers; they were the most appreciative of his service. Anything to keep them from having to deal with these strange machines themselves! Often, people just wanted directions, and Mort soon became an expert on Detroit streets and avenues.

Finally, there were the smooth-talking crooks. Mort learned about them the hard way in his first month. He'd been working at the Grand River station when a well-dressed man pulled in with a nice car, bought about $1.25 in gas and asked if Mort could change a $20. Mort did so. Then the man seemed to suddenly remember, "Oh, I've got just the right amount here" he said, handing it over. "Just give me back my $20." Mort did, and the man was already two blocks away before Mort realized he'd been taken. *Never again!* he vowed. Since then, he'd lost count of how many customers had tried that trick. Never the same guy twice, of course, and always well-dressed. He warned David, who admitted sheepishly that he'd been suckered too. "We ought to keep a bouncer around," he said, "for punching those guys in the face."

10.

As the Twenties moved on, Mort and Miriam's home life was almost completely taken up by their children. By the time he and Miriam had bathed the kids, read them stories and put them to bed, Mort was usually too tired to keep up with his reading project and Miriam too tired to go over the partners' books. That would wait until Sundays. Sadly, Mort noticed that he and Miriam spent less time talking about current events and ideas. She had developed her own interests: reading, of course, but also bridge and mahjong, a board game that had become quite a fad in these years. Mort's interests were less social; his business, of course, reading when he could find time for it, a book club at the JCC and classical music (they still attended the symphony). Together, they could enjoy programs in their own living room. The crystal sets of 1920 had evolved into radios that broadcast news, concerts, but mostly half-hour and fifteen-minute programs — comedies, romances, adventure serials — and irritating commercials. Their floor-length Philco became the proud centerpiece of their living room.

Before Andrew's birth in 1924, they had put a down payment on a roomier two-flat, which provided a regular income from the downstairs flat. Its locale on Tyler Street was shady and tree lined. They could also afford a housekeeper to come in once a week. With her parents babysitting, Miriam had time to shop and run errands on Dexter Avenue and join her friends for their weekly bridge and mahjong games at the Jewish Center on Davison Avenue.

In 1925, Mort's sister Anna wrote to announce that their younger brother, Saul, had married a girl from Pinsk, and the couple had moved to Moscow, where Saul worked in a tool factory. He had become a devoted Communist.

So now it falls to me to take care of Mother and Father. Mother is still quite ill. Father is old and difficult. It is hard finding help to run the farm.

The sadness and resignation in Anna's letter were painful.

One reason Mort and Miriam didn't discuss current events much was there seemed fewer to discuss. The later Twenties seemed remarkably free of wars and disasters, except for the flood of 1927, which didn't affect Detroit. Lindbergh's successful Atlantic flight and celebrated return were briefly distracting. Baseball fans like David went to Tigers games, especially to watch Babe Ruth hit home runs — he hit sixty in 1927. But Mort wasn't a big sports fan. Prohibition continued, and mobsters like the Purple Gang were murderously competing for the big profits. David said often that he was lucky to be out of it, and the Gang left their gas stations alone. People seemed to be drinking and giving parties more than ever. Generally, times were good; one obvious sign was all the new cars Detroit was selling. They could be seen parading down Woodward Avenue, the city's central north-south thoroughfare.

There was one other distinctive feature about the late Twenties, however: the stock market, which had been rising steadily most of the decade, now really took off.

"It's unbelievable!" David said at dinner one evening in 1928. "You could buy RCA for $60 a share in January, and now — what is it, six months later? — it's selling for $80! Think of that! It's risen a third in just six months! And the same is true for all the other stocks. I tell you, people are making a fortune on the market. I get tips from my barber!"

"Are you still buying on margin?" Mort asked.

"But natch," David replied. "Hey, I wait four weeks, and the market's rise has covered what I owe! It's just amazing."

"*If* it keeps going like this," Mort inserted.

Now, both Miriam and David objected, "You're always the pessimist!" Miriam chastised him. It wasn't teasing anymore; she was clearly fed up with his gloominess. "I know you don't believe in buying on margin. Okay. But we could still take advantage of this market if we paid full price."

"You should listen to your wife, Mort," David put in.

"But I do own stocks," Mort said defensively, "and I've been adding to them gradually."

"But now is the time to get in big," David continued. "Get in while the getting's good."

"Is there a particular stock you recommend?"

"I'll check with my broker and get back to you. I'll look for a conservative one," David teased, winking at Miriam.

One afternoon, in late October 1929, David called from the station on Brooklyn. "Have you heard the news? Wall

Street's crashed! It's a real panic. Stock prices are going down like crazy. My broker's already called twice wanting more margin on several stocks."

"Can you put it up?"

"Unfortunately, no. This caught me up short."

"Does that mean you'll lose them?"

"Looks that way."

Mort took a deep breath. "I'll be glad to loan you money, David, to try to cover the losses. How much are we talking about?"

"The broker wants about two thousand."

"Two thousand?! I don't have anywhere near that kind of money. I think I have about five hundred in our checking account and another eight hundred in our savings. What about five or six hundred?"

"That would help a lot, Mort."

"Okay. You're at the Brooklyn Station? I can meet you there in a half hour with a check. Then you can wire the money to your broker."

"I'll be here. Thanks, Mort. I hate to do this to you. You're a pal."

"Happy to do it, David. I won't even say 'I told you so.'"

"You just did."

"Yes, I guess I did. Well, not again."

After he hung up, he realized that he hadn't cleared this large loan with Miriam. He hoped she wouldn't object.

11.

The stock market crash was only the beginning of troubles for the country and for what would later be called 'the economy'. It didn't happen all at once. It didn't even begin on Black Thursday and the following Tuesday. The market had had some earlier breaks, like warning tremors of a coming earthquake, but it seemed to recover. After the October crash, it even had a mini boom over the winter but then crashed much harder the following spring of 1930. The real problem wasn't the market, Mort explained over dinner — he had been mulling this over for several months. It was people's psychology, their expectations.

"Let's say you're thinking about buying a car on payments. So long as you have your job and conditions are okay, you go ahead and buy. You expect a regular paycheck to enable your payments. But if things look shaky, as they did after the Crash, and your job no longer looks secure, you decide to play it safe and put off buying. Now, multiply that decision by millions of other ones for all kinds of products that aren't strictly necessary."

Miriam and David tried to look interested. They had heard Mort's lectures before.

"Okay, now imagine the psychology of a manufacturer who has to decide how much to produce for the next six months, or whether to build that new plant to produce even more. He's seen the Crash also, and it shakes his confidence. Perhaps the company's sales for the last six months have declined. So, if he *expects* sales to go down even more, not only does he cut back on production and not build that new plant, he decides to lay off some of his workers to cut expenses. So, now you have more people out of work, and the cycle continues. You see, both the buying and producing decisions are based on expectations of how conditions will be in the future. And those expectations are largely psychological; they're based on the buyer's or producer's confidence. The stock market kept climbing in the last few years not because businesses were making so much more money but because people just *expected* stocks to keep climbing."

"So, you're saying it was like a house of cards," Miriam said.

"Exactly. With nothing to support it but expectations. And those can change overnight. One strong jolt like the October crash, and the house comes tumbling down."

David had been quiet, listening. He offered no wisecracks. His natural ebullience had diminished markedly since the Crash. Finally, he spoke.

"So then the big question is, when will this turn around? When will people's expectations change?"

"I don't have a crystal ball for that one," Mort shrugged. "But you'll notice that President Hoover is playing the expectations game when he announces, 'Prosperity is just around the corner.'"

"Yeah," Miriam put in. "Unfortunately, no one believes him. He's just trying to buck us up."

"I could say something that rhymes with 'buck,' which describes what he's really doing to us," David said. "But that's not true either. So far as I can tell, he's really not doing much of anything."

"Perhaps he doesn't know what to do, despite his rosy predictions," Miriam said. "You know, they've interviewed some of the big industrial moguls, like Ford and Firestone — you know, the ones who are always asked for their opinions by reporters — and *they* sound as stumped as everyone else."

"I hate to continue the gloom," Mort hesitated, "but at a lot of the big intersections downtown, you can see men selling apples for five cents. I've looked at these men when I bought their apples. They're wearing suits and ties and nice overcoats. They probably had good jobs not long ago."

"Well, at least you didn't lose your stocks," David said, "since you owned them outright."

"True, but they're not worth much now. Like you, I took quite a hit," Mort replied. "I figure the best strategy is to hold on to them and hope they'll go back up eventually. You see," he said, turning to Miriam, "I'm not always a pessimist. But it may take a while. And that's provided we don't need the money we'd get for selling them."

"And thanks to you," David said, "I still have a lot of mine. Say," he tried to sound light-hearted, "wasn't there some fable like this? About a reckless creature versus a safe one?"

"The grasshopper and the ant," Miriam said. "*Aesop's Fables.*"

"Well, I know which one I was. I know I teased you a lot about your conservative buying, Mort. Looks like you were right, and I was wrong."

"There's no need to beat yourself up, David," Miriam said patting his hand. "As Mort says, we didn't have a crystal ball."

"Well, at least our business looks okay — for now."

"Let's hope it stays that way."

"I'll drink to that," David said, holding out his empty wine glass.

Their business did survive the early Depression — suffered, but survived. People who had cars still needed gas, and saving a penny or two on each gallon was more attractive than ever. One significant change, though, was how much people bought. In the Twenties 'fill 'er up' was the typical order; now drivers tried to get by on half a tank or even two gallons at a time. That brought in more cars, since they would get low on gas sooner, but gallon sales didn't increase. And putting just a half dollar's worth in each tank was time-consuming and irritating for the partners.

"You should have seen it," Mort complained to Miriam one night. "We had a line of cars for the Fort Street station, but each one wanted just three or four gallons of gas."

"Well, that's all they could afford," Miriam replied. Her tone didn't sound sympathetic. "They're probably living hand to mouth and need the gas just to get to work. If they have work. No more pleasure rides or visiting Aunt Martha in Kalamazoo."

"No," Mort said sadly. "Those days are over for now."

"But *Happy days are here again*!" Miriam said, mocking Franklin Roosevelt's theme song that autumn.

"Hey, don't make fun of Roosevelt," Mort said. "At least, he represents something new. Besides, I assumed you were voting Democratic, like I am."

"Since when have you become a Democrat? I thought you voted for Coolidge and Hoover."

"I did. But Hoover has really disappointed me. Things are so bad now, with the banks closing and all, that anyone seems better than Hoover."

"So, hooray for Franklin D. Anyone!" Miriam declared, cutting off the discussion by leaving the room to see about Andrew's bath. Their relationship had changed over the past several years, Mort was forced to recognize, even as their lives had become more comfortable. Miriam was often irritated by his habits, especially his desire to explain what he was learning in books or current events. She had become tired of being a passive audience or discussing subjects that she didn't really care about. She had once shared David's amusement at Mort's cautious business behavior. Now, she grudgingly admitted he had been right, but that didn't make him any more attractive. Their passion in bed had cooled too.

Both seemed to accept these changes in their marriage, and Mort found himself taking more interest in the children. Edward was eleven now, Sarah ten and Andrew eight. All three were intelligent, and only Andrew was difficult, in being rebellious sometimes. Edward was like his father: serious, hardworking and perhaps lacking in humor. In school, he earned all 'A's and was drawn to the sciences and mechanical devices. He'd already taken apart the family radio and reassembled it to work even better. After school (he was in the 6th grade at Macculloch Elementary), he had a large paper route, just as his father had decades earlier and was proud of his regular earnings each week. Though Mort never admitted it to anyone, he had hoped the boy would take up a sport in school. It was so American.

Sarah resembled her Aunt Chava in her passion for classical music, which exceeded even her parents' love of it. Like her aunt, she had immediately taken to the violin, and, with Chava's instruction and much practice, she was playing proficiently by the time she was nine. Her aunt had settled for giving lessons to immigrants like herself and to their children, like Sarah, because no better jobs were available to women musicians. Recently, she had taken the bold step of opening her own studio that doubled as her apartment. Sarah had higher ambitions. Even at ten, she wanted to become a concert violinist one day.

"Another Heifetz," Miriam said sardonically.

"Well, why not?" Mort rushed to her defense, since he knew Sarah was listening. "There are women pianists, so why not a woman violinist?"

All Sarah's free time was devoted to practicing. *It's good we own this two-flat*, Mort reflected, *where no one can evict us. Even I'm getting tired of* Humoresque.

Andrew was least like his parents. If anyone, it was David Riskin he most resembled in personality. Andy always took things easy. His quick wit made him popular in class. He was funny but also mischievous, already skillful in getting his sister blamed for his pranks or for the chores he didn't do. He was the same at school, never the one to be caught for something he started.

The parents were glad when Roosevelt was elected in '32, but surprised, like so many others, by the blizzard of 'New Deal' programs he immediately rushed through Congress.

"I can't make it out," Mort admitted over their weekly dinner with David. "He wants to control wages and prices with this NRA, which I doubt will work, but he also wants to create more jobs to put more money in people's pockets."

"What's wrong with that?" David asked. He winked at Miriam, who smiled.

"Don't get him started," she warned.

"What's wrong with that," Mort continued, knowing they were egging him on, "is they're contradictory. More income from more jobs will push prices higher. It will have to — they've never been this low. And higher prices will destroy price controls."

"Perhaps you should write Roosevelt," Miriam suggested, obviously bored. "He's gathering a bunch of intellectuals to advise him."

"Yeah," David put in. "The paper calls it his 'brain trust'."

"What I really don't understand," Mort said, ignoring them, "is this triple-A bill. If I read it correctly, it proposes to pay farmers for *not* growing certain crops. That's just crazy!"

"I think it's great!" David said. "I'm applying tomorrow for not growing rutabagas on the roof of my apartment building. Think what I'll make for the thousands I could have grown!"

"Well, I still appreciate Roosevelt's efforts," Miriam said, "even if his programs confuse our resident expert. At least he stopped the bank failures. I was really afraid ours would fail. And what would we have done then?"

"You mean you don't hide your money under the mattress?" David winked again. "That's where I keep mine, and there's so little of it, the mattress isn't even lumpy."

"Be patient," Mort advised. "Times will get better and so will our income from the stations."

"I'll have a white beard before that time comes," David replied. "I haven't been able to pay back much of your loan, I realize."

Mort raised his hand to stop him. "Don't worry about it. I'm not charging you a pound of flesh, am I?" No one was laughing. *I've always been a flop at jokes*, he thought.

"The important thing is that we hang on to our stations."

12.

They did hang on, barely, closing the unprofitable stations, opening new ones, but generally keeping the total number at about four or five. They'd been in business together for over twelve years and would have stayed partners indefinitely if Mort hadn't decided to go home early one day with a headache.

The kids were at school, and it wasn't the housekeeper's day, so the scurrying noises he heard as he unlocked the downstairs door were strange. After he climbed the steps to the upper flat and unlocked that door, there was more scurrying and hushed voices. He opened the door to see Miriam and David standing, their clothing disheveled, David's shirt not even tucked in, his coat on the dining room chair. Miriam was wearing a nightgown. They both looked guilty and abashed.

No one said anything for many long seconds. Finally, Mort broke the silence.

"I see," was all he said. Then a pause. "How long has this been going on?" The odd thing was he didn't feel angry, just let down, disappointed. Several things now made sense, fell into place. The winks, Miriam often touching David's hand at dinners, her increasing impatience with Mort and increasing sympathy for David, and of course David's unfailing presence for their weekly dinners together, not to mention his going out with them. He'd even become 'Uncle David' to the children.

Miriam started to answer, but David spoke over her. "I'm sorry, Mort. You can't know how sorry I am. I feel like the total rat I've been."

"You didn't answer my question," Mort said coldly. "How long?"

"I don't know," David replied, looking down. "Several years."

"Years!" Mort couldn't hold back.

Miriam started to respond, but again David stopped

her. "Well, you've noticed I never married. You probably assumed it was because I was the 'confirmed bachelor' who didn't want to be tied down. The real reason was because I fell in love with Miriam, not that long after you first introduced us. And no other girl came close to measuring up to her. You don't know how lucky you were — are — to have her. How envious I was."

"And what about you?" Mort turned to face Miriam squarely. "Were you in love with him all that time? All the time we were married?"

She lifted her head to meet his eye. "No, of course not. I sensed something of how he felt, of course, but I tried to downplay it and attribute it to his fondness for you."

"For me?" Mort was incredulous.

"I was just the wife of his best friend. That's how I thought of it for a few years. But gradually I realized that I was beginning to feel the same way toward David."

"When did you first... get together?" Mort hated feeling like a prosecutor, but he had to know.

"I don't know," David said looking at Miriam now. "Was it..."

"It was about 1923," she said.

"1923!" Mort repeated, astonished. "Before Andrew was born?" The realization hit him. "Before you became pregnant with Andrew? Then Andrew is...?"

Miriam explained, "We're not certain he was David's. He might have been yours."

"Well, that explains why we always thought he had David's personality."

"So, what do we do now?" David asked hesitantly.

"What do we do?" Mort replied. "Well, we can't go on as if this never happened."

"No," Miriam said. "And in a way I'm glad that it has

— your discovering us. I'm sorry, Mort, I never meant to hurt you. But I'm glad it's out in the open after all this time. At least we won't be sneaking around anymore. You don't know how often, especially in the last few years, I wanted to broach the subject of our marriage. Now we have to face it. I want a divorce. I think it's the best way. I loved you once. I don't know why I stopped, I really don't, but I have. I'm sure you could sense it these past few years."

"A divorce so you can marry David?" Mort couldn't keep himself from asking.

"One thing at a time," Miriam replied. "We'll see how we feel later."

All David could say was, "I'm sorry, Mort. I'm really sorry. Sorry I betrayed you. Especially after you were so good to me about rescuing my stocks. But I'm not sorry for loving Miriam. I couldn't help that. And besides…" He started to giggle from nervousness, the giggle one sometimes hears at funerals, from the absurdity of the whole situation, from the trite, theatrical cliché that had now become their reality, "She was great in bed!"

Breaking up their partnership wasn't difficult because they had never legalized it. They simply divided the stations — Mort took over the first two, David the second two. David kept the *$AVON GAS!* name, since he had come up with it. Mort used the more prosaic *DISCOUNT GAS* for his stations. And both men went back to the dreary work of operating a station. No more driving from one to another in their business suits. Both quietly planned to expand on their own, or perhaps find a new partner.

Breaking up Mort and Miriam's partnership was a more complicated business. She couldn't just move into

David's apartment; there were the children to consider. But her living with Mort was now intolerable. Mort's first act was to order separate beds and throw out their double bed. He spoke to her only when necessary, always politely, always coldly. Edward and Sarah, of course, immediately knew something was very wrong and waited to be told what. When neither parent was forthcoming, Edward finally asked his father.

Mort was laconic; there wasn't much he could say until he knew what Miriam planned to do.

"Your mother and I haven't been getting along," he said. "You've seen that. So, we're trying not to make it worse. That's why we talk to each other so little."

"Are you going to get a divorce?"

"We don't know yet. Probably. But we haven't worked out what we're going to do."

"What about us?"

"What do you mean?" He knew, of course, what Edward meant.

"If you two separate, who will we live with? And do we have any say in the matter?"

"We haven't gotten to that point. Yet. Don't worry, we'll talk to you and Sarah and Andrew about that when the time comes. If it comes."

"I'm really glad to hear that," Edward said coldly, walking away.

Finally, about three weeks after the discovery, Miriam called for a meeting and included David. The children were sent to the movies.

"Mort," she said with no preamble, "David and I have discussed this…"

"I'm glad you two have," Mort said bitterly. "You

certainly haven't discussed it with me."

"That's what this meeting is for," she continued, unruffled. David, obviously feeling like the third party he was, stayed silent.

"Let's start with some facts," Miriam said briskly. "Fact one: we can no longer live together. Neither of us wants to. The marriage can't be fixed. It's over. Fact two: I can't just bring the children and move in with David. For one thing, his apartment is too small. And it would upset the children terribly to move abruptly. That leave us two possibilities," she continued as if giving a lecture. "Either you move out and find a place of your own or I will."

"Just like that? What about the children?"

"I want to keep the children," Miriam said.

"Have you talked about it with them?"

"I tried to, individually. Not Andrew — he's still too young to understand. But neither Edward nor Sarah expressed any strong preference for who they want to live with."

"Just a minute. Something you said doesn't make sense." Mort was glad to revert to his familiar role as analyzer. "If you move out, you'll have to find another three-bedroom flat or house if you take the children. Meanwhile, I'd be living here where I don't need three bedrooms. The obvious conclusion is that *I* move out, provided, of course, that I move without the children."

"I'm glad you reached that conclusion," Miriam said. "That's how I felt, too. But I didn't want to seem as if I were kicking you out."

"But what if I don't want to give up the children? Or what if they, or one of them, wants to stay with me?"

"Then things get messy," Miriam said. "We'd have to settle that in court."

"Yes, I can see that."

"How do you feel about who gets the children?"

"I don't know how I feel," Mort said honestly. "What they want has a lot to do with it."

"Yes," Miriam agreed.

She turned to a new subject. "You would also be paying me child support regularly."

"What about alimony?"

"Well, under the circumstances, I'm not sure I could claim it even if I wanted to, since our desire for divorce is mutual."

"And because *your* infidelity caused it," Mort added belligerently. His patience had about expired.

"Let's not start pointing fingers right now. We're trying to be rational in working this out."

"Where does David come in? Will you two be living together?"

"That doesn't concern you," Miriam snapped. Mort started to object that it did indeed concern him as the children's father, but Miriam overrode his objection. "I don't know if we'll live together. We'll see."

"Yes, we'll see," David finally spoke up. Mort sensed how dominant Miriam was in their relationship. *I wonder if she started the affair*, he mused. *She thinks she's in control, but she may not realize what she's getting into, what with David's irresponsibility. God, what a mess.*

As it turned out, the children were divided in their wishes. Edward, to Mort's surprise and Miriam's, wanted to stay with him; he hadn't noticed that Edward's relationship with his mother hadn't been very affectionate for some time. *Had he known about the affair?* All agreed that Andrew stay with his mother. If he were really David's child, it seemed more natural. Also, Mort worried that even the possibility that David was the father might bias him, Mort, against Andrew in subtle ways. Sarah was the difficult case since she loved both her parents equally. She was also the most upset about the family's breakup. Miriam argued that she would benefit from living with a sibling to keep her from becoming too self-involved in her musical obsession. But, as Mort pointed out, the same argument applied to Edward. Finally, the parents decided that Sarah would stay with Miriam since Mort might have less understanding in raising a girl, especially one as sensitive as Sarah. Mort insisted on having liberal visiting time.

"I suppose we have to hire custody attorneys and start the whole legal business," he said sadly.

"I already have, and I have a name for you to contact," Miriam said.

"You make it easy."

"I want this settled," Miriam said matter-of-factly.

When it was settled, several months later, Mort would have Sarah and Andrew every other weekend, the dates to be mutually agreed upon. Edward would go to Miriam on the weekends in between so that he could also be with his siblings. Mort and Edward found a three-bedroom flat in the Dexter area. Its mortgage payments were not much more than the rent on a two-bedroom apartment, and Edward could still attend Durfee Junior High, where he had started that fall and had already made friends. The third bedroom would do double duty: a room where Sarah could stay during her visits (while Andrew would sleep on a trundle in Edward's room) and a place to house Mort's books. As before, Edward's mechanical tinkerings would be relegated to the basement, where Mort had set up a workbench and desk lamp. The large labor market made it easy to find a housekeeper who was willing to make dinners. An added benefit — Elsie was good-natured.

David kept his apartment but spent even more time with Miriam and her children. He was still 'Uncle David' to them, but Sarah sensed he was more than that to her mother. They tried to be discreet about their coupling, Miriam going to David's apartment when he could get away from work. In the evenings, when the children had a sitter, the couple often went back to his apartment instead of going out.

Though the complications of this settlement seemed smoothed over, Mort couldn't help feeling despondent. He was glad that Edward wanted to live with him; he was drawn to the boy's intellectual seriousness and well understood his self-consciousness about being a little pudgy. But being separated from Sarah and Andrew made it virtually certain that Mort would become a stranger in their lives, a friendly stranger perhaps, who bought them ice cream, but still a stranger. He had never felt as close to them as he did to Edward, and he blamed himself for this failure. *Did Miriam have similar feelings?* he wondered.

There was one other thing Mort regretted. Now that his partnership with David had ended, there was no reason for meeting with him and Miriam to go over the books, followed by a deli dinner. He had enjoyed those times with the whole family and David present, the easy give-and-take of a relaxed dinner. Now, those dinners would cease. The funny thing was, he didn't hate either Miriam or David. He just felt sad that his relationships with them had broken up.

At about this time, late 1933, Mort received a disturbing letter from Anna in Motal. It came through Uncle Yitzhak because his family didn't know Mort's new address in Detroit. As usual, it was written in Yiddish in her neat cursive.

I hope you and your family are well. Here, things are confused and not good. We have heard that across the border in Ukraine people are starving. One farmer escaped (they are not allowed to leave the country) and he made it to Motal. He was all skin and bones. He said that Stalin actually created this famine by taking all of the wheat the farmers grew. All of it! It was to punish them for not wanting collective farms. People there are actually starving, he said, whole towns of them. I don't think this will happen to us because Motal is now part of Poland. Father and Mother are both too weak to travel. Mother has been sick a long time. Father is just too old and very difficult. We hope things are better for you in America than for us here. I'm sorry I couldn't write a happier letter.

Your loving sister, Anna
Much love and many kisses to Miriam, Edward, Sarah, and Andrew. We would love to have pictures of them.

After discussing the letter with Uncle Yitzhak, Mort drove home, thinking about the family, particularly Anna. He wondered if there was any way that he could get them out of Poland. Getting them a visa would be extremely difficult with the quotas in place and would take months, maybe years. Could he smuggle them out with bribes?

Even if that were possible, he wouldn't be able to smuggle them *in* to this country. Finally, even though the chances were daunting, he decided to apply to the State Department for two entrance visas. He assumed that, from what Anna said, their mother probably wouldn't survive by the time the visas arrived. His father probably wouldn't come, but Mort would have an extra visa ready in case the old man perversely changed his mind. Mort hoped he wouldn't.

In the application letter, he documented that he had a steady income sufficient to take care of them until his sister found work, so they wouldn't be a burden to the State. He even sent a copy of the letter to the influential Rabbi Stephen Wise in New York, asking if he could intercede on Mort's behalf. Even if the application went nowhere, it would ease his conscience to know that he had tried. If the visas did come through, he would contact Jewish aid societies to see about getting a job for Anna.

As if these problems in Poland and Ukraine weren't enough, a dire situation had arisen in Germany. The Nazis, as everyone called them, had taken power there. After years of their Storm Troopers harassing German Jews — beating them up, organizing boycotts of their stores, blaming them for Germany's problems — the Nazi leader Adolph Hitler was made Chancellor in January 1933, a few months before Franklin Roosevelt became President.

Different as they were, the two leaders shared one similarity; they both owed their rise to power to the Depression, to the millions who were out of work in both countries. And both were devoting major efforts to putting their citizens back to work. Some in America — newspaper analysts, even some rabbis — predicted Hitler would settle down after becoming Chancellor and turn his attention away from the Jews and toward Germany's problems. But this hope proved fatuous. For Hitler, the Jews *were* Germany's biggest problem, and his rants against them only intensified now that he was in power.

Thank goodness the family doesn't live there, Mort thought. But their situation in Poland was also precarious, where anti-Semitic attacks were frequent. *Had Stalin also gone mad? Was the whole world going mad? Everywhere, it seemed, anti-Semitism was on the rise. The Germans hate us. The Russians hate us. The Poles hate us. They especially.* And even in America sentiment against Jews was rising. The quota law showed it. It also appeared in small but stinging reminders. Some apartment buildings, even in the Dexter area, had 'for rent' signs that added: 'No Jews or dogs'.

The next summer, during one of his weekends with Sarah and Andrew, Mort took all three children to Boblo Island, a popular destination for Detroiters with its own amusement park. The island was on the Canadian side of the Detroit River just east of Grosse Ile, and part of the fun was getting there. A huge triple-deck steamboat ferried passengers from the foot of Woodward Avenue to the island while entertaining them with band music and refreshments. The kids were the perfect ages for enjoying the island's amusement park; they even prevailed on Mort to join them on 'The Sky Streak' roller coaster, a decision he immediately regretted on the coaster's first downhill rush and wild turn. *It defies physics*, Mort gasped fearfully, trying to keep down his hotdog lunch. He much preferred the quieter fun of the Ferris wheel and renting a boat to navigate the island's waterway. Everyone returned to Detroit exhausted, sunburned and happy.

Apart from this outing and one to Belle Isle, which could delight all three children, Mort had trouble thinking of entertainments that both Sarah and Andrew would enjoy. If he took them to the symphony or art museum, which he knew Sarah would love, Andrew was bored and made rude remarks about the paintings of nudes (patrons nearby frowned at his loud mention of 'titties'). If he took them to a Tigers baseball game, Andrew would be in seventh heaven, but Sarah would complain about the hard seats as she read her novel. Mort solved the problem by alternating the children's visits and the types of entertainment. That way, each could sleep in the extra bedroom, and he would have more one-on-one time with them.

13.

In his spare moments, usually while waiting at one of his gas stations for the manager to be free, Mort had taken to jotting down his reflections in a pocket notebook. He admired short, pithy observations and had recently come across a book of them, *Pensées*, by the French philosopher, Blaise Pascal. Here are some of Mort's.

There is only one 'me'. Everyone else in the world is a 'you'. But every 'you' is a 'me' to himself. So, here are all these 'me's walking around, each the most important person in the universe, each seeing everyone else as a 'you'. No wonder there's so much conflict.

We're told to love your neighbor as yourself. But that's impossible, since he's a 'you', not a 'me' except to himself. Yet love does exist. I know this. And it needn't be just between two people. You can love your dog or cat, and it loves you back. You can even love a plant, watering it carefully, nurturing it, and I believe that plant feels your love too. You can also overwater it — and overlove your pet or your child, ruining them.

Love is like gravity: it's an attractive force that pulls two beings toward each other. Gravity is a strong enough force to pull planets toward the sun (but not into it fortunately!) and pull one star toward another. It can even bend light, I've read. Is there an opposite force, akin to hate, that drives stars apart, that drives people apart, so that all they have for comfort is their isolated 'me'?

But the self-love of 'me' is not completely isolated. It resides at the center of concentric circles determined by an ever-weakening love-attraction force. The innermost of these 'me' love circles is the beloved. Family is next. One's identification with a religion may be a circle (I am a Jew. I care what happens to Jews I've never met in a country I've never lived in). And the most distant of these circles, I believe, is one's country. Yet people have always been willing to die for that distant and abstruse 'me', that projection of 'me'. Even I was during the Great War. Well, it does provide protection from other collections of 'you's'.

With Roosevelt's New Deal, conditions in America slowly improved over the next two years. According to the government's statistics (which Mort realized might be biased), unemployment had gone down and personal and business income up. There were fewer evictions and foreclosures. Evidence on the streets confirmed this: fewer bread lines and 'Hoovervilles', and the sickening sight of people's belongings piled on the curb was less common. In 1935, FDR, as he was now known everywhere, got Congress to pass a massive public works bill called the WPA. Using unemployed workers, it built new roads, highways, bridges, schools, hospitals, city halls, county and federal buildings and new parks. Artists were employed to paint murals on post office walls; playwrights, actors and stage people were employed to write and give performances of plays and circuses in towns that never had them before; writers were employed to write travel guides for each state and major city. Even folklorists and historians found work in collecting folk songs, describing local customs, even interviewing former slaves. One of Mort's unemployed writer friends, Eddie Avener told him joyously, "The Writers' Project hired me to help out on their guide to Michigan. They don't pay much, but it's enough to keep me going and even gives me time to work on my novel." The best thing about the WPA, besides putting money into people's pockets and taking them off the dole, was that these projects were beneficial, not just make-work. They made Mort into a fervent Roosevelt supporter.

As economic conditions improved, so did business at Mort's gas stations. It wasn't quite back to the freewheeling 'fill 'er up' days of the Twenties, but people were definitely putting more gas in their tanks. Gradually, Mort made enough money to open a third station on Forest Avenue. He also made the bold move of buying the most profitable of his three stations when land values were still cheap. Since he could deduct the mortgage payments as a business expense, his income actually rose from the decision, and he soon set about buying another of the three. This required getting an accountant to do his taxes, but that service, too, saved him more money than it cost. He also decided to hire his own bookkeeper and manager, Joan Waritzki, to keep track of sales and supplies. That freed his evenings and gave him more time to read. The biggest problem remained the same: finding honest and competent people to run the stations. But in 1935, there was no shortage of candidates, and through trial and error, he eventually found good ones. Gradually, he was returning to his (and David's) original dream of driving from one station to another in his business suit. And he had even gone up a notch in his choice of cars — from a Chevy to a Buick.

He learned from Miriam that David's two stations were doing okay but not flourishing. What surprised Mort was not this news, but that Miriam shared it with him. They had little time to talk when they were dropping off or picking up the kids, but they squeezed in a few minutes while Sarah and Andrew were packing.

She and David were still 'thinking about' getting married, Miriam said, but she hinted that all was not well with them, not only because David wasn't making as much as she'd hoped, but because he had trouble hanging on to the dollars he did make. Once, she let it slip that he liked to gamble and played poker regularly with a group she wouldn't entertain at her home.

"You know, at one time I admired David for taking chances in your business, while you seemed like such an old fuddy-duddy, too conservative to take risks. It made him seem, I don't know, more dashing, more fun."

"And now?"

"Not so much," was all Miriam would say.

Sarah and Andrew, conversely, seemed to be thriving. Sarah was playing in a youth orchestra (Detroit, which had suffered so much during the worst years of the Depression, was now able to give free concerts in the park with WPA money and hired the orchestra — until the musicians' union objected). Often, Sarah's rehearsals and lessons on Saturdays cut into the time she was to spend with Mort. *I still don't feel I know her very well*, he thought sadly.

"She wants to be a performer, not just a teacher," Miriam told him.

"Maybe she can achieve it," Mort said. "Things are opening up for women. I noticed that the Detroit Symphony has a few women musicians. And maybe these new municipal orchestras will hire more women."

"We'll see."

Andrew, meanwhile, was playing baseball in the warm months, basketball at the Jewish Center in the cold ones. Fanatically devoted to sports, at which he was graceful and skilled, he was the most American of the children with almost no sense of being an immigrant's child. Miriam said he was too slick, too confident with others for his own good. *She's always critical*, Mort thought. Determined to get closer to the boy, Mort bought a baseball glove and, though he was clumsy and not even interested in baseball, he took Andrew to the park on their weekends together to play catch or chase after Andrew's batted balls. When it was Mort's turn to bat, he often swung and missed while Andrew snickered in the outfield. If they found a pickup game, Mort gratefully watched from the sidelines.

14.

One Sunday afternoon after Mort returned the kids, he and Miriam had a few minutes alone. Sarah and Andrew were sprawled before the family radio, listening to *Amos and Andy*. David was at the track.

"He goes there often, nearly every Sunday," she acknowledged.

"How does he do?"

"He won't tell me, but I suspect he loses a lot more than he wins."

"That's too bad." Mort said it without gloating. He felt genuinely bad for Miriam. And to show he harbored no bitterness toward the couple, he now made a proposal that surprised her.

"I'd really like it if we could renew our Sunday dinners with the whole family, including David. I really miss the lively conversation and repartee, even if some of it's barbed. And I especially miss the feeling of the family being together. The divorce has torn it apart." He had expected Miriam to reject the proposal out of hand. But she said nothing, so he continued, "We could just extend the time when we return the children on Sundays to include an early dinner. We could get deli, just as we did after those Sunday business meetings, so no one would have to cook. And I could pick up a dessert from Sanders, cake or ice cream. For the dinners at my place, I'd like to invite Chava too."

It was now Miriam's turn to surprise. She agreed to the proposal. "I miss those conversations too," she admitted.

At the first of these dinners in September, David held the

floor. His natural enthusiasm had received a huge boost that fall when the Detroit Tigers won the American League pennant for the second straight year. The previous year, 1934, they had lost the World Series to St. Louis in a bitter seven-game match, but this year they stood a fine chance of winning it against the Chicago Cubs. David raved about Hank Greenberg, who was not only the Tigers' outstanding home run hitter, but Jewish to boot.

"You should see him when he stands in the batter's box," David said, his eyes shining. "He's so big! Boy, there's one Jew that the *goys* aren't going to mess with! And can he hit that ball! Thirty-six homeruns this season, tied for the league's best!"

"He also hit .328 and led the league in RBIs and extra base hits," Andrew put in, proudly displaying his mastery of baseball minutiae.

Now, if he just doesn't refuse again to play on the High Holy Days!" David continued.

"Did he do that?" Miriam asked.

"You bet he did, on *Yom Kippur,* anyway. Don't you remember all the fuss about it? He asked his rabbi whether he should play, and they arrived at a compromise. He played on *Rosh Hashanah*, but not on *Yom Kippur*. People here were outraged by it, but some in the newspapers respected his decision. The Tigers won the pennant anyway. But this year, *Yom Kippur* will happen during the World Series, if it goes that long."

"Well, let's hope he plays," Mort said.

"I'm going to try to take Miriam and the kids to see one of the Series games if I can get tickets." David said. "It's something they'll always remember. You want to come too, Mort?" he added awkwardly.

"Thanks, but you'll probably have enough trouble just

getting tickets for five."

"Four, you mean," Sarah corrected. "I'm not really interested."

"No surprise there," Andrew muttered.

"No need to be rude, dear," Miriam said sharply to Sarah.

"Was I? Sorry."

She's in her own world, Mort thought. *Doesn't really care much for any of us.*

Miriam spoke up, hesitantly. "David, won't these tickets be expensive? If you can get them. I'm no baseball fan, so just try for three."

That must have been hard for her, Mort thought. *Hinting at their financial troubles. Poor David. He tries to do the right thing by the kids, and gets caught up in family complications. Look at him — all his enthusiasm's gone.*

"For that matter," Edward spoke up, "I don't really need to go either. I'm all for the Tigers, but I'm not a big sports person. If you can find an extra ticket, that would be great. But don't worry about it if you can't." It was a long speech for Edward.

"Five down from six! Four, down from five!" Andrew imitated an auction barker. "Three, do I hear three? Now it's down to two!"

As it turned out, it was zero. The Tigers did win the World Series that year. Greenberg was in uniform on *Yom Kippur*, but a fractured wrist forced him to sit out the game; the Tigers won it anyway. But David couldn't get even two tickets. The games were already sold out.

Besides the WPA and the Tigers winning the World Series, 1935 proved to be a momentous year for Mort in a more personal way. Long after he had given up on the matter, the State Department finally began to act on the visas he had applied for a year and a half earlier. His letter to Rabbi Wise apparently had made a difference. As the Rabbi informed him in a separate letter, he had used contacts and pressure to get the wheels turning. Now, Mort was invited to meet with a State Department representative in Detroit's Federal Building. He learned at this meeting that, by a lucky turn, not all the visas allocated for Poland had been given out because applications for them had dropped. Apparently, many found the hurdles the Department had created too daunting. And Poland required an exit visa that was equally daunting. Mort brought with him documents showing his financial ability to support two more members of his family, plus a testimonial letter from Uncle Yitzhak about their good character, as well as a similar letter from his local rabbi, though the rabbi had never met the family. The State Department official was especially impressed when Mort told him that he planned to go to Poland personally to bring Anna and his father to America. Mort hadn't really thought about this until he was driving to this appointment — it just occurred to him as the right thing to do.

Otherwise, it would be like throwing them to the wolves to expect them to negotiate with officials of a hostile country.

Obviously, bribes would have to be paid — that's where Mort came in.

"What about language difficulties?" the official asked.

"I thought about that and plan to bring a translator with me, a U.S. citizen, to help with the Polish and Yiddish; I'll pay for his passage both ways."

Actually, he hadn't given it any thought, just decided on the spot. His mind was working in new ways he wasn't accustomed to; it was exhilarating. The official stamped the visas and handed them to Mort.

"These are good for six months," he said. "Good luck with your plans."

Leaving the Federal Building, Mort found a Western Union office and took some blank cables. The following Sunday, he went to Uncle Yitzhak and explained his plan.

The uncle was astonished. "You received the entrance visas? That's a miracle!"

"Now we must inform Anna immediately, so she can work on getting the documents they'll need for exit visas. I have these telegram blanks from Western Union. Do you think you could print the messages in Yiddish for them? I understand the language but can't speak or write it very well."

"Of course, I can. I know Yiddish, and I know how to print."

"We'll try to use as few words as possible. Write,

I am coming to bring you out of Poland.

No, cross that out. Tell them,

I am coming to bring you and father to America. I have entrance visas. Now, you must get the documents for exit visas. I will come in November. Write back immediately. Love, Mordecai.

Do you have all that?"

"I'm printing, I'm printing!" Uncle Yitzhak said, with his head down. "There!" He read it back to Mort.

"Perfect! Now, how will we get the telegram to them?"

"Well, we can't just put their town's name on it. It would probably take three months for someone to deliver it by donkey cart. Why not send it care of Rabbi Hirsch at the Motal synagogue? Even if he has already retired, the current rabbi can have someone take it to them."

"That makes sense," Mort said.

"How will you communicate with them and with the Polish officials?" Yitzhak asked. "You don't speak Polish. The Jews in Motal speak Yiddish, I'm sure; Anna's letters were in Yiddish. How well do you understand it?"

"Listening to it, pretty well," Mort replied. "But I haven't spoken it in decades and am pretty rusty. But you can speak it fluently, can't you, Uncle?"

"Yes. I also know some Russian but very little Polish."

"Would you consider coming with me? I'll pay for all your expenses."

"What about my job at the factory?"

Mort was crestfallen. "I forgot about that." *The idea had seemed so brilliant.*

"Well, don't worry about it. I'm sixty-five now. It's time I retired."

"Do you mean it? You would do that?"

"Why not? Listen. I took in you and Chava for my brother all these years ago. Personally, I think he's a *putz*, but family is family. If I could do that for two of his children, why not for another one? It's too bad we couldn't bring out your mother, may she rest in peace."

Mort nodded. Anna had told them of his mother's death the previous year.

"What about Schmuel?" Yitzhak asked.

"I'm assuming he won't want to come. But we have the extra visa for him if he does."

"Of course, he won't. What did I tell you? He's a *putz.* So, when do we leave?"

Before Mort could answer that question, he had three things to do: get passports for himself and Uncle Yitzhak; see that his stations would be well taken care of in his absence; and inform his family of his plans, including having Edward stay with Miriam's family. The first was easy. Regarding his stations, he followed the same protocol he used on his vacations. The proprietors of the three stations would take their receipts each afternoon to the bank and deposit them in special accounts Mort had set up. It would be easier to keep track of them that way. They were also to inform his bookkeeper of items they needed and provide her with sales receipts when possible. She would continue ordering and paying bills for the gasoline and supplies. The system had worked for his one-week vacations; why not for four weeks? As Uncle Yitzhak had promised, he retired from his job at the Cadillac Assembly Plant on Fort Street. His children were now grown and supporting themselves. And he had set aside money anticipating his retirement, so he and Minna wouldn't starve.

Informing his family wasn't easy. He had told them, of course, about Anna's letters and her increasingly hopeless situation in Poland. But they were shocked by his plan to bring her to Detroit himself. Miriam, in particular, was petulant.

"I don't understand. Why do *you* have to be the one to go bring them out? What about your responsibilities to your work? To your family?" This, with a nod toward

118

Edward. The others seemed to lean in closer to hear his answer, since Miriam, as usual, had perfectly expressed their own reservations.

Stay calm, Mort told himself, *stay calm and logical*.

"To your first point, Miriam, I'm going myself — correction — Uncle Yitzhak and I are going — because no one else can do so, and Anna isn't capable of going by herself and overcoming the barriers blocking exit from Poland. We've already obtained the entrance visas to America, but she'll also need an exit visa. The whole thing shouldn't take more than a month and may be much shorter."

"You keep saying 'Anna.'" Miriam said. "What about your father?"

"He's already said he won't come, and he's a stubborn old guy. Just in case he changes his mind, we have an entrance visa for him. Regarding my business, I've already arranged to have my station managers handle the receipts and bank deposits just as they do during my vacations. It worked then, and I don't see why three extra weeks should make the system fail."

"Will you sweeten their deal?" David asked. "Give them a bonus?"

"Yes." He felt no need to explain further; *it was none of their business*.

"As for my responsibilities to my family, I realize that I'm imposing on you when I ask this, Miriam, but I'd like to have Edward stay with you while I'm gone. He's a responsible boy, so I don't think he'd be a burden. I guess Andrew would have to share his bedroom, so *he* might feel burdened."

"Heck, no!" Andrew piped up. "I could play basketball with him!"

"Good. Then that's settled. I realize that you'd have to cook for one more, Miriam—"

"That's not a problem," she shook her head.

"And look on the bright side," Mort continued. "You'll remind Edward what an accomplished cook you are. He may never want Elsie's cooking again." As usual, his humor fell flat.

"I hate this talking about me as if I weren't here," Edward said, "as if I were a ghost."

"Sorry, Edward. It can't be helped," Mort replied.

Now, it was Sarah's turn. "So, you're actually going to Poland to bring Aunt Anna to America to stay permanently? This sounds like a rescue mission. When did you turn into a white knight, father?" Her tone wasn't sarcastic; it was genuinely curious and a little admiring.

"It's nothing that heroic, Sarah. I just saw that it had to be done, and there was no one else to do it. If anyone, Uncle Yitzhak is the heroic one for deciding to retire and come with me." All agreed.

Part II: The First Rescue

Poland and Germany, 1935

They left in early November after the passports arrived. Anna had written back joyously that she couldn't wait to see her brother and Uncle Yitzhak. She was eager to come to America. But their father kept insisting he wouldn't come. Also, she had tried to get police certifications of their good behavior needed for exit visas, but hadn't yet succeeded. True to form, Mort had done his homework and studied the newest map of Eastern Europe he could find. He even bought a pocket copy to take with him. Motal was still part of Poland. The most direct route to it was to land at the port of Danzig, which was now a 'free city' administered by Poland, then take trains to Warsaw, Brest and on to Pinsk. They would get off before Pinsk at Ivanova, a tiny village about twenty miles south of Motal. He hoped there was a connecting line to the town; if not, they'd have to take a horse and wagon, just as he and Chava had done back in 1912.

Checking the ocean liners, he found it was mostly German ships that sailed to Danzig after stopping at Hamburg or Bremen. Taking a German ship made Mort uneasy, given the country's attitude toward Jews. *But after all*, he reasoned, *it's just transportation. He was an American citizen, not German, And if we pay our fare and mind our own business, what could they do? Plus, we'd be landing outside the country*. The Baltic American Line seemed the most promising. Mort assumed it would take the rest of November to get to Motal, make sure the exit visas were in order, return to

Danzig and sail back. In case they had unforeseen problems, he didn't book return passage; he could do that later, perhaps in Warsaw.

They traveled by train to New York and stayed overnight at the Rivard, the same hotel where Mort and Miriam had stayed on their honeymoon in 1920. It looked a bit down at the heel, but it was only for a night. Their ship was scheduled to depart on November 3rd at 10 a.m. Both Mort and Yitzhak were excited to be departing; to be among the eager crowds, going up the covered gangway, to be treated with respect. They had both ridden steerage coming to America and weren't even allowed to come on deck until the last day. Now they could stroll comfortably on the second-class deck, watch the shuffleboard and deck tennis games, and read or just look at the sea from their blanketed deck chairs. Just strolling around the perimeter of the ship took nearly twenty minutes. As their ship pulled slowly out of the harbor, they both watched the Statue of Liberty gradually disappearing. Mort felt a twinge of doubt. *Was he crazy to be leaving this secure haven for the turmoil of hate-filled Europe?*

As they unpacked in their small stateroom, Mort joked, "I didn't bring a tux because I didn't think we'd need one for dinner in second class. Anyhow, I don't own one."

"I'm so glad," Uncle Yitzhak laughed. "Mine would have had moth holes — if I had one."

A steward knocked on their door to ask, in German-accented English, if everything was all right or if they needed anything. When they thanked him, "No," he bowed slightly and clicked his heels.

Although it was a November crossing, the weather

was pleasant and there were no storms. The food was first-rate and plentiful. There were even some nightly entertainments. In exchange for a free ride, musicians gave concerts, playing German music, of course, and a theatre troupe of young people performed comedies. *Too bad it's not Shakespeare*, Mort thought; *still, it was entertaining*.

After ten days of mostly blue sky, they arrived at Danzig and carried their suitcases down the gangway. It felt odd to be on a floor that didn't rock. The Customs officials were Polish, but Mort noticed several official-looking Germans standing around, wearing swastika armbands. *Is that because the ship was German?* he wondered. *Or does Germany have designs on this port?*

"Do you want to handle this?" he asked Uncle Yitzhak, as they approached the Customs table.

"My Polish isn't good enough," Yitzhak whispered.

"Okay." Mort played the realistic role of a language-bereft American tourist, and the officials promptly produced someone who spoke English. As he looked through their luggage, Mort started to explain their travel plans, but the official, balding and middle-aged, interrupted him irritably.

"You'll need to get transit visas for yourselves and for your father and sister. We don't handle exit visas. For those, you'll need to go to the State Bureau for Travel Documents in Warsaw. We can provide the transit visas, but it will take a while."

"How long?"

"That depends," the man said eyeing him. "It might take many hours."

Mort took out his wallet, removed twenty dollars' worth of Polish *zlotys* and handed it to the man. "Will this help?"

"Yes," the man said, pocketing the money, "that will help. The transit visas themselves cost five *zlotys* each. Come back in two hours, and we'll have them done. But first write down the names you want on the visas. And get in that line over there to have your passports stamped."

As they shifted to the other line, Mort wondered how big the bribe should have been to get the visas right away.

"I hadn't expected transit visas," he said to his uncle. "Didn't even know they existed."

"Any way they can milk you for more money," Yitzhak murmured. "Perhaps they also require toilet visas."

"Bureaucracy is a curse the world over. He said we'll need to get the exit visas in Warsaw, from — what did he call it? — the State Office for Travel Documents. No, Bureau. The State *Bureau* for Travel Documents. Let's find a bank to get more Polish *zlotys*. I exchanged about $100 on the ship, but that won't last very long. At least, we won't have to buy rubles too."

"Yes," Yitzhak agreed, "paying bribes in only one currency is much more efficient."

The train station was close by, and they bought tickets for Warsaw, connecting to Brest and Pinsk. The next Warsaw train wouldn't leave until 14:10 — it was now 11:00 — so they had plenty of time for a leisurely lunch and even a stroll around town. The Warsaw-Brest train left at 18:00 and wouldn't get into Brest until 21:30. Prudently, Mort found a tourist office in the train station to reserve a hotel room in Brest for the night. The tourist officer, a young woman in blonde braids with pasty white skin, studied him without smiling.

"You are a Jew?" she asked in English.

Mort immediately felt a surge of anger.

"It doesn't matter what I am. I asked you to book a hotel room. Can you do it?"

"Of course," the woman said, feigning surprise that he was offended. "There's a second-class hotel by the train station. Will that do?"

"Yes," Mort said, "that will do." The sooner he left this bitch, the better.

She typed up the reservation slip and handed it to him without a word.

"Thanks," he said, as curtly as he could, and turned away to where his uncle was waiting.

"Let's go find a bank and a restaurant," he said with forced cheerfulness. "Are you hungry?"

"I am always hungry," Yitzhak said.

"We don't need to eat at the station restaurant, since we have almost three hours to kill. We can look for a decent place."

"That would be fine," Yitzhak said. "Perhaps we can find one that serves a nice Polish stew."

The restaurant they chose barely lived up to Mort's sense of 'decent', but they were satisfied and had plenty of time for that walk. Danzig's old town was picturesque: narrow buildings with peaked gables on twisting, cobblestone streets. It felt medieval to Mort, and he half expected to see a crowd of people come around the corner carrying torches. Then he remembered the torchlight parades of the Nazis that he'd seen in newsreels. *Primitive*, he concluded. *Primitive emotions. Primitive actions. And they don't change, not in Europe anyway. Thank God for America.*

The transit visas were ready, but the train took three hours to get to Warsaw. *I wonder if this passes for an express*, Mort thought. At least, their compartment was comfortable and uncrowded. At Warsaw, they changed to the Brest train. This one was considerably shabbier and made numerous stops along the way. *The local*, he thought and was glad he had made hotel reservations. *I hope they hold them.*

In Brest that night, they found their hotel easily — it was across the street from the train station. Their room had twin beds. *That bitch at the tourist office actually did something right*, Mort conceded grudgingly. He went downstairs to ask if there was a café nearby that was still open. The clerk, who spoke English, told him the train station restaurant was always open, but there was also a Rathskeller down the street that didn't close until midnight. One could eat there, the clerk added, provided one liked sausage.

When he returned to the room, he found Uncle Yitzhak holding his shoe and stalking a cockroach.

"This may be a second-class hotel," he said, "but they have first-class cockroaches. I have not seen them this big since we left Mott Street in New York."

"Well, it's only for a night. We can live with it," Mort said.

"I believe you said the same thing at the hotel in New York."

"Cheer up, Uncle. Things will probably be worse where the family lives." He explained about dinner.

"I would like to bathe first — I haven't in several days — the showers were always in demand on the ship," Yitzhak explained. "I'm assuming that the roaches in the bathroom will at least be cleaner. They might have bathed."

As they left the hotel for the Rathskeller, Mort noticed several women lounging in the small lobby. *So, it's a brothel too*, he realized. *Perfect for the traveling man.* The Rathskeller was easy to find with its well-lit sign on the dark street. Inside, it was noisy, smoky, brightly lit and cheerful. An oom-pa-pa band was playing in one corner, and at some long tables, drunken men were singing loudly, swaying together as they swung their beer steins.

"I hope you like beer, Uncle," Mort said, "and sausage."

"What I like doesn't matter," his uncle replied resignedly. "If that's what they have, that's what they have."

Later, as they left feeling considerably better, Mort was careful to check the dark street and make sure they weren't being followed. *What a disaster if we were robbed*, he thought. He hadn't anticipated getting a money belt. No one followed them, however, and no one else was on the dark street as they walked back to their hotel as quickly as he could make Uncle Yitzhak move. The old boy was singing to himself one of the oom-pa-pa songs. *The first chance I get, probably in Warsaw, I'll buy that belt.* He prayed the beds didn't have bedbugs.

The following morning, Mort found that the train to Pinsk wouldn't leave until 13:00. *Stuck again*, he sighed. The ticket agent fortunately wasn't busy and, though his English was poor, confirmed to Mort on a map that he should indeed get off at Ivanova to get to Motal. The town's Polish spelling was difficult, and Mort wrote it down. He ran his finger back and forth on the map between Ivanova and Motal.

"Train?"

The clerk nodded. "*Tak. Pociąg.*" It sounded like "poch-yong." Mort repeated it until the clerk nodded again. *Well, that was good news*, Mort thought. *We won't need to ride a wagon those twenty miles.*

Since they had plenty of time to kill, they strolled through Brest looking for a café.

"How did you sleep, Uncle?"

"We slept fine," Yitzhak replied, scratching under his arms, "once I got used to feeding our little friends." Mort nodded, feeling his own bites. *Second class hotel*, he snorted to himself. *Wonder what a third class would have. Probably scorpions. Well, I shouldn't compare it to America. We're a rich country, New York especially. Poland is a poor one. How in the world did they manage to win that war against the Soviets and expand their territory so far east? But as Uncle said, one less country, one less set of rules and fewer palms to grease.*

On a main street, they found a restaurant that seemed to be doing good business. "Now, this will be a challenge, to tell the waitress what we want," Mort said, once they were seated.

"Perhaps we could draw a picture," Uncle Yitzhak replied.

"Excellent idea!" Mort said, "I know you were kidding, but I think it might work." He immediately got out his note pad and drew a crude picture of fried eggs, toast and a steaming cup of coffee. When the waitress came over — there were no menus — he showed her the picture, and she immediately brightened.

"*Tak, Tak!*" she said, nodding happily. Then she pointed to the cup. "Kawa?" Since it sounded more like 'coffee' than 'tea', Mort nodded. The breakfast was the best meal they'd had in days.

After another leisurely stroll, they returned to their room and wrote some postcards they had bought at the station. They waited as long as they could before checking out, since they knew they'd only have to wait in the train station. "Besides," Yitzhak explained, "I want to say goodbye to all my little friends here."

"Except for the ones you bring with you."

At the station restaurant, they bought hard rolls and stuffed them into their pockets. "Who knows when we'll be eating again?" Mort said. "Or where." Finally, the train pulled in — the same type of shabby train they'd taken to Brest. *Even sounds old-fashioned, with its high-pitched steam whistle*, Mort thought. On board, he found the conductor and pointed on his pocket map to about where Ivanova should be.

God, he thought, *I wish I knew the Polish word for exit*.

Instead he just gestured from himself to somewhere off the train. The conductor understood.

"*Tak.* Ivanova." Then he said something rapid-fire in Polish, which Mort hoped meant, "I will tell you when we get there."

When Mort made the same back and forth finger motion between Ivanova and Motal on the map while inflecting '*poch-yong*' into a question, the conductor nodded, "*Tak.*"

The train to Pinsk was definitely the local and stopped at every town en route. Finally, as they approached Ivanova, the conductor knocked on their compartment door and said loudly and repeatedly, "Ivanova." He gestured for them to get off.

Mort and Uncle Yitzhak were waiting with their suitcases when the train pulled into the little whistle stop of Ivanova. They were the only ones to exit, and when the train pulled away after watering up, they were standing alone on the rickety station platform. On the platform was a small one-room building. No one was there. It was so quiet with the train gone they could hear the wind blowing and crows cawing as they flew over the wheat fields nearby.

"Well, now what do we do?" Mort asked.

"We wait, of course."

"Wait where?" Mort asked. "There isn't even a bench."

Uncle Yitzhak peered through the dirty station window. "I think there's one inside."

"Fat lot of good that does us," Mort said, trying the station door. "Locked, of course."

"My guess," Yitzhak said, 'is that the station agent comes maybe a half hour before a train is due. To put out the water for the steam engine. Why should he waste his time here otherwise?"

"Makes sense," Mort said glumly. "Only, we don't know when that will be. Let's look around."

They noticed right away that the track their train had taken was bisected by another track heading roughly north-south. "This must be the track to Motal," Mort said. "Wonder how often that train runs."

"Well, we'll never find out standing here," Yitzhak said. He looked over to the village of Ivanova nearby the station. "Why don't we walk into town? We're there already. Maybe we'll get lucky and find someone who speaks English."

"I wouldn't bet on it. Should we leave our bags here?" Mort asked, already knowing the answer.

"I wouldn't advise it," Yitzhak replied. "I imagine people here are more honest than in New York, but why tempt fate? C'mon, you're a young man. If I can carry my suitcase, you can carry yours."

The two got down off the train platform and trudged to the village.

To the few people they encountered as they walked, Mort and Yitzhak couldn't have stood out more, wearing suits and hats and carrying suitcases. The locals gawked at them as if they had just landed from Mars, but when the two approached them, they ducked their heads and suddenly got busy, moving away.

"What are they afraid of?" Mort wondered aloud.

"They probably think we're from the government. Who else would wear suits around here? And that can't be good for them. Just keep walking. We'll see more people when we get to Broadway and 42nd Street."

Ivanova had only one street, and that one was muddy and rutted. There were a few stores on it, notably a grocery with a horse and wagon parked in front of it and a building that might have been a government office that was shuttered. It had announcements in Polish script nailed to the walls. In the grocery, dark and dusty with a wooden floor and barrels of foodstuffs here and there, Uncle Yitzhak tried out his Russian. That was a mistake at first, since of all the governments that had recently controlled Ivanova — Russian, German and Polish — people distrusted Russians the most. There were three people in the store, all wearing caps or hats, all with beards. Two apparently were shopping or just chatting; one older man, who sat on a barrel, was apparently the proprietor. The two customers studiously ignored Uncle Yitzhak's question "Can someone please tell me about the trains here?" After almost a minute, the proprietor spoke up in Russian.

"Who are you two? You're not from around here, that's certain."

"We have come a long ways," Yitzhak replied, "from America."

"America?" the proprietor and the two others said simultaneously. They might have said "From the *moon*?" All three moved closer to Yitzhak to hear him now.

"Yes, America. My nephew and I are trying to get to Motal. We have family there, and we want to visit them."

"So, you want to get to Motal?" the proprietor repeated, making it official.

"Who are your relatives in Motal?" one customer interjected in Russian. "Maybe we know them."

"Yes, we want to get to Motal," Yitzhak said, ignoring the customer. "Is there a train that goes there? We saw a track heading north."

The three townspeople now buzzed hurriedly among themselves, apparently debating how best to convey the information Yitzhak had requested. Mort thought he heard Yiddish.

"We haven't had anyone from America visit this town in I don't know how long. Many years, decades even," the proprietor said. "We thought you were officials from Brest or Warsaw, until you spoke Russian. That language is outlawed now, you know. You're not from Russia, are you?"

"No, we are not officials, and we are not from Russia. We are Americans," Yitzhak answered patiently. "Is there a train to Motal?"

The customer who had spoken before answered. "A train? Yes, of course, there's a train. You saw the track, didn't you? It doesn't run very often. Once every other day. Isn't that right?" he said to the others gathered close.

"Yes, yes, of course. Every other day," they agreed. "To Motal, it comes from the south, from Rudsk, I think," the bolder one added.

Uncle Yitzhak took a deep breath. "When is the next

time it will come?"

The proprietor, as if he had called a meeting, now addressed the other two townspeople. "When did it last come?"

"Yesterday. I know for a fact it was yesterday."

"Yesterday?" the other customer said. "You're crazy! Two days ago. It came on Monday."

"No, it didn't," the first one said.

At this point, Mort muttered to Uncle Yitzhak. "They must be Jewish. They're arguing about nothing."

The proprietor lifted his head when he heard the word 'Jewish'.

"Excuse me, did you say 'Jewish'?" he said in Russian to Mort. The word sounded a little like *"Yin-yay"* or *"Yin-nay."*

"He did," Yitzhak said, now speaking Yiddish. "We are Jews. My name is Yitzhak Stein, and this is Mordecai Stein," he said, conveniently forgetting Mort's Americanized version.

All three townspeople started smiling and nodding. The Yiddish and the Hebrew names were like magic words that opened doors. Uncle Yitzhak and Mort were *landsmen.* The boldest one was suspicious, however. "If you are Jews, why don't you have beards?"

"In America, most Jews don't wear beards," Yitzhak explained.

"Don't wear beards? Strange."

"We, too, are Jewish," the proprietor said. Many in this town are. In Motal too."

"The train," Yitzhak said gently. "Please tell us about the train."

The three townspeople huddled and finally agreed.

"Yesterday. It came yesterday at 14:00."

"No, 14:30!" the argumentative one corrected.

"Will you please, please, shut up, Avram," the proprietor said. "It makes no difference."

Uncle Yitzhak interrupted and spoke with exaggerated slowness and emphasis to keep them focused. "So, the *next* train to Motal will come *tomorrow, Thursday*, *at about 14:00 or 14:30*?"

"Yes, of course," the proprietor said. "Why do you speak this way, so slowly? We're not stupid, you know."

"I know that," Yitzhak said. "Excuse me. Now, we have a problem, my nephew and I. We need to stay somewhere overnight to catch this train to Motal tomorrow."

"You can stay with me," one of the men said. "I can house you and your nephew both for the night."

"In your shack?" the one called Avram said scornfully. "Where would they sleep? In the stable like Jesus, who was a Jew, you know," he said to Uncle Yitzhak.

"Yes, I know," Yitzhak sighed.

"Well, is your hovel any better?" the first one challenged.

"I can at least put them in a bedroom," Avram said pridefully. "My son's." He turned to Yitzhak. "My son has left home. He works in Minsk. He is—"

Yitzhak raised his hand, like a judge or an umpire settling a dispute. "How about this?" he asked in Yiddish. "My nephew will stay with… I'm sorry, what is your name?"

"Moishe. Moishe Beidner."

"With Mr. Beidner—"

"Listen to him," the others said. "*Mister* Beidner."

"And I will stay with, is it Avram?"

"Yes," Avram said, drawing himself to his full height. "Avram Farber."

"Good," Uncle Yitzhak said in a voice that settled the matter. "And I will stay with Avram Farber. For one night."

"Why only one?" Avram asked. "You could stay a week."

"Idiot!" the proprietor exploded. "Because they want to get to Motal sometime this year. Like tomorrow."

"All right, all right," Avram said, sounding hurt. "I was just offering."

"Well, no one wants your offer, beyond tonight," Beidner said.

"Thank you so much, gentlemen," Uncle Yitzhak said, forcefully interrupting them. "Now if you could kindly take us to your homes. We are very tired."

"You see?" the proprietor said. "While you were gassing about nothing, they were falling down on their feet."

"I was not gassing—"

"Who are your relatives in Motal?"

At this point, Uncle Yitzhak took Mort's arm firmly and steered him out of the grocery store.

Late the next morning, he met Uncle Yitzhak at the train station. They exchanged stories about their night as guests of Ivanova's Jewish community.

"It wasn't at all bad," Uncle Yitzhak said. "Just as Avram promised, I slept in a bed. I and my little friends. I'm afraid I left a few there, but it couldn't be helped. Perhaps I picked up some new ones, I don't know. They fed me a very nice dinner: bread, soup, and greens. But this morning I had fresh eggs!"

"My experience was exactly the same," Mort replied. "except that I slept on a straw mat, obviously saved for guests. It wasn't so bad, and it was damn nice of them to put us up. They wouldn't accept any money for it, of course."

"Not from me either," Yitzhak said. "Now we must wait two or three hours until that train to Motal comes — if it comes."

"Just be glad we're not going by horse and cart," Mort said. "That would take half the day."

"I wish we had a chess set, even checkers."

"I'd settle for a newspaper."

"In what? Polish or Russian? You can't read either of them."

"That's true," Mort admitted.

Just as the townspeople had said, the train, all two cars of it, came in at about 14:00. A half hour before that, the station master arrived, alerted about the new passengers from America. He examined their tickets and stamped them, then filled the water tank and shifted the signal for the train to stop. Gratefully, Mort and Yitzhak sat down on the bench inside the station for the final half hour.

The train moved so slowly, it seemed to Mort that he could keep up if he ran alongside. Though their car was hot, they had to keep the windows closed to keep engine steam from blowing back into the car. The twenty miles to Motal crept by with agonizing slowness. As they passed farms on the outskirts, Mort studied them carefully, wondering if one was his family's — or had been. None looked familiar, and he no longer knew where it was located. But the town's rabbi could tell him since he had passed along the cable to Anna. Mort had expected to feel nostalgic about coming back and seeing the shtetl where he grew up. He wasn't. As a boy, he had had few occasions to visit the town, a long walk from the farm. The family didn't go to synagogue, and when his parents rode in to shop on market days, they seldom took the children. Apparently, when he left with his sister at age thirteen, he put the town out of his mind.

Motal was a little bigger than Ivanova. Instead of a single muddy street, there was a muddy town square. But wooden sidewalks surrounded it. Mort noticed a church with a tall spire at one end of the square. Russian Eastern Orthodox, he guessed. A few dismal houses, dark with thatched roofs, could be seen just behind the square.

After the two men descended and the train tootled off, they had no trouble getting directions to the synagogue. Uncle Yitzhak simply spoke in Yiddish to the first person he saw with a beard. The synagogue was just off the square on a kind of spur. It was not large but more imposing than the other buildings on the square (except the church) since it was made of cement, not wood. As they walked to it, a group of schoolboys came running out a side door, swinging their prayerbooks on straps. *Cheder* must have just let out. Mort checked his watch. It was just past 4 p.m. The schoolboys stopped in midflight to study these strange men in suits. Yitzhak spoke to them, and they pointed to the synagogue. Yes, Rabbi Hirsch was there.

The rabbi was straightening up the study room as they entered. He was short and slightly stooped, with a gray beard, and was humming to himself. He looked startled to be overheard.

"Hello," Uncle Yitzhak said briskly in Yiddish. "Peace be with you. We come from America, and we come to see Anna and Schmuel Stein. I am Yitzhak Stein, Schmuel's brother, and this is my nephew, Mordecai Stein, his son. Several weeks ago, we sent a telegram here for Anna, which you kindly delivered."

"Ah, yes, I remember," the rabbi brightened. "Yes, I delivered it. They no longer live on that farm — a good thing, as it would have taken me close to an hour to walk out to it. They live in a small house off the square." He turned toward Mort. "You know, of course, that your mother, Rachel Stein, may she rest in peace, passed away last year."

"Yes, thank you. We knew that," Yitzhak responded. "My nephew's Yiddish isn't so good. That's why he's silent."

Just to show he could speak, Mort asked in halting Yiddish, "Could you please show us where they live?"

"Yes, of course," the rabbi said. "Just give me a minute to finish straightening up here. The boys leave the school such a mess. Did you just come for a visit?"

"No," Yitzhak said. "We came to bring them to America."

"America?" the rabbi smiled. "Really? You came all this way just to bring them yourselves?"

"Yes," Mort said in English, eager to explain. "We didn't feel they could make the journey on their own. And we brought their entrance visas for America."

"Slow down!" Yitzhak said. "I'm trying to get it all."

"Sorry."

The rabbi finished putting books away and faced them squarely. "I think I should tell you, before I take you there, that Schmuel — your brother? — is really in no condition to travel. He's an old man, sickly. And besides, he does not want to leave. He told me about the cable — I hadn't opened it — and that he would refuse to go. He said he was born here, and he wants to die here."

"Yes, we know that," Yitzhak responded. "But just in

case, we obtained two entrance visas and two transit visas. If he refuses to go, so be it. We can't force him."

"No, of course not," the rabbi agreed. "And Schmuel can be — how should I put it? — a rather difficult man. Stubborn."

"Cantankerous," Mort added in English.

Yitzhak took out a handkerchief to mop his brow. "This translating is a hot business."

The rabbi led them out of the synagogue into the darkening day. It had gotten cold, and a storm looked to be building.

"Looks like we'll have our first snow of the year," the rabbi said, studying the slate gray sky.

"Uncle," Mort said as the three walked, "please ask the rabbi how they support themselves now that they're not running the farm." Yitzhak complied.

The rabbi hesitated, then said "Well, I give them some tasks to do around here. Schmuel acts like a *shamas*. Anna leads the congregation in songs. Teaches songs in Sunday School also."

Mort said harshly in English, "What he's not saying is that they're living on charity. Don't translate that."

The rabbi continued, "You see, it was very hard for them when they could no longer operate their farm. Schmuel had no man to help him, and he is weak now from old age. His son had left home several years ago. He lives in Moscow, I understand. So, they had to give up the farm a few years ago. And they had no other way to support themselves."

"I see," said Yitzhak.

"There," the rabbi pointed to a small house. "That's where they live. I will introduce you, so that your arrival won't be too much of a shock. But first let me invite you two for dinner tonight. Tomorrow night, too — Shabbat — if you're still here. The Steins eat with us most nights."

"That's very good of you, rabbi." Yitzhak said.

"*A dank*," Mort added. The rabbi smiled and nodded.

Mort didn't recognize the woman who opened the door, but he knew it must be Anna. *Why should I recognize her?* he asked himself. *I haven't seen her in over twenty years. She was a child when I left. Now, with graying hair and a tentative, undernourished appearance, she looked much older than her thirty-two years. More like sixty-two*, he thought sadly.

But at this moment she was truly animated — overjoyed — as the rabbi was introducing them. She clapped her hands, ran out and hugged Mort first and then Uncle Yitzhak. Responding to her rapid, excited Yiddish, Mort held up his hand.

"Please slow down! My Yiddish is not very good." Anna's hand flew to her mouth; she complied immediately.

"Who's there, Anna?" a querulous voice called from the house. "Who is it?"

"It's your brother and son — Uncle Yitzhak and Mordecai — come from America!" she called through the door. "They've finally come! They're here! With the rabbi."

"Well, bring them in!" the voice commanded. "Don't let them gather dust out there."

The rabbi made a graceful exit at this point, and Anna, Yitzhak and Mort entered the house. It was dim inside, and Mort squinted while his eyes adjusted. There wasn't much to take in: one main room and what looked like a small adjoining bedroom. At the back of the main room was a rough-hewn table and two chairs. In front was a couch of some sort and a rocking chair. There was a cold fireplace in the wall by the rocker. No kitchen was visible, but some bread and jam, a water jug and two glasses were on the table.

Destitute, Mort thought, *utterly destitute.*

His father, who had been lying on the sofa, now sat up, rose slowly and tottered toward the men. "It's been a long time, Yitzhak," he said, simulating a hug.

Yitzhak returned it, feigning warmth. "Hello, brother. Yes, a long time."

"And you," Schmuel said, turning to look at Mort. "You are Mord'cai, my firstborn?"

Mort nodded, trying to adjust to his father's appearance. He had remembered him, dimly, as thin but wiry, muscular and vigorous from the daily farm chores. Here was a gaunt old man, so skinny he seemed almost skeletal, a few wisps of white hair on his bald head, his cheeks gray and whiskery, a scraggly white beard on his chin like a billy goat's, his veiny neck sticking out of a soiled work shirt, and an incongruous paunch above what looked like filthy trousers. More than anything, he looked sickly. His eyes were rheumy, sunk deep in their sockets, his cheeks also sunken, his forced smile revealing few teeth and dark gums.

"I've aged, haven't I?" he bluntly addressed Mort's open-mouthed stare. "Well, we all have, even you. I can't even remember what you looked like when you left, how long ago was it? More than twenty years ago?"

"Twenty-three," Mort said in English.

"Why don't you speak in Yiddish?"

Yitzhak interceded. "Your son understands some Yiddish, but he doesn't speak it well."

"They don't speak it in America?"

"He doesn't. Neither do I for that matter, except occasionally."

"So, my own son comes to visit me," Schmuel said, shaking his head sadly, "yet he can't talk to me? *Meshuga*."

"That's why I'm here," Yitzhak said. "To help him."

"I thought you came to bring me to America. Anna and me."

"We have. We've even obtained entrance visas for both of you."

Anna clapped her hands again like a joyous child, but Schmuel frowned. He was lying down again on the sofa, leaving the two men standing.

"Well, Anna may go with you, but I'm not. Didn't she tell you that when you sent that telegram?"

"She did. But we thought you might change your mind."

"And why should I? I never wanted to go. That's why I just sent Mordecai." Here he turned frowning to Mort. "Didn't I also send someone else with you? A daughter?"

"Chava," Mort said.

"Ah, Chava," his father said, the name sounding as if it came from a long way back in his memory.

"How is Chava?" Anna asked. "My big sister."

"She is good," Mordecai said.

"She lives in an apartment in Detroit, as we do, and gives violin lessons," Yitzhak said.

"Violin? She must play well," Schmuel said. "But like I was saying, I have no interest in going to America. I was born in this country, and I will die here."

So die, Mort thought savagely. *Who wants you?* Then he felt ashamed.

In this manner — haltingly, with Uncle Yitzhak having to translate Mort's English — they exchanged information about themselves, mostly about Mort's and Yitzhak's families. Anna had almost nothing to say about herself, and Schmuel didn't care to talk much, except to bark a comment now and then. He didn't seem particularly interested in his American offspring. Instead, he told them what they already knew. He never even mentioned his late wife.

"You probably know that Saul is in Moscow with his wife."

"Yes, Anna told us in a letter."

"Well, I couldn't very well run the farm after he left. Couldn't afford to hire help. Had to give it up when I got weak." Schmuel's dropping of 'I' made Mort think he was sending a telegram. *Trying to save words. Why? They don't cost him anything. He probably resented Saul's leaving the farm, just as Saul probably resented being forced to work on it. So, no more farm.*

"Is it all right if we sit down?" Yitzhak asked.

"All right?" Shmuel replied, "Of course it's all right. Sit! Sit!" They sat gingerly on the sofa, trying to avoid Schmuel's spread out legs.

"You must excuse me," Schmuel said formally, "I am a very weak man. I lie down on this sofa all day. I get up only to eat and to — what's the polite word?" Yitzhak told him. "Yes, to do that."

"Ask Anna about the exit documents," Mort said to Yitzhak, who complied. Mort had already forced himself to adjust to being mostly silent, waiting for Yitzhak to speak, intercede.

"I went to the commissioner here," Anna said, "and I brought the rabbi who speaks Polish. The commissioner said I needed a paper saying that I was a good citizen and had no jail offenses. He could provide it."

"But did he?" Yitzhak asked.

"Well, no. He said you should come and see him when you arrive."

"You know why he's waiting," Mort said, miming with his hand out.

"He's a *gonif*," Schmuel said. "He wants to be paid off."

"We expected that," Yitzhak replied, turning back to Anna. "When can we see him? Is he there now? When does he come in?"

"He comes in about twice a week," Anna said. "I think he'll be there Monday morning. Tomorrow is Friday, isn't it?"

"Yes, tomorrow is Friday," Yitzhak said. "What time does he arrive?"

Anna shrugged. "I don't know."

"He comes in when he comes in," Schmuel said. "Who can tell? You'll have to pay him something."

"We know," Yitzhak said and turned back to Anna. "One more thing… the train to Ivanova. We know it runs every other day. We took it today, from Ivanova. Will it run on Saturday?"

"You ask so many questions," Schmuel said. "Are you sure you don't work for the government?"

"I don't think so," Anna said, trying to recall. "I think it just runs on Tuesdays and Thursdays."

"So, we won't be able to leave until next Tuesday. Well, at least that will give us time to get this document if the commissioner doesn't come tomorrow."

"You could always take a horse and wagon," Schmuel said. "I know a farmer who regularly drives past Ivanova to Pinsk on Mondays. It's only about thirty-five kilometers."

"Well, we'll see," Yitzhak replied. "One final question." He addressed this one directly to Schmuel. "The rabbi told us you eat your meals with him and invited us to join you tonight."

"Yes," Schmuel said. "That's good. He's a kind man, Rabbi Hirsh. He feeds us well."

"What time should we be there?" Yitzhak asked.

"We go... I don't know. What time do we go, Anna?"

"Six o'clock."

Yitzhak took out his pocket watch. "It's about 5:30 now. We'll meet you at the synagogue at 6:00. The rabbi lives there, right?"

"Of course," Schmuel said. "Where else should he live?"

"In the meantime, we'll walk around the town."

"That won't take long," Schmuel said.

"Can we leave our suitcases here?"

"Of course. Did you think I would sell them?"

"Can I go with you?" Anna asked eagerly. "There's so much I want to hear about my family... your children, and yours," she said, nodding to Mort. "Also, about America. I cannot believe I'm really going after all these years."

"And leaving your poor father to die alone," came from the couch.

"Of course, we'll walk together."

"And leave me here alone?" Schmuel's voice was whiny.

"Oh, Papa. It's just for half an hour."

"Well, supposing I die during that time. Who'll be here to say *Kaddish*?"

"You won't die, Schmuel," Yitzhak said. "You will probably live forever and drive all of us to early deaths."

"All right. But don't say I didn't warn you."

"Let's go." Yitzhak got up. The others followed.

Sitting around the rabbi's table, Mort and Yitzhak felt grimy from traveling and having no chance to shower. At least, they could wash their hands. The dinner was modest but well-cooked, a stew of some sort.

"I must apologize for the meager dinner," Rabbi Hirsh said, after leading the prayer for breaking bread. "I didn't know you were coming. Fortunately, we had enough." His wife smiled but said nothing.

As they ate, Yitzhak asked about the Polish commissioner's schedule.

"I think he'll be here Monday. For a few hours in the morning."

"We would be very grateful if you would accompany us to see him, since you speak Polish. I speak only a little."

"I will try," the rabbi responded, "provided it doesn't conflict with morning prayers, and I have no house calls to make. You probably don't know this," the rabbi continued, "but the Poles have been trying to get Jews to migrate to Palestine."

"They've become Zionists?" Uncle Yitzhak was astonished.

"In effect, they have," the rabbi laughed. "You know that our great Zionist, Chaim Weitzman, came from this town."

"I had heard that," Yitzhak replied.

"Our most famous resident. Well, as I was saying, the Polish government secretly supports the migration. They've even contacted rabbis from this area to enlist our support. We should make announcements in synagogue and encourage people to go."

"Imagine that," Yitzhak said.

"It's not because they love us, you may be sure," Rabbi Hirsh continued. "They want to get rid of us. When they expanded to the east after the war with the Soviets, they inherited all the Jews who live in this region, hundreds of thousands, I'm told. So now they've become the Zionists' best friends."

At this, Mort had to interject. "Then they certainly shouldn't hold back on providing an exit visa for Anna."

"So long as you grease their palms," Yitzhak said in English and translated. He was proud of his American expression.

The rest of the dinner was taken up by questions the rabbi and Anna asked about America. Schmuel listened but said almost nothing. He seemed to frown with disapproval at everything he heard. At the end, Yitzhak addressed a final question to the rabbi and seemed a little embarrassed.

"I hate to ask, rabbi, but could you find a place where we could sleep for the next few nights? Through Monday night, I would think."

"I will ask the congregation tomorrow night at Shabbat service. I'm sure many will volunteer. Who knows? You might even get better meals than I could provide. In the meantime, you can stay here. We can set up two pallets in the school room for tonight. And tomorrow, you can bathe and go to *Mikvah* if you like." Mort realized he hadn't bathed since the night before he and Yitzhak disembarked. *I must be pretty ripe*, he thought.

"That would be fine, rabbi," Yitzhak was saying. "Mort and I thank you so much for your kindness."

"Don't mention it," Rabbi Hirsh said. "It's what one Jew should do for another."

Like caring for my family, Mort thought with a pang.

The Shabbat service Friday night did more than just find Mort and Yitzhak a home for the next few nights. It made them the main attraction. Rabbi Hirsch skipped his concluding sermon, introduced them to the congregation and explained their purpose in Motal. He invited them up to the *bima.* The congregation, men and women sitting separated, were fascinated not so much by the two men taking Anna away — she deserved to be rescued from that *alte kaker* — but simply by their coming from America. Yitzhak, at least, seemed familiar, speaking Yiddish. But neither he nor Mort had a beard. And indoors, except at the synagogue, they removed their hats. Jews are like that in America, the wiser ones explained to the others. That's being modern — American. Still, they had plenty of questions about America, since most had relatives, even family members, living there. Yitzhak answered each question patiently — or at least tried to, since those who assumed they knew all about America tried to answer first. That sometimes started argumentative exchanges, such as,

"I wasn't asking you; I was asking *him.*"

"Do you always need to put in your two kopeks, mister know-it-all?"

"Why isn't your nephew speaking? Is he mute?"

Yitzhak explained.

"Not speak Yiddish, and he's a Jew? What do Jews speak in America?"

"They speak American, you dummy."

"Like Germany. The educated Jews speak German."

"The educated German Jews would be smart to get out. This Hitler is a maniac. The Germans are the biggest Jew-haters."

"What are you talking about? The Poles are the biggest anti-Semites by a big margin."

"What makes you such an expert?"

So it went for at least half an hour. One serious question came from a soft-spoken man. "I have read that some Jews in America don't go to *shul*. In fact, they try to hide the fact they're Jewish and act like *goyim*. Is that true?"

"They can't hide their *schmeckels*," someone cracked, to laughter.

Mort responded slowly in Yiddish, then switched to English while Yitzhak translated, "Yes, it is true for some. But there are also Jews who are modern but still consider themselves Jews. I don't go to *shul*, and, as you see, I don't speak very good Yiddish. But I think of myself as a Jew."

"Not a very good Jew," someone in the audience muttered.

The homes where Yitzhak and Mort stayed were among the nicest in the village — not that they were much better than the poorest, except for Anna and Schmuel's hovel. The rabbi directed them to the *Mikvah* Friday morning after they had washed themselves with soap. Mort, the baths, after three grimy days, were especially welcome. They ate well, too, especially Shabbat dinner with the rabbi. His wife made a roast chicken, and the two Americans and Anna ate avidly. Schmuel picked at his dinner. The family where Mort stayed had a daughter, whom he guessed to be about seventeen. All the time he was there, she couldn't take her eyes off him. *I thought unmarried daughters were supposed to be shy*, he smiled to himself. *This one practically throws herself at me, though I'm much too old for her. Maybe, she's hoping I'll take her to America. Hmm, maybe that wouldn't be such a bad idea. Go on! Are you crazy?*

The rest of the family — the father, who ran the town grocery store, mother, a younger daughter and a boy about sixteen — were pleasant enough. Mort tried to help with chores around the house, so as not to seem so much of a mooch, but the language problems and his city clumsiness and inexperience kept him from doing much. He couldn't milk a cow, though the older daughter tried to show him how. And the family didn't want their special guest doing household chores. So, he had much time on his hands and no way to spend it except taking walks. At dinner, he could respond to their curious questions only in short sentences. He dearly wished Yitzhak were present, but his uncle was housed with a different family.

Monday couldn't come soon enough. The Polish commissioner did indeed come Monday morning. Mort and Yitzhak met at the synagogue, and, together with Anna and Rabbi Hirsch, they walked to the village office. The commissioner, grossly overweight, looked startled to see such a crowd come into his small office, but the rabbi, tactful as ever, set him at ease and explained the two strangers' intention and the need for that good conduct document for Anna.

"Yes, yes," the commissioner said. "I remember now her asking for it. I didn't have the right form with me then, but I think I may have it now. Let me check," he said, shuffling through papers in his desk. Mort knew he was lying and decided it was time to let the money talk.

He took twenty dollars in Polish *zlotys* from his wallet and put them on the table. "Rabbi, please tell him, that this contribution is our thanks for his efforts."

The official smiled on seeing the money and picked it up. "Thank you." He went back to searching. "Ah, here it is," he said, pulling it up and displaying it triumphantly. Now, I just need to ask the young lady some questions. Rabbi, would you please help translate?"

Yitzhak signaled Mort to step away with him and let the other two answer the questions. They waited in chairs by the wall. It went very smoothly and took only a few minutes.

"There!" the commissioner said, stamping the document firmly and signing it. "That should do it," he said, handing it to Anna with a greasy smile.

Mort said to the rabbi, "Please ask him if any other documents are needed for an exit permit." The rabbi complied.

"No, but they will ask you at the Warsaw office how much money you are taking out of the country. They have a limit. I think it's two hundred *zlotys*."

"Don't worry," Mort said, "that won't be a problem." The rabbi translated.

Now that the official business was completed, the commissioner wanted to chat and show he was truly a nice man. And who else would he have to talk to while in this shtetl office?

He conversed with the rabbi, who translated.

"Where will you leave from after you get your exit visa?"

The rabbi looked at Mort, who just said, "Danzig."

The official suddenly frowned. "That may be a problem. Danzig's port closed two days ago. There is a labor strike. The dock workers — dirty reds, all of them — are on strike, and no ships are coming in or going out."

When Rabbi Hirsh translated, Mort said, "What about German ports like Bremen?"

"About Bremen I wouldn't know," the official said. "But I wouldn't advise your going into that country. You are Jews, aren't you?"

"Yes," the rabbi answered, and Mort said to close this discussion, "Thank you. We'll make that decision later." Now that they had the certificate, he was anxious to leave before this slob devised another means of getting more money.

He started to rise, but Yitzhak gently pulled him back down. "Let's find out about the trains," he suggested.

"Good idea! I hadn't thought of that."

Yitzhak asked the rabbi in Yiddish, who asked the commissioner in Polish about the Motal train to Ivanova and the Pinsk train to Brest.

"I have train schedules on that wall," the official pointed, "but they're hard to read. I think I have some in my desk I can help you with." He started searching.

Amazing what twenty dollars will buy you, Mort thought.

"Yes, here are some schedules," the commissioner said producing them. Now, he sounded well-organized and efficient. "Let's begin with the Pinsk-Brest train. Let's see... it runs at the same time each weekday. It leaves Pinsk (probably coming from Minsk) at 09:30 and arrives in Brest at 11:00. You said you wanted to get it at Ivanova? It would *probably* stop there at, I'd guess 10:00, a half-hour after leaving Pinsk. Since it's 09:30 right now, you cannot take that train today if you try to get to Ivanova by train. I believe the train that goes to Ivanova from Motal runs twice a week, Tuesdays and Thursdays. It stops here about 11:00, sometimes earlier, sometimes later."

Yitzhak groaned. "Then we'd have to stay overnight in Ivanova to catch that Pinsk train on Wednesday"

"It looks that way," the official said, "unless you found another way to get to Ivanova. But permit me to offer you an alternative. I could *drive* the three of you to Brest this afternoon. I just have to go to Pinsk at about eleven and stay for about two hours. You could ride with me. It wouldn't cost you much, not much more than the train, and you wouldn't have to bother with these two trains and the overnight at all."

"That's wonderful!" Mort exclaimed after the translations were made. "So, we would leave Motal with you at—"

"10:30. In about a half hour."

"How much would it cost us?"

"Let's see," the official said, calculating.

He's figuring how much he can take us for, Mort thought glumly. *Even if it's a lot, though, it would be much more convenient than waiting overnight for slow trains*.

The official finished figuring and cleared his throat. "For each of you, I could do it for, say, 100 *zlotys*, 300 altogether."

That's about $75, $25 each, Mort calculated. He spoke to Uncle Yitzhak. "It's pretty reasonable considering we wouldn't have to stay overnight here and in Ivanova."

"I agree wholeheartedly," Yitzhak said. "I'm glad you want to do it. I don't think I could take another night of those Ivanova *nudniks* arguing with each other."

"Okay," Mort nodded directly to the commissioner,

and said, "We'll do it." He took out his wallet again, counted out three hundred *zlotys* and handed it over.

"Excellent!" the commissioner said. "You'll enjoy the ride, I guarantee it!"

That guarantee was false; they might have enjoyed it had they not been so crowded. The commissioner's car, a European make Mort didn't recognize, held two people comfortably in the front, but the back seat had almost no leg room. Mort deferred the best seat to his uncle. In the back seat, he sat with his knees drawn up to his chin. Anna didn't seem to mind being crowded; she had never ridden in an automobile before, and this was the first of many new adventures for her. Her eyes were wide as she took in the car and stared out of the windows. The car's age was indeterminate, but its shock absorbers were old and the road to Pinsk bumpy. *Potholes you could disappear in*, Mort grimaced. When he gratefully exited the car in Pinsk, it felt like someone had been kicking him in the kidneys the whole trip. The commissioner had stuffed two of their suitcases in the trunk and roped Anna's satchel to the roof. Before he entered his office in Pinsk, he pointed to his watch and said "*godzina pierwsza*" emphatically. Then he held up one finger. Though this was clear enough, Mort was uneasy not having the rabbi nearby to translate.

"Why don't we find a café and get an early lunch?" Mort suggested to Yitzhak. "We won't get into Brest until mid-afternoon." Anna nodded vigorously when Yitzhak translated.

This must be the big city for her, Mort thought. *I wonder if what she's suffered with our father has affected her mind. She seems a bit simple.*

They strolled leisurely around Pinsk's streets. After Ivanova and Motal, it did seem more like a town and had streets and shops. They found a café easily. "We could do what we did before," Mort said to Yitzhak "and draw what we want."

"I've already had breakfast," Yitzhak said, "and how do you draw stew?"

"Easy," Mort said, "draw a bowl with steam lines coming from it. Just for good measure, he drew some chunks in the bowl."

"They might take that for just soup."

"That's true. Could you live with soup?"

"I'd rather have stew," Yitzhak grumbled. "But very well." He asked Anna what she wanted. She shrugged, then said that anything would be fine.

When the waitress came, there was no problem. After she saw the drawing, they could easily distinguish between her choices of *Zupa* and *gulasz*. They guessed that *chleb* was bread, and the waitress understood 'coffee'.

The rest of the trip was uneventful. Since they were ready earlier than one o'clock, and the commissioner had finished his work, they left early. This time, Mort studied the countryside: apart from the few towns, it was nothing but wheat fields or sunflowers as far as the eye could see.

They pulled into Brest about 13:45, and the commissioner drove them directly to the train station, which now looked familiar. Mort extracted the luggage; a brisk handshake, and they were free.

The next train for Warsaw left at 14:30 and wouldn't arrive until 17:30. "We can stay overnight in Warsaw," Mort said, and go to the government office when it opens the next day, probably at ten. Meanwhile, I'll try to make reservations for a hotel."

"You're getting to be very skillful about traveling," Yitzhak commented, as he translated for Anna. She had been studying the train station. *It must look huge to her*, Mort thought. *Imagine what Warsaw will look like.* He bought the train tickets to Warsaw and was directed to the station's tourist office. Like the one in Danzig, the travel officer spoke English, only she was much friendlier than the other one. Yes, she could get them a nice hotel room in Warsaw.

"With three single beds?"

"That would be difficult," the woman said.

"All right, then, two rooms, one with two single beds. And the hotel must not have cockroaches," he added bluntly.

The woman was taken aback. "No, of course not. This will be a nice hotel. Second class." When she handed him the reservation slip, Mort asked about the Danzig strike the commissioner had spoken of. "Yes, it is true," the agent said. "The port is closed."

"We want to sail on the first ship available to America after Wednesday. From the closest port."

"That would be Bremen. Let me look up what ships are leaving Bremen for America."

After a few minutes, she returned and said, "There is a fine ship leaving Bremen on Friday morning. It would arrive in Baltimore in only nine days. I could book your passage."

Mort was tempted but decided to wait until Anna had her exit visa. He thanked the woman and reported his findings to Yitzhak. "Okay, we're set for the night in Warsaw. I got a separate room for Anna. The travel agent swore the hotel wouldn't have roaches."

"What about bedbugs?"

"I would think if it doesn't have one, it won't have the other."

"We'll see," Yitzhak said, skeptically. "Do you really want to go through Germany?"

"We would just be traveling through. We could take an overnight train straight through and wouldn't have to stop before Bremen."

"But we'll have to go through their border. They might make trouble for us."

"I think we'll be okay. And we have an extra day to spare before the ship leaves. Maybe we'll get lucky, and they'll settle the strike tomorrow."

"And maybe we'll win the Irish Sweepstakes. All right, Mort. You're the boss."

In Warsaw, Anna was overwhelmed by the big city and its five- and six-story buildings. Mort and Yitzhak had to continually tug on her arm to shake her out of an open-mouthed stare and get her moving, even just to walk to the taxi stand outside the train station. Mort handed the driver the reservation slip and off they went, twisting and turning in Warsaw's rush-hour traffic. Soon, the cab pulled up in front of their hotel, which looked nice enough from the outside. The driver seemed a bit impatient as Mort slowly counted out the *zlotys* and guessed at an appropriate tip. As they carried their bags inside — *a first-class hotel would have wheeled them in on one of those big, shiny trolleys*, Mort thought — Uncle Yitzhak explained to Anna that she would have her own room. She looked as if he had given her an expensive present.

"All to myself?" she asked.

This hotel did seem nicer than the one in Brest, and

both men had the luxury of a bug-free bath in the bathroom at the end of the hall. Yitzhak explained to Anna that she could have a bath too, and that he would stand guard outside the bathroom until she finished. He also explained how the toilet worked. Fortunately, it was in a separate room from the tub.

Before they went out to search for a restaurant, Mort stopped at the desk and asked, in the sentence the commissioner had taught him, if anyone spoke English. One did, and he directed them to a good restaurant a few blocks away. This one had menus, and Uncle Yitzhak could get his beloved stew. He asked Anna what her favorite food was, but the restaurant did not have *gefilte fish*. They ordered her white fish instead with potatoes and a vegetable.

"How about some wine," Mort suggested, "to celebrate our coming this far?"

"Can we just order a glass, not a bottle? Yitzhak asked. "You remember what happened the last time I drank too much — at your wedding? I drink very little since then."

"That was whiskey," Mort said, "but I'll see if we can get just a glass each."

The waitress did not speak English, but the manager spoke enough to get them what they wanted. The wine was excellent and tasted of plums. The dinner was also very good. After, they walked around the neighborhood.

"Keep your eyes peeled for shops with women's clothes," Mort told Yitzhak. "I want Anna to buy some new clothes for herself. I felt that satchel — she barely brought anything with her."

"That's because she didn't have anything to bring."

Anna knew they were talking about her and looked embarrassed.

The next day, Tuesday, after a light breakfast in the hotel restaurant, they took Anna to the shop they had found and explained that she needed to pick out some clothes — a few dresses, underwear, stockings, perhaps a hat. They also took her to a shoe store. Anna seemed dazed. She had never bought clothes for herself — she just wore the clothes Chava left behind and then village hand-me-downs. Even when his farm was prosperous, Schmuel was too stingy to take her to Pinsk to buy new clothes. Soon enough, though, Anna adjusted to this unimaginable luxury and was carefully examining dresses. It took well over an hour, and they carried her treasures back to the hotel.

They next had to find the State Bureau for Travel Documents. The hotel clerk who spoke English wasn't there, but another told them that it was located in the central government building, about half a mile from the hotel. He gave careful directions, and they found it without difficulty. The Bureau was on the second floor and a receptionist steered them to the office handling visas and passports. Others were ahead of them to see the chief clerk. When it was their turn, they were ushered into the clerk's office. Again, their language luck held, as his assistant, a comely young woman with dark features and jet-black hair, spoke excellent English.

Mort explained their original aim and how they planned to change their exit from Poland. She listened politely and looked sympathetic.

"Yes," she said, "this strike is upsetting a lot of people's travel plans. It is very distressing. But your plan to travel to Bremen changes your situation very much."

"How is that?" Mort asked uneasily. "We brought with us the good conduct form required for the exit visa for my sister."

"That is good. We will have no problem providing that visa for her. May I have it please?" She continued, "But to travel through Germany, she will need a *German* transit visa, which you can get at the border crossing, and a German exit visa."

"Good lord!" Mort interjected. *We'd be dealing with the Nazis as well as the bureaucrats!*

"You see, right now, so far as the Germans are concerned, your sister is stateless, while you men are protected by your American passports. The Germans are sticklers about enforcing the rules, even though they change them from day to day, especially for Jews." She didn't say this snidely.

She continued, "But if we could get her a temporary passport — getting a permanent one would take weeks — then she would have the same protection and could travel through the country, provided she didn't intend to settle there."

"That's not likely," Mort said grimly. "But can she really get this temporary passport? It sounds like a lifesaver."

The assistant smiled. "I don't see why not. We just need to photograph her and fill out the document. It won't have a nice cover on it like yours do, but it would still be official for one month."

"That would be wonderful!" Mort said. "How do we begin?"

Anna was steered to a nearby room to be photographed. The setup reminded Mort of the photos available in the five-and-ten stores, where you sat in a curtained booth. Meanwhile, the assistant filled out the Polish exit visa and the temporary passport. "I need some information about her," she said, "and she'll need to sign it." Mort provided the information; he wasn't sure of Anna's age but figured a close approximation would do. The assistant had never heard of Motal.

While she was writing, Mort couldn't resist asking, "You are different from the other government clerks we've dealt with. Why are you being so nice to us?"

The assistant looked up and smiled. "Perhaps because I understand the situation you're facing in traveling through Germany."

"*You're* Jewish, too?" Mort was incredulous.

She nodded and kept writing.

The chief clerk walked over from his desk to see what the delay was. Apparently, a few people were waiting in line. He said something sharp to her in Polish, and she responded just as sharply. The man glared at Anna, Mort and Yitzhak, but didn't stop the proceedings. He just shook his head and took the next person waiting in line.

In less than a half hour, the documents were complete, Anna's photo pasted in the appropriate place. Mort was astonished. *Once the wheels of bureaucracy get moving, they really move! Especially if someone is on your side.* As they prepared to leave, the assistant spoke to Mort.

"Let me give you a word of advice in dealing with the Germans. If they start to become difficult about the temporary passport, then *you* become difficult and demand that the American consul in Berlin be contacted immediately. They would never call him, of course, but it might stop them from harassing you. Their officials can be bullies, you see, but they are afraid of real trouble. Just to be sure, you should carry the consul's name and telephone number. I think we have it here somewhere."

"How can I thank you for this?" Mort said earnestly,

thinking I know how to thank the other officials. With *zlotys*. That would probably offend her.

"You have thanked me. That is enough," the woman said. "Good luck to you all, and bon voyage."

He wanted to embrace her and suddenly realized it was because he was physically attracted to her. She was young and quite pretty after all — and Jewish. *And she wasn't wearing a wedding ring!* Impulsively, he said "I would like to write to you when I get back to the States. Not just a thank you note, a letter. Would I be too forward to ask for your name and address?" He produced his notepad.

The woman looked surprised and a little baffled. But she complied, writing hurriedly.

Next came the train tickets to Bremen, via Berlin, and the steamship tickets. A tourist office near the government building would take care of both. The train trip was about nineteen hours *if* all went well. The ship that the tourist agent in Brest had mentioned, aptly named *The Bremen,* left that port for Baltimore on Friday at 10:00. At the travel office, Mort spoke with a clerk about schedules and fares, then returned to the other two to discuss their options.

"I figure we could take a night sleeper tonight. It leaves the main station at 21:00. *If* we aren't delayed, it would get into Bremen about 16:00 the next afternoon, Wednesday. We'd have an extra day and a half margin this way."

"We may need it if the Germans give us trouble," Uncle Yitzhak said. "Are you also going to buy the steamship tickets now?"

"What?" Mort wasn't paying attention.

"The steamship tickets," Yitzhak repeated. "Are we going to buy them now?"

"Well, yes. We need to reserve our berths. Let's hope they're not booked up."

As Mort walked back to the travel agent, Yitzhak wondered about the difference in his behavior. Formerly, he was alert and always thinking ahead. Now, he seemed distracted. *He's probably worried about going through Germany*, Yitzhak concluded.

When Mort came back with the tickets several minutes later, he looked a bit relieved, as if now the matter was settled.

"The steamship has berths and so does the sleeper to Bremen. We don't need to be at the station until 20:45 tonight, so we have all afternoon in Warsaw. Let's go back to the hotel, freshen up, have lunch somewhere nearby, maybe a nap, and I'll find out from the concierge if there's anything interesting going on this afternoon."

"That's quite a plan," Yitzhak said. "We'll be paying for a second night at the hotel, you know."

"Can't be helped," Mort replied. "We still need the facilities of the hotel, and we can't very well carry our suitcases around all day."

When Yitzhak glanced at him, he noticed Mort studying, not the tickets, but the name and address the assistant had given him, the assistant who had helped them so much at the Travel Bureau and was so pretty. Her name was Magda Karlinsky.

There was a Tuesday afternoon concert available, the hotel concierge informed them, which suited the men just fine. Mort already enjoyed classical music, though it saddened him to associate it with Miriam. *Well, that chapter of my life is pretty much over*, he reflected. The concert featured the Symphony Orchestra of Warsaw playing Mozart and Brahms. For Anna, going to the concert was, like almost everything else since she left Motal, an entirely new experience and gave her a chance to wear some of her new clothes. They not only made her look more attractive and younger, they also began to change her manner. They made her less shy, a bit more self-confident. She was smiling more.

Following a pleasant dinner, they caught the night train from the main station in plenty of time. From walking so much in Warsaw and the heavy food of their dinner, they were tired and turned in early. Several hours later, Mort, lying cramped in his berth, heard the train screeching gradually to a halt. A conductor passing through the car called out in Polish, "We are coming to the border. Please have your passports ready." Mort guessed at the meaning, scrambled to get dressed and alerted Yitzhak and Anna to do the same. He was furious with himself for not anticipating this stop and didn't want to be interrogated in his pajamas.

Two German officials went through the sleeper car, looking at documents. They wore uniforms and had swastika armbands. But realizing they were disturbing the passengers' sleep, they moved quickly and asked few questions — until they looked at Anna's temporary passport. This looked strange to them, and one handed it to the other, asking questions.

Mort had already prepared a question for them from a travel dictionary he picked up in Warsaw, "*Sprechen Sie English?*"

"*Nein*," one German said.

"*Ein Bisschen*," the other said.

"*Sie ist mein* — what was that word he had memorized? — *Schwester.*"

"Yes," the official understood, "but this whatever it is, it is not a regular passport."

Mort decided to try the other official's English. "It is a *temporary* passport she received in Warsaw. We are just passing through Germany to sail at Bremen."

It was too much for the other German's weak English, and he shrugged, confused.

"Perhaps I can help," a passenger nearby spoke up. He translated Mort's explanation. When he got to the word 'temporary' — *vorübergehend* — the officials lit up.

"Ah so," one said, and handed the passport back to Anna, who looked frightened. They moved on, and Mort thanked the bilingual passenger profusely.

"Don't mention it," the man said with an American casualness. "These krauts can be pretty officious. Well, good night. See you in Berlin."

"The train stops there, I suppose," Mort said.

"Oh yes. And the inspection there will be much more thorough."

"I hope you'll be able to translate for us there. We'd be very grateful if you could."

"I'll try if I'm nearby," the man said, turning away. "Better get some sleep."

Getting to Berlin from the border took another five hours. Mort awakened Yitzhak and Anna early, so that they could be dressed and have breakfast before stopping.

"I'm not looking forward to this," Yitzhak muttered as the train slowed going into Berlin's *Anhalter Bahnhof.*

"You think I am?" Mort replied.

All the passengers were required to exit the train and

have their papers examined in a large transit office adjoining the main waiting room. Their documents had already been collected, and the travelers sat on benches waiting for their names to be called. Mort scanned the waiting passengers nervously. The bilingual American was sitting across the room. He waved when Mort caught his eye, but his shrug said, "There's not much I can do for you from over here." While they waited, Mort studied the surroundings. There were desks behind which sat the German officials, in black S.S. uniforms. In the corners were red Nazi flags hanging on stanchions. On the wall was a framed picture of Adolph Hitler, standing with his elbow bent, hand on hip, looking impatiently into the distance. *A true visionary*, Mort thought bitterly.

The officials dealt with the waiting passengers expeditiously, calling them to one of several desks in the room. Finally, one called out, "Morton Stein, Yitzhak Stein and Anna Stein." The three rose and approached the desk as if facing the judge for a death sentence. Mort immediately asked if anyone spoke English.

"Why don't *you* speak German?" the official snapped back. "Why must *we* accommodate you, a Jew?"

So, it begins already, Mort tensed. He said nothing, just stared at the official.

"All right," the official said. "Since you are all pathetically ignorant, *we* will help you." He called over another official, who took the adjoining seat after looking the three supplicants up and down.

The first official studied the American passports. "They don't have a 'J'," he grumbled. "How is anyone to know you are Jews — except by your names, of course?"

"The Americans are a backward nation," the other official joked. He was younger and looked less stern.

"What is your destination?" the first official spoke to Yitzhak. The second translated each of the questions and answers.

"Bremen."

"Why Bremen?"

"We are taking a ship to America from there."

"Good. Then you don't plan to stay in Germany?"

"Only in Bremen until the ship leaves — on Friday."

The first official gave a disapproving "Hmph," stamped Yitzhak's passport and handed it to him. He then turned to Mort after examining his passport. "And you," he sneered. "Same story? We know how you Jews stick together in your stories."

"Yes," Mort said. *Say as little as possible*, he cautioned himself — *for now.*

The first official snorted, stamped the passport and handed it over. Then he studied Anna's temporary passport.

Now the shit's going to hit the fan, Mort grimaced, bracing himself.

"What in the world is this?" the first official asked, addressing Anna and pretending he had never seen such a document.

"It is a Polish temporary passport," Mort interjected. "My sister lived in what is now Poland, and we just received it in Warsaw."

"Why can't she answer?" the first official barked. "Is she mute?"

"No, she's not mute," Mort responded back. "Just shy."

"Shy," the first official muttered. "I never heard of a Jewess being shy." Grudgingly, he addressed Mort. "You say she received this in Warsaw? I thought the Poles

167

didn't consider Jews full citizens."

Just as in your country, Mort wanted to respond, but kept his mouth shut.

"She received it yesterday in Warsaw. She is accompanying us to Bremen and to America. She doesn't plan to stay in Germany, in Bremen, any longer than is necessary." *Who would want to?* he thought.

When the other official had finished translating, the first one shook his head. "I don't think we can approve this. You will have to wait while I telephone my superior. You'll have to take a later train to Bremen."

Now or never, Mort decided. "And while you're asking your superior, I demand to speak to the American consul in Berlin! He will want to know about this."

"You are *demanding* of us? Just who do you think you are? You Americans think you own the world. Well, you don't own us! And Jews, no less!"

The room had suddenly quieted, and everyone still there was watching this confrontation.

You're in this far, Mort steeled himself. *Don't back down*. "Nevertheless, I insist on speaking to the American consul if you are going to hold up our certification."

"You arrogant Jews! We know how to deal with you." the first official sputtered.

"But the American is correct," a third voice interjected in German. Mort turned. It was the American who had helped them on the train. He spoke in rapid, authoritative German to the first official. "It just so happens that I am the son-in-law of that American consul in Berlin, Mr. George Messersmith. My name is Randolph Hathaway. And this American is correct. You have no justification for denying approval of this temporary passport. And if you do, *I* will call my father-in-law, and there will be a real stink!" The final word came out *stunk*. "Do you want me to call him now?"

The first official started sweating and said in an altogether different voice, "There is no need for that, Herr Hathaway. We were simply unfamiliar with this kind of passport and felt we needed permission to approve it. I think, under the circumstances, we'll be able to do so," he concluded, stamping the document and pushing it toward Anna — pushing because she was too scared to reach for it. Yitzhak took it and handed it to her.

As the official called the next name, the four of them left the office. "You've saved us again!" Mort said breathlessly.

"I enjoyed it," the young man said. These krauts are bullies until someone proves he's a bigger bully."

"Is your father-in-law really the American consul?" Uncle Yitzhak asked in awe.

"What do *you* think?" the young man laughed.

"We cannot thank you enough," Mort said. "Truly. Can we at least buy you a drink on the train? Or lunch?"

"Thanks, no. Like I said, I enjoyed it. Glad to help," the young man said, walking away.

"C'mon, let's get out of here before fish-face over there changes his mind," Mort said, steering the other two to the outer doors. Yitzhak looked plainly relieved. Anna was still stunned. She only partly grasped what was going on, but sensed that they were, for the moment, safe. She spoke in rapid Yiddish to Yitzhak, who briefly summarized the confrontation. They were careful to keep their voices low. It was not a good place to speak Yiddish.

The train made it to Bremen in four hours, arriving in the early afternoon. The city looked more modern than

Danzig, but the group had no time for sightseeing. Mort found the tourist office in the station and asked for hotel reservations.

"I'm afraid the good hotels are all booked solid," the young attendant said, in fluent English. "We can get you a third-class hotel or a pension. The pension comes with a breakfast, but the rooms are small and there are time restrictions." He explained, "You have to be in by a certain time, say 22:00, and then they lock up for the night. They also have time limits on when breakfast is served. Not after 9:00, in some of them."

"That will be all right," Mort decided. "We'll need two rooms for two nights. Two single beds in one room, if possible.

"I can reserve the rooms, but I won't know the bedding arrangement," the attendant responded.

"That's okay. Just book them, please," Mort said.

The pension was on the outskirts of town. and the cab driver didn't find it right away. It was a two-story home on a residential street of gabled houses, quiet and neat with flower boxes outside the windows. The owner showed the Steins their rooms, which looked spotlessly clean. The beds, one double for each room, had comforters on them instead of blankets.

"I guess we'll have to share a double," Mort said to Yitzhak.

"I don't mind if you don't," Yitzhak said. "But Minna tells me I snore sometimes. Besides, as you like to say, "It's only for a night — two nights." Mort helped him finish the quote, and they both laughed. Anna was again amazed that she had a comfortable room and bed all to herself. Yitzhak again noticed that Mort seemed distracted, as if mulling over something.

Using his travel dictionary, Mort asked about a restaurant, and the owner wrote down the address of one nearby. *He probably steers all his guests to that one and gets a kickback,* Mort thought, responding, *"Danke."* *We even have time for a bath before dinner.*

The continental breakfast the following morning was in the pension's dining room, and along with the other guests, the Steins sat around the large table sipping the strong coffee and munching on the fresh rolls. "What, no eggs?" Yitzhak joked in English. A few guests who knew English frowned at him, and Mort shushed him.

After breakfast, they sat in comfortable chairs on the sunny front porch, and Mort made an announcement.

"I've decided not to go with you to America. Not on this ship, anyway. I wanted to wait to tell you this until I knew you were both safe and the trip is secure. I'm going back to Warsaw."

"Why, in God's name?" Yitzhak demanded after he translated for Anna, who also looked shocked. "You're leaving us?" He still couldn't comprehend the announcement.

"Yes," Mort explained patiently. "I've been thinking about this ever since we left Warsaw. That's where I'm going. I want to see Magda again to see if I can interest her in coming with me back to America — as my wife."

"As your *wife*?" Yitzhak was incredulous. "She's a young girl! You think she's going to drop everything — her job, her life in Warsaw, perhaps her family — and go off with you, someone she barely knows, to a foreign country, a *distant* country."

"I know it sounds crazy…" Mort said.

"Not sounds. *Is*!" Yitzhak interjected. His vehemence startled Mort; he had never seen Uncle Yitzhak so worked up over anything.

171

"But I was really attracted to her when we were in Warsaw, not just because she helped us so much, but to her as a person."

"And as a Jew," Yitzhak added.

"Yes, also as a Jew. Why not?"

"What about your steamship ticket?"

"I think I can return it today. Or get a voucher for a later trip."

"And what about Anna? She's why you came all this way in the first place."

"I'm leaving her in your care, Uncle Yitzhak. You and Aunt Minna have space in your flat; you could put her up for a few weeks, couldn't you? Until I return? I wouldn't be able to communicate with her very well if she stayed in my flat, not until she learns some English."

"Or until your Yiddish improves. So, that's all the time you plan to spend courting your new beloved, a few weeks?"

"I think that by that time — or even sooner — I'll know if she's interested, seriously, and *she'll* know if she wants to return with me — as my wife."

"Well, if you ask me—" Yitzhak said.

"And I wasn't," Mort tried to stop him.

"If you ask me, I think it's crazy. *Meshugah.* This is so unlike you, Mort. It's so — what's the right word?"

"Impulsive?"

"Impulsive."

"Look, Uncle. I'm thirty-seven years old. I'm divorced. If I'm going to remarry and possibly start a new family, I need to do it soon. This woman really knocked me over. Call it infatuation if you wish. But I think she's just what I'm looking for. And I didn't even know I was looking until I met her! She's intelligent, pretty, speaks English perfectly, and she's Jewish."

"Yes, but what do you have to offer her? A middle-aged American who runs three gas stations and lives in an industrial city in the Midwest. Why should she give up her single life and a good job in a cosmopolitan city for *that*?"

"I've asked myself precisely that question, Uncle, and I'm going to find out the answer from her. If worse comes to worst and she's not interested, I'll take the next boat back to America. I'll write Miriam about my staying longer, not about why. I had already told her we might be gone the whole month."

"So, I'm to watch over Anna until you return?" Yitzhak said.

"I do appreciate it, Uncle. I know this is crazy. But I have to do it. Have to try at least. Or the rest of my life, I'll be wondering 'what if?' What if I had tried? What then? I'm not going to spend all those years regretting that I *didn't* try. Can't you understand?"

"Yes, I understand," Yitzhak nodded. "You're a fool. But love often makes people fools. Especially this kind of love. You're just one more." He briefly explained to Anna Mort's decision. She looked stunned.

In their pension room, Mort checked on his money — he had brought enough for an entire month of hotel rooms, travel, and meals. He gave a big chunk to Yitzhak for expenses in getting Anna and himself back to Detroit and advised him, "Please get her into an adult education class right away. She's got to learn basic English as soon as possible."

Yitzhak nodded.

"The ship departs at 10:00, Friday morning. I'll take

the extra entrance visa with me — in case I get lucky and Magda agrees to go. Good luck, you two!"

He stood and hugged them both. Tears silently slid down Anna's cheeks. Mort now spoke to her directly. "Don't worry, sister. I will be back in a few weeks, and then you will stay with me and my son, Edward. Uncle Yitzhak will watch over you 'til then. Have a safe trip, you two."

He checked again on his papers, took his suitcase and left.

After returning his steamship ticket, Mort taxied directly to the train station. The Warsaw train took eleven hours, much faster than the overnight train they had taken, and if he hurried, he could catch the next one at eleven. At the train station tourist office, he just had time to book the same hotel in Warsaw they had stayed at before.

Traveling alone with a valid American passport, he didn't expect problems with the Germans. In his train compartment he settled back and contemplated what had just transpired with Yitzhak and Anna and what lay ahead tomorrow in Warsaw. He also studied sentences in German to explain where he was going.

The trip proved uneventful. At the Berlin station, a different official gave a cursory look at his passport and stamped it. No questions, no hostility, no obstructions. The same held true for the border check, but he breathed easier when the train had crossed into Poland. No more menacing swastika armbands and flags. The train pulled into Warsaw at 22:00, and the hotel had his room ready. There was even a tavern nearby that served food.

He had considered how he would approach Magda the first time. The great imponderable was how she would react seeing him. As he approached the Bureau for Travel

Documents the next morning, he felt a little short of breath and not just from climbing the stairs. When he entered, he saw her immediately, just as beautiful as he remembered her, and his heart melted. She was working with a couple, her head down, writing something. When she raised it and saw him, her face brightened immediately, and she smiled at him. But she also looked surprised, a bit taken aback. He waited patiently for her to finish with her clients and declined help from the supervisor, who studied him for a moment. The couple got up, thanking her, and he walked directly to her desk before someone else might fill the opening. She smiled again as he approached.

"Hello. It's Mr. Stein, isn't it? I'm surprised to see you again. Did everything go all right?"

"Hello, Miss Karlinsky," he responded, feeling very formal. "Yes, everything went well. My uncle and sister are on their way to America. I'll tell you about it later. I know you don't have time to talk with me right now, but is there a time later today when you'll be free for a little while?"

"My lunch break is at noon," she said. "Come then."

"I will," he said and left the office before her supervisor could come over.

He was there promptly at noon, after killing hours walking around Warsaw and window-shopping. He found a shop that sold suitcases and travel paraphernalia, where he bought a money belt. At the Travel Bureau, he waited at the door while she closed up her desk and came out to him with a smile.

"Now, Mr. Stein, you must tell me what happened," she said, as they walked downstairs together to the main door.

"I will," he said, feeling his heart beating fast, "but please call me Mort. And I'll use Magda, if that's okay. First, tell me where you'd like to go for lunch."

"I usually just get coffee nearby, since I bring my own lunch," she said, holding up the bag. "But today, let's go to a café I know, since you need lunch too. I'll save this one for later."

The café was crowded but not so noisy that they couldn't talk. Mort told her briefly about the two confrontations with German officials and the timely intervention of the young American. Magda laughed when he described how the American had bluffed the Nazi officials.

"True to form for these Germans," she said. "Bullies when they can get away with it, cowards when they can't. But why aren't you with your uncle and sister?"

Mort took a deep breath and explained, trying not to sound gushy, that he felt he had to see her again, even if it meant taking a later ship to America. He knew better than to mention his goal of bringing her to America or their marrying.

When she replied, she wasn't smiling, but not frowning either, just serious.

"I'm deeply flattered, Mort. Truly, I am. But you do not even know me. You know nothing about me. I may be married and have six children, for all you know."

"Are you?" he laughed.

"No, I'm not married. Or have even one child."

"Do you have a boyfriend?"

"I go out often with different young men, mostly old friends from the *liceum* and a few from the office. No one that you would consider a boyfriend."

Mort hadn't realized he'd been holding his breath until

she answered. Now, he exhaled with relief and said, "I can't tell you how glad I am to learn that. You see, I would like to go out with you. That's why I came back."

At this point their food arrived, but Mort hardly looked at it.

Magda seemed incredulous as she started eating. "You came all the way back to Warsaw just to go out with me?"

"I know it sounds crazy," Mort admitted. "But you see, I'm very much attracted to you. And if we went out a few times, you could decide if you feel the same way about me — if you haven't already decided to avoid this crazy man."

They both laughed. Then Magda said seriously, "You're much older than I am. As I recall, your passport said you were born in 1898. That would make you — thirty-seven?"

"Yes. I'm astonished that you remember my birth year."

"Yes. Well, I'm twenty-two."

"Fifteen years is a big gap, I admit. Listen, Magda. I'll make this promise. Go out with me one time, and if you're not interested after that, or you still think I'm too old for you, I promise to leave you alone and go back to America on the next ship available."

"I'll accept, provided you let me ask you about yourself. Then I'll decide."

"Please do ask."

"Are you married? One man I went out with was married but didn't tell me, until later." She recalled it with a laugh.

"I'm divorced. Have been for almost two years."

"Children?"

"Three. A son, fourteen, who lives with me. A daughter,

thirteen, and a second son about eleven. They live with their mother. We all live in Detroit."

"It's funny, I would have expected New York."

"Jews live all over America, not just in New York. I've lived in Detroit almost since I came to America in 1912. From Russia."

"And what about the relatives you were traveling with?"

"My uncle Yitzhak has his own flat — apartment — with his wife, a few blocks away. His children are grown and living elsewhere. My sister, Anna, the one helped with the temporary passport, will be staying with me, at least until she learns English and finds work for herself — or gets married. That might be quite a while."

"So, you live with one son and soon with your sister? You are already a family. And you support your other two children, yes?" Magda asked without enthusiasm.

"I pay child support, yes. I realize it would not be a carefree situation for you — if things should get that far. But my son who lives with me is easy to get along with. He's serious, like me." She laughed at that.

"I also have another sister, who came with me to America. She lives alone and is self-supporting."

"Like me," Magda said with a hint of a smile. "What do you do in Detroit?"

"I control three gasoline — petrol — stations. I don't actually pump gas unless one of the managers is ill. I plan to acquire more stations if things continue to go well. I'm not rich, but I make a pretty nice living from the stations. There, does that qualify me for one date?" he tried to sound light-hearted to cover his sense of foreboding.

But Magda laughed. "Yes," she said, "I think it does."

With a huge sense of relief, Mort turned to his lunch.

They went out Saturday night. Mort had planned to take Magda to a concert or ballet, but then decided a good dinner in a first-class restaurant would give them more chance to talk and get to know each other. This time it was Magda's turn. She was obviously proud of her *liceum* education and her fluency in English, which helped land her current job at the Bureau. Her family of wealthy sophisticated Jews from Warsaw was worlds apart from Mort's shtetl origins in Russia. It was not uncommon for them to have *soirées* or musical evenings at their apartment, she said. Their open-mindedness enabled her to live separately in an apartment, a freedom unheard of for unmarried Jewish women from shtetls. She was more political than Mort, a socialist who had to conceal her views as an employee of this right-wing government. She had expected her job to be tedious and brief, just a stop gap until she went back to school to get a *licencjat* degree so that she could teach English. But she found that she rather enjoyed untangling the bureaucratic twists of document requirements for people, like the Steins, who were often anxious, sometimes desperate. The salary was adequate, so she stayed on.

"That is my life — so far," she concluded. "Am I boring you with all this talk about myself?"

"Not at all. It's helping me know you better. But tell me, don't you encounter resistance at work being Jewish? Or to your ambitions to teach?"

"It's there, of course, but the Poles direct most of their anti-Semitism against the poor Jews of Galicia. In pogroms. The government's attitude is to try to get the Jews to resettle in Palestine. They've even secretly made efforts to support Zionists. Except that nothing is secret in a government office," she laughed.

"I heard the same thing from a rabbi in Motal — that's near Pinsk. They're trying to get rabbis to help them."

"Well, at least they're not beating us up on the street or denying us our civil rights, like our enlightened neighbors to the west are doing," Magda said.

"Not yet, anyway."

"You are cynical."

"No," Mort said, "just realistic. I can't get those Nazis and swastikas out of my head after that train trip through Germany."

"Can a socialist get on with a cynic?"

"If I were a cynic, would I have come back to Warsaw? I wouldn't even believe that such a thing as love exists." It had just slipped out, but he saw its effect: Magda lost her smile and looked uneasy. Quickly, he moved away from it. "In America, you can be a Jew and a socialist, and no one will bother you. In fact, some of my more idealistic friends are communists. And our president is a liberal."

"Yes, Roosevelt," she said. "We think highly of him, my friends. You make America sound appealing."

Might as well come out with it, he thought.

"It's because one day soon I hope to persuade you to come to America. With me."

"Morton—"

"Please, call me Mort."

"Mort, you are moving much too quickly. I don't have those kinds of feelings for you."

"Yes, but you might if we keep seeing each other."

"Ah, I see I was wrong," she laughed. "You're not a cynic. You're a romantic."

"I never thought of myself that way at all — until I met you. My Uncle Yitzhak said I was being impulsive to come back here. Crazy. Mostly, I tend to be cautious and conservative. In fact, that was one reason my wife left me. She wanted a more exciting life. She took up with my former business partner who is often reckless."

"And is she happier now?"

"No." They both laughed.

"It's a nice night," Magda said. "Why don't we walk around a little? I'd like to hear more about you."

"That's fine." He signaled the waiter for the check.

After Magda's discomfort over his romantic blundering about love, Mort was surprised that she kissed him goodnight. He had expected — and feared — the firm handshake that would signal the end of their brief encounter. *You shouldn't make too much of that kiss*, he told himself. *She's a modern woman, after all, who lives apart from her family, supports herself with a job and has romances and affairs of her choosing. Her friends were intellectuals, writers and artists — all leftists.* Compared to them, he felt a little stodgy and — he had to admit it — old. Her attitude toward most things was breezy and insouciant, taking them as they came. She went to socialist rallies, yes, but she could have gone just as easily to a chamber music concert.

After their first date, Mort moved out of the hotel and into a less expensive pension. He had planned to stay there a few weeks. But after their second date the following Sunday night, he had to admit to himself that his dream of making Magda the second Mrs. Stein was absurd. She had taken him to a party given by friends, who greeted him casually enough, if not with distinctly friendly overtures. They were curious, mainly. He knew that he really stood out from them, not because he was so English-dependent — most of them spoke English — but because he was so much older and more conventional. In his coat and tie, he was uncomfortable sitting on the floor. When they shared a marijuana cigarette, he passed it along, fearing how it might affect him.

In America, he recalled, *only jazz musicians smoke these things, or so I've heard. Yes,* he bitterly admitted to himself afterwards, *I am stodgy.*

He sensed that Magda felt this way about him too, though she was too tactful to say it. Instead, she just made jokes about her 'bohemian' friends as he walked her home.

"Passing around marijuana — really!"

"But you smoked it, I noticed," he couldn't keep from saying.

"Well, of course. It was there."

When he confessed how out of place he felt among her friends, she didn't try to reassure him. Since she obviously felt the same way about his age and stodginess, he realized there was no hope. His dream of sweeping her off her feet and taking her back to America as his wife was just that, a dream. *Hopelessly unrealistic. Like some fantasy from the movies*, he thought bitterly. *Realistically, she would have felt stranded and isolated in America as the wife of an owner of gas stations*. When he said good night, they both knew it was for the last time, and he thanked her formally for the two dates.

The next morning, he awakened as if from an illness — he was brisk and purposeful. The dock strike had been settled, and he booked the first ship leaving Danzig. There was one leaving Wednesday evening, so he checked out of his pension immediately. Better to leave now and put this foolish business behind him permanently. The train trip, five hours, seemed short and uncomplicated after the grueling one to Bremen. These actions, if intended as an amputation, still could not keep him from brooding over his foolishness as the train clicked along. It hadn't all been bad, though. Their first date was pleasant enough. And as he had told Uncle Yitzhak, if he hadn't at least *tried* to pursue this romantic dream, he might always regret it. Now, he was back to being Morton Stein — safe, conservative, practical, dull.

Detroit, 1935-37

On the ship home, Mort Stein had plenty of time to read and to think about his gas stations. The three were doing all right — the country was still in the Depression, after all. But they needed something to improve business. Mort had noticed that some grocery stores gave out S&H green stamps with purchases. Once customers had pasted the required number of stamps into books, they could redeem them for household items: toasters, irons and the like. It was a good device for building customer loyalty, since not every store gave out stamps. *I could give out S&H stamps*, Mort thought, *or, better yet, my own stamps and leave out the middleman. Then they could just pick up their prizes at one of my stations instead of going to an S&H redemption center. Anyhow, it's worth looking into.*

When the ship docked in Baltimore in early December, he wasn't surprised that no one met him at the pier, even though he had cabled ahead to Uncle Yitzhak. *Who'd want to make this trip just to escort me back to Detroit? They're all busy with their own lives.* Passing through Customs, he was glad to put behind him the travel reminder of Nazi Germany — the swastika stamped into his passport — and re-enter the Land of the

Free. America had never looked sweeter to him than it did this day, as people waited for their routine Customs inspections without the looming menace of arbitrary arrest by uniformed men in jackboots and armbands, not to mention the fear of being harassed because he was a Jew. In place of the portrait of an aggressive Adolph Hitler was the benign, fatherly portrait of Franklin Roosevelt. He was back.

Baltimore, he discovered, was an inconvenient port for getting to Detroit. Since the trains typically stopped in New York, and the soonest transfer would arrive in Detroit in the wee hours, Mort decided to stay overnight in New York, try to catch a concert that night, and take the first train to Detroit next morning. He was in luck. The New York Philharmonic-Symphony, under Toscanini, was performing an all-Beethoven program at Carnegie Hall. Even his distant upper balcony seat did not detract from hearing stellar performances. No one, it seemed, could conduct Beethoven with the same driving intensity as Toscanini. Mort left the hall with themes of the *Eroica* coursing through his mind.

After the eleven-hour train ride, which he passed reading Hemingway's *A Farewell to Arms*, he taxied to his flat and called Miriam to arrange for Edward's return. Since it wasn't too late, she suggested he come over now. David would be there, she said, and they all wanted to hear about his adventures. Miriam even provided a light supper, and over the wine Mort brought, he related some of his and Uncle Yitzhak's experiences but left out his failed romance with Magda.

"I see that your little fling with that government clerk didn't work out," Miriam remarked. "Too bad." Her venom was evident. *Was she actually jealous?* he

184

wondered. Did she miss him? Mort could tell that his children, except for Andrew, wanted to hear more about that romance, but he was laconic.

"Yes, a quixotic notion." He was proud of his literary allusions.

David wanted to know all about his encounters with the Nazis. "*The Free Press* doesn't print many stories about them." And even Edward asked some questions about them. The family also wanted to hear about Motal, Anna and Schmuel, but Mort deflected their questions, pleading fatigue. Dead on his feet from the traveling and wine, he was eager for his own bed. But before he could leave, David took him aside while Miriam finished packing Edward's suitcase.

"Listen, Mort, I was wondering if you'd consider renewing our partnership. Now that you and Miriam are divorced, we could put that business behind us and just be business partners. I think with our combined stations — you have three, right? And I still have the same two — we could be more successful than ever, a major chain that people could easily recognize. What do you think?"

"I think I'm dead tired, David, and can't think about that now. I'll consider it, though, and let you know." The proposal caught him off guard and irritated him. *Just like David to pop this on me when I haven't even unpacked*, he thought. As he left with Edward, he wondered where Miriam stood on this plan. Maybe she had put him up to it. *Was that why she disappeared so conveniently to finish packing Edward's bag?*

Readjusting to his former life was easy. One unexpected pleasure was driving his car again after a month of relying on train schedules and travel permits. What a sense of freedom to go where you want, when you want! Edward seemed pleased to be back at their flat — the bus to Durfee Junior High was easier to catch, and he was glad to have his old room back instead of sharing one with Andrew. But that sense of spaciousness was cut short when he learned that Mort was preparing to have Anna live with them. True, there was a spare bedroom where Sarah slept when visiting (now, she'd get the couch). To Mort, the move seemed the right thing to do. Bringing Anna to the States had been his idea, after all, and it wasn't fair to saddle Uncle Yitzhak and Aunt Minna any longer with this responsibility.

Chava had already made Yitzhak and Minna's lives easier. Eager to see her sister after twenty-three years, she met Anna and Yitzhak at the train station. Her fluent Yiddish, which she needed to converse with many of her violin students, proved a great relief to her aunt and uncle, especially when the three took Anna shopping to help ease her into American life. Just teaching her how to safely cross Dexter Avenue and judge the speed of oncoming traffic required Yitzhak's nervous instructions. But seeing Anna marvel at the plentiful apples, oranges and bananas at the grocery store made the effort worthwhile. Yitzhak enrolled her in a Jewish Center language class, and she was learning quickly under his patient guidance in providing the names of household objects (Mort's earlier fears that her restrictive life in Motal might have made her simple were, to his relief, unfounded).

As soon as they could, Mort and Chava threw Anna a party to welcome her to her new homeland and introduce her to the family group. It started awkwardly. After the introductions, Anna and Chava fell to conversing so happily in rapid Yiddish that Miriam and the kids felt like outsiders, the children frankly bored. To fill the gap, Mort and Uncle Yitzhak recounted their adventures in rescuing Anna, dramatizing the menace of the Nazi passport inspectors and the fortunate intervention by the bilingual American. They also recounted the silly bickerings of the Jews at the Ivanova grocery and the Motal Shabbat service. To Mort's surprise, even his children were laughing at his and Yitzhak's imitations of the various voices. Though he described his father's crankiness and refusal to leave Motal, he left out Schmuel and Anna's destitution. Silently, he resolved to send the rabbi some money for Schmuel's upkeep. Now, as the family was enjoying cake and coffee, Chava approached Mort with a proposal.

"Since Anna and I both speak Yiddish, why shouldn't she live with me? I have a spare bedroom in my flat, and I think we'll get along fine. If you'd like to, you could contribute to her upkeep."

The suggestion delighted Mort since it solved several problems at once. He would now have his extra bedroom free for Sarah's and Andrew's visits. And he would be spared the difficult months of communicating with Anna while she was learning English. And Anna would have Chava's company instead of hours alone at Mort's flat. Looking ahead, Mort envisioned that he and Edward could help Chava by taking Anna out on weekends to introduce her to more aspects of American life — movies, sports, even politics (Roosevelt was running for reelection). Most important, Anna was all for living with her sister. So, it was settled on the spot.

Now, Mort had to consider David's proposal. It was certainly tempting to combine their stations, but there were several questions to resolve. *Would they share the proceeds equally?* That seemed unfair since Mort had an extra station, acquired during the split-up. A better alternative would be for each partner to keep the earnings from his own stations.

Would David pull his weight in the shared tasks and routines? Was he reliable? The answers to these questions, Mort knew, were most likely negative. David couldn't be relied on as a partner. But rejecting him after this much time had elapsed since their blowup seemed spiteful. David would always need a shove to pull his weight. But in the past, he never seemed to resent or resist that push. And he often came up with good ideas. So, despite his trepidations, Mort informed David that they would again be partners beginning with the new year, 1936. Miriam, he hoped, would return to keeping the books and managing the orders for the partners; their Sunday afternoon conferences would resume; and Mort would have to release Joan Waritzki. Though this arrangement cut short the children's weekends with the 'other' parent, Mort made up for it by taking them out to Sunday brunch.

Over the next weeks, Mort resumed the routine of supervising his stations. There had been no disasters or screwups in his absence; it had all gone as planned. David liked the incentive of the stamps, and Mort soon found supplies of them and a reasonable printer. Soon, all their stations featured glassware, bowls, toasters and electric irons in the store windows in place of the pyramids of motor oil. New signs announced the premiums. The managers grumbled a bit about having to count out the stamps, but Mort noticed that business improved somewhat and that, according to the managers, the same customers kept coming back. Mort even took home some of the prizes he'd bought to try them out. That was how he discovered the dangerous toaster. A cheapie, it didn't pop up the toast. Instead, the user had to open the side and extract it. Waiting too long meant burnt toast, as Mort learned the hard way. *I could be sued for starting a house fire,* he worried. *Better offer pop-ups.*

Miriam was dumbfounded and grateful for Mort's decision to take David back. She told him that the idea was strictly David's and that she was certain that Mort would reject it. Was she trying to warn him? Mort wondered. She also told him that they had finally decided to get married. Decided shortly after Mort's decision. She knew that, by himself, David would never be very successful, but the prospects looked better now that they were partners again. *In other words*, Mort thought, *so long as I'm there to give him a regular kick in the pants.* He wondered what kind of stepfather David would be to the children.

The news from Germany continued to be grim. Just before Mort and Uncle Yitzhak left for Europe, Germany had proclaimed the 'Nuremberg Laws' stripping German Jews of citizenship and moving toward a completely segregated society. Already banned from most occupations, Jews were now prohibited from marrying or having sexual relations with Aryans. They were restricted from German schools and universities, from 'German' apartment buildings, from attending 'German' theatre and concerts, from entering many parks, even from sitting on public benches reserved for Aryans.

"Why do they stay?" Mort demanded at a family Sunday dinner. "Why don't they just get out and leave the damned country?"

"It may not be so easy," Miriam replied. "You saw yourself how difficult it is to get travel and exit visas. And where would they go? To be blunt, who wants them? Certainly not America with its immigration restrictions. You saw how long it took to get visas for Anna and your father."

"Well, something has to be done. We can't just sit here and cluck our tongues," Mort said.

"What do you propose?" David asked.

"I don't know. I haven't worked anything out yet. But I'm going to find out which Jewish agencies help refugees or lobby for immigration reform and join them. Or at least donate money to them."

"Where will you find time to help them, with managing your stations?" David asked.

"Don't worry, David. I'll find the time. Our partnership won't suffer."

And he did find time. Shortly after that dinner, he did some research and found that the central agency in charge of helping European Jews to emigrate was the International Jewish Relief Organization, the JRO. Mort contacted their representatives in New York but discovered, to his disappointment, that there wasn't much he could do from Detroit except to donate money or try to raise it among Jewish groups. The real work went on in New York, Washington and especially in Paris, their main European office. Once again, Mort was limited by his ignorance of other languages and, of course, by his work responsibilities. Partly to compensate for his sense of being ineffectual, he decided to donate a regular percentage of his income to the JRO — *a tithe* he thought sardonically — and to contact rabbis in the Detroit area about speaking to their congregations to raise money. And he decided to do something else in his spare time: learn German.

In the meantime, Miriam and David went ahead with their plans to marry. It was a simple ceremony at City Hall, followed by a reception at Miriam's flat. Mort hoped that this time Uncle Yitzhak wouldn't fall into the cake — a more modest but better-tasting one from Sanders. Looking at the assembled Steins at the reception — Uncle Yitzhak and Aunt Minna, Chava and Anna, Edward, Sarah and Andrew — Mort felt surprising pride. They really did form a family, and he had a lot to do with having created it and bringing it together.

Paradoxically, Miriam and David's wedding also underscored Mort's own sense of being single and, he admitted to himself, feeling lonely at times for female companionship. His impulsive return to Warsaw to court Magda had surprised him as much as it did his family. Previously he had repressed this loneliness as he struggled to make his stations survive the Depression. But the Magda affair, as he now called it, forced him to recognize it. *I need to go out more*, he thought. *But what am I after? Or rather, whom? I'm not a womanizer who's going to chase after every loose woman I can find. I want a woman — no, a soul-mate — someone I can talk to, someone who'll share my feelings and is interested in ideas and the world situation. And someone to put up with your lectures*, his self-critical side added. *Sex, too, would be nice. But where would I find such a woman? And, if I did, why should she be interested in me?*

He studied himself critically in the mirror. *I'm aging — thirty-eight — middle-aged. My hairline is receding, and my hair is thinning. I'm not paunchy; that's good. But I'm not exactly a 'catch', as my ex-wife would have said. I need to go out more if I'm going to meet someone, go to lectures at the JCC, maybe join some social groups. That would mean giving up some of my reading time in the evenings. Finding the time will be the biggest problem. Well, you can't have it all*, he concluded.

Finding a third gas station for David was a simple matter. Several were for rent in the Depression year of 1936, and the partners picked out a nice one at the corner of Dexter and Elmhurst — a very short drive for either. It didn't have a repair garage, so there would be less to keep track of that way. All the stations now used the *$AVON GAS!* name, and Mort had some colorful signs installed. They all gave out stamps and premiums, and after a few months for the new rental to catch on, all were making money.

Mort was determined to follow through on his vows to help Jews in Germany. He started a separate savings account for his weekly tithes and made a quick trip to the New York office of the JRO to learn about their operations. That would prepare him for the fundraising speeches he planned to give. After checking his background, the JRO welcomed him and encouraged his fundraising plans. With one exception, the rabbis he contacted in Detroit were all for these speeches. The holdout was an Orthodox rabbi of a tiny *shul* who believed that fundraising was inappropriate at a religious service, at which little English was spoken anyway.

Most rabbis had already appealed to their congregations for contributions to the JRO and other aid groups. But these appeals were sporadic, and they knew they couldn't make them too often without irritating their congregations and seeming too political. The rabbis realized, too, that their congregations were divided, just as national Jewish leaders were, on what should be done. Most agreed with Rabbi Stephen Wise that the U.S., and American Jews in particular, must actively resist Nazi persecution with boycotts, protest marches and the like; that the State Department must be lobbied vigorously to liberalize its immigration policies for refugees; that Hollywood should make anti-Nazi films; and that the JRO should do whatever was possible, even resorting to bribes and smuggling, to bring German Jews out of that hateful country. But a sizable minority of Jews in these congregations felt that opposing Germany vigorously would only make things worse for the German Jews, whom the Nazis would punish in revenge. Jewish activism in America, this group argued, with some justification, would also play into the hands of domestic anti-Semites like Father Coughlin and Senator Borah, who tirelessly claimed that Jews were selfishly trying to get the United States into another war. Keep a low profile was their conclusion. Zionists favored a third approach: devote all efforts to creating a Jewish homeland in Palestine. This meant actively opposing England, Palestine's mandated controller, since it tightly restricted Jewish emigration there.

Mort realized that he would encounter these alternative views in the question-and-answer sessions following his appeals. The Zionist approach, however, could be merged with the JRO's, since both groups worked to get Jews out of Germany. And the JRO was not at all opposed to helping Jews get to Palestine if that was their goal. But they also worked on getting other countries to accept them: Cuba, Bolivia, Brazil and the Dominican Republic in this hemisphere, and, closer to Germany, Switzerland, the Netherlands, France and the Scandinavian countries. In all but Switzerland, the JRO had successfully relocated thousands of Jews.

Mort's first speech was to Congregation Shaarey Zedek, one of the oldest and most prominent Conservative synagogues in Detroit. It occupied a distinguished place on the city's affluent Chicago Boulevard, and its new rabbi was in complete agreement with the JRO's approach. Mort, who hadn't attended Jewish services anywhere, was stunned by the size and ornateness of the sanctuary. Besides the stained-glass windows, there were very large lamps of stained glass hanging down from the high ceiling. The sanctuary seemed large enough to hold a thousand people, though far fewer were attending the Saturday morning service. Fortunately, there was a microphone at the podium so he wouldn't have to raise his voice. As the rabbi introduced him, Mort wished that he had started with a smaller congregation to warm up his speech-making techniques. But once he began, by reviewing the steadily intensifying Nazi persecutions, he put his heart into the speech and concluded with what he knew was on everybody's mind: What horror would the Nazis embark on next? How much more could the German Jews stand? About half the 1933 Jewish population had already left Germany. But those remaining, perhaps as many as 150,000, were the poorest Jews, least likely to find a way out by themselves. And most did want to leave, that was clear. Couldn't the good people of Congregation Shaarey Zedek open their hearts as well as their wallets to help these people? The JRO was providing ways to do this. But it needed money.

When he finished, the rabbi smoothly took up the cause with a practical flourish, informing his flock that he had set up some tables at the exits for their donations.

"Don't let their enthusiasm cool," he whispered to Mort off-mike and winked. The speech, though it had a few rough spots, was successful. It raised over $300.

In the weeks and months following, Mort continued making speeches. He contacted every synagogue in the city, from small Orthodox ones to imposing Reform temples. Though there was no Q&A session after the Shaarey Zedek speech, other speeches, especially at the smaller, more intimate synagogues, produced a lively discussion afterwards. Gradually, Mort became comfortable — and effective — speaking ad lib at these sessions.

His plan to learn German was also progressing. Though private programs like Berlitz were available, Mort didn't want just 'tourist German' but to learn the language thoroughly and become fluent. So, he signed up for a night class at Wayne University and devoted his evenings to studying the *Der-Die-Das* and later to mastering the intricacies of separable verbs. True to form, he carefully made and memorized long vocabulary lists. He had to repress his residual knowledge of Yiddish because of its similarity to German. If he had any future encounters with the Nazis, just one Yiddish word slipping into his speech would be fatal. After six months of classes, he realized that he needed to practice in a German-speaking environment. Joining a German club in the city, however, was not an option since at least some of the members were likely to be pro-Nazi. So, he settled for hiring a tutor part time, an impoverished Wayne University student, with whom he could speak his new language.

New York, 1937

Mort was careful not to talk about his language lessons to Miriam and David. They would have been appalled, or worse, derisive, if they knew his intent. In brief it was this: just as he had gone into Poland to bring his sister from Motal, he now wanted to go, undercover, into Germany to directly aid the Jews there, perhaps even bring some out if that was possible. Tentatively, he had discussed his aim with the JRO people in New York when he had traveled there to be approved as a fund-raiser. Not surprisingly, they were skeptical and discouraging. Leave it to our professionals. You're an amateur, and you don't even know German. How could you possibly get around in Germany without knowing the language? You'd only get yourself in trouble, and as a Jew, that's catastrophic. Later, when they saw his determination and growing mastery of German, they were less reluctant and directed him to one of their people, Arno Steelbach, who traveled back and forth between New York and Paris. Mort made an appointment, which required another trip to New York.

Steelbach was a vigorous, middle-aged man, balding but muscular, with an inquisitive squint, as if sizing up his conversant each moment. Though well-dressed, he seemed always to have a five o'clock shadow. He wasted little time in laying out the difficulties Mort would face going into Germany.

"First off, you'll have to have a cover, a completely different identity. A new Aryan name and documents showing it, possibly a new look though you don't look particularly Jewish, and most important, a plausible and agreeable reason for being in Germany. Usually, posing as a businessman or trade official is the best cover, since, despite its international belligerence, Germany wants and needs to trade with other countries for raw materials. Your background file says that you own gas stations in

Detroit, so you must know something about oil production and sales. That would be the most logical business for your cover. You'd be, say, the president of a small oil company — we couldn't use the big ones since they'd deny knowing you — and you're in Germany to drum up business. You can ship them oil on tanker ships, that sort of thing. Right now, they get most of their oil from Romania, but they're always on the lookout for new sources in case the old ones disappear in a war. Then, we'd have to establish this dummy company with a pseudo-office and would-be receptionist in New York, just in case the Gestapo checks your background."

Mort's head was spinning. "I hadn't realized it would take all this," he admitted.

"That's just the beginning," Steelbach continued, eyeing him. "We'd have to set up meetings with one of their trade officials — good Nazis all."

"Who do you mean by 'we'?"

"We have a friend in the State Department with trade contacts in Germany. Then, it depends on what sort of job you'd be doing." He suddenly switched to German, studying Mort to see how he handled it. "Smuggling money in and out of the country is probably where we'd begin. It's a lot easier than trying to get people out, that is, if you don't get caught."

"How does it work?" Mort responded in German.

"Basically, we'd sew the money you bring in into the lining of your overcoat or suit jacket. You'd have to sew it in if you're smuggling money out of Germany. You'd be smuggling it in, to needy families, smuggling it out for families already emigrating, rich Jews, probably."

"What's the penalty if I get caught?"

"That depends on whether they find out you're Jewish.

If they do, it's a concentration camp, for sure. And the State Department won't bargain for you since no government agency sent you in the first place. You might simply be shot as a spy. If they don't realize you're Jewish, you'd probably be imprisoned for breaking German currency laws. And you'd be interrogated."

"Tortured?"

"Probably not," Steelbach switched back to English, "since Germany wants to keep on good relations with the States — for now."

"So, the moral of the story is: don't get caught."

"Right. By the way, you speak German with an accent. But that probably won't arouse suspicion since you'd be an American businessman."

"What about people? Will I ever get the chance to bring someone out of the country?"

"That depends on a lot of factors I can't answer now, such as how you do with your initial assignments and who we're trying to get out. Also, how much our Paris people trust you. The Paris office would be your base, at least initially."

"Why only 'initially'?"

"Well, think about it, Morton. If the Gestapo were checking you out after your first trip — or even before it — they'd put a tail on you. If you led them directly to the Paris JRO office, they'd know you were a phony, and, worse, a Jew. End of your spy career."

"I see," said Mort thoughtfully. "So then I'd need to have clandestine meetings with the Parisian JRO officials."

"Right. At local cafés or some place."

"This sounds more and more like espionage than humanitarian aid."

"Unfortunately," Steelbach said, with a tone of wrapping

it up, "with the Nazis in control, there's no difference between the two. I'll see you again in a few months when you've had more time to consider your plans."

"You mean, to see if I get cold feet and come to my senses."

"Correct. By the way, will your business in Detroit be okay while you travel?"

"I have a business partner who can watch over it," Mort lied.

"That's good. We prefer that you conceal the real purpose of your travel from your family and business acquaintances — the fewer people that know, the better. But we realize that that may not always be possible. It's good that you're single. If you were married, we wouldn't hire you. Too difficult to conceal it from your wife. And fewer people to suffer if you were apprehended."

"That's a pleasant thought. I do have a fifteen-year-old son who lives with me. But he could live with his mother for that time."

"Well, that is a complication since you'd have to invent more stories. But it's not an insurmountable problem. Okay, I'll contact you in a few months to come to New York. Meanwhile, I'll give the JRO office here my assessment, which is generally favorable. You're willing; you speak German well; you're relatively unencumbered but naïve about the ins and outs of smuggling. You'd need a thorough course before we'd send you out."

"Thanks for sharing that with me, your evaluation I mean. Now I won't have to wonder about it."

"Don't mention it," Steelbach said, disappearing down the hallway.

Before he left New York, Mort was hoping to hear another concert conducted by Toscanini. Now, however, the

Philharmonic-Symphony had a new conductor, John Barbirolli, an Englishman. His all-British concert featured Elgar's *Second Symphony*, a work Mort had never heard before, and he came away disappointed by both the music and the conducting.

Back in Detroit, Mort had plenty of time to get cold feet about his European project, but he didn't. He was determined to see this through, to know that he made a personal difference in helping Jews against the Nazis. His experience in Europe bringing Anna back had changed him, had shown him he was capable of undertaking a bold project. It had also shown him first-hand the Nazi menace. His language practice with Alex Seebold, the Wayne University student, continued, and he came to like the young man. Their meetings went better once he persuaded Alex that it would be more comfortable to meet at Mort's flat than in his cramped room. They conversed in German about every subject they could think of. Alex, fortunately, had a keen interest in international affairs, and Mort easily passed himself off as a businessman who needed to learn German to expand his business. After a few months, they went out with Alex's German friends, who were impressed by Mort's command of the language. They went to German restaurants and cafés. Mort was careful to avoid political discussions, not so easy when everyone had strong pro or con views of Hitler.

His gasoline business, meanwhile, was thriving. David seemed determined to recapture Mort's trust and justify his decision to resume the partnership. He supervised his three stations carefully and met with Mort and Miriam each Sunday to go over receipts, orders and expenses. At these meetings, Mort was all business and refrained from asking David privately about how his marriage was going. He still remained 'Uncle David' to the children.

Sarah, now fifteen, was advancing steadily on the violin. She still played in the Michigan Youth Orchestra, a WPA project which the musicians' union permitted to perform in numerous Michigan cities and towns. Her ambition was to spend her summers at the National Music Camp at Interlochen, Michigan and maybe even attend their high school on scholarship. When Mort had described hearing Toscanini and Barbirolli conduct in New York, she was all ears, but she didn't seem interested in much else. Certainly not in boys, Miriam told him. "I guess I should be grateful," she said. "Most girls her age are boy-crazy and become a real handful, worrying all the time about their looks and clothes." But if Sarah was easy on Miriam's clothes budget, the cost of her music lessons more than made up for it. She 'took' with the concertmaster of the Detroit Symphony, having long since outgrown Chava as her teacher.

"It would be years," Miriam sighed, "before she could get some sort of a self-supporting position as a musician. Teaching wasn't good enough; no, she has to *perform.*" To Mort, she seemed a pleasant girl, rather plain looking, as if she didn't care much about her appearance. But he really knew little about her outside of her passion for music.

Andrew's personality was more outgoing and engaging. The thirteen-year-old was the image of the all-American boy who lived for sports. He was especially good at baseball, playing third base in an after-school league. He also was adept at basketball, though he wasn't tall. He told Mort he would like to play hockey too, but the equipment was expensive and finding a frozen pond for skating was dicey. *I can see why he feels close to David*, Mort thought sadly. *I just never took to American sports, while David is a sports* maven. He could converse easily with Andrew about the Tigers and their prospects. Mort couldn't help comparing his two sons. Andrew was far more talkative than Edward and seemed more self-confident, but Mort wondered how much of this was a façade. He was certainly the charmer of the family, though. At the Sunday dinners, he often had the family laughing about his escapades at school.

And what about Edward? Mort asked himself. *How well do I really know him? How are my trips away affecting him?* Edward was now sixteen, a sophomore at Central High. When Mort had driven him there or had attended PTA open houses, he was deeply impressed with the campus, combining Central High, Durfee Junior High, and Roosevelt Elementary. Central, in particular, was an architectural gem, designed lavishly in Collegiate Gothic. At the PTA meeting in the school's spacious library, Mort admired the vaulted ceiling with wooden beams and the leaded gothic windows. *The city certainly didn't cheap out when it built this campus in the Twenties*, he mused. *They wanted to make it a showplace, and they had the tax revenues to do it. No longer.*

Edward seemed to thrive at Central. His grades were consistently 'A's, and, unlike his younger brother, he was never in trouble. Although he didn't go out for sports, he joined some school clubs and especially enjoyed the Electronics Club. He had progressed from tinkering with radios to repairing them on weekends for family and friends. Once he turned sixteen, he began working after school, repairing radios at the Philco Store on Dexter Avenue and making more than he had as a newsboy. He wasn't talkative, but Mort noticed that he followed current events closely. Their dinner conversations were often about these events, especially the Nazis, and Edward offered insightful opinions. *He's mature for his age*, Mort concluded. He would have liked to share with Edward his plans to help German Jews directly but didn't feel he could — yet. Fortunately, Edward didn't question Mort's explanations that his trips to New York were 'about business'. Regarding his learning German with the college tutor, Mort just said that an educated man should speak more than one language.

It was David and Miriam who proved more problematic in Mort's concealing the reason for his trips to New York. He simply told them that he needed to discuss with the JRO officers new fundraising ideas and an expanded role for himself. David said little about the absences from work, since he still felt indebted to Mort. In the meantime, Mort kept making Friday night and Saturday fundraising speeches at Jewish synagogues and Jewish Centers in and around Detroit. The donations increased as the news from Germany grew steadily more dire.

Finally, in the fall of 1937, the JRO decided he was ready for his first trip. He would travel to Paris via steamer and train and report to the Parisian branch of the JRO for assignments. There would be no cover identity — yet. Since he might be gone more than a month — the round trip alone would take well over two weeks — he knew that despite the JRO's preference for secrecy, he'd have to explain his plans to the family, because his absence would impose some burdens on them. A Sunday dinner, when David and the children were assembled, was the perfect venue. Of course, they all knew about and approved his fundraising, but they were shocked by his new intentions. Even his mastery of German surprised them (all but Edward) but conveyed his seriousness. He got through the predictable questions:

"How long will you be gone?"

"About a month or a little longer."

"Edward will stay with me, I assume?" (This from Miriam)

"Yes, just as he does on his visits."

"Good."

In particular, they wanted to know what kind of work he'd be doing. Mort was intentionally vague. "Mostly helping out the JRO in Paris in whatever errands they need done, like carrying money to groups helping Jewish refugees." He omitted his ambition to rescue German Jews, but his mastery of German suggested more was at stake.

"Will you be going into Germany?" David asked. "That's pretty risky, isn't it?"

"I think I'll be okay as an American citizen. We still have an ambassador and consulate there."

"The Nazis may not be too keen on you when they see your last name," David replied.

"Well, if I do go into the country, the JRO might give me a cover identity."

"Like a spy," David murmured. He was confident that he could supervise all six stations. "As long as you don't fall off the earth or rot in a Nazi concentration camp." But Miriam was worried.

"It's just not like you to do this, Mort. You used to be so, what shall I say, so cautious and conservative. Of course, I'm happy to have Edward here. But still..."

"It would just be for a month or so, Miriam. And

Edward gets along well with his brother and sister. He's a good boy, very responsible."

"I know that, Mort," she replied. "It's *you* I'm concerned about. You're like a different person, taking these risks. What's gotten into you?"

"Well, if you really must know, I think it was that trip to Motal to bring back Anna. It changed me. Showed me I could take on new challenges — with help, of course. By the way, please don't talk about my trip to your friends. The fewer people who know, the better."

What worried him was not Miriam's skepticism — that was predictable. It was David's matter-of-fact acceptance of his greater business responsibilities. *Could he handle them?* He would have to depend on the station managers, as Mort had done earlier.

When he talked about his plans to Edward later that night, his son surprised him with an enthusiastic response.

"I think it's great, Dad, that you're doing this. I don't mind staying at Mom's place.

"It might be longer than a month, you know."

"That's okay. Will you really be going into Germany?"

"I don't know. Hard to say. It would just be to do money transfers."

"That's really neat. You'd be like a spy."

"I'd rather you not think of me that way, Edward. I'm just trying to help German Jews and Jewish refugees." But he could see an unfamiliar look in Edward's expression; he seemed proud of his father.

Part III: The Second Rescue

Paris, late fall 1937

The JRO office in Paris was one flight up on a side street in the 3rd arrondissement. The receptionist greeted Mort warmly and asked about his trip. He knew better than to describe how stormy it had been, how seasick he had been. He just murmured, "Fine. Just fine." He hadn't expected a large office. After the Nazis bombed its Berlin office, the JRO kept a low profile everywhere and needed to keep down expenses. But Mort was surprised that, except for the receptionist, it was empty.

"People are on various assignments," she explained. Her name was Hilda; she was middle-aged and spoke English with a heavy Eastern European accent. "But they've been expecting you, and I think Mr. Slonsky will call in this afternoon to see if you've arrived." She took down Mort's hotel and its telephone number. "I'll notify you of your appointment," she concluded.

Business-like, Mort thought, walking back to his small hotel a few blocks away. Since the JRO couldn't afford to pay for his travel or hotel, he had selected it after reading *Fodor's* and a few other guide books. It seemed adequate, if a bit shabby and cramped, and it served a continental breakfast. Most important, it was close to the JRO office.

Mort decided to visit the Louvre and returned in late afternoon, his head swimming with images of overly large historical paintings and flesh-filled Rubenses. A telephone message was waiting for him. It was from a Meyer Slonsky and gave him a number to call.

Mort called, and the two arranged to meet for dinner near

Mort's hotel. The restaurant was small, unpretentious and uncrowded, and there was Slonsky, waving him to his table. He was a small, middle-aged man with thick, graying hair. Mort might have taken him for a schoolteacher, except for the two small scars on his face. After the introductory small talk and after they had ordered (Mort, relying on his menu French to order *coq au vin*), Slonsky got down to business.

"We've read over your record, Mr. Stein, and we're impressed with your seriousness." Mort wondered who 'we' were — *a board of directors?*

"Your fundraising in Detroit has been very much appreciated. "But you have had no experience in the kind of work we do, especially in Germany. So, before we can entrust you with a mission there, and with carrying, say, 10,000 *Deutschmarks*, we need to season you, so to speak, with some easier assignments here in France and in friendly countries."

"You're also checking me out to see if I'm honest and competent," Mort added.

"Of course," Slonsky nodded with a small smile. "That goes without saying. Regarding the competency, do you speak any languages other than German and English?"

"I understand some Yiddish, no other languages."

"I see. So, if we were to send you on a simple assignment here in France or the Netherlands, you'd have to pose as an ignorant tourist and depend on someone else speaking English."

"That wouldn't be a pose," Mort acknowledged, embarrassed. "You see, I was preparing solely for trips into Germany."

"But even there — I should say *especially* there — experience is essential. Linguistic mastery alone isn't enough.

So, your first assignment will be relatively simple, here in France, to carry some money to a local refugee group in Rouen and return. If you left early, you could get it done in a day. If that goes well, we'll assign you a more involved task, perhaps accompanying some refugee children on a train to Lisbon."

"Will I also be going to Germany? I can only stay a few weeks."

"I understand you have time constraints since you must return to your business in Detroit. Ah, here's our dinner," his face brightened.

Mort decided to postpone further questions and enjoy his dinner.

The next morning, early, he reported to the JRO office where Slonsky handed him a sealed envelope.

"This contains 10,000 *francs*. You are to deliver it to the French Aid Group for Refugees in Rouen at 14A Avenue Delacroix. Here is a city map marking your route from the train station to the Refugee Office. You turn over the *francs* to Mlle. Renée Corvant. Get a receipt — make sure you get that receipt — and return. Simple as that."

"What if Miss Corvant isn't there? Can anyone else receive the money?"

"She'll be there. They're counting on this transfer, since their office is almost broke and they have a number of refugee families to care for. Your taking it there, by the way, saves me the trouble, which I appreciate. There's always more work to be done here in coordinating our many assignments and tasks."

"Just out of curiosity," Mort asked, "how many people work out of this office carrying out assignments?"

He considered the question innocent, but Slonsky

shook his head vigorously.

"I'm sorry, I can't reveal that. Frankly, the less you know about our operations, the better. I don't mean this to sound like a spy novel, but we do know there are Gestapo agents who would like to know that information. And in the unlikely event you were apprehended, even by the French police, the less you know the better."

"Could that possibly happen in France, I mean about the Gestapo?"

"It's unlikely, but not unheard of. One of our couriers was kidnapped by two Gestapo agents, who drove him to a remote location and beat him severely to make him reveal our operations in Germany. Fortunately for us, he had no knowledge to reveal. But we learned a lesson at his expense."

"Were those agents ever apprehended?"

"Oh no. They disappeared across the border and were no doubt replaced by other agents. I'm not telling you this to scare you, just to explain why we must be careful. After your first trip into Germany, for example, you won't be able to come directly to this office anymore. If you were spotted doing so, it would destroy your cover identity since we wouldn't be expected to deal with American oilmen."

"I see. How should I contact you, or this office, when I return?"

"Just use the phone number I left. If I'm not in and it's during business hours, you can call the office here. But don't come there directly until we tell you."

"All right," Mort said, rising. "I think I understand."

"I hope things go well," Slonsky said seriously, extending his hand.

"Thank you," Mort said, shaking it and equally serious. "So do I."

It did go well, much to Mort's surprise. He didn't have to wait long for a train to Rouen next morning. The hour-and-a-half ride was pleasant — no squalling kids in his compartment — and the map was easy to follow. Mort felt a bit naked without luggage, however. *I should have brought a briefcase to look like a businessman*, he thought. *I'll have to find one somewhere.*

The office was a little storefront just off a busy shopping street, and Mlle. Corvant, a pleasant lady in her forties with her brown hair pulled back in a bun, had been expecting him. She greeted him in English.

"You are new?" she smiled with crooked teeth as she took the envelope and handed him the receipt. "I don't think I've seen you before."

"Yes," Mort replied cautiously. "My first time."

"You had a nice trip?" She seemed to want a conversation, perhaps to exercise her English. Mort, remembering his conversation with Slonsky, was disinclined.

"Very nice, thank you. I should be getting back."

"*Au revoir.*" Her tone was a bit colder.

Outside, Mort chastised himself. *Did I really need to be curt with her? Interesting, she didn't ask my name. What is my name? Stein, I guess — no need for an alias here in France. And it must match my passport and driver's license in case I'm picked up. What would the police want with me, anyway? I'm just a dumb American tourist out sight-seeing.*

He noticed from a clock on the street that it was nearly noon. *Perhaps I should stop somewhere for lunch before catching the train back.* He saw a café across the street and studied the menu outside. A signboard advertised a *prix fixe* lunch: soup, bread and salad. *Perfect!* he thought, ducking in. *Prix fixe. Looks like an ad a moyle would put out: We fix pricks here.*

As he walked back to the train, he was pleased with how smoothly everything had gone. Almost, but not quite. He had the uncomfortable feeling — not definite, but still discernable — that he was being followed. He had first sensed it walking to the refugee aid office; it returned after he left it and was there now as he walked to the train station. But when he stopped to look in a shop window that reflected behind him, he saw nothing. Just to be sure, though, when he came to a large department store, he ducked into it quickly and even more quickly (without running) made his way through the shoppers, turning down several aisles while searching for a side exit. Finding one, he was out in a flash and took the next street over to the train station. The feeling diminished. *Did I lose him? Was it real? If so, who was it?*

In the station, he was careful to choose a waiting bench against a wall, so that he could see all the people approaching the ticket window. No one looked suspicious. Relaxing, he waited for the train. But then it occurred to him, *if someone were following me, he could guess that I'd be taking the return train and just wait out of sight.*

During the return ride, he kept chastising himself. *Stop imagining things! You are not in a spy novel. There's no one. And why would someone follow you in France, anyway?* Then he remembered Slonsky's story about the two Gestapo agents beating up the JRO courier. *Well*, he sighed, *this is what you put in for. You'd better get used to it. And learn to think on your feet.*

When the train pulled into the Gare d'Orsay, he hopped down and looked around. No one unusual. Just people heading toward the exit. He started walking that way and noticed a small man walking briskly past him.

Obviously in a hurry, Mort thought. Then the man suddenly wheeled in front of Mort and blocked his path.

"Hello. You don't know me. No, you don't know me at all, but I work for the JRO too. Yes, also. My name is Lazar. I've been following you. But you already knew that. Yes, you knew that. Good job, losing me in the department store! Good job, yes. I just assumed you'd go right back to the station, and right back to the station you went!"

"Why were you following me?" Mort asked, astonished. The man's manner was strange.

"Oh, Mr. Slonsky told me to. Yes, he told me. I do favors for him, you see. All kinds of favors. This was sort of a test to see if you'd notice. A test. Well, I can say that you passed with high marks. You passed it, certainly. You not only noticed, you lost me for a while. Yes, you lost me. And that's not easy, let me tell you. No, not easy at all. I'm a good tailer. One of the best."

As the little man spoke, Mort could discern several odd features. He didn't look directly at Mort but seemed to be talking almost to himself, with his eyes blinking rapidly as he kept repeating himself. *I guess he's better at tailing than talking*, Mort concluded. *What a collection of tics!*

"Well, you can now tell Mr. Slonsky that I passed the test and am back in Paris. He knows how to reach me." Mort turned away from the little man, as if looking for fresh air.

"Oh, I'll do that. I'll surely do that right away," Lazar called after him.

When Slonsky called him later that day, he wasn't apologetic. "We needed to see if you could tell you were being followed and how you'd behave if you did realize it," he explained. "It's just another way we check you out to see if you could handle an assignment in Germany, where you almost certainly will be followed."

"So, I passed?"

"You did."

"That Lazar fellow is quite a character."

"Yes, we like Leonard and assign him to tasks like that. Also courier jobs if they're not too involved."

"He's good at tailing," Mort said. "I never actually saw him until he confronted me."

"Yes," Slonsky agreed. "We have another job for you if you're interested. Much more involved than the first one, but not in Germany. You'd be escorting about a dozen children from Paris to Lisbon. You'd have help, of course — another of our people. And you'd be met in Lisbon by one of our people there. Interested?"

"How old are the children? A dozen, you said?"

"Eleven, to be precise. Their ages range from about eight or nine to thirteen."

"How long do you think the whole thing would take?"

"The train travel time is about twenty hours. You'd take an overnight. And you'd need to pick up the children and escort them to and from the train stations — and make the return trip, of course. All told, I'd say at least three days."

"You still don't think I'm ready for something in Germany?"

"Well, let's just say, we'd like you to have more seasoning."

"You make me sound like a turkey."

"Ha-ha," Slonsky said mirthlessly. "Very funny. Well?"

"Well, I must go by your judgment, of course, regarding my so-called seasoning. But you know I'm anxious to try the big-time before I head back to the States."

"We know. If this escorting job goes well, I think the next assignment will be in Germany — if Mr. Steelbach agrees."

"That's good. I haven't that much time left before I need to return."

"Here's an idea," Slonsky said. "If you need to get back soon, you could take the same steamer as the children. It stops in Cuba before going up the coast to dock in Baltimore. That would save you the trip back to Paris and to a port."

"And I'd be supervising them on the voyage?" Mort sounded unenthused.

"Not by yourself. But if you were on the boat, you could help the women we've assigned to accompany them."

"You said the kids are now in Paris. I assume France isn't their native land."

"It is for two of them. Their parents just feel the Western Hemisphere is safer than Europe. They plan to follow soon. The rest of them are from Germany. We couldn't get their parents out — yet — but we were able to bring out the children."

"Well, that's what I wanted to do anyway," Mort said, thinking out loud. "So, it would be like I was at least doing half the job to accompany them back to — Cuba, did you say? Of course, someone else did the hard part in getting them out of Germany."

"But we need to accompany them the entire route," Slonsky sounded a little tired of Mort's back-and-forth. "So, are you interested?"

"Yes, I guess so. And I might as well sail back with them since I'm not ready yet for any assignments in

Germany."

"Excellent! I'll notify the others that you've accepted, and I'll make your travel arrangements."

"When do I pick them up?"

"In two days. You'll be working with Fräulein Schiller — I should say Mlle. Schiller since she lives full time in Paris. I'll call you tomorrow with more specific information about where to meet them. We'll make your travel arrangements and have travel visas for you. Again, thank you very much, Mr. Stein. We realize it's not quite what you wanted. But you're getting there. Next time — your next trip, I hope — you'll almost certainly be able to go into Germany. Barring an unforeseen war, that is."

"Just one last question," Mort said almost as an afterthought. "Why Cuba?"

"Because it will accept refugees. Your country, unfortunately, will not — not without visas that are almost unobtainable."

"Okay. I'll wait for your call."

"It will come about 10 o'clock, I'd say. So, be near your phone."

"Right."

"Oh, one other thing, Mr. Stein, since I probably won't meet with you again while you're here this time."

"Yes?"

"Learn French."

The refugee center was in Belleville, a working-class neighborhood so far from the nearest Metro that Stein soaked his shoes walking in the rain. *Don't the gutters work in this quarter?* he wondered grumpily. Sheltering his street map under his umbrella, he made his way slowly until he found it — a dreary, nondescript two-story building on a dreary, nondescript street. Inside the front door, however, the center teemed with noise and excitement. Several children were playing indoor soccer (*football, I must remember,* Stein told himself) in an empty room off to one side. Mlle. Schiller was waiting for him in the hallway.

"Mr. Stein?" she said, extending her hand, smiling.

"Yes," he smiled back, forgetting his wet socks. She was young, about twenty-five with dark features, but quite different from Magda's. Her hair was long, dark brown, and she wore a simple, flowered dress.

"It's not easy to find this place," Stein said, shaking the rain off his umbrella and shedding his hat and overcoat.

"No," she agreed in a musical voice. "The agency pinches its pennies. This place is both large and affordable, but far out."

"So, when do we gather the children?" Mort asked, thinking of the Metro connections to the train.

"They are ready to go — have been ready for over an hour. But I must first introduce you to them. First, let me introduce myself. I am Bette Schiller. Please call me Bette. Mademoiselle Schiller sounds so formal." She pronounced it as Bett-ah.

"How do you do, I'm Mort Stein. "You said Mademoiselle, but Schiller sounds German."

"I am from Hamburg and have lived in Paris since 1933."

"Since Hitler took power," Mort added.

"Yes, of course, that's why I'm here. I'm Jewish."

"So am I. My first name used to be Mordecai before I shortened it. Just call me Mort."

"Do you speak French?"

"No, unfortunately. Mr. Slonsky advised me to learn it

when I go back to the States."

"It is no problem," she smiled. "I'm fluent in French and Spanish. I studied Romance languages at the *Hockshule* in Hamburg."

"And English, too, I see. You speak it well. That will be very convenient, since I'm an ignoramus except for German. In fact, if you like, we could converse in German so that I keep my skills sharp."

"Perhaps on the ship," she smiled. "Now, we must meet the children." *Did she always smile this much?* Mort wondered.

They were waiting in the adjoining room, eleven children with their meagre baggage lined up against the wall. They had been washed, combed, and the younger ones were being read a story in German by another attendant of the shelter. When Bette and Mort came in, they looked up expectantly, eagerly.

"Children," Bette said in German, "I'd like you to meet Mr. Stein. He's going to be coming with us on the train to Lisbon and on the boat—" (here, she looked to Mort, who nodded) "—to Cuba. Please stand and tell Mr. Stein your names." She repeated it in French.

The children did so obediently. Mort noticed that two of the children were much better dressed than the others and introduced themselves in French. The others, whose clothes were shabby, even if they had been expensive when new, introduced themselves in German. There were several sibling pairs, one child usually speaking for both. To each speaking child he replied "Hello" and used the child's name.

"Well, I guess we might as well get started," Bette said. "Please put on your jackets and overshoes, since it's raining out. When we get to the train station, we'll have a white rope for you to hold on to so that no one gets lost or left behind." She quickly translated into French, while Mort looked on, marveling at her fluency and calm. Being around so many children made him nervous. *What if one had an accident in their pants?* What would he do? Fortunately, Bette seemed to have the situation under control. A bus was waiting for them at the front door. *At least we won't have to walk to the Metro*, Mort thought.

The trip to the Gare d'Orsay was uneventful. Mort went among the seats, trying to learn the children's names, silently creating mnemonic or visual associations. Franz — torn jacket — and Lisa, his younger sister, holding on to his hand for dear life. Pierre and his sister Marguerite — the only two French children, well-dressed. Pierre — arrogant, probably looks down his French nose at the more ragged German kids.

When the bus pulled up in front of the station, Bette took command immediately and vigorously. She told the children to be on their best behavior and produced the white rope she had spoken of. Once inside, they were to hold on and follow along.

"But first, does anyone need to use the rest room?"

Two hands went up, one young boy, one girl.

"Very well," Bette said. "We will move to the side of the main hall. Then I will take Frieda to the rest room. When I return, Mr. Stein will take Nachum. You can wait that long, can't you Nachum? Good. All right, please step off the bus carefully. It might be slippery. Then we go through the doors and get together on the other side to hold the rope." The children were obedient and well-behaved, although the older boys looked a little put out having to do such a babyish thing as holding a rope.

After Mort led him to the rest room, eight-year-old Nachum promptly peed on his shoes. *The tall urinals must have intimidated him*, Mort guessed. Cursing silently, he grabbed as much toilet paper as he could — there were no paper towels — and wiped off the boy's shoes. *They'll still smell like piss*, he knew, *until we can really wash them, perhaps on the train.* Bette and the children were waiting for them when they returned.

"I was afraid you had some trouble," Bette smiled. *Why is she smiling?* he wondered. *Do I look that flustered?*

"No, just some bad aim and a quick cleanup."

"You'll have to get used to that with the younger ones. These are new experiences for some of them. And adult accommodations are intimidating, especially after what they've been through."

Mort didn't comment, didn't want to consider what they've been through.

They found benches near the gates to wait — the train wasn't due for an hour. Bette opened a shopping bag she'd been carrying and began to pass out sandwiches.

"They'll need something to drink," she told Mort. Can you go to the food kiosk and bring back eleven cartons of milk and eleven straws? No, twelve."

"Oh, sure," Mort said. "I used to juggle in the circus. I'll stuff them into my overcoat pockets, I guess. When do we eat?"

"Later," she smiled again. "After we get everyone in their seats on the train. There's a dining car we can go to."

"I'll look forward to that," Mort smiled back.

Getting the kids into two train compartments wasn't difficult except for negotiating who wanted to sit with whom. Bette sorted it out. The train to Lisbon was only moderately crowded. After the kids were settled and given some picture magazines Bette had bought at a kiosk, she led the younger children, three at a time, to familiarize themselves with using the tiny rest room.

Then, after Mort washed off Nachum's shoes, he and Bette took turns visiting the dining car. The arrangement disappointed Mort, but the children couldn't be left alone. At least, he could sit with Bette afterwards, and they conversed in English, confident the children wouldn't understand.

"Well, we're over the first hurdle," Bette said, with that omnipresent smile. "Except for rest room trips that need supervising — and that's only a problem for the three youngest — we're in the clear until dinner time and bedtime. I'll buy some snacks for them at about three. So, Mr. Stein, what made you decide to come along? You're a businessman, not a teacher, Mr. Slonsky tells me."

"I came over to help Jews get out of Germany," Mort answered, knowing it sounded pretentious. "But since Slonsky feels I'm not ready for that kind of assignment, he's giving me smaller ones outside of Germany, delivering money and such. He mentioned this one, and I accepted."

"I wouldn't call this assignment small. I hope you don't regret it," she said, without smiling.

"Well, it *has* been a long time since I've been with young children — mine are in their teens now. But one adjusts. And if it helps our refugees, then fine, that's what I came for."

"You're a good man — I'd say a remarkable man — to drop what you were doing and come all this way to help. We don't get many like that. Nearly all of the JRO volunteers are from European countries."

"And recent émigrés from Germany?" Mort said looking directly at her.

"Yes, most of them," she returned his look.

"I'd like to hear your story, Bette, if you don't mind telling it."

"There's not much to tell. I think I told you that I studied languages at the *Hockshule* in Hamburg. My parents are both schoolteachers, by the way. And they felt — we all felt — there was no place for Jews in Germany once Hitler was made Chancellor."

"You were certainly right about that. It's taken most German Jews a lot longer to learn that. Too long. They've had to put up with so much. And now they're not even considered citizens. They have no rights."

"You must realize, Mr. Stein—"

"Mort. Please."

"Mort. You must understand that German Jews felt that Germany was their homeland — and many still feel that way. They were good Germans. Many, like my father, fought in the German Army in the Great War. If your President started making hateful speeches against American Jews and passing laws against them, would you consider leaving your country?"

"No, you're right about that. We'd try to replace him with someone else in the next election. But once Hitler took power, he wasn't about to let democratic voting kick him out. I guess that's the difference."

"It was bad for Jews even before Hitler took power," Bette said, remembering. "One of my brothers was beaten up on the street by a gang of SA thugs. I was constantly being insulted and shunned by my school chums. You understand, not being invited to parties, or worse. That sounds trivial, but it matters a lot to a young girl. My parents also received increasing disrespect from their students — and in Germany that's shocking. German students are taught from kindergarten to show respect for their teachers. We stand when they enter the room."

"American students sure don't," Mort laughed. "But I still think your parents were — what is the right word, 'prescient'? — to get out when they did. So, you all live in Paris now?"

"Yes. My parents have found comparable teaching positions. In fact, my father is now an administrator (I don't know what you call the position in America) at his *lycée*. I was going to continue on to university, but my volunteering with the JRO became a full-time job."

"Do you still live with your parents?" Mort immediately regretted the question. "I'm sorry, that's a rather intrusive question."

"Not at all," Bette smiled. "Yes, I still live with them. I have two brothers also, although the younger one, Andras, is going into the French Army."

"They don't discriminate against foreigners, then?"

"Not the Army. Besides, we're not foreigners now. We've become French citizens."

"Your brother might be fighting one day against his original homeland."

"France is now his homeland. For all of us," she said, raising her chin a little. It was a cute chin. "What about you, Mort?"

"It was Mordecai when my sister and I emigrated to America in 1912 — from Russia. I'm thirty-nine. I live in Detroit, and I run a string of gasoline — you'd say 'petrol' — stations with a partner. I'm divorced some three years now and have three children. The oldest lives with me. He's sixteen."

"What made you want to give up your work in Detroit and come here to help German Jews?"

"Well, first, I didn't give it up. My partner is running the business until I return. We share the supervisions. I'm not a religious Jew, but I couldn't stand reading about what the Nazis were doing to our people and felt that I had to do something more than just contribute money to refugee organizations. I learned about the JRO — I like to research things to learn about them — and what vital work they're doing. So, I began by making fundraising speeches in Jewish synagogues and centers in Detroit. Then, after speaking with JRO officials in New York, I decided to come over myself after learning German. By the way, I'd still like it if we spoke it to each other, to keep me in practice."

"We'd have to do so quietly," Bette said. "The French despise the Germans. We don't want to be taken for spies."

"No, certainly not," Mort smiled. "If you don't mind me asking, how old are you? I did tell you my age."

"Twenty-five." She smiled. Was she blushing a little?

"A nice age," he smiled back. *Too bad I'm too old for her*, he regretted. *She seems perfect. I always find that I'm looking even when I'm not aware of it.*

To avoid a crowd at dinner, the group entered the dining car at 17:00 before it officially opened; Bette had gotten permission. She sat with the six younger children at two tables. Mort took the five older ones: the French pair, two boys about eleven and a girl about ten. They easily understood his German and seemed familiar with dining cars, all except the youngest girl. Mort told them, "You can order spaghetti and meat sauce or soup and a salad."

"Can't we order steak?" the French boy said, taunting.

"No," Mort replied, already hating him. "We're on a limited budget." He had discussed the choices with Bette. "And order only what you're going to eat." His mother's admonition came back: 'It's a sin to waste food'. He ordered coffee for himself. He noticed that Pierre, the French boy, had ordered a mineral water. *He's trying to look grown up*, Mort thought. *In America, he'd be cut down to size but quick.*

The meal went smoothly; everyone found something they could eat, and no one was ill.

Back in their cars, Mort studied the countryside. They were passing through the wine country just north of Bordeaux; workers by the dozens were in the vineyards carefully pulling grapes off the vines and filling wheelbarrows between the rows. He wished he could film them with a movie camera. But the better alternative was to order some Bordeaux with dinner tonight; even the *vin ordinaire* should be good now. The dining car closed at 19:30. Bette suggested they eat separately, beginning at 18:00, so that they'd have time to prepare the children for bed, escort rest room stops and take them to the sleeper car. *What a collection of chores I've signed up for*, Mort sighed, *even though lovely Bette is doing the lion's share of the work. Lioness's*, he corrected himself.

He missed having Bette to talk to over his dinner of trout almondine, sautéed Brussels sprouts and a quarter-liter of white Bordeaux. But after they had both dined, they still had a little time to continue getting to know each other. It was only Bette's second trip to the West, and she hadn't seen very much beyond New York. She was curious about Mort's hometown. "All I know is that they make autos there," she laughed.

"It's true, they do. Several types in several factories. I used to work in one in my teens, on the assembly line."

"I don't imagine that it was much fun."

"I didn't work there for fun. The family I stayed with needed the money. But working there, I met another guy with the idea of going into the petrol business, once we had enough working capital. And eventually, we saved enough to do it. Not a terribly interesting story."

"But an American success story, nevertheless," Bette smiled. "Are you anxious to get back?"

"Not particularly. My partner is taking care of the business now. And I have to admit that my brief experiences here, delivering money and such, have been a lot more exciting than the life I led in Detroit."

Bette frowned. "But surely you're not doing this for excitement?"

"No," Mort agreed. "But that was an unexpected benefit." Then he said impulsively, "It's too bad I'm so much older than you, Bette. I'm very much attracted to you. You don't need to respond to that, but I just thought you'd like to know."

Bette smiled but said only, "There's no need to rush things, Mort. We have a long voyage ahead of us."

Our entire lives, it might have been, Mort thought wistfully.

But then, Bette added something that electrified him: "And I don't think you're too old for me."

Looking back, Mort concluded that his romance with Bette could not have had a better setting — or greater impetus — than an ocean voyage. They were constantly together for eleven days, even though they spent much of that time taking care of their eleven charges. Unlike his trip to Europe a few weeks earlier, this one found calm seas. Better still, the JRO office in Lisbon provided an additional chaperone — a middle-aged French mother, which enabled Mort and Bette to spend more time alone, enjoying the voyage, enjoying each other's company. Mme. Sadir's presence also relieved the strain Mort was under in constantly helping to monitor eleven children. Bette no doubt felt the same relief. By the third day, she and Mort were holding hands as they strolled the steamer, a French ship, while Mme. Sadir looked on, beaming. By the fifth day, they were lovers, Bette slipping quietly into Mort's tiny stateroom one moonless night.

They talked about their immediate future, after the children were safely landed in Cuba. Mort, feeling that this was perhaps his last chance for a serious, long-term relationship with someone he both loved and deeply respected, wanted Bette to come back with him to Detroit. He realized at the same time how foolish his desire was, just as it had been with Magda, to expect that this young woman would just drop everything — her work and life in Paris — and leave her family so abruptly. Even if she loved him, it was impossible — and unreasonable to expect it. So, reluctantly, he accepted the inevitable; he would disembark at Baltimore and return to Detroit. She would stay on board and return to Paris. As Europe was moving inexorably toward war — Hitler had already occupied the Rhineland and had sent planes and pilots to Spain — Bette felt more needed than ever in helping Jewish refugees. And Mort knew he could impose no further on David to run their gas stations. The best he could promise Bette was that he would return as soon as he could. They kissed goodbye at the Baltimore port.

Detroit, 1937-38

The family seemed relieved to see him again, David most of all, in being freed of his extra responsibilities. How well he had done with the six stations would take a while to determine. Edward and Miriam were glad to return to their normal accommodations. Over a carryout Sunday dinner, Mort described his adventures in France. He mentioned Bette but didn't go into detail, knowing Miriam would intuit much left unsaid. So far as he could tell, she and David seemed relatively happy as a married couple.

An entirely different topic usurped the family discussion that night and removed him from center stage — jazz versus classical music. It began, typically, with a sarcastic dart by Andrew, aimed at his sister's 'square' love of 'long-haired' music. Sarah shot back that Andrew was incapable of appreciating deeper art and that jazz was an excuse for sloppy rhythms and sloppy intonations. That got David started, he who had introduced Mort and Miriam to Detroit jazz back in the 1920s.

"You're way underselling jazz, Sarah," he said. "Just turn on the radio at night and what do you hear? Not Toscanini playing at Wherever-it-is Hall, but Benny Goodman, or Duke Ellington, or Artie Shaw, or Count Basie and their orchestras playing live dance music from a big hotel. The kids love this music; that's what they dance to; that's what they fill the halls to listen to — swing jazz is really hot right now. And even though I'm an old fogey from an older generation, I must admit I really like it. I'm even trying to teach your mother some steps, so that we can swing dance when we go out."

"I can just see you two doing *The Big Apple*," Andrew teased.

Miriam now objected on both counts, "Go out? When was the last time we did that?" And I don't remember you trying to teach me any steps."

"Well, I was planning to," David amended, sheepishly. "But I've been too busy with the stations. We'll cut a rug yet."

"Nice, Uncle David," Andrew jibed. "You almost sound like a real hep cat."

Mort couldn't resist putting in his two cents, "Sarah, I don't think it's fair to call jazz rhythms sloppy. From what I've been able to determine, that syncopated rhythm is really at the heart of jazz." He would like to have mentioned his first exposure to it at the whorehouse David had taken him to back in 1920 but couldn't, of course. Instead, his scholarly interjection had a predictably soporific effect on the debate. It died.

Before things settled back into normality, he felt obliged to share with his family his future plans — that he wanted to return to France just as soon as he had mastered the language, and that effort would require an intensive course. At the latest, he hoped to return in the summer or early fall of 1938. No one was happy with the news, but Mort had anticipated this and planned out some scenarios to make his absence less burdensome. Edward would be turning seventeen in October; he was in his senior year at Central High and could drive himself to school with Mort's car. Edward's grin showed how much that prospect pleased him. He would stay at his home this time, not crowd Miriam and David's flat. And Anna would stay with him — Mort had already arranged this. Not that Edward really needed any overseeing, but Mort wanted no trouble with school authorities should they discover Eward was living alone. Anna was pleased to come over for the month or two Mort would be gone. Her English had rapidly improved; she could do the shopping, and Elsie would make dinners for both of them. Or Chava could have them both over to her flat. Edward, low-key as always, seemed to accept the proposal willingly, but Mort could see he'd need to talk with the boy to sound him out.

David was obviously unhappy with another long interruption of their partnership.

"Look, Mort," he said when they were alone, "You've got to decide where your loyalties are. If you keep running off to Europe for months at a time, why hang on to the stations? You know I can't run all six by myself."

"I've thought seriously about pulling out of the partnership, David, and selling the two stations I own and letting the lease run out on the third. That would leave you with your three unless you could buy mine."

"I don't have that kind of money right now," David said.

Was his tone resentful or just sad? Mort wondered.

"I think a better alternative, David, would be for me to do what I did before: have my three managers run their own stations, for a bonus, and you check up on them to make sure everything's kosher."

"How long would you be away?"

"I'd guess two months at most. Frankly, I want to hang on to my stations until I can see better where I stand." *With Bette*, he thought. "No use burning your bridges behind you."

"Well, as long as you don't make a regular thing of these trips..." David's voice trailed off. He obviously still felt indebted to Mort, which kept him from taking a stronger stand.

Mort knew that there was no point in revealing to David, or to anyone else, how uncertain he was about his future. There were so many variables. His relationship with Bette, of course. If things worked out, where would they live? How would his assignments go, and what would happen in Europe generally? How long could he devote himself to helping Jewish refugees in his present situation?

Making David supervisor of his stations, at least nominally, also raised questions. Was he putting a fox in charge of the henhouse? He didn't think his managers were skimming, but what about David himself? Well, he'd have to depend on Miriam's bookkeeping to keep him honest.

He had dinner with his sisters to describe his plan in more detail and to see how they were getting along. Chava made them an excellent dinner of gefilte fish, roast chicken and kugel. Mort brought a good white wine. Chava's violin teaching was going well, she said. She had several regular students and was gaining more new ones than losing old ones. Her calendar was virtually full. She was proud of how Sarah was progressing and brought Mort up to date. Sarah had spent the summer at Interlochen on scholarship. Though she still had over a year left of high school, she already planned to apply for a scholarship to some of the best music schools in the country: Indiana University, Oberlin College, and of course Julliard. Her teacher, Richard Neubauer, would no doubt write her a strong recommendation.

"And he's somebody," Chava added, "concertmaster for Detroit. Sarah has a brilliant future ahead of her as a violinist, not just as a teacher, but with an orchestra."

Mort was pleased with the news but still felt guilty about not being more of a father to Sarah. *Well, maybe she didn't really need me*, he concluded; *she's been self-motivated from the get-go and knew what she wanted. I wonder how she gets along with Miriam and David, though.*

Anna was also progressing steadily, not just in learning English but in working for the Jewish Welfare Agency, where she helped newer immigrants acclimate to America. Her English that night was still unsteady and far from fluent. But she was determined to keep using it rather than fall back on Yiddish. It slowed their conversations to a crawl, Chava told him, but in a few more months she should be fluent.

"So, how do you like living in Detroit?" Mort asked her, speaking slowly. "Quite a change from Motal, eh?"

"It is a very big change," Anna responded carefully. "Everything is different. Everything! But I am get — getting — to know it and to understand it."

"But do you *like* it?" Mort asked. "The pace must seem much, much faster than in Motal."

Anna turned to Chava. "What is 'pace'?"

"Speed. How fast things are going. Like automobiles on the road and shopping in stores."

"Yes," Anna nodded to Mort. "The *pace* is much fastest."

"Faster," Chava corrected.

"Yes, faster."

In the same manner, she described her work at the Jewish Welfare Agency, where her Yiddish came in handy in communicating with recent immigrants.

"But I tell them, my 'clients', that they must learn English right... away. As soon as it is possible. Just as I am."

"That's fine, Anna, just fine!" Mort said. "I'm so glad you are adjusting."

Anna gave Chava a puzzled look.

"Adjusting," Chava said, sounding like a dictionary, "when you become comfortable with your new home."

"Ah," Anna nodded vigorously. "Yes, I am *adjusting*." She smiled at Edward. "And I am looking forward to staying with you when your father is in Europe."

"I really appreciate that, Anna," Mort said. "And you also Chava, for having Edward over for dinner sometimes. Miriam will also. Please understand that I'm not doing this — going to Europe — for fun, but to help our people, now that they need help. I can't just sit back and do nothing."

"We know that, Mort. I think what you're doing is very good," Chava said. "Just as when you went to bring Anna to Detroit. We don't see it as a burden."

"I'm glad that you understand, Chava. Frankly, Miriam and David weren't exactly thrilled with my plans. But with Anna to look after him, I'm sure Edward will be fine."

"I'll be okay, Dad," Edward said, uncomfortable to be talked about in third person.

In the final months of 1937 and the spring of 1938, Mort worked hard at his business and, at the same time, enrolled in an intensive French course at the French Academy in Detroit. Resuming his supervision of the gas stations was easy; the hard part was evaluating why the profits from his three seemed to dip while David was in control. Had he been skimming? Well, he wasn't about to confront David now; he needed him to keep these stations in the chain. He noted, wryly, that his profits rose with his return.

The French course was ideal; it moved quickly and expected students to devote their free time to study. Intensely motivated from his recent experience, Mort threw himself into learning the language. The only hard part was pronunciation, since it required an experienced French speaker to correct him. As with his German learning, after he mastered the basics and could start putting sentences together, he hired a French major at Wayne University to be a paid conversant. To avoid any entanglements, he met the young lady in a public place, usually a café.

Meanwhile, the news from Europe was getting worse. After a relatively quiescent year, Nazi troops marched into Austria in March 1938 to effect a so-called union with Germany, or *Anschluss*. But it was really a takeover, which expanded Germany's size and population considerably. It also brought almost 200,000 Austrian Jews under Nazi control. Not satisfied with that expansion, Hitler began making demands on Czechoslovakia that summer to cede to Germany the Sudetenland, the western border regions where about three million Germans lived. Confident that France and England would not intervene, he threatened war if he didn't get his way. None of this could be good for German and Austrian Jews, Mort knew. Nazified Austria was hurriedly applying Germany's anti-Semitic edicts and thuggish treatment of its Jews. *I've got to get back as soon as possible,* Mort concluded.

But there was his son to think about. *What kind of father am I to be away so often?* Mort asked himself. *These are pivotal years for Edward. He said he'd be okay, but was that bravado? Doesn't he need me here for stability and guidance?* He knew the answer to the guidance question was no. Edward was self-directed and had his own plans. *But we still need to talk.*

When they did, Edward surprised and disappointed Mort by declaring that he wasn't interested in going on to college.

"You know I've always liked mechanical devices, especially radios. Understanding how they work and fixing them. I'm as good as any repairman at the Dexter Philco store right now. But the device of the future is going to be television."

"What's that?" Mort wasn't ashamed to show his ignorance.

"It's like radio, only it receives visual signals from a transmitter, so you can see things happening on a television screen — like movies in miniature, but they're happening live on the screen."

"Why haven't I heard of this before?" Mort wondered aloud.

"There's no setup right now to send the television signals or airwaves, just a few experimental devices. But that was once true of radio and look how that caught on. If I'm one of the first to understand how television works, I figure I could write my own ticket, either at the transmitting end in broadcasting stations or in the production of television sets to receive the transmissions."

"It's all a little confusing," Mort admitted.

"It's the future, Dad. And right now, colleges don't teach courses like that. I'd have to find some kind of specialized training. And who knows where that would be, or when?"

"What will you do in the immediate future, when you graduate Central?"

"Short term, I'll keep working for Philco repair. I think I can be promoted to supervisor once I graduate."

"What about this trip abroad I'm planning? How do you feel about that?"

"Well, of course I'd rather have you here," Edward said diplomatically. "But I think what you're doing is admirable and necessary. Don't worry about me, I'll be fine. And you'll be gone a few months at most, right?"

"I think so. But this time I hope to go into Germany, so it might be riskier."

"Go for it, Dad. I'll be fine."

"How's your social life going? Got a girlfriend?"

"I've been dating a few girls, nothing serious. Having your car when you were away really helped."

"I'll bet it did," Mort said, imagining backseat trysts in parked cars. "But nothing serious?"

"No, Dad. Nothing serious."

As the summer of 1938 reached its full height and Detroit sweltered in torrid heat, Mort's thoughts kept turning to Europe, the JRO and Bette. They had exchanged letters, more informative than romantic. Bette was busier than ever, performing several necessary duties for the JRO — transferring money to smaller refugee centers in France, Belgium and Holland — and working at the refugee centers in Paris. Those centers were now crowded, as Austrian Jews who could get out fled their homeland for safer havens. Sometimes, Bette escorted Jewish refugee children to Atlantic ports but did not sail with them. The port refugee centers provided escorts. The problem was with the receiving end. Fewer and fewer countries were willing to take even the children. Cuba was now expressing reluctance to take any more refugees, adults or children. That left only the Dominican Republic and Bolivia. England blocked transfers to Palestine and to its own shores. And to Mort's thorough disgust, so did the United States. The State Department had not only refused to loosen its restrictive quotas, it seemed actually to increase the requirements of those fortunate enough to qualify for immigration. Meanwhile, the threat of a European war that summer intensified; England and France were calling up their reserves and drilling intensively. German troops were massing on French borders.

Finally, Mort decided that his conversational French, though far from ideal, was sufficient to get him through border crossings and dealings with French officials. He booked passage on a French ship that sailed in early September and would arrive at Le Havre on the 15th. Even if France and England did go to war against Germany that fall, he assumed that with an American passport, he could safely return.

Paris, fall 1938

The trip abroad was a paradox of lovely weather and a tense mood of passengers feeling they were sailing into harm's way. The crowds at the bars were bigger, the laughter at dinner tables shriller. When Mort landed, he took the train directly to Paris and returned to the same hotel near the JRO office. He was eager to see what missions he could carry out for the JRO and even more eager to see Bette again.

They'd been expecting him and planned a meeting at the JRO for ten o'clock the next day. This time, Arno Steelbach was present, along with Meyer Slonsky.

"Welcome back, Mr. Stein," Slonsky began. "I trust you had a good trip. Did you learn French?"

"Yes. Not as well as I know German, but enough to deal with French officials at borders, I think."

"Not ideal, but we can live with it."

"So, what do you have for me? Will I be going into Germany?"

"You will," Slonsky responded. "We're envisioning a four-part trip. First, you will carry money to Hanover. Second, you'll meet with a German trade representative in Frankfurt to solidify your cover identity. Third, you will meet briefly with a Jewish family in Frankfurt and prepare to smuggle out much of their money. Finally, and most important, you will escort two young children on the pretense that you are a close friend of the family and are taking them to meet their grandparents in Saarbrücken. You will take them to the train station there, where our people will meet you."

"Why Saarbrücken?"

"It's on one of the shortest routes to France and, most important, you won't have to cross a large body of water if you have to cross the border on foot."

Mort took that in. "That's quite an assignment. Looks like I'm making up for lost time."

"Let's just say that with the worsening political situation, our tasks have multiplied, and we can't spread them out as we'd like to into separate trips. I'll spend more time with you later, going over details of each phase of your trip. By the way, this is the last time you can come to this JRO office. We'll meet elsewhere from now on."

Steelbach had been silent until now, studying Mort. Now, he spoke out.

"What kind of physical shape are you in, Mort? Do you know any self-defense if you had to fight?"

The question punctured Mort's enthusiasm. He hadn't

banked on having to fight with his fists. "I wouldn't say I'm in great condition. I don't work out at gyms, no time for that. And no, I don't know self-defense if you mean judo."

"What I mean is killing a Nazi agent if it's a case of him or you. Have you ever used a gun?"

"No. I wasn't in the Army during the war."

"Well, you won't be carrying one," Steelbach reassured him. "Too dangerous if you're caught with it. Still, knowing judo would be useful if you find yourself in a tight spot."

"Such as when?"

"Such as escorting your charges on foot across a border and being stopped by a German guard."

"Do you think that's likely?"

"It's happened before."

"Well, I wouldn't mind taking a quick course in judo, but..."

"Never mind," Slonsky interrupted. "We haven't time for that. Have you followed any recent news on board ship? Hitler's threatening war if he doesn't get the Sudetenland. The Czechs are resisting. And England and France are, as usual, shilly-shallying. The whole thing might blow up into a war in the next few weeks."

"Rotten time to be in Germany," Mort acknowledged. "Still, I'm ready to risk it."

"What you're ready to risk doesn't concern us," Slonsky said. "It's what we need to do that matters. Let's talk about your cover identity."

He produced an American passport and travel visas and handed them to Mort. "Here you are, Mr. Christopher Danforth. You are now the president of a small American oil company, Danforth Oil, and you have come to Germany via France to scare up some business. We'll need to add your photo to the passport. We can take it here this morning. Then our expert forger can stamp it appropriately."

"Nothing is supposed to result from my contact with the trade rep, correct?"

"Correct. It shouldn't last more than a few hours. Its whole purpose is to give you a plausible reason for being in Germany that you can tell the officials at the borders and — let's hope this doesn't happen — to any other German official who questions you."

"Like a Gestapo agent?"

"Like a Gestapo agent," Slonsky nodded. "In the meantime, I'd suggest that you invent and memorize a biography for Mr. Danforth, so you can explain, for example, why you don't have a Texas accent. Your business is located in Houston, by the way, but you have a branch office in New York."

"Are you circumcised?" Steelbach blurted out.

"Well, yes." Mort replied, taken aback.

"That's not good if the Germans suspect you're Jewish. Circumcision is uncommon in Europe except for Jews. You don't look Jewish — that's good. But if the Gestapo was determined to find out..."

"We'll just have to risk it," Slonsky said. "Let's get back to the cover story. In case the Gestapo checks out your background, we have a special phone line for these situations at the JRO office in New York. When that phone rings, our receptionist will act like a Danforth Oil receptionist and pretend that it's the New York branch of your business."

"That's clever," Mort said, "but what if the Gestapo is checking on a different operation using the same number?"

"Our receptionist will probably answer by asking

"Whom did you wish to speak to?" or something like that. She knows what she's doing. The important thing is that the call would be coming in on a separate phone, which she knows is coming from Germany."

"I see. I'll need to know her name in case the German trade rep mentions it."

"We'll let you know in good time," Slonsky said.

"How soon will I leave?"

"It's difficult to say. The appointment with the trade rep still has to be made, and others must be informed of your visits and when to expect you."

"Like the parents of the two children?"

"And the people connected with your money transfers."

"One last question," Mort said, holding his breath, "Is Bette Schiller in town now? I accompanied her in taking the refugee children to Cuba."

"We know," Slonsky smiled. It was pleasant to see him smile — the two little scars on his cheeks were lost in the smile's creases. "Yes, she's in town. She's moved, you know. Our receptionist will check with her and, if she approves, Hilda will give you her new telephone number."

Why shouldn't she approve? Mort wondered. *Has she met someone else?* To Slonsky, he just said, "You're being very careful. I knew about the move, but not the new phone number."

They went to the Paris Opera to hear Donizetti's *Lucia.*

Remarkable, Mort reflected, *to be in the middle of a war scare, yet life goes on as normal. The opera, concerts, museums — no closures.* In fact, the cafés were crowded and never looked livelier. He had expected Bette to be a music lover — it was one more passion they shared. Their passion in bed later that night was another and even more delightful than it had been in the ship's cramped quarters. Her new apartment was small but had a double bed.

Relaxing afterwards, they talked in general terms about his assignments. Bette was deeply impressed with his quick return to Europe.

"I must admit," she confessed with a smile, "I hadn't expected to see you again."

"What you mean is, I got my jollies the first time around, including sleeping with you, and that would be enough for me."

"Yes, something like that, although not so ugly as you phrase it. I'm just so glad you're back," she snuggled into him.

"For now, at least. We still need to talk about the future. Our future."

"But how can we, when everything is so uncertain? Please, let's not get too serious right now, I was so enjoying the moment."

"I realize I'm not a great lover, Bette. Probably haven't had enough practice."

"You were fine, darling. And I don't want you practicing on other women."

"Will you be here in Paris for the time being?"

"Of course. Where would I be? Paris is my home."

"Lucky girl. A lot more exciting place than Detroit."

"But Detroit is safer. And you have your business there. And your children."

"Now, who's being serious?"

"All right, you caught me. We'll talk about those things later."

"One thing I do have to ask, Bette. What if war breaks out?"

"What if it does? It's nothing I can control. Or you. I'll still be in Paris. But I hope you're not in Germany if it happens. They will close the borders."

"I'll get out somehow. Perhaps by going to Switzerland. That country will stay out of it, I'm sure."

"Yes. Switzerland is wiser than the rest of Europe. They make cuckoo-clocks, not war."

"'Cuckoo' is how I feel about you."

"How is that?"

"An American expression for being a little crazy."

"So, you have lost your mind, Mr. Stein?"

"Over you darling. Over you."

They embraced again.

For his money transfers he had to buy a new sport coat a size larger than he usually wore. When it was ready, he took it — and 10,000 *Deutschmarks* he'd been given — to a tailor the JRO had selected. A laconic little man with a bent back, the tailor needed no explanations; he had done this sewing many times. As Mort watched, he sewed two extra compartments inside the lining of jacket, one on each side. He kept the stitches from showing on the outside.

"It's easier in the winter, when we use overcoats," the tailor said in French. "But you'd sweat like a bull in heat if you wore one now."

"I'll probably just bring along a light topcoat in case it turns cold."

"As you wish. You must keep wearing this jacket all the times you're out."

"I will," Mort said, watching him. Finally, he took the *Deutschmarks* Mort had ready — large denominations, Mort noted — and fitted them perfectly into the new compartments.

"*Voilà!*" the tailor said, sewing the pockets closed. That will hold perfectly unless you start using your jacket like a bullfighter's cape."

"You must enjoy bullfights," Mort said. "That's two bullfighting comparisons you've made."

"Never saw one," the tailor responded dourly. "And I don't care to. Barbaric sport, if that's what it is. The Spaniards are even crazier than the Boche."

So, I can use the same pockets for the money I take out of Germany, Mort was thinking. *Just need to stitch them closed.*

"Make sure to keep your coat buttoned at all times," the tailor cautioned. "You don't want anyone to notice those compartments and rob you."

"Or arrest me."

"Obviously." The tailor was through and showed he wasn't expecting to be paid. As if reading Mort's mind, he explained. "I do this for myself. It's a small thing, but something I can do to help my people."

"You are helping," Mort said. "Helping a lot."

"Goodbye," the tailor said. "And safe travels!"

The French 'goodbye' is so much more optimistic, Mort thought, walking out. *'Until we meet again'. Likewise, the German 'Auf Wiedersehen'. Well, I hope to, little tailor, whose name I never learned. I hope to.*

Five days later, Mort was still waiting to begin when the European war threat came to a head. On September 24th, the Czechs ordered a general mobilization; forty-seven divisions, of which thirty-seven were stationed on the border with Germany. Situated in the mountains, they seemed capable of putting up a good defense if Germany invaded. The same day, France issued a partial mobilization. *I don't know what 'partial' means*, Mort thought, reading the new bulletins pinned to kiosks and pasted on walls. But he saw French Army trucks loaded with soldiers racing down the boulevards. The train stations, too, were mobbed with French soldiers just called up. They looked none too eager to be going off. *Not like the last war, when pretty girls threw flowers for their caps.*

Slonsky had already contacted him over the telephone to meet him at a nearby café.

"Our plans are now on hold," he announced, "until we see what happens. Obviously, if there's a war, we can't send you. France would be in it, and the border with Germany would close. We'll just have to wait and see."

Mort's disappointment was palpable.

"All right," he said. "So, I guess we wait. Do you want the money back now?"

"Yes, there's no point in your keeping it, where it may get stolen. And it may be a while yet before you can go, if at all. We'll have to see how this plays out."

It played out in Munich, in a last-ditch conference on September 29th proposed by Neville Chamberlain, Prime Minister of England, and attended by Hitler, Deladier of France and Mussolini of Italy. Notably not permitted to attend (except to wait at a nearby hotel to be told the results) were the representatives of Czechoslovakia, whose territorial integrity was being decided upon. In brief, Hitler was given the Sudetenland as an appeasement; Czechoslovakia protested bitterly but had no say in the final decision. Chamberlain returned by plane to England, waving a piece of paper as he disembarked — a piece of paper he and Hitler had signed, which expressed their countries' mutual 'desire never to go to war with one another' and 'to use negotiation in all future disagreements'. Spared from war, the populations of England and Europe collectively exhaled in relief — all except the

Czechs. Chamberlain had belittled the cause of the whole affair as 'a quarrel in a far-away country between people of whom we know nothing'. He was now celebrated as the man of the hour for having achieved what he called 'peace in our time'. Others, like Winston Churchill, saw it as a humiliating capitulation to Hitler and a betrayal of Czechoslovakia.

Mort, Arno Steelbach and Meyer Slonsky listened to Prime Minister Deladier explaining the agreement on the radio as they sat in a French café.

"He doesn't sound happy about it," Slonsky said.

"He ought to be ashamed," Steelbach replied angrily. "Selling out Czechoslovakia that way. I read that Chamberlain thinks they've bought peace. What they've really done is to show Hitler that he can get away with it, with *any* demand or any action, no matter how outrageous, and England and France won't have the balls to stop him with their armies."

"What armies?" Slonsky challenged. "The English aren't ready for war, and Chamberlain knows it. He's buying time."

"At whose expense? Well, at least the French have a decent-sized Army and good weapons."

"But will they fight?" Mort wondered. "The mobilized soldiers I saw at the train station did not look very eager. No bands or flowers this time."

"Who knows how long France will put up with these humiliations?" Slonsky replied.

"Where does all this leave my missions?" Mort asked.

"Well, I don't see why they can't go forward," Slonsky

replied. The borders are still open. We're still waiting to hear back from our State Department contact about the meeting he's setting up with the German trade representative."

And who knows when that will be? Mort thought grimly.

"Monsieur Stei-i-n?" The sing-song voice of the concierge accompanied her tapping on Mort's door. "There's someone here to see you."

It startled Mort, who had settled in for the night. It was 10:30. after all. Groggily, he thought it might be Bette but couldn't remember if he had told her where he was staying. *Why would she be dropping in like this? She has her own place.* When he went downstairs, he found Arno Steelbach waiting in the lobby.

Typically, Steelbach wasted no words. "Do you like jazz, Mr. Stein? I'm on my way to a jazz club and thought you might want to come."

Mort wasn't sure which surprised him more: Steelbach, Mr. all-business, paying him a social call or his suggesting a jazz club. *Target shooting would be more in his line.*

"I do like jazz, Mr. Steelbach," Mort responded, "but I don't follow it much. I went to some jazz clubs in Detroit in the Twenties, but that's about it."

"Well, it's time to catch up, then. There's a jazz club in Paris that's really something. Called 'The Hot Club.' Features a guitar player who plays with just three fingers. Have you ever heard of Django Reinhardt?"

"No. But that's not surprising. I couldn't name you any jazz musicians playing today except maybe Benny Goodman. My son is the real jazz maven."

"Well, this will give you something to tell him about," Steelbach said. "Want to come? C'mon Stein, you need a break from politics and the Nazis."

Being with Bette is my break, Mort wanted to say, but he said only, "Okay, I'll come. Just give me five minutes to get dressed."

The club was in the basement of a respectable-looking building. As Mort expected, it was smoky and noisy. *Hell*, he thought as they found a table, *I might as well smoke, I've inhaled so much cigarette smoke in all these clubs, cafés and restaurants*. On the makeshift stage, a quintet was playing an oldie from the 1920s, *Dinah*. What stood out for Mort was that it featured a fiddle player, as well as Reinhardt playing what sounded and looked like a mandolin. His playing was lyrical but also improvisatory, as he weaved arabesques around the simple melody. Mort liked it and told Steelbach so. *Imagine, playing with just three fingers!*

"Some of his recordings have made it back to the States," Steelbach replied. "He's much admired here. In fact, a lot of jazz musicians from the States visit here to jam with the group. Now, should we order some drinks? Ever have Pernod?"

When Mort got back to his room, his head was spinning from the drinks, but the music he'd heard was worth tomorrow morning's hangover. Now he had something to tell the family that wasn't just about Toscanini and symphonies. *Sarah might not care, but Andrew would be enthralled!*

It was well into October before the business meeting was confirmed. In the meantime, Mort had been carrying out small assignments, carrying money to various locales in France, Belgium and the Netherlands. He rather enjoyed using his new identity at the borders and wearing his new jacket with the money pouches. Slonsky and Steelbach met him at their favorite café.

"It's been arranged," Slonsky announced. "You will meet with Herr Wilhelm von Mecklin, a German trade representative, in Frankfurt to discuss a possible deal.

"*von* Mecklin. So, he's from an aristocratic family?"

"We have no way of knowing," Slonsky replied, with a trace of irritability.

"How did they set up this meeting?"

"I think I told you," Steelbach replied. "We have a friend in the economic section of the State Department. If he ever gets caught, he'll probably lose his job. He's done this sort of thing for us before. Different covers with different contacts."

"You will meet him on 10 November, a Thursday," Slonsky said. "He'll call for you at your hotel in Frankfurt, the Bristol, about 10:00.

"November 10th? Why the delay?" Mort asked. He was getting antsy about waiting — almost two full months since he'd arrived.

"Who knows?" Slonsky replied. Mecklin's probably a busy man, what with his trade duties and reporting regularly to the Gestapo."

"He's an agent?"

"Undoubtedly. So, watch what you say to him. Stick strictly to your story and don't ad lib too much."

"What about my courier missions?"

"You'll do one before meeting him, carrying in money to Hanover, and two after: carrying out money and escorting two children past the border at Saarbrücken."

Steelbach spoke up. "I'd say you should enter Germany on Tuesday, 8 November, to deliver the money. Now let's go over the details of each assignment."

A week later, at another café meeting, Slonsky removed some materials from his briefcase.

"We had a prospectus for Danforth Oil printed up, so that you can give Herr Mecklin a copy. Please memorize it. Also these business cards." Mort was impressed with Slonsky's foresight and thoroughness. Even before coming over, Mort had begun to research the things he'd need to know to project his business identity convincingly. He studied oil production and transport — where the crude oil was typically drilled (he chose some place called Midland, Texas), where it was refined and shipped (Houston), how many barrels an oil tanker typically held (anywhere between 100,000 and 150,000 depending on the ship), and, most important, the per-barrel price on the open market. For this last, he had studied *The Wall Street Journal*.

He noticed a sheaf of papers next to the business cards. Slonsky explained, "This is a dummy annual report with your company's name printed to replace the original company. We don't expect you to show this to Mecklin; in fact, you shouldn't. But it's the kind of reading a business executive would have in his briefcase, as well as a popular novel and perhaps a pint of whiskey."

"You think of everything," Mort marveled.

"We try to. The cards have on them our special telephone line in New York, in case Mecklin or his Gestapo buddies try to call. By the way, exchanging business cards is an important custom in Europe, an icebreaker. So, have yours ready, also at the border."

"I just have one question — for now," Mort said. "If I'm successful in interesting Mecklin in a deal — we won't close it, of course, on my brief visit — won't he be mightily pissed off when he finds that he can't get hold of me afterwards or that I've just disappeared? Won't he feel he's been deceived and alert the Gestapo of same?"

"Yes, of course. We realize that the number of times we can set up these phony meetings is limited. We've already done a few in widely different realms. We once had someone posing as an athletics executive contact his counterpart in Germany to set up a possible competition. The Gestapo is bound to get wise and issue warnings to Germans dealing with foreigners. So far, though, we're in the clear."

The day before Mort was to leave, Slonsky called him with menacing news.

"You've probably heard that a young Jewish refugee, here in Paris, shot and killed a German diplomat at the German embassy here. It was in all the French papers. Apparently, the boy was taking revenge for the Nazis deporting his Polish parents back to Poland. Needless to say, Germany is in an uproar over this, especially because the boy was Jewish."

"So, my missions are cancelled?" *How many more times will this happen?* Mort wondered glumly.

Slonsky's answer surprised him. "No, I think we can still go ahead. After all, none of this should affect an American businessman coming into Germany to do business. Just don't get caught."

"Thanks, I'll try not to," Mort couldn't keep the sardonic tone out of his voice. "I'm leaving on the 9:15 train."

"The tailor sewed in the money again?"

"Yes, it's secure. He does nice work, by the way. I'll have someone else sew in the new money I take out of Germany."

"I'm sure you'll find someone reliable, possibly Frau Goldstein herself. It's half her money, after all. Well, good luck to you. You won't be able to contact us from Germany, though the people you'll work with will know how to reach us."

"That's comforting."

"So, *mazel tov* and goodbye."

"Until we meet again."

The Missions

The train from Paris to Saarbrücken, a two-and-a-half-hour trip, was on time and speedy. After he had lifted his suitcase to the rack overhead, feeling the weight of his two jacket pockets stuffed with money, Mort settled in with the European edition of the *New York Herald*, too old to carry the assassination story. He had left his Morton Stein passport at the hotel and carried no other identification cards in his wallet. *I'm Christopher Danforth, do or die*, he thought. *Well, let's drop that cliché.* Before he left, remembering the trouble he'd narrowly escaped in Berlin escorting his sister, he wrote down the name and phone number of the American consul in Berlin. *But can he help an American with a phony identity and who is obviously lying? Let's hope it doesn't come to that.*

Crossing the French border before Saarbrücken was routine. On the German side, as Mort expected, he had to exit the train to be interviewed by German border officials. Though he could feel anxiety starting to build in his stomach, this time it was different. He had his knowledge of German as a defense. He could understand

and talk back if he had to. *How vulnerable he'd been on that earlier trip!*

As he approached the desk, he studied the German official sitting there, a squat little man with a split mustache, its waxed ends turned up like Kaiser Wilhelm's. He was studying the passport picture and comparing it to Mort's looks.

"Name?"

"Christopher Danforth."

"Occupation?"

"Businessman."

"Religion?"

"Protestant."

"Where are you going in Germany?"

"First to Hanover, then to Frankfurt."

"For what purpose?"

"Business meetings." He was ready with information about the von Mecklin meeting if needed. *What about Hanover, though?*

"How long do you plan to be in Germany altogether?"

"I'd say about four or five days."

"How much money are you bringing into the country?" Mort felt his stomach tighten.

"About two hundred *Deutschmarks*, to cover my expenses."

"That should be more than enough, Herr Danforth." He looked closely at Mort's face, then, glancing at the line of people waiting behind him, decided.

"Have a pleasant trip, Mr. Danforth," he said, stamping the passport and handing it to Mort.

In the Saarbrücken train station, the German newspapers at the newsstand were all screaming about the assassination of Ernst vom Rath.

'𝕴𝖊𝖜 𝕸𝖚𝖗𝖉𝖊𝖗𝖘 𝕲𝖊𝖗𝖒𝖆𝖓 𝕯𝖎𝖕𝖑𝖔𝖒𝖆𝖙!' was a typical headline.

'𝕯𝖎𝖕𝖑𝖔𝖒𝖆𝖙 𝖒𝖚𝖗𝖉𝖊𝖗𝖊𝕯. 𝕴𝖊𝖜 𝖗𝖊𝖘𝖕𝖔𝖓𝖘𝖎𝖇𝖑𝖊!' shouted another.

'𝕴𝖊𝖜𝖘 𝖒𝖚𝖘𝖙 𝖇𝖊 𝖕𝖚𝖓𝖎𝖘𝖍𝖊𝕯 𝖋𝖔𝖗 𝖙𝖍𝖎𝖘 𝖔𝖚𝖙𝖗𝖆𝖌𝖊𝖔𝖚𝖘 𝖆𝖈𝖙!' bellowed a third.

Mort took one from the stand to read while finishing the Mannheim leg, about two hours. *Well*, he reminded himself, *I'm just an American businessman with no particular interest in this murder or in the revenge being demanded against the Jews. I hope von Mecklin doesn't want to talk about it.*

In Mannheim, Mort had to change trains for Hanover, a three-and-a-half-hour trip. During the stopover, he had a pleasant lunch at the Mannheim station restaurant. *As long as you stick to German food, it's not bad*, he concluded, *though Schnitzel and Spätzle can get old pretty quickly*. Alone in his compartment of the Hanover train, he imagined a nonsense ditty to go with the clicking of the wheels over the tracks: *It's Schnitzel mit Spätzle und Spätzle mit Schnitzel...* He started to doze.

When he awoke with a start, he saw that another man had entered his compartment. He was sitting opposite him by the window and studying him.

"Ah, I must have dozed off," Mort said in German.

"You did," the man replied. Like Mort, he was in his late-thirties and well-dressed, with sandy hair clipped short and pleasant features. Aryan features. Mort thought about his own hair, wished it were lighter.

"It must have been that heavy lunch I had at the station," Mort said.

"No doubt. But you see, we Germans are used to taking

our big meal in the early afternoon. You Americans — am I right in guessing you're American from your accent? — you Americans prefer to have your big meal at six or seven."

"That is true," Mort said, eager to get the topic away from himself. "Going far?"

"Just to Frankfurt," the man said. "And yourself?"

"To Hanover." He didn't see any need to dissemble about his destination. *More lies, more lies to get trapped in*, he cautioned himself.

"A long ride," the man said indifferently. "Business?"

"Yes," Mort replied, intentionally cutting it short, and turning to his newspaper.

The man took the hint and began reading his own paper, a different one but with the same anti-Semitic headlines in boldface Gothic.

When Mort finished his paper, he put it into his briefcase and took out the novel he had brought with him, Margaret Mitchell's *Gone with the Wind.* He was aware the man was still studying him surreptitiously over the newspaper. But now he exclaimed, "Ah, I see you are reading *Gone With the Wind* — in English. So, I was right; you are American. By coincidence, I too am reading that novel, and I like it very much. It is very — what would be the right word in English? — *melodramatic.*"

"Yes," Mort said, resisting the invitation to switch to English. "She describes things very well."

"I find it very interesting how she depicts the Black slaves," the man said with a small smile. "How happy they all seem, working long hours in backbreaking labor without pay for this rich White family. How devoted they are to them."

"She romanticizes history," Mort said. "I don't believe it

was really like that."

"But it is true, isn't it," the man continued, "that you Americans do not treat your Black people very well. I've read that in your American South, everything is separated. Separate restrooms for White and Black, separate sections in movie theatres, in restaurants, on buses, even water fountains. Yet Americans protest the loudest about how we Germans treat our Jews, applying the same principles of separation because that is how the majority — we Aryans — prefer it. Don't you think that is slightly hypocritical?"

Mort was determined not to get into a debate with this man who seemed so self-assured, so knowing. But he had to reply. "You've described our South, but not other parts of America, where Negroes have the same rights as White people. They can live where they want, go where they want, and so forth."

"Is that really true?" the man said with a smile. "If I were a Negro, could I buy the house next to yours? Or get the same kind of work in your company, working alongside White people?"

"I really don't know," Mort said coldly, trying to cut it off. "I haven't made a study of it."

"Well," the man said, ignoring Mort's curtness, "curiously enough, I have. And all around the world, countries practice the same kinds of separation that we Germans practice. The South Africans practice 'apartheid' — I believe that is the correct word — to separate their Black people. The Indians keep their 'untouchables' apart — even their name tells you that. The Hindus and the Moslems despise each other and refuse to mix. So, I personally think that this is a natural way of co-existing. Or, if you prefer, the natural right of the strongest to dictate terms of natural separation of people they don't care to associate with."

"The *Untermenschen*?"

"Yes, exactly! The *Untermenschen.*"

Mort knew he shouldn't let himself be sucked in. But he couldn't hold back. "And how do you think the *Untermenschen* feel about this?"

The man studied Mort more frankly. "I really don't know. Nor do I care. Do you know how the Black people in your country feel about being separated and not having the same privileges?"

"No," Mort admitted, "I don't know. I've never spoken to one about it."

"My point exactly," the man said, as if calling 'Checkmate!' We of the *Übermenschen* set the rules, have always set the rules. And the central rule is separation. It may not seem fair to the *Untermenschen.* But when has history ever been fair? It is always a struggle" — he used the word *Kampf* — "between the stronger and the weaker."

"What you say is very interesting," Mort said, determined to cut it off. "But if you don't mind..." He turned to his book.

"No, of course not," the man said. He seemed incapable of being offended. And besides, he had bested Mort in the debate, hands down. He had successfully defended German racial policy against this American Jew in disguise.

When the train reached Frankfurt, the other man prepared to leave.

"Goodbye," he said to Mort, with a nod of his head. "I enjoyed our discussion. Perhaps we'll meet again." There was that little smile again as he left.

Mort waited a minute for the man to disappear. At first, he was furious with himself for being identified so easily as an American. *Of course, my accent gave me away. But did I need to be reading an American novel?*

He was on the verge of disposing of it but then stopped himself. *Take it easy! Reading an American novel would be perfectly natural for an American businessman.* The man's knowing air was unsettling, however. *Do you suppose he knew I was Jewish? That damn superior little smile! And what was that about seeing me again? Was he a Gestapo agent? Are they on to me already? Calm down and focus on your missions.* He went back to the novel and waited for the train to pull out. So far, he was alone in his compartment.

It was 17:45 when the train arrived at Hanover, but there was still daylight for Mort to make his way to the address Slonsky had given him. He could have settled himself in his hotel first, but he wanted to turn over the money as soon as possible and have it off his person. Also, offices were closing. But he was careful to check his suitcase at the station, since carrying it around would attract attention. *Too bad — that would require an extra trip back to retrieve it.* Since the address he had memorized was across town, he took a cab. Without thinking, he had expected he'd be going to some sort of a welfare office, as in Paris and Rouen, until he remembered that the Germans provided no welfare for Jews, nor allowed Jewish workers at a government office. The cab took him to a private home on a tree-lined street of middling homes, neither ornate nor run down. In the sunset, a few children were on a lawn nearby kicking a soccer ball.

Mort walked up the front walk and rang the bell. The door opened immediately, and a middle-aged Jewish-looking woman welcomed him in after looking up and down the street. She'd obviously been expecting him.

Mort said only, "You are Helena Schreiber?" The

woman nodded and showed Mort her identity card, stamped with a large 'J'.

"I've come from the Jewish Relief Organization in Paris, and I have a delivery for you," Mort said, taking off his suit coat. He felt under the lining for the first packet, cut its cover flap with a small scissors Frau Schreiber provided, extracted the German bills and handed them to her. Then he did likewise for the other sewn-in pocket.

"That should be 10,000 *Deutschmarks*."

"Yes," she said, taking the pile immediately to a desk and locking it in a drawer. "Let me write you a receipt," she said.

Mort started to thank her, then caught himself. "Thanks, but I think it's better that I don't have evidence on me that I was carrying this much money."

"Yes, of course," she agreed. "What was I thinking of?" A tremulous smile tried to lighten her seriousness. "Thank you so much for bringing the money all this way. It was very brave of you. We Jews here in Hanover have a great need of it."

"How will you distribute it?" Mort was curious.

"We have numerous couriers to take it to locations in the city and surrounding towns, as far away as Bielefeld and Magdeburg."

"I'd like to hear more," Mort said. "but I don't think I should linger. And I still have to get to my hotel. What's the fastest way to get to a cab or tram stop?"

"There's a tram stop a few blocks away on Rodenbacherstrasse. You simply turn right at the corner on Amsdorf and keep walking until you reach Rodenbacher. When you leave, make sure no one is following you."

"I'll be careful," Mort said. "I could have just had the

taxi wait for me, but I thought that might look suspicious."

"Everything looks suspicious these days to the Gestapo and to our nosy neighbors," the woman said. "Well, thank you again for bringing the money and have a safe trip back. God be with you."

"Thank you," Mort said, thinking, *Yes, God and luck be with me. I can't tell her that this is only the first of several stops. She may know that already.*

"Good luck to you," he said, leaving. He was immensely relieved to be free of the 10,000 *Deutschmarks*.

There were no cabs where he hit Rodenbacher, so he stepped up on the first tram and asked the driver if it went to the *Bahnhof*.

"You want the next tram," the driver said. "21B. That will take you there."

"Many thanks," Mort said, stepping down.

While waiting for 21B, he was glad that the JRO office in Paris had reserved his room. Pretending to search for the tram, he scanned the line forming behind him. Everyone seemed preoccupied, several reading newspapers with the screaming headlines. Eventually, the tram arrived and took him back to the train station. Getting off, Mort looked to see if anyone else got off. There was only a young couple, so he felt relatively sure that he wasn't being followed. Breathing easier, he retrieved his bag and took a cab to his hotel. The *Metropolitan* was nice, somewhere between first and second class, and it had a restaurant. Checking in as Christopher Danforth, Mort saw no one in the lobby glancing at him. So far, so good. He didn't like leaving his passport at the desk, but that was the rule. Mort had resolved to keep the lowest of profiles and not search for good restaurants in Hanover or Frankfurt. In fact, he ordered dinner sent up to his room. He wanted no more encounters with Nazis trying to justify their *Übermenschen* policies or studying him. *My looks and my books*.

The next morning, following an American-style breakfast he had sent up to his room, he checked out. He wasn't surprised at the sizable hotel bill, for which he'd be reimbursed later, but was miffed by the service charge for having his dinner sent up when it had been barely lukewarm. *Schnitzel* again, this time with red cabbage. At least, the breakfast was good.

"Here you are, Herr Danforth," the desk clerk said politely, handing Mort his receipt and passport. "We hope you enjoyed your stay." *I suppose they routinely turned passports over to the local Gestapo agent who checked hotel guest lists*, Mort thought. It fell open to his picture and stamped visas and had lost the shiny newness it had had in Paris. *Well, if there was going to be trouble, it would have happened last night — or right now!* As he turned away from the desk, he casually surveyed the lobby. No one looking at him. No one approaching him.

He took a cab to the train station and checked on the next train for Frankfurt. *Ten minutes — too soon. And what's your rush?* he told himself. *You have all day to get there. You aren't meeting Mecklin until tomorrow morning. Better to take the 11:15 train and stretch things out*. He checked his suitcase and, ignoring his earlier resolve, decided to walk to the *Altstadt*, a short stroll but well worth it for its scenic buildings. Mort was reminded of Danzig. *Such lovely old towns — and such awful people!*

As he strolled back to the station, he noticed uncovered trucks going in various directions and carrying uniformed men. *Black uniforms. S.S.*, he realized. *Normal transport? Or is something going on?* While walking, he kept searching for angled shop windows where he could see behind himself. Nothing, at least nothing he could detect. *Paranoia must be one of the side benefits of this job*, he thought. *Slonsky didn't prepare me for that.*

The train to Frankfurt would take about three and a half hours. *That will bring me to the hotel about 15:00,* Mort calculated. *Perfect! I can catch a nap, then have a leisurely dinner and read my novel. Must get a good night's sleep to be sharp for Mecklin. He's to call — when? — I think it's for 10:00 tomorrow.*

The train ride was uneventful — a beautiful word to Mort — but crowded and unpleasant. His compartment was full, with a family of four and another passenger, an old lady in a heavy coat. Getting there first, Mort took a seat by the window. The children, he estimated, were about six or seven, and squirmed about, eager for the train to leave. When it did, they ran out into the corridor to watch the fields moving by from the other side. Quickly bored, they piled back into the compartment, where the mother immediately began removing a wurst from her large bag, as well as bread and a small knife. Efficiently, she pulled hunks of the bread and cut slices of the wurst.

What, no mustard? Mort thought nastily. The smell of the wurst quickly permeated the compartment — *the worst of the wurst*, Mort couldn't resist it, which reminded him he was getting hungry. *When did the dining car open? Probably not for half an hour, at noon. Just have to tough it out.* He tried to read his novel. The mother had by now extracted a chunk of cheese, a particularly smelly cheese, which she cut skillfully and

261

handed slices to the children and to her husband, who had been reading his newspaper. *Above it all*, Mort thought. The children simply added the cheese to their wurst sandwiches and kept chewing. *How much more time?* Mort wondered, looking at his watch. *Twenty-five minutes. Twenty-five hours, seems like. Wish this compartment had better ventilation.* He could have gotten up and lifted the window but didn't want to make a fuss and step over one child sprawled in front of him. *Well, this makes up for having nearly empty compartments in the trains coming up — empty except for that man who wanted to debate me, the man with that superior little smile.*

Finally, at the stroke of noon, Mort got up, made his way past the children, whom he would have gladly stepped on, and exited the smelly compartment. *Freedom and fresh air — well, corridor air — at last!* he exulted, noting that a man from the next compartment exited when he did. *Probably hungry too*, Mort guessed, as they made their way down the corridor to the dining car. When he got there, it had just opened and there were several open tables. Mort chose a table for two in the rear and promptly started reading his novel. He wanted no conversations, pleasant or otherwise, with other passengers. He was also determined to drag out the lunch for as long as possible. *That family is probably going all the way to Frankfurt*, he thought grimly. *It would be just my luck. Anyhow, it would be the German thing to do to have a large lunch with several courses and coffee and cake afterwards. Just fitting right in*, he smiled to himself. *Though I won't fit into my older clothes if I keep this up. Just this large coat.*

As it turned out, he was wrong about the family. They got off at Kassel. Mort felt a palpable sense of relief and sensed that the other passenger, the old lady, did also.

"Thank goodness they're gone!" he said in German. She nodded but said nothing.

Odd duck, he thought. He took out his novel again and promptly dozed off, stuffed by the large lunch and dessert he'd consumed in the diner. At least it wasn't *Schnitzel* again, but fried trout and boiled potatoes.

At the Frankfurt station, he held the door open for the old lady, who was also getting off. Again, she nodded and barely uttered a *"Danke." Friendly sort*, Mort thought. *Maybe she's had a stroke or a speech impediment and can't talk.*

The station wasn't crowded at 15:00 and neither were the streets outside. But once again, Mort noticed considerable activity in trucks carrying the S.S. Some trucks were headed down the avenues, but some were stopping in the area, as S.S. detachments dismounted and were assembling. *What is going on?* Mort wondered.

When he settled into his cab, he asked the driver, "Is something going on? I noticed a lot of the S.S. out there."

"I wouldn't know," the driver responded curtly.

Now, Mort was sure something was happening. *The citizens are clamming up. See no evil... Well, thanks, buddy. You just reduced your tip.*

The Bristol was definitely a first-class hotel, and the doorman immediately met the cab and took Mort's suitcase as he paid the driver. *Of course*, Mort thought. *This is where a German trade rep would expect a Texas oilman to stay.* Checking in was a breeze, and they showed him to a nice room on the top floor with French windows that opened out on a small balcony overlooking a major avenue. From the balcony, Mort could see far down the street in either direction and a long way over other buildings. *Now for that nap*, he thought. His dozing on the train had been brief, part of his mind feeling he needed to keep track of who entered his compartment or looked in.

When he awakened, it was almost five. He decided on a hot bath to iron out the kinks of travel. Then, he'd order up a whiskey and relax on the balcony, watching the sunset. Later, he could review his prospectus and figure out a rough estimate on how many barrels he could ship and at what price.

The bath was delicious, but as he was drying off, thinking about dinner, he heard noises coming from the street below. He quickly dressed and went out onto the balcony. Down the street, several blocks away, a building was on fire, flames leaping out of its upper windows. A crowd had gathered to watch it burn. The odd thing was that there were no sirens, no fire trucks coming. In the twilight, he thought he could just make out the black uniforms of S.S. men around the building; they looked like beetles. That wasn't all. Nearer the hotel on the avenue, crowds had gathered at several fashionable stores, including one featuring furs in its windows. Those windows were now being smashed by members of the crowd. The S.S., standing nearby, seemed to be directing it, rather than trying to stop it. The crash of broken windows was, in fact, coming from several directions at once, a cacophony of shattering. On other store windows, Mort observed people painting 'JUDE!' in large white letters. A few policemen watched the crowd from a distance without intervening.

So, that's what this is, Mort thought, the gravity of it sinking in — *an organized pogrom. That's why the S.S. men were in the trucks. They were directing it. This must*

264

be happening in several parts of the city. *Just this city?* He had seen them in Hanover too. *Why these particular cities?*

Then came the chilling realization. *It's not just these cities. It must be happening all over Germany.* He remembered the newspaper headline he had seen yesterday: "𝕵𝖊𝖜𝖘 𝖒𝖚𝖘𝖙 𝖇𝖊 𝖕𝖚𝖓𝖎𝖘𝖍𝖊𝖉 𝖋𝖔𝖗 𝖙𝖍𝖎𝖘 𝖔𝖚𝖙𝖗𝖆𝖌𝖊𝖔𝖚𝖘 𝖆𝖈𝖙!"

So, this was the punishment, this planned violence. Planned at the top — who else could organize the S.S. this way? Broken windows and painted names he might have expected. *But what was the building burning in the distance?*

Shaken, he started to phone for that whiskey — *a double would be even better* — but then stopped himself. *How would it look to the staff? Why should a Texas oilman, a Gentile, be particularly shaken by what he'd just seen on the street. Who most likely would be shaken up to see this violence perpetrated against Jews? Better not order a double.*

By now, it was dark, and Mort expected the crowds to break up. *They've had their jollies. Time to go home to their Frauen and boast about their heroism.* But the actions didn't stop. If anything, they got worse. Standing on the balcony, Mort could smell smoke and see in the distance fires in several parts of the city, but particularly in one district.

The Jewish quarter? Of course. But what were they burning? The building he'd originally seen was too big to be a home. In fact, it towered over the stores in its stately dignity. *A shul!* he realized. *They're setting the synagogues on fire! And burning everything inside — the Torahs!*

Below his balcony on the street, he could see detachments of S.S. arresting people and herding them into police vans. A few fights had broken out, but they didn't last long. The S.S. had the weapons, and Mort thought he could even hear the faint thuds of clubs denting skulls. In the distance a shot rang out. Then, a few minutes later, another. *So, they're shooting Jews on the street*, Mort thought, sickened. *Out-and-out murder.* Now he could hear sirens — of more police vans coming to arrest Jews. *To take them — where? Surely, there were too many Jews in a city like this to be held in the local jails. Where, then? And — God, Almighty! — I'm in the middle of this!*

The sleep he had hoped for that night dissipated into sporadic dozing, interrupted by street noises: shouts and sirens. In the morning, a pall of smoke hung over the city, and he could still see some fires from his balcony. Shaken, he showered quickly and ordered up breakfast.

Remember! he told himself repeatedly, *a Texas oilman would not be especially upset by all this, just curious.*

Shortly after ten, he received the call he'd been waiting for — von Mecklin calling from the lobby. Would it be convenient for Herr Danforth to come down now? Mecklin was waiting near the elevators. A balding man of medium height, with light brown hair, well-dressed in a blue business suit. He identified Mort immediately, smiled and gave a formal nod, extending his hand.

"Herr Danforth? I hope you had a good trip."

"Very nice, thank you. Is it Herr von Mecklin or just Herr Mecklin?"

"Either way is fine," Mecklin laughed. "I've been called far worse. Should we get some coffee in the dining room?" he gestured. "Come to think of it, have you had breakfast?"

"Yes, thank you," Mort said, noting the other's careful manners. "Have you?"

Mecklin nodded as they were seated near a window. *For once, I don't want to look outside*, Mort thought.

Mort immediately handed Mecklin his business card and received Mecklin's in turn. Then, over coffee, he presented Mecklin with a copy of his company's prospectus.

"As you can see, we're not a large company. But we have been steadily expanding and hope to continue to do so with new clients in Europe, particularly your country."

"I certainly hope we can help you realize that ambition," Mecklin said. "I hope I'm not being impolite, but I am curious. Your German has, as I would have expected, an American accent but not one that sounds like it's from your South. Are you a native Texan?"

"No, I moved there as an adult," Mort said, having rehearsed this answer. "Originally, I'm from Detroit."

"Ah," Mecklin smiled, "the motor city."

"Yes." Mort quickly shifted the conversation off himself. "Now, as I understand it, Germany gets most of her oil right now from Romania, the Ploesti oil fields."

"That is correct," Mecklin nodded. "And secondarily from Russia, although their tanker fleet is old and few in number."

"Well, ours is not," Mort said. "We lease a fleet of up-to-date tankers to send our oil all over the world, though most of it goes to Europe and South America."

For the next hour, they talked business: how many thousands of barrels Germany was looking to import; the approximate price it was willing to pay; tanker space and shipping routes. And the key question: Could Danforth

Oil meet these expectations on a continuous basis? For the approximate costs of a typical tanker full, Mort did some quick math in a small notebook he had brought for the purpose and presented the page to Mecklin for comparisons with Germany's present providers.

Throughout their meeting, Mecklin had been pleasant, well-informed and businesslike. Unlike the man on the train, he wasn't studying Mort. And except for the icebreaker about his accent, he did not ask Mort any questions about his personal life or even about his travels in Germany. He seemed to accept Mort's credentials at face value. Finally, as they seemed to have exhausted the topics pertaining to a sale, Mort produced a large note pad and wrote up a tentative offer.

"We have formal sales proposals, of course, but I just wanted to sketch this one out so that you could consider it."

"Of course," Mecklin said, taking the sheet. "I don't have final authority to approve something this big. In fact, I am just the first link in a chain — I guess that's how you'd phrase it. It must be approved by many people above me."

Including your asshole Fuhrer? Mort thought. But he said, "I understand completely. I too, must run our final proposal by our financial people, though I don't expect any problems there."

As the two rose from the table, Mecklin looked at his watch. "It's nearly twelve. Would you be my guest for lunch? There's a very good restaurant down the avenue a few blocks."

"I would be most pleased," Mort said, trying to sound formal.

As the two approached the hotel's revolving door, Mecklin stopped Mort. "How stupid of me! I forgot what we'd encounter today if we walked out on the street. You've probably already heard some of the commotion. It's a retaliation against the Jews. I don't know if you'd find it very pleasant making our way past broken glass."

Does he know I'm Jewish? Mort worried in a panic. *No, he's just being thoughtful. Or doesn't want to see me vomit.* "No, it's quite all right. Really. We'll walk to our restaurant."

This is going to be difficult, but I must see it through and not flinch. Just how difficult he hadn't imagined. When they'd gone a block, skirting piles of shattered storefront glass, they approached a crowd circling an old, bearded man on his knees scrubbing the sidewalk with a brush while the crowd jeered. Mort felt sick.

"It's in retaliation for the assassination of our Paris diplomat," Mecklin explained.

"Well," Mort replied, hating himself for what he was going to say, "they brought it on themselves. They should have known what to expect if they murder a German official."

"You're quite right," Mecklin said, steering them into the restaurant, the windows of which were intact.

Well, if he ever doubted my being a Gentile before, that should nail it, Mort thought. *My God, this dissembling is awful!* He was also unnerved by someone he saw just behind the circle surrounding the old Jew. In her heavy, oatmeal-textured coat, she looked familiar. *Of course!* It was the old lady who had ridden in his train compartment to Frankfurt. She was looking directly at him and smiling.

He had no appetite and ordered the lightest lunch he could find on the sizable menu. "I had a large breakfast," he explained to Mecklin. When the food arrived, he forced himself to eat. Now that they had finished their business meeting, Mecklin was chatty and curious to learn more about Mort's personal life and background.

So that you can report it to the Gestapo? For each question, however, Mort steered the conversation back to Mecklin, even though he realized his "How about you?" appeared mechanical. *Remember not to use* 'du', he told himself. *We're still on formal terms.* What he learned about Mecklin was as superficial as what he told the German: a degree in business administration from the Munich Business School, several years in the oil business, eventually a seat on the German Trade Commission (its name in German was one long word), married with two children and living in a Frankfurt suburb.

What he didn't tell me, of course, Mort thought, *was when he joined the Nazi Party and if he holds rank in the Gestapo or is just one of their drop-in informers.*

The meal concluded, the two made conventional plans for renewed contact. Each would use the telephone number provided on their business cards. They shook hands outside and went their separate ways. Mort was immensely relieved. *I'm pretty sure it went all right — I don't think I bungled anything.* In a way, he felt guilty about deceiving Mecklin. *He seemed nice enough, but he's going to be really pissed when he finds out that Christopher Danforth has disappeared. Hold on to his business card, though. It may come in handy.*

He made his way carefully back to the Bristol. The old Jew who had scrubbed the sidewalk was gone, as was the crowd around him and the old lady. But there were other actions up and down the street and more sounds of shattering glass.

What bastards! Mort thought, entering the hotel. *And*

not just the S.S. and the Gestapo. Ordinary citizens were enjoying this persecution. What swine they were!

His next assignment was also in Frankfurt, more precisely, in one of its wealthy suburbs. He was to go to the home of a Jewish family and carry out of the country the money they gave him, just as he had carried *in* the money for his Hanover contact. He was scheduled to meet them at 2 p.m. — just enough time to get there in a cab. As it wended its way through the curving, tree-lined streets, Mort studied the imposing mansions set back behind wide lawns, shrubbery and wrought iron fences. Three-story, brick homes with polished wooden doors beneath archways. Prominent bay windows. In front of some homes, servants clipping hedges.

Mort paid off the cab, opened the metal gate and went up the winding walkway. No one answered the door immediately. Eventually, a servant did and showed him in. Coming down the curving staircase was a short, overweight man in a bathrobe, *or perhaps it was more of a smoking jacket*, Mort thought. *We're not going formal for this one.*

"Mr. Danforth?" the man inquired, approaching and putting out a stubby hand. "I'm Hermann Goldstein." Mort identified himself.

"Shall we proceed to our apartment?" the man said turning for Mort to follow him. *Apartment?* Mort thought. *You mean, you don't own this whole mansion?*

As they climbed, the man had obviously read Mort's thoughts. "This used to be my family's home — the entire house. But the Nazis have taken it from us and allowed us to use only the top floor. The rest of it they have rented out to business offices and other families."

He stopped at the first landing to catch his breath, then they continued climbing, and the man continued talking. "They did the same thing with my business. They have an Aryan running it, and I was given a low-level job — and a pittance for a salary."

"What is your business?" Mort asked.

"Export-import," Goldstein replied. "We were once the largest importer of furniture in western Germany. And we had a thriving export business as well — before Hitler."

B.H. Would that be the new B.C.? Mort wondered.

By now, the man was speaking only in short fragments; his labored breathing prevented anything more. He stopped frequently to catch his breath. Mort, too, was feeling winded.

When they reached the top floor, they rested and then entered a spacious room stuffed with furniture from larger rooms. On one sofa sat a pleasant looking middle-aged woman, who rose to greet them.

"This is my wife, Rosa," the man got out between gasps. He immediately sat. "You must excuse me, Herr Danforth. I am an asthmatic, and this climb is very difficult for me. Not that the Nazis care, of course."

Meanwhile, Frau Goldstein approached Mort and greeted him. "It was awfully good of you to come, Herr Danforth."

"Rosa," Goldstein called from his chair, "Danforth is just his pretend name. What's your real name?" he called to Mort.

None of your damn business, Mort thought.

"Let's just stick with Danforth. It's simpler."

"Of course," man replied. "Pardon me for being nosy. You're right. One can't be too careful these days. Well," he said, rising and breathing almost normally, "let's get on with it."

He moved to an ornate desk — *looks like something from Louis XV with all those gilt curlicues*, Mort guessed. Goldstein unlocked a drawer with a key on his watch chain and took out several packets of money.

"Your agency told me to convert my money to large bills so that they wouldn't be too bulky. You have no idea how hard it was to get those large bills. I couldn't do it myself, of course. Jews can't even go into banks now. I had some Gentile friends I trust — former employees — make these conversions in several different banks."

While he spoke, Mort had taken off his sport coat and opened the secret pockets.

"There's about 60,000 *Deutschmarks* here." Goldstein pointed to twelve packets spread on the desktop.

"I don't think I can carry all that," Mort said. "I just have these two pockets inside my coat. Let's see how much we can squeeze in."

"I had hoped you could take it all," the man said peevishly.

If you don't shut up, Mort thought, *I may not take any. Why am I helping this guy? Just because he's Jewish and the Nazis won't let him take out all his precious money himself? Weren't there needier cases he could be helping? Wasn't just about every case needier than this guy's?*

When Mort finished stuffing the two pockets, there were still several packets on the table.

"Hell," the man said, "that's only about half."

"Well, I'm sorry, but that's all I can carry. I can't very well stuff the rest in my pockets and hope to get through the border. They'd arrest me in a minute."

"Please excuse my husband," Mrs. Goldstein said

gently. "He sometimes gets obsessed with the question of money."

"If it were your money, you'd care too, Rosa!"

By now, Mort wanted to be through with this repulsive little man. He turned to Frau Goldstein. "Could you please help me sew the pockets closed? Or perhaps have one of your servants do so?"

"We no longer have servants," Goldstein snapped.

"Of course, I can do it," Frau Goldstein said. "Let me just find some needle and thread."

While she was gone, Mort asked Goldstein the obvious question, "When are you and Frau Goldstein planning to leave Germany?"

"Very soon. In the next few days."

"Are you going straight to Paris?"

"We don't know yet."

Though the answer was reasonable under the circumstances, Mort thought he was being cagey. *Just as well I don't know*, he concluded.

Frau Goldstein returned and set about immediately sewing the pockets closed. While she did so, she said, "It is so good of you to do this for us, Herr Danforth. We realize that you are taking a big risk."

"Yes," Goldstein put in. "We appreciate it."

How, Mort wondered, *could such a nice lady, such a gracious lady, end up with such a jerk? Was it his money? I doubt it. Oh, well.*

When she had finished, he put on his jacket. If fit tightly and bulged over the hidden pockets.

Shit! Anyone looking closely will notice these bulges, he thought. He took it off again and, even though the flaps were sewn shut, he was able to fish out one packet of bills from each pocket and return it to the desk.

"I'm sorry," he said, addressing them both, "but I really can't take any more without it showing."

"That's perfectly all right," Mrs. Goldstein said. "We understand."

Mr. Goldstein said nothing.

"Wait a minute," Goldstein said, as Mort was preparing to leave. "I want a receipt."

He counted the money remaining on the desk and subtracted. "You're taking about 20,000 *Deutschmarks*." Mort quickly signed for it.

As Mort left the room, he turned to the little man.

"Tell me, Herr Goldstein, do you work at being obnoxious, or does it come naturally?"

The nearest cab or tram stop was at least a half hour's walk, but Mort didn't mind. It was a pleasant day, and he needed the exercise. Besides, he couldn't wait to leave. He would return to the Bristol.

I hope to hell the pogrom is over, he thought. *Funny, the two didn't mention it. Not once. Maybe they never left their apartment and didn't hear about it. You'd think they could smell the smoke, though.*

He was glad his final mission, bringing out the two children, was set for tomorrow. Today's assignments were enough for one day. Now, he just wanted a nap, a bath and dinner.

As Mort understood the plan to transport the children, they would take the train to Saarbrücken via Mannheim, about a three-hour trip with a change of trains and a twenty-minute stopover in Mannheim. Once they arrived at the Saarbrücken station, they'd be met by two JRO people who would drive them as close to the border as possible, then hide the car and guide them on foot across the unguarded border. Another JRO person would meet them on the French side and accompany Mort and the children to the nearby train stop, while the first two would recross the border and return to their car. The rest of the ride to Paris, about three hours, would be easy. And someone would meet them at the Gare de l'Est. The plan had been performed successfully many times, Slonsky had assured Mort. To cross the border unseen, they needed to arrive in Saarbrücken at night. So, allowing for travel time, the change of trains and the stopover, they would need to leave Frankfurt at about 15:00. The family had been briefed on the schedule.

After Mort had breakfast and checked out, he cabbed to the train station, checked the times and purchased three tickets for the 15:20 train. Then he checked his bag, left the station and walked towards where the smoke was still curled in the sky, the Jewish section of Frankfurt. Going there was probably unwise, especially if he were being followed, but he had to see for himself the damage the Nazis had done.

He expected bad and found worse. Two more synagogues burned down and numerous shops with broken or defaced windows. A Jewish store owner told him of beatings and arrests of Jews on the streets. Some had been killed. Some may be sent to concentration camps, rumor had it.

"It was awful, just awful," he said near tears. "I saw people I've known for years — Gentiles who worked nearby — throwing chairs through windows, setting stores on fire. I just cannot understand it. The Germans are usually so law-abiding." What Mort saw and heard strengthened his resolve to carry through his mission regardless of the danger.

The Fassinger home was near Grüneburgpark, and after Mort's cab arrived at about 14:30, he told it to wait. The family was expecting him. He introduced himself and was ushered into the living room where the father and the two young children were waiting. Their little suitcases were already packed and standing by the front door. Frau Fassinger introduced her children while her husband looked on unsmiling.

"This is Bruno, and this is his sister, Bonita. Say hello to Herr Danforth, children." She waited while they mumbled their hellos. Mort squatted to gently greet them using their names. Bonita looked to be about five, Bruno seven — younger than the children he had helped escort to Cuba.

Frau Fassinger continued, "Herr Danforth is doing us a very big favor, children. He is accompanying you to your new home in Paris, France."

Before she could say more, Bonita started to wail and clung tightly to her mother's dress. "But I don't want to go, Mummy! I want to stay here with you."

"Why can't you come with us?" Bruno asked.

Herr Fassinger answered gently. "We've already explained why, Bruno. Your mother and I can't leave just yet. The government won't let us. But we'll be coming just as soon as we can. And you'll have a very nice home in Paris with lots of children your own age to play with. Think of that, Bruno, you'll have football games all the time!"

"Is it a long way to Paris, Daddy?" Bonita asked, her voice shaky.

"Not so very long, dear heart. Probably all day today on the train and into the evening. Then you'll be there."

"And you promise you'll come soon?" Bruno asked.

"Yes, dear, we promise," his mother said gently. "But in the meantime, you must be very brave and not cry or complain. You must do just what Herr Danforth tells you to do. He's a nice man and wants you to be safe and happy. Remember, we'll be apart only for a little while."

Mort struggled to overcome the lump in his throat. When he could speak, he briefly reiterated the itinerary and plan to the Fassingers and checked that they had the correct phone numbers for the JRO.

"If anyone asks us, I'm escorting the children to see their grandparents in Saarbrücken—"

"But our grandparents don't live in Saarbrücken," Bonita objected. "Bubbi lives in Frankfurt. And Zadeh isn't alive anymore."

"We know, sweetheart, we know," Mr. Fassinger said, kneeling to get on her level. Thinking of the waiting cab, Mort shifted his weight. "This is just a game we must play with the officials on the train if they ask us," Mr. Fassinger continued. We have to fool them into thinking that's why you're going to Saarbrücken. And you must help Herr Danforth play that game."

"Isn't that lying?" Bonita asked. "You told us never to lie."

"This is one time when it's all right, darling," Frau Fassinger reassured her. "You must get ready to leave now." Mort could hear the tremor in her voice. *She's just barely hanging on*, he realized. *They must be brave in front of the children, but as soon as we leave, they'll break down; I'm sure of that.*

The goodbyes at the door were intense, but brief. The parents knew that lingering would just make things worse. Outside, there was no delay in bundling the children into the cab's back seat with their tiny suitcases.

How awful this all is, Mort thought, *children forcibly separated from their parents. For their own safety. Would they ever meet again? What a barbaric place this is — and yet so civilized on the surface with cabs, hotels, orchestras.*

The first part of the trip, the train to Mannheim, went smoothly. Their compartment wasn't crowded, and Frau Fassinger had provided coloring books and a few crayons to keep the children busy. She also squeezed two story books into their suitcases, which Mort extracted with some difficulty but was glad to have. After about an hour's ride, they exited at Mannheim and waited in the station for the Saarbrücken train. Mort gave Bonita careful instructions about using the rest room, while he waited with Bruno. *How I wish I had Bette with me,* he thought. *God, I hope she doesn't make a mess!* She didn't, and neither did Bruno when it was his turn. Mort, himself, would wait until they were safely ensconced on the Saarbrücken train.

On that train, the trouble began. It started innocuously. The conductor, entering the compartment to check their tickets and visas, made a huge fuss over the children.

"Ach, how darling the little ones are! So nicely dressed. Where are you going, *kinder*?"

"We're going to visit our grandparents in Saarbrücken," Bruno recited.

"Ah, that is so nice. And they are such darlings! I have grandchildren of my own," he beamed at them. To Mort, he was a little less twinkling. "I notice you have a different last name," he said after inspecting their travel visas.

"Yes," Mort said as casually as he could, "I am escorting them, because their father, my business associate, couldn't get away from work, and I was going this way."

"I see," said the conductor, reaching into his pocket. He presented each child with a sucker. "Here you are, my sweethearts, something to make your trip sweeter. *Auf wiedersehen!*"

Five minutes later, an older woman entered their compartment without a suitcase and sat opposite them. Mort silently gasped — he was sure it was the old woman who had ridden with him on the Hanover train to Frankfurt and who had smiled at him during the pogrom outside the Bristol Hotel. She had on the same oatmeal-textured coat with the large pockets and wore the same hat. *She must be tailing me*, Mort realized with alarm. *The conductor must have told her about the different names on the visas, that twinkling son-of-a-bitch!* Then the full gravity struck him — *She's Gestapo!* She smiled at the children, but when her glance fell on Mort it was not friendly. She extracted a small book from her coat pocket and started reading. Mort kept his head down and worked with the children on their coloring books, his mind racing. *How can I leave them to use the toilet? She might arrest them while I'm gone and remove them! It's a risk I'll have to take. It's me she's tailing, anyway.* He made the fastest rest stop he could remember and was relieved to find the children just as he left them. The old lady was still there, of course.

When the food cart came by, Mort bought sandwiches and drinks for the children and himself.

"But I don't like cheese sandwiches," Bonita complained in a whiny voice.

"Just eat your sandwich, Bonita, and be quiet," Bruno told her quietly. She complied.

"That's good, children," Mort whispered to them. "Good job, Bruno," he said even more softly. He went back to quietly reading them their stories. Eventually, Bonita fell asleep.

As they neared Saarbrücken, the old lady made no pretense at reading and stared steadily at Mort, as if daring him to do something or say something.

From this almost absolute calm, events suddenly exploded into action. Their compartment door opened suddenly and two young people, a teenage boy and girl entered. They were dressed in dark clothing, carrying a small satchel.

"The Gestapo is waiting for you at the Saarbrücken station!" the boy said, in English. "We're getting off at the next stop!"

Mort pointed. "This old lady is Gestapo! She's followed me."

Simultaneously, she started to rise and put her hand in her coat pocket. Instantly, the boy smacked her hard with the back of his hand, knocking her back onto the seat. "Pull down the shade, Sylvia!" he commanded, while yanking the old woman's hand out of her pocket and squeezing it so tightly that she gave a cry. Mort imagined that he could hear bones break.

"Tape, Sylvia, get the tape from the bag!" the boy commanded. Holding the old woman's arm with one hand, he reached into her pocket and extracted a small pistol. "Hold on to this!" he commanded Mort, tossing the pistol. The children, meanwhile, were dumbstruck with amazement, terror and fascination. They had moved as far away on the seat as they could get.

With the tape Sylvia handed him from their small satchel, the boy quickly and skillfully taped around the old lady's mouth, avoiding her bite and leaving room for her to breathe through her nose. Then he taped her wrists behind her back. She cried out when he touched the hand he had squeezed.

"Hurry!" Sylvia urged.

"I'm going as fast as I can," the boy responded. He was now taping the old lady's feet together. She tried to kick him until he pinched her calf hard. When that was done, he tied the taped hands to the feet with several rounds of tape. That made the old lady seem to bend backwards in pain. He shoved her to a lying position on the seat and told her in German, "You make a noise, and I'll break your jaw, you Nazi bitch."

"What happens when we get off?" Mort had recovered himself enough to ask.

"We're getting off with you. Can't say more now."

It seemed a small miracle to Mort that the conductor did not come by to announce the station. As the train slowed, Mort had the children and their little suitcases, as well as his own, ready in the aisle. The young couple were waiting in the compartment until the train was stopping, then came out.

Then Mort saw the conductor hurrying toward them from the other end of the car. "But this is not your stop!" he cried. "This is not Saarbrücken!"

"It's our stop, now!" Mort called back to him, as the boy and girl quickly hopped onto the platform and Mort passed the children to them, then tossed them their suitcases, handed over his own, and then jumped off himself holding his briefcase.

"We're parked nearby," the boy said. "We must hurry! The conductor will alert the Gestapo at the Saarbrücken station, and the police will come looking for us."

"I am so grateful to you for alerting us and doing this—" Mort started to say.

"Nothing at all," Sylvia said, as if tying up Gestapo agents and disarming them were a routine part of their job.

Their car was in the station parking lot, as if they were no more than a couple of commuters. "We were going to meet you at the Saarbrücken station when we saw the Gestapo and police gathering," the boy said over his shoulder. "Your conductor must have tipped them off."

"Or that bitch who was following me," Mort added. "I've seen her now three different times."

"They like to use old people for those jobs," Sylvia said. "Less suspicious."

"When I saw her come into our compartment today, I knew we were in trouble."

The boy continued, "So, my friend Johann drove us to two stations ahead to get us on the train there so we could warn you. Then he parked at this station and walked the rest of the way to where we'll meet him. That old lady and the conductor must be having a fine time right now," the boy laughed. "I think I broke a bone in her hand. But at least we got that gun from her." Mort touched it in his pocket. The metal felt cold.

"Do you want it? I didn't think I should carry one."

"We already have one," the boy said. "In the satchel."

Mort was impressed. "You came prepared."

"You'd better be if you're dealing with the Gestapo. They don't fool around."

"Where are we going?" Mort noticed the car had turned off the two-lane road and was now traveling along a dirt one.

"A trail we use to get people across the border," the boy responded. "I'm afraid I won't be able to drive you all the way. We'll have to walk the last 500 meters or so. We've already crossed the Saar River."

Mort turned to the children, who were still frightened and holding hands tightly. "Did you hear that, children? We're going to go for a nice nighttime walk with Sylvia and — I'm sorry, I don't know your name."

"Call me Bertrand."

"And with Herr Bertrand."

By now, the dirt road ended. "All right," Bertrand said, "We must get out now. Then I'm going to pull the car into this brush and cover it up."

There was no trail. Bertrand and Sylvia led the group over ground that rose and fell. The children followed, carrying their suitcases. Mort brought up the rear carrying his suitcase and briefcase. *No matter how short this walk is*, he knew, stumbling when the ground dropped suddenly, *this is not going to be easy. I got spoiled having other people carry my suitcase. If I survive this, I must get in better shape.*

Bruno started to say something, but Bertrand turned immediately and whispered, "No talking now, children. We must be absolutely quiet. We don't want the boogeyman to hear us."

That should do the trick, Mort smiled to himself. *Now, they're scared shitless.*

In the dark, he felt the ground drop abruptly. He stumbled and nearly dropped the suitcase.

"Sssh!" Sylvia whispered. "We're nearly there."

Despite his efforts, Mort had fallen well behind the others. His breathing was labored.

Why the hell did I pack so damn much? And I'm also carrying Goldstein's money, that prick.

At that moment a figure sprang up out of hiding in

front of Mort but behind the others.

"Halt!" he commanded. "Stop right there!"

His back is to me, Mort thought. *Now's my chance!* With his full weight he ran against the figure, knocking him over downhill. "Run!" Mort shouted to the others. "Go!"

Bertrand and Sylvia immediately scooped up the children and started running. Mort came upon the sprawled border guard as he was beginning to pick himself up and kicked him as hard as he could in the face. Twice. The man groaned and dropped to the ground. Mort saw his rifle lying nearby and grabbed it, as he started running after the group. *Better I should have it than him*, he thought. *What a sight I must be, suitcase and briefcase in one hand, rifle in the other!*

Fifty yards on, the group was waiting for him. And there was a new person with them, a man. "We made it!" Sylvia said. "We're in France." The words never sounded sweeter. "This is Johann," she continued. "He'll take you the rest of the way to the train station. We must go back to get our car."

"But you're going to run into that guard," Mort said. "Here's his rifle, by the way."

"Thanks," Bertrand said, taking it. "We might need that."

"How will you avoid the police?" Mort asked.

"Don't worry. So far, they haven't found our route. Running into that border guard was a fluke. Nice work tripping him up, by the way. Did you also have special training?"

"No," said Mort. "I'm just a businessman."

"Well, you did well," Sylvia said. She gave him a quick kiss on the cheek and also kissed the children. "Goodbye, dear ones. Go with Herr Danforth and do what he tells you."

"Watch out for that guard," Mort warned. "He'll be ready to kill you if he finds you."

"Don't worry. We've done this before." Bertrand replied.

"We must be going now," Johann said.

"Come, children," Mort said. "Follow Herr Johann, and I'll be right behind you."

The two groups silently separated.

"Good luck and thanks!" Mort called to the disappearing couple in a stage whisper.

"Thanks. To you too!" Sylvia's voice came back.

After they had gone a little way, Johann turned back to the others. "It's not far to the station. Perhaps 500 meters."

I've heard that before, Mort thought grimly. They had to stop well before the station because the children were exhausted. Johann took up Bruno, and Mort did likewise with Bonita. *There's got to be an easier way*, he thought. "Would you like to ride on my shoulders?" he asked her. She nodded shyly, afraid to admit she was afraid. He kneeled and lifted her on. "Here we go!" *What's the German for 'upsy-daisy'?* Carefully, he rose again, took his suitcase and briefcase and her little bag, and the group continued. *I must not stumble*, Mort thought, *I must not!*

Soon, the station was in sight, brightly lit. It was an uphill climb, but Mort made it without stumbling. Every time he hit a bump, Bonita giggled. *She's enjoying this!* Mort realized. *Her piggy-back ride for the night.*

In the station, Johann said a brief goodbye.

"What will happen to Bertrand and Sylvia? Where will they go?" Mort whispered.

"Back to their homes," Johann was intentionally vague. "They'll be all right. We've done this several times."

"Goodbye and thank you again," Mort said, shaking his hand.

When Johann was gone, he checked on the next train to Paris. 21:00. It was now 20:35. It seemed like at least three hours had passed since Bertrand and Sylvia had burst into the compartment. He bought three tickets and returned to the children. They were the only ones waiting in the station. Of course, they both needed to use the toilet. Mort told Bonita to go first since there was only one rest room.

After all the excitement of the border crossing, he felt a huge letdown emotionally. He also noticed he was trembling — or shivering from the cold. And he was famished. But he had lots of time to review the events.

The only thing I would do differently would be to charge that guard with the suitcase. That would have really sent him flying. But running into him with full force was good enough. Could the Germans apprehend us here? How could they? We're in France where they have no authority. Just wait for the train and don't think about how hungry you are. The kids are probably hungry too, but they haven't complained. Good kids.

He pulled the story book from Bruno's suitcase and started reading them a story. They were out in two minutes, sleeping on the hard bench.

At French Customs, the sleepy officials studied their visas and Mort's passport.

"Why are your names different?" one bored official asked. Mort gave him the prepared story, only now in French and the grandparents now lived in Paris rather than Saarbrücken.

"I'm surprised the Boche didn't stop you," he said. "They're always on the lookout for Jewish children being smuggled out." He was eyeing the children. "But so long as they have travel visas for France, we have no problem with them. And your passport is good," he said, handing over the papers."

"Thank you," Mort said. *If he had made a fuss, I don't know what I'd have done at this point — either cry or attack him.*

By 23:30, the train finally arrived at Gare de l'Est, and Mort escorted the sleepy children, carefully lifting them and their little suitcases off the train into the waiting hands of the welcoming committee on the platform: Bette, Slonsky, and a woman he didn't know.

Bette gave him a quick kiss and squeezed his hand. As the women fussed over the children and gave them rolls that they carried, Slonsky said to him, "Excellent work! We received a signal from our people in Saarbrücken that you made it through. You can fill us in on the details tomorrow morning. It's okay to come to the JRO office since you've already blown your cover. See you at ten?"

"That's fine," Mort said. "What about Goldstein's money?"

"Bring it with you tomorrow." They were already leaving.

Mort fell asleep in the cab taking him back to his hotel.

The next morning, he was late for the ten o'clock meeting, but he didn't care. He had slept like the dead — overslept — and had his American breakfast in a nearby restaurant. Arno Steelbach was waiting with Slonsky. Right away, Mort cut open his concealed pockets, removed the money packets and handed them over, glad to be free of that responsibility. He mentioned, almost laughing, how angry Goldstein was that Mort couldn't carry out more money. Then he reviewed the trip, mentioning the suspicious, argumentative man on the Frankfurt train and, of course, the old Gestapo woman that Bertrand had taken care of.

When he had finished narrating their close escape on foot, Steelbach didn't look pleased and spoke up. "Well, you made a real dog's breakfast of that escape. Now, we can't use Saarbrücken anymore. Our agents there were lucky to escape with their lives, which would have been forfeit, you realize, had they been caught."

"They were splendid," Mort put in before defending himself. "I did the best I could. I really don't know how they got on to me."

"They were probably on to you before you left Paris," Slonsky observed dryly. "For long distances, they work in tandem You probably never saw the one tailing you from Paris to Saarbrücken. The second one — the man who conversed with you — was probably higher-ranking Gestapo and decided to have some fun debating you. Then he turned you over to the old lady."

"What did you see regarding the *Kristallnacht*?" Steelbach wanted to know. "That's what the bastards are calling it now. Likewise, the press."

"Just what I told you. Synagogues on fire; Jewish shop windows broken or defaced; Jews arrested, beaten up, humiliated on the streets — the old man having to scrub the sidewalk."

"They've sent many thousands of Jews to concentration camps in that action," Steelbach said.

"And killed at least a hundred, we've determined," Slonsky added. "It looks to us here like the Nazis have passed some sort of turning point regarding the Jews. They're no longer satisfied with denying them citizenship and basic rights. Now, they're finding excuses to kill or imprison them. Our work has become all the more important."

"And all the more difficult, since we can no longer use Saarbrücken as a crossing point," Steelbach added.

"It wasn't my fault that we got stopped," Mort said defensively. "And at least we did get the children through."

"Yes, you did," Slonsky agreed, "and that's to be commended. So, what are your plans now?"

Mort sensed dismissal. "Should I assume I'm no longer of value to you for missions into Germany?"

Slonsky considered, then said, "That is correct for the time being. You are now known to the Gestapo. They probably have your picture — they sometimes carry miniature cameras, you know. And we'll no longer be able to pull that traveling businessman ruse — at least not in Western Germany where you used it. And probably not anywhere else. Still, you've done an excellent job. You carried out all four assignments. But now it's time to think about going home."

Yes, thought Mort. *With or without Bette.* He had to admit to himself that he was relieved to have finished being a secret agent. *Not really in my line, a middle-aged businessman with a heart murmur. Better to leave it for younger people like Bertrand and Sylvia. Still, I did what I came here to do. I'll have that to remember during my boring life.*

"What about the children's parents?" he asked. "The Fassingers. Can they get out?"

"It's doubtful," Slonsky replied. "The Germans make it more difficult each day. I frankly don't understand why, since they want to get rid of their Jews. They should be making it easier to leave, not harder."

"Poor kids. So, they're effectively orphans."

"For now. But they're safe."

Safety comes at a high price these days, Mort reflected. *With sorrow*.

Seeing Bette again was a pure delight. She was fascinated by all the details of his missions, laughed at his characterization of Goldstein and almost gasped when he described how the border guard sprang up out of hiding. A line from Shakespeare popped out of his memory: *She loved me for the dangers I had passed, and I loved her that she did pity them. Othello, about courting Desdemona*, he recalled. *Well, that one didn't work out so well*, he thought.

"My brave darling," she said, embracing him. I never would have guessed that you had it in you to take on such dangerous work. That was wonderful how you knocked over that border guard and grabbed his rifle!"

"Well, Bertrand and Sylvia were the real heroes. They rescued us from that old Gestapo lady and kept us from being apprehended at Saarbrücken. Such gutsy kids! Boy, there's one old lady who won't forget them, even after her hand heals. Now, what about us?"

"What do you mean, 'what about us?'" Bette sounded a little uneasy. "We're together again, aren't we?" They'd been talking in Bette's bed.

"Yes, and it's lovely — for now. But what about the future?"

"Don't think about the future, darling Mort. You can't control it anyway. Live for now, the present. And we have each other, here and now."

"It's a lovely thought, Bette, but I have to return to America. My kids are there. And my business. Would you consider coming with me, either as you are now, or as Mrs. Morton Stein?"

Just like that, with no prior planning, Mort Stein had proposed. *It seemed like the right time to ask*, he told himself. *We have to settle this one way or the other. And I don't want to lose her.*

"How could I do that, darling? Leave my work? My parents? Leave Paris?"

The triple whammy, Mort sighed to himself. *I've heard this before.*

"You could find the same kind of work in America, in Detroit. Working with relief agencies, I mean. It's true there's no JRO office in Detroit, but there are other Jewish relief agencies. And I'm pretty sure I could get entrance visas for your parents, since the JRO has contacts in the State Department. That is, if they want to come."

"I don't think they would," Bette said. "They're already settled here and have good jobs."

"There are all kinds of teaching jobs available in Detroit. And administrative jobs," Mort said, knowing he was bluffing and feeling like a salesman making a pitch, responding point by point to a customer's objections. It was a losing proposition. "Your parents speak English, I think you said once."

"Yes, they're fluent," Bette said. "You'll see that when you come over for dinner. But would they want to give up what they already have?"

"I don't know. You'd have to ask them if *you* wanted to come yourself."

She furrowed her brow. "It's all pretty sudden. Give me some time to think about it."

"How much time? I hate to press you, but I have to return soon. I've been away almost two months. So, I need to know. We could get married here before we leave and start the process for getting your American citizenship."

"It's a pretty big step. Several, in fact."

"Do you love me?" Mort asked. *Might as well play my ace. Or is it a deuce? Nothing to lose.*

Bette hesitated. "Yes, Mort, I think I do, even though I haven't known you that long."

"In this world, and in these times, it's hard to know people a long time. At least you've seen that I'm pretty good with children."

"That's true," Bette agreed. "Let me think about it, dear heart."

"The funny thing is," Mort said, "is that I didn't think about it — not consciously — before I asked you. I just knew I wanted to do it, to propose."

"That is funny," Bette agreed.

"Now, what were you saying about your parents having me to dinner?"

They were together often in the next few days, but Mort knew better than to nag Bette about deciding. That Sunday night, her parents invited him to dinner. They were cordial to him, interested in his background and reasons for helping the JRO, and Madame Schiller's dinner was delicious. Finally, about three days after he had proposed, Bette gave him her decision.

"I love you, darling, but I just don't think I can leave right now. And my parents don't want to, just as I'd expected."

"What did they think about your marrying me?"

"They like you, you know that. But they think you're too old for me. And you have a family in the United

States. I don't agree with them about your being too old; I've told you that. Still, I just don't think I can right now. I'm needed here. And here is where I want to be."

It felt like he had swallowed a lead weight. "I see," he said. "Just one last question. You know and I know that there's going to be a war. Hitler will never stop until England and France stand up to him. It may come this year or next year. Over the rest of Czechoslovakia or over Poland or some other place. But it's coming, that's for sure."

"We know that," Bette sounded a little impatient. "What's your question?"

"What if Hitler attacks France — and wins? What will you do then?"

"That isn't clear right now. We'll have to see how things play out. At worst, I suppose we'd try to get out of France."

"Along with countless others," Mort added. "And where would you go? At least, I'm offering you a way out now, to a much safer place. That safety might not matter much to you — you're young — but I bet it would matter to your parents."

"Don't you think they've already considered those dangers, that we all have?"

"And they still want to stay?"

"They don't want to move — again — be uprooted again. They're not young, Mort, and they've already had to completely — I don't know what the right word is — reassemble? — reassemble their whole lives and professions, even their speech, to make one escape. I honestly don't know if they could handle another."

"I understand, Bette. But the Germans might not leave them a choice if they invade."

"They know that. Believe me, they know it. It's a question of having the will to uproot themselves *before* being forced to. And I certainly can't force them to do so."

"I understand, Bette. Well, I tried."

"Yes, you tried. Now stop wrinkling your brow and give me a big hug. Or have you decided to drop me because I won't marry you?"

"No, no. You know I still love you, Bette. I really wonder if I'll ever find anyone else as nice as you. As close to my heart as you are."

"You will Mort. Once you get resettled in Detroit. Eventually, you'll meet a nice Jewish woman who isn't living on the edge of a precipice, and you can settle down with her, in safe America."

"Maybe, but I can't see it," Mort said.

He had been in Europe for exactly two months, longer than he'd planned, and he was anxious to get back to Detroit. But before he left, he visited the refugee children's center in Paris, the same one he had gone to before to help escort the eleven children. He wanted to check on how Bruno and Bonita were getting along. When he arrived, Bruno was outside, kicking a soccer ball with several other boys in the small back yard. Bonita was playing with some other girls in a room. The woman in charge of the center assured him that the two children had acclimated well and had made friends. But they were homesick for their parents and asked constantly when they were coming. It was painful not to give them a definite answer. The woman sighed. "But that is what all these children have had to go through — those who still have living parents, that is. We can only hope that the Fassingers will find some way to get here."

"*Yes,*" Mort thought gloomily, *some way before the roof*

caves in and there's another war. But how? Well, that's one I can't solve, or even work on. Someone else will have to help them. But how? he kept wondering. *How?*

Slonsky and the other JRO people, including Bette, threw him a going away party the day before his boat train left Paris. It was in the JRO offices and was quite merry, with champagne and cognac, as well as a nice rum cake from a nearby bakery.

"We appreciate very much what you have done," Slonsky said. "You have helped more than you realize. Not just with the money transfers. These children you helped bring out — they will grow into adults and have children of their own. And so on. The benefits will keep multiplying. And you helped make that possible."

Even Arno Steelbach had dropped his acerbic attitude toward Mort's rescue mission and was friendly.

"Goodbye, Mr. Stein. I'm sorry I was so critical about the rescue mission. The problems you ran into couldn't be helped. And you performed very well indeed, thinking on your feet. That border guard will remember your shoes, I'm sure," he laughed. "So, happy landings in Detroit, and please don't stop raising money for us. We need it now more than ever."

"I really wish I could stay to keep helping," Mort responded. "But..." he shrugged.

"We understand completely," Slonsky replied.

Bette had been standing beside him, quietly. Now she took him to a quiet corner.

"Will I see you again?"

"How about tonight? My last night."

"Of course. Pick me up at seven," she gave his hand a squeeze.

They went to Bette's favorite restaurant, had a quiet meal, then back to her apartment to make love and say goodbye. The parting wasn't as difficult as Mort had expected. They had both steeled themselves for it, Mort having reluctantly accepted the inevitable.

"If you change your mind," he said, feigning light-heartedness, "my train for Le Havre leaves at eight-thirty. The captain can marry us on board the ship."

"Please don't be funny," Bette said. "It's not a time for humor. And please don't forget me. I'll write. You write, too."

"Of course," Mort agreed, wondering how long that would last.

Then he went back to his hotel to pack. *Tomorrow would be a long day.*

Part IV: A New Life

Morton Stein married exactly as Bette had predicted, except that his bride, Deborah Hofstadter, was just discovering her Jewish heritage. In fact, that was how they met. She had attended a fundraiser he gave in January 1939 at a Reform temple she was considering joining. Temple Beth-El, on Woodward Avenue, was fifteen miles from her home in Birmingham, a wealthy suburb where many auto executives but almost no Jews lived. Socially, the locales were worlds apart. At the end of Mort's talk she had asked some questions, and when he met with the audience, she asked him some more and gave him a check. She was about his age, not beautiful, but her dark blue eyes exuded warmth. Before the evening ended, they were having coffee together.

Deborah was a widow; her late husband, a General Motors executive, had died of a heart attack in his early fifties. She had no children. After they'd gone out a few times, she told Mort, "I'm not looking to have any children of my own. I hope that won't be a problem."

"I don't see why it should be," Mort replied taking her hand. "I feel that I've already paid my dues raising three kids, well, one since my divorce."

Deborah worked in public relations for Chevrolet in the GM Building on Grand Boulevard. It was only after her husband's death that she began to explore her Jewish roots by attending adult education courses in Jewish history and culture. Her parents were Jewish, but thoroughly assimilated. She had been raised in a secular home, celebrated Christmas culturally and, as part of her late husband's circle, had casually absorbed, or at least heard often, its anti-Semitism.

"It was water off a duck's back," she assured Mort.

Deborah saw her rediscovery as making a definite break from that executive culture of country clubs and cocktail gossip. Since Mort was beginning his own Jewish rediscovery, they found they were not just compatible but sharing a mutual journey. She was fascinated by Mort's adventures in Europe.

The two went out often in the months following their first meeting. They discovered other shared interests: classical music, reading and history, good food and wine. Deborah was a first-rate cook — it was one of her hobbies — and Mort was glad to have her over to practice it and, of course, get to know Edward. He was more cautious about introducing her to the rest of the family until he was sure the relationship would take. He'd been burned before. Finally, in March, they began to discuss marriage. Apart from a few close friends, Deborah wasn't interested in keeping her social ties to her late husband's friends; seeing some of them at work was enough. And she knew what they'd think about her marrying a Jew. The date was set for early April, followed by a honeymoon to Miami Beach.

By now, mid-March, Miriam and David had invited the couple and Edward to a Sunday dinner at their flat, and Mort was keen to see how the family would react to Deborah. It went well, and he was pleased. Even Sarah seemed interested. Miriam kept her acerbic tongue under control as she provided a fine dinner. Afterward, Deborah confessed that she thought it a little odd that he was still seeing his ex-wife socially, until Mort explained that she met with David and himself on Sundays to go over the books and that the dinners that followed were a tradition.

Separately, he had Uncle Yitzhak and Aunt Minna, as

well as Chava and Anna, come for dinner to sample Deborah's cooking. As always, Yitzhak was the life of the party, regaling them with his adventures learning golf in his retirement.

They decided to reinforce their discovery of Jewish traditions by having a Jewish wedding instead of a civil ceremony. This meant finding a Reform rabbi willing to marry them since neither was yet a practicing Jew. Mort did insist on one tradition, however: stepping on the glass and breaking it at the end of the ceremony.

"It adds a dramatic touch," he explained. "And it drives off the evil spirits," he added with a wink.

"It does seem medieval," Deborah agreed doubtfully, "but sure, why not?" After the marriage in the rabbi's study, the extended family, including Miriam and David, went to Lelli's, an Italian restaurant that had just opened on Grand Boulevard, which Deborah had discovered. It was outstanding, a blend of Italian food and perfectly grilled steaks.

Three weeks before the marriage, Europe experienced another war crisis. Destroying the Munich agreement, Hitler occupied the remainder of Czechoslovakia. Now, finally, he had forced England and France to draw the line; any further German aggression meant war. It was clear that Hitler had his eye on Poland next, especially the international port of Danzig and its land corridor, quirky artifacts of the Versailles Treaty. Poland was where the issue of war or peace would be decided, Mort observed to Deborah. The question was when. He still tended to turn his observations of current events into mini-lectures, but so far Deborah had tolerated them well and responded with her own views. Essentially, the two thought alike. Deborah said she sympathized with his guilt about not being with the JRO in Paris as war loomed — sympathized in theory. But she obviously wanted her new husband to stay with her in Detroit. And that was what he wanted too, he reluctantly admitted to himself. The reasons for staying put were just too weighty to ignore. As he reflected on his experiences in Germany, especially his narrow escape, he realized that he was too old for such risks. He had responsibilities to other people: to his children and now to Deborah. And responsibilities to his business and to David. He couldn't keep taking leaves of absence. He cited those reasons in reassuring Deborah.

His business continued to do well, especially after Mort resumed the reins of his three stations. When he suspected that one of his managers was skimming, he patiently went over receipts, deposits and gallons purchased with the man, instead of accusing him. When the man couldn't explain the discrepancies, Mort just stared at him while he sweated.

"You were skimming, weren't you?" Mort finally asked. "How much? $10 a day? $15?"

The man confessed, and Mort fired him. He hated doing that, not only because the man had worked for him for several years, but because now he'd have to interview replacements.

Meeting with David each week to go over receipts and expenditures, Mort was more convinced than ever that David, too, was putting his hand in the till. The profits on his three stations were always about $100 a week less than Mort's.

Well, Mort thought, *that's his problem — and Miriam's*. He was glad he had insisted when they resumed their partnership that each keep the profits on his own stations rather than pool them.

He's probably trying to cover his gambling debts, Mort guessed. *Poor Miriam. Does she know she married a loser? Of course she does.*

He wasn't the least bit surprised, therefore, when Miriam announced at a Sunday dinner that she had intended to go back to work as a secretary for the law firm where she had worked years earlier. A friend had told her about the opening, and the firm was happy to have her back. She would try to keep doing the partners' bookkeeping too — for the time being. Sarah and Andrew were old enough to be on their own after school. Mort doubted that but said nothing except to wish her good luck. David was silent during Miriam's announcement. *He looks abashed,* Mort thought.

After their marriage and honeymoon, Deborah sold her home in Birmingham and moved into Mort's flat in the Dexter-Davison neighborhood. *I wonder how many women would have been willing to make that kind of move,* he reflected, *from an upper-class Gentile neighborhood to a middle-class Jewish one.* Deborah — he preferred her full name to 'Deb' or 'Debbie', which her late husband and their friends had called her — immediately set about redecorating the flat: tastefully, but thoroughly. Money was not an issue given her salary, the proceeds from her home sale and her inheritance, though Mort insisted on paying his share of the improvements. Just as with the gas stations, he opposed combining their assets: Deborah's money should be kept separately. He couldn't explain why, exactly, just that he didn't want her to feel that he was taking advantage of her wealth.

Neither Mort nor Edward minded seeing their bachelor quarters, with its haphazard collection of worn furniture and few kitchen utensils, transformed by new paint, carpeting, furniture and up-to-date cookware from Hudson's. Deborah did retain Elsie, their housekeeper and cook, since Deborah's job at GM left her only the weekends free. One advantage of her new home, however, was a much shorter commute.

"Just a few minutes!" she marveled. "Before, we always ate at eight o'clock or ate out. Now, we can eat at seven or even six, like other people."

Mort's family took to Deborah immediately, especially after she had them over for one of her gourmet meals. But more than that, they were drawn to her genuine warmth. The exception, predictably, was Miriam. She sniffed as she looked at the new furniture and redecoration.

"So, you married into money," she said to Mort when they were alone. "Well, good for you. I'm happy for you."

"No, you're not," Mort shot back. "You're jealous. And you know damn well I didn't marry her for her money. I didn't even know about it when I proposed. And anyway, I'm not hurting." This last was obviously a dart, since he knew that Miriam and David were just getting by, and Miriam's new job didn't pay much. They carefully excluded David's haphazard earnings from the discussion. Though Miriam didn't say so explicitly, she wasn't especially pleased to see Deborah accompany Mort and Edward at the carry-out Sunday meals at her flat. In turn, Deborah sensed Miriam's coolness and found a plausible reason for not accompanying him: a Sunday bridge club, about her only remaining tie to her Birmingham friends.

Since returning to Europe was no longer feasible, Mort threw himself into the one thing he could do for European Jews, fundraising, and into the recovery of his own Jewishness. Thinking about his previously secular attitudes, he realized that for years he'd had little say over them; they were largely shaped first by his stingy father, who wouldn't even pay for his son's *Cheder* and *Bar Mitzvah*, and second by Miriam, who had reneged on raising their children Jewish. He and Deborah decided to start attending Friday night services regularly at Temple Beth-El. It was the logical choice; its rabbi had married them, so they already felt a part of its congregation. And its Reform service was nearly all in English. There, and at the JCC courses on Monday nights, they found other couples who were also rediscovering their roots. And so, they gradually became part of a social network of these 'renewed' Jews.

Mort knew there was trouble as soon as he heard Elsie's voice on the phone. She almost never called him since he was hard to reach, usually at one or another of his three stations or in transit.

"I'm sorry to bother you, Mr. Stein, but there are two men here from the government, and they want to see Edward!"

"Edward? What for?"

"They won't tell me, Mr. Stein. They're from the FBI!" Her alarm was audible.

My God! What had he done? "All right, Elsie. Tell them I'll be there in about ten minutes. Could you make them some coffee while they wait?"

What could Edward have done? Mort wondered as he drove hurriedly home. *It was only a week ago that he had graduated from Central High* magna cum laude. All the family had proudly watched him accept his honors and celebrated afterwards at Mort and Deborah's home. *And now this? The boy was never in trouble. Never. And the FBI for God's sake! What in the world's going on?*

They were FBI, all right. Two men in dark suits and white shirts, one flashing his ID to Mort.

"What's this all about?" Mort asked, after identifying himself.

One of them explained, "Your son apparently published an article in a technical journal, and the article made reference to a device that's still considered secret by our government. That's all the technical people would tell us."

Thinking back, Mort recalled Edward mentioning an article he had recently published. Typically, Edward had been matter-of-fact, referring to it almost in passing. Mort had planned to read it though he couldn't make heads or tails of Edward's summary. *Could that have caused all this fuss?*

The agent continued, "They'd like to meet with your son to find out how he came upon this information. Does he work in a laboratory? Where is he right now?"

"Right now, he's working in the repair department of Philco Radio on Dexter Avenue. I'll call him. It's not far from here, and he can be home in ten minutes."

"That won't be necessary, for now. You see, we're just sort of the advance guard in this matter, Mr. Stein, to make sure there's nothing illegal going on. It's the two technical people who want to talk with him. When does he come home from work?"

"I don't know exactly." He turned toward Elsie, who was listening from the kitchen.

"4:30, five o'clock at the latest," she said through the open door.

"Very well," the two men stood as if to go. "The two

technical people will be here at five. Meanwhile, we just have a few questions. Routine."

"My son's a good boy," Mort interjected. "He's just graduated from Central High. *Magna cum laude*. He's never been in any kind of trouble. Never."

"We know. We checked. Does Edward have a laboratory somewhere, say in the basement?"

"Well, I wouldn't call it a laboratory exactly, but, yes, it's in the basement. I'll show you."

When they had seen the scattered collection of radio tubes, wires, antennae, tools and the oscilloscope on a table, surrounded by various technical magazines, they weren't impressed. "That's all there is?"

"That's it," Mort replied.

"Does Edward belong to any political groups?"

"You mean, like the Communist Party?" Mort couldn't resist the sarcasm. "C'mon. He's just a high school student. Or was."

"Well, we noticed that you, Mr. Stein, have made several trips to Europe in the past few years."

Mort briefly explained the trips.

"You're not an agent working for another country?"

"No, certainly not. And if I were, do you think I'd admit it?"

"But Stein is a German name."

"It's also a Jewish name. I was born in Russia, and I emigrated in 1912. I still have my naturalization papers. I hate the Germans, the Nazis."

"All right, I think we've covered the basics," the leader of the two said. "Thank you for your time, Mr. Stein. The technical people will be here at five."

Before they arrived, Edward, coming in at 4:30, just had time to explain to Mort the basic principles of radar and the gist of the article he'd published in *Technology Today*.

"It has to do with how powerful the radio waves are which a transmitter sends out. Obviously, the stronger the better, since they can go out further before bouncing back after they hit something. My article was about something I had read about somewhere — I think it was a British journal. Anyhow, it's called a 'cavity magnetron', and it has the potential to increase the power of the radio waves many times."

To Mort, it sounded like something out of *Buck Rogers*.

"You didn't build one of these magnetrons, did you?" he asked.

"Oh no," Edward said. "That would require a lot more technology and materials and tools than I have. That's laboratory stuff. My article was just theoretical."

"Well, it obviously made an impression on somebody, or the FBI wouldn't have been talking to us."

"Suppose so," was all Edward would say. Mort called Deborah at work to prepare her for what she'd encounter.

The two men arrived promptly at 5:00. One wore a rumpled brown suit, the other a blue suit with white socks. They looked to be in their thirties and certainly didn't look like police. They introduced themselves — one was from General Electric Corporation, the other from Bell Labs. Edward showed them his messy lab. Essentially, they wanted to know how he had learned about the cavity magnetron and how he knew so much about radar. Edward, obviously flattered, explained how his long interest in radio waves had morphed into the newly developing radar. The acronym still sounded weird to Mort. *Like a science fiction 'ray gun'.*

"My writing about the magnetron was just speculative," Edward concluded.

"Let me ask you gentlemen something that's been worrying me," Mort interjected. "Has my son violated some sort of state secret by publishing this article? That's what the two FBI men implied."

The two men looked at each other briefly, then the blue suit spoke up. "Technically no, Mr. Stein. The magnetron isn't *our* secret because we haven't yet built one. Yet. But—" and here he took in everybody in the room — "this must remain confidential. The British *have* developed a magnetron, a good one, and are applying it to the new radar stations they're building on their coast. In case war comes. One of their scientists was the one who spotted Edward's article and immediately contacted us. You see, unofficially Bell Labs and General Electric are working with the British on this device, though the Brits' research is clearly in the forefront. So, we contacted the FBI and here we are. Our collaboration, by the way, is not something we're making public. So again, this is strictly confidential."

The other man turned toward Edward. "If you don't mind telling us, what are your plans now that you've graduated? Are you going to college?"

Edward told them what he'd earlier told Mort about not going to college. "I'd like to find a corporation or a research agency to work for, where I could learn more about radar and maybe help develop it."

The two men smiled. Brown suit spoke up. "I don't think you'll have a problem finding a position, Edward. Usually, we prefer to have employees with a college degree. But anyone who has developed this level of expertise on his own, as you have, would obviously be slowed down by college. And with the way things are in the world today, we don't need slowness. We need speed." Here, he looked at his partner, who nodded. "So, I think you can expect to hear from us in the very near future about a job offer. And to calm our friends across the ocean, please don't publish any more speculative articles."

The two men rose, shook hands with Edward and Mort and left, just as Deborah was coming in. The family collapsed into excited talk, and Edward just smiled like the Cheshire Cat.

Three weeks later, just as the corporate men had predicted, Edward received an invitation for a formal interview at General Electric in Schenectady, New York. A job offer soon followed. From the $50 a week he was making as supervisor at Philco Repair, he'd now be making $150.

"It means I'd be living in Schenectady, but that's no problem," Edward said. "Just think of the research lab and materials I'd have at hand. Not to mention working with their top researchers! It's like a dream come true!" Mort had never seen him so excited. "They want me to start in two weeks," Edward continued, "so I better start packing."

"And all because you published one article," Mort said with wonderment.

"Well, I would probably have applied there anyway even if I hadn't published it. But it really sped things up."

Several weeks later, after Edward had settled into his new job and, with Mort's help, found a one-bedroom apartment over a store, he called his family long distance with exciting news. "They want me to go to England, with a few of my colleagues, to inspect how England is developing its radar stations! That's confidential, of course."

"That's wonderful, Edward!" Deborah replied, sharing the receiver with Mort. "We're so happy for you! When do you leave?"

"I don't know yet. It's all very hush-hush. Officially, America is not England's ally, remember. But unofficially, we are. And we're trying to get up to speed ASAP on stuff like radar. But we still keep it on the QT."

Mort was struck not only by how fast General Electric — really, the government — was moving, but also at Edward's professional use of 'colleagues' and his offhand abbreviations — 'ASAP', 'QT' — obviously, the lingo of his workplace. Mort and Deborah were still acclimating to his absence. Suddenly, there was another empty bedroom in the flat. (Deborah confessed she didn't mind seeing the clutter and dust of his basement 'lab' gone). It had all happened so suddenly.

One day he's a high school student, Mort mused, *the next he's a researcher, a 'colleague', traveling to England to study England's secret defensive weapon, and all at the government's expense. It's all very disorienting. Well, perhaps that's how the family had felt about my trips to Europe — a sudden change from the predictable Mort.*

Edward's news also drove home how imminent the next war seemed for England. *They're not just going to wait around for Hitler to bomb them*, Mort thought. *They're taking measures now. They're getting ready. And I suppose that secretly, that's what we're doing too — belatedly — in research anyway. On the 'QT'. But on the surface — building up our Army and weapons — it looks like we're doing absolutely nothing.*

In early August, a postcard from Edward arrived postmarked London. It was typically laconic.

England is cool.

Well, at least he's safely across, Mort thought. *Wonder how long he'll stay?*

Mort had a few friends whom he considered leftists: communists or fellow travelers. Those few had often justified their pro-communism by citing Russia's 'Popular Front' — its implacable opposition to Nazi Germany at a time when the Western democracies did nothing to oppose Hitler. Russia's support of the Spanish Republic in the Spanish Civil War, his friends said, was a perfect example of its anti-fascism. Hitler and Mussolini aided Franco's fascists, of course. But when Stalin signed a 'Non-Aggression Pact' with Nazi Germany in late August 1939, Mort's communist friends were dumbfounded. One even resigned from the Party. Mort, too, was confused by Stalin's about-face. *How could Russia, after years of proclaiming its anti-fascism, now shake hands with the devil?*

A little over a week later, on September first, Germany invaded Poland. Two days later, England and France fulfilled their pledges to embattled Poland and declared war on Germany. Now it was partly clear — to Mort and to the world — why the former enemies signed the Non-Aggression Pact. Hitler wanted to make sure his invasion of Poland would not be opposed by Russia. A few weeks later, when the German Army stopped short of occupying all of Poland, Russian troops moved into the eastern part. Now, Russia's benefit from the Pact became clearer. *Essentially, they just carved up the country between them,*

Mort concluded. And Stalin still wasn't through — Russian armies occupied the Baltic countries: Lithuania, Latvia and Estonia. In late November, Russia even invaded Finland, but that one didn't go well for them initially. The Finns fought back effectively by putting their soldiers on skis in the winter weather.

The one thing Mort couldn't understand as he read the news stories that fall was why Hitler would want Poland in the first place. It contained about three million Jews, a large percentage living on the German side. Here was Germany, a country that hated and persecuted Jews, that had tried to force them out and had largely succeeded, reducing its Jewish population by half since Hitler took power. And it now inherited a million or more Jews.

What would they do with them all? Mort wondered with dread. *Even Poland hadn't been successful in trying to rid itself of its Jews*, he recalled. And now all the Jews in these countries — as well as in Austria and Czechoslovakia — were essentially trapped. The borders were closed. Emigration, such as it was, had stopped. *What could agencies like the JRO do?*

The German Army had sliced through its half of Poland with ease. *What a pathetic situation*, Mort thought, *Polish cavalry opposing Hitler's tanks*. Germany gave a preview of how it would fight this new war in its merciless bombing of Warsaw, a bombing of civilians. *Magda was right in the center of it*, Mort realized with a start. *Did she survive the bombings? Perhaps her family was able to escape. But to where? More likely, they were trapped in their own country, facing the Nazis. Was this what Paris could expect? And London? And scores of other French and English cities?* Mort had read that England was already evacuating its children to safer, more remote areas.

And what about America? President Roosevelt had called it a European war, which America did not want to get involved in. Well, he got that right, Mort thought glumly. *No one here cares who Hitler invades or what he does to the Jews, just so long as* we're *safe, so long as we can still go to baseball games, listen to our favorite radio shows, and go to the movies. So long as we have enough to eat. In fact, we can even profit from Europe's misfortune by selling arms to the Allies, just as we did in World War I. Only the current neutrality laws prevented this, but how long will those last? And everyone, it seemed, remembered their disillusionment about Wilson's grandiose ambitions that led America into the Great War. We were suckered by the British and the French — that's the prevailing attitude now. But not this time. This time, we'll stay out and keep staying out.*

As much as Mort wanted to see America oppose Hitler and side with the Allies, he could understand this profound distrust and isolationism. *But what if England and France couldn't stand up to Hitler?* He recalled Arno Steelbach's confidence that the French had the weapons and manpower to stop Hitler. *I wonder if he still feels that way.*

Mort had already written to Bette in April, telling her of his marriage. A return letter, some weeks later, was brief. She was happy for his marriage, of course — hadn't she predicted it before he left? — and wished them well. Meanwhile, her work for the JRO continued. That was all. Now, in late September, Mort wrote her again asking how she and the JRO were adjusting to wartime conditions. Bette's reply sounded depressed.

Everybody is waiting. Just waiting to see what the Germans will do next. They already have Poland. But they seem in no hurry to follow up with another invasion before winter. No doubt, we will be next — or the Low Countries. But when? The French soldiers wait behind their Maginot Line in the East. My younger brother is there. The Brits have sent an "expeditionary force" of soldiers. tanks and planes to the northern border. Otherwise, nothing happens.

The JRO still helps refugees in the free countries, so I am busy as a courier and escort. We can do nothing for Jews where Germany controls. In fact, we lost two of our agents, who were captured in Germany when the war broke out. You were lucky to get out when you did, Mort. My parents still teach in the Parisian schools — I cannot get them to relocate now, before it is too late, just as I told you before you left. Paris is their home, they say, and Paris is where they'll stay. We'll see.

Now that you're married, I don't expect to see you anymore. Your actions in Germany were the adventures of a single man, and a rather reckless one at that. No wife in her right mind would let her husband go to a war zone and do such things now. I certainly wouldn't. So, good luck, Mort. I enjoyed knowing you.

Remember me,
Your Bette

P.S. I am training to use a rifle and pistol.

Mort showed Bette's letter to Deborah, who had already guessed that he'd had an affair with her. She was sympathetic and not a trace jealous. "What a brave girl, staying in harm's way."

"She won't leave without her parents," Mort replied. "I tried to persuade her to come to the States."

"As your wife?"

"Well, yes."

"Oh, so I'm second-hand goods?" Deborah feigned offense. "Well, I admire your ex-girlfriend. I think she's in for a rough time of it. And she knows it too, training with firearms."

"The whole damn continent is in for a rough time of it."

"Just to be clear. You really aren't thinking of going back, are you, Mort?"

"No. I think that phase of my involvement is over. All I could do there is what she's doing. Act as a courier or escort refugee children."

"Well, that's necessary, too."

"Are you telling me I should do it?"

"Of course not. Bette's right. I want you here, with me, safe and sound."

"Well, safe at least. My friends and family would have doubted the 'sound' from my previous trips. Besides, I'm an old married man now."

"And getting paunchy," she teased, poking his stomach.

1942

Mort's resolve not to go abroad any more lasted about three years. In that interval he watched the war steadily worsen, swallowing Denmark, Norway, the Low Countries, and most of France, engulfing England and Russia and finally reaching across the Pacific to snare the once 'safe' United States. He'd been at Miriam's on Sunday afternoon when the news about Pearl Harbor interrupted the football game David and Andrew had been listening to. Immediately, Mort's thoughts turned to his children. Edward was probably safe from the Draft, exempted by his government research job at General Electric. And Andrew, at seventeen, was still too young by a few years (Eleven months later, the draft age was lowered to eighteen).

The events of the year that followed, 1942, proved to be a roller coaster ride of extremes, some catastrophic. In the first three months, the news was consistently bad, as Japan, a country Mort had paid little attention to previously given his near obsession with Germany, won victory after victory in the Pacific. That summer and fall, German armies cut ever deeper into Russia until their offensive finally met effective Russian resistance at Stalingrad and became a siege. Beginning in June, the news seemed to brighten. The U.S. Navy won a major victory over the Japanese fleet at Midway, sinking four of its aircraft carriers. Two months later, the Marines successfully landed at Guadalcanal, a small island in the Solomons chain, giving the Japanese Army its first reversal. And in the fall, the Allies took the offensive in North Africa. The British, under Montgomery, successfully attacked Rommel's Afrika Korps at El Alamein, and the Americans landed in force in Morocco and Algeria. Meanwhile, Russia counter-attacked at Stalingrad and surrounded an entire German Army. By the end of the year, both Germany and Japan seemed to be on the defensive. *Were these the turning points?* Mort wondered. Churchill was more measured in calling them 'not the beginning of the end', but 'the end of the beginning'.

The news closer to home, however, was profoundly

disturbing. First, Edward announced that he'd decided to give up his exemption and enlist in the Navy. Before Mort could object, Edward explained that he was going to take advantage of the Navy's new V-12 program for advanced study at college. He would study meteorology — weather prediction — as it pertained to radar, about which he was now an expert. In fact, he was part of the developmental team that had created and installed advanced radar sets on Navy ships. His goal, he said, was to be the chief meteorologist on one of the major ships, perhaps even for an entire task force.

By far, the most disturbing news for Mort came from New York on July 3rd. He had been speaking long distance with the head of the JRO in New York, Menachem Shulman, about expanding his fundraising territory, when Shulman asked him if he had read the story yesterday in the *New York Times* about the 'camps'.

Mort knew about Germany's concentration camps, of course, but these were different, Schulman said. These camps, located in Poland, were devoted strictly to the mass murder of Jews by using poison gas or carbon monoxide. 700,000 Jews, perhaps over a million, had already been murdered and many thousands more were being killed each day. The stories of eyewitnesses had made it to the West via Switzerland to confirm what the Germans were doing. Sadly, the *Times* had reported the story in a brief article on page six. Stunned, Mort hung up. It was too late to find the paper on the newsstands, so he went to the library to read it. Four months later, Rabbi Stephen Wise announced similar findings to the Associated Press. Only now, the number murdered was set at two million. Several newspapers in the U.S. carried the story, some on their front page, but not as a headline story.

When Mort announced his discovery at the next family supper at Miriam's — this time he insisted on bringing Deborah, too — he followed it by saying, "I can't stand by while this is happening! I just can't! I have to go back and see if I can help get some Jews to safety."

"But how in the world would you do that?" Miriam asked, her incredulity obvious. "All the borders are closed. The Nazis control most of France, and from what you've said before, the French police work hand in glove with them in the French section. Assuming you could get over — a big assumption — where would you even take them, the Jews?"

"There are only two places, so far as I can tell," Mort replied. "Portugal or Switzerland. Both are difficult to reach. Portugal, over the Pyrenees and through Spain. Switzerland, across the French border."

"And you don't even know Spanish, do you?" Miriam's voice had risen. Deborah, meanwhile, stayed silent.

"No," Mort said sadly. "I don't. That's a major stumbling block. But perhaps I could take a quick Berlitz course in Spanish. I already know French and German. And Yiddish. Spanish shouldn't be hard to pick up after that. There are others doing this smuggling too, across borders. It's largely a matter of bribing the border guards. But I do have to learn their language."

"Their language is greenbacks," David remarked. "And who's going to run your gas stations while you're gone? I can't look after all six by myself. I tried that before, remember, and it didn't work out too well." He didn't ask what everyone was thinking: *What if you don't come back?*

"I'll cross that bridge when I come to it," Mort said. "We'll figure out something. David, this is too crucial to be stopped by these practical considerations. Ordinarily, they'd be enough to stop me. Stop anyone. But not now. Not when thousands of Jews — thousands! — are being murdered every day. And the Allies are doing nothing about it."

"What can they do? Drop parachute troops on these camps?"

"You're right, of course," Mort replied. "There's not much they can do, for now. That's another reason *I* must do something. I don't mean to sound like — I don't know what — a martyr or a hero. It's just that I can't sit back and watch this happen, now that we know for sure that it *is* happening. I just can't."

It was Deborah's turn to speak up. "Mort, darling," she said quietly, putting her hand on his arm, "we do need to discuss this. In private."

"We will, Deborah, we will. Right away. It's just I was so upset hearing the news. In the past, when I heard things like this — Anna's problems in Poland, the Jews in Germany — I knew instinctively what I had to do. That's how I feel now. Perhaps I'll come to my senses after we've talked. I can't leave right away, that's sure. I need to learn some Spanish."

"And Portuguese?" Sarah asked.

"I don't know. It all sounds pretty impossible." Mort's manic intensity had shriveled to depression.

"It *is* impossible." Miriam said decisively. "Now, if you've finished ruining our dinner... I don't mean to sound callous—"

"You do," Sarah said. Her tone was contemptuous.

"But there's nothing we can do about it, awful as it is," Miriam finished. "Now, can we have our dessert and coffee and talk about something else?"

"What else is there?" Andrew said. Even his high spirits had been crushed.

Subdued, the family cleared the table while Miriam brought out cake and coffee.

When Mort and Deborah returned home after his announcement, Deborah was noticeably less gentle than she had been at Miriam's.

"You *promised* me that you were through with those trips," she said, almost as soon as they hung up their coats. "And now this? Mort, this is really too much! You're going to get yourself killed or captured by the Nazis. You'll end up in one of those same camps that you're trying to rescue Jews from!"

"I promised not to go before I learned about these mass murders," Mort replied. "It's different now, drastically different."

"It's also 'different' because you're four years older than the last time you went. You're in no condition to do this sort of work, to risk your life this way. And it's not fair to me! Mort, I don't want to become a widow again."

The discussion continued for a time, but Mort's heart wasn't in it. Deborah was right, of course. (He was beginning to discover that she was usually right in the few instances where they disagreed). The wartime conditions made rescues far more difficult and dangerous. Hiking over the Pyrenees, for God's sake! He was in no condition to do that, and he knew it. He also knew he'd been lucky last time — *damn lucky!* he thought — not to be caught even though the Gestapo was on to him. And if he were caught this time, he was a dead man, no questions asked.

He'd already gone to Europe twice for the JRO,

couriered money, escorted refugee children across the ocean, and directly smuggled two children out of Germany. It was a record to be proud of. Hadn't he already done enough? Better to do what he could do: continue raising money that would be sent where it was needed. But his old approach now seemed inadequate, too narrow. He looked for other agencies as well as the JRO that were helping to resettle refugees, and he found that the Jewish Federation was a good umbrella group for these agencies. Even before these horrific revelations, Mort had been contemplating a major career change that would free him from the gas stations and enable him to work full-time for one of these agencies, perhaps coordinating their fundraising activities or perhaps as an administrator. He had already applied to the JRO and several other agencies for such work. But he knew such jobs were scarce.

The see-saw of 1942 still wasn't finished with Mort, and as happened so often, the bad news came by telephone. Miriam was calling, obviously upset.

"David's been arrested! Apparently, he took some money under the table for gas. That's all I've been able to find out."

So why are you calling me? Mort thought bitterly. *Am I Mr. Fix-It?* But he said, "All right, Miriam, calm down."

"I'd have called the attorney I work for, but I didn't want him to know. It's so embarrassing!"

"But it's okay if I notify *my* attorney, is that it?"

"Please don't bicker with me, Mort. I feel bad enough having to call you. But we must do *something*."

"Do you know where they're holding David?"

"I think at the Twelfth Street Station."

"Well, I'm pretty sure they'll release him on bail after they've gotten all the information," Mort said. "We'll have to put up bail, of course."

"I know, Mort. That's also why I called you. We barely have any savings to cover something like this." He suspected she was exaggerating. She had been working full-time for over two years, and she didn't gamble away her salary or let David get his hands on it. *But her salary was probably low, and she had two teenagers to raise even with his child support...*

"All right, Miriam. You needn't worry. We're not about to let David rot in a cell. Though perhaps that's where the jerk belongs."

"You didn't have to say that," she sniffed.

"No, I didn't have to. I wanted to."

It didn't surprise him in the least that David was black marketing his gas to make extra money. With gas rationing in place since December 1st, David's stations were probably barely breaking even. The income from Mort's own stations had sharply dropped. *Fill 'er up!* had disappeared as a command, just as it had a decade earlier during the Depression. Now, four gallons a week was the most that people with 'A' stickers (the majority) could get — *if* they had sufficient ration coupons. Mort himself had a 'B' sticker (eight gallons), given to businessmen whose jobs required much driving. He himself had been approached a week earlier when he was subbing for one of his managers. A customer offered him five dollars to sell the gas without coupons. Without thinking, Mort said, "No way!" and the driver went off in a huff. Later, Mort wondered if he had refused out of patriotism or from fear of being caught.

David was probably snared by an OPA inspector

posing as a customer, Mort guessed. *I wonder how much he was making under the table before he was nabbed. It couldn't have been much since rationing was less than three weeks old in Detroit. What a schlemiel! Still, the temptation was there for every pump jockey. Many must have yielded, and many more still would. A whole industry of illegal selling. And not just gas. What about tires and meat and coffee?*

David was home by five that evening, sprung by Mort's hundred dollars and looking thoroughly humiliated. Not from being caught — that was just bad luck— but from having to accept Mort's charity. David's case, Mort's attorney assured him, would not go to trial. This was his first offense, and he had a clean record. He'd pay a stiff fine is all.

But this was the last straw for Mort. He was blunt about it, and he didn't care if Miriam and the children were listening.

"I know you've been skimming for years. But I didn't say anything because they were your stations, most of the time. But this is the limit, David. I'm going to break up the partnership for good. I'm pulling out. You can keep your stations, burn them down for all I care. But I'm going to sell the two I own and let the lease run out on the third. I'm through with the gas business, and I'm through with you as a partner."

"I kind of expected you'd do that," David said quietly, "breaking up the partnership, I mean."

"It's been coming for a long time. Only other things kept getting in the way."

"Like your numerous trips to Europe?" David said. His rejoinder fell flat.

"There's no point in going over that now."

"What will you do now?" Miriam inquired. She seemed genuinely curious.

"I've been planning this move for some time," Mort replied, "and talking to the JRO people in New York about a permanent position. Other agencies too. Either I'd become a coordinator of fundraising or some other kind of administrator working in New York or Washington. There aren't many positions available, of course, but I have experience handling donations and a good track record with the JRO." He stopped abruptly, realizing that this wasn't the time to talk about himself.

"Better hold on to your stations until those golden job offers come in," Miriam remarked.

Early in 1943, Menachem Shulman called with news. Arno Steelbach was now conducting their operations exclusively in Europe, leaving his New York duties open. It was simply too difficult logistically to go back and forth. Would Mort be interested in filling that role in New York, plus handling all the fundraising operations?

Mort kept down his excitement. "It sounds like you're combining two jobs into one."

"Well, in a sense, we are," Schulman conceded. "But our coordinator of the fundraising was a part-time position previously."

"I'd have to give up my gas stations. What would the new position pay?"

Shulman named a figure higher than what Mort was earning. *Of course, the cost of living would be higher in New York*, Mort thought. *But still...* Deborah had told him she'd like living there.

"I'd like to discuss it with my wife," Mort said. "Can I let you know tomorrow?"

"Of course," Shulman said.

It didn't take long for Mort and Deborah to decide. This was the position he had wanted for some time. Deborah said she was ready to give up her job at GM; what with the labor shortage brought on by the war, she shouldn't have much trouble finding work in New York, though it might not be the same PR work she did before. Edward had already left home and was now in the Navy. Sarah was at Indiana, and Andrew would soon be drafted. *Anyhow, they were Miriam and David's lookout now.*

So, there was really nothing to keep them in Detroit. And living in New York would be more exciting. The next day, Mort gave Shulman an emphatic "Yes," and the couple set about planning their move. Selling their flat would be a piece of cake, given the housing shortage in Detroit, and Mort was confident he could find buyers for the two gas stations he owned outright. Finding a pleasant two-bedroom apartment in New York, however, would take longer and require an intensive search, hence a short visit. And moving itself would be difficult with all the labor, fuel and truck shortages. All told, they could move by late spring, summer at the latest.

He wouldn't be sorry to give up the gas stations. It had been a good business overall and had supported him and his family for over two decades. But his heart was no longer in it. Conversely, the new job with the JRO was precisely what he wanted to be doing. He had long considered himself the linchpin of the family. But were they still a family with the children going their separate ways? So, he wasn't really breaking it up. And Mort would be glad to be shut of David's constant mishaps.

He had lived in Detroit for thirty years, and he had come to love the city, its peculiar identity in the way its strivings for 'culture' bumped up against its gritty, working-class diversity. But it was time to move on, and with Deborah, he felt ready to begin a new phase of his life and career.

Part V: The Stein Children:
Three Decisive Encounters

Andrew Stein, March 1943

Andy Stein was a natural athlete. Though he wasn't tall enough to star in high school basketball (he did well at guard), or heavy enough for football, he was agile and quick. Baseball was his game; he had started playing in the third grade and never stopped, always advancing. He intuitively knew how to respond and where to move to field a hard-hit ground ball at third base almost before he heard the crack of the bat. Even before high school, he had stood out in the after-school leagues. His visual acuity and fast swing made him a good hitter, though not a power hitter, and he taught himself to hit a curveball by the time he was thirteen. In the tenth grade at Central High, he had no trouble making junior varsity, and the coach quickly moved him up to varsity to fill the slot of the graduating third baseman. In his two years on the Central varsity team, he batted .373 and .398 and set the school record for doubles and stolen bases. The .398 average earned him a spot on the all-city team and the attention of a few scouts.

As Miriam had predicted to Mort, Andy was popular with girls. He exuded self-confidence where other boys were shy and bumbling. He was never at a loss for words and teased girls, even the pretty ones, just enough to pique their attention and flatter their vanity without annoying them. 'Glib' perfectly described Andy's personality. The word's negative connotations — insincere and superficial — unfortunately also applied. In elementary school, he was expert at starting something — a smart remark others repeated, a parody of a hated teacher — but getting out of it before he was caught. It was the slower ones who repeated the joke who were punished. Those successful escapes epitomized Andy's weakest quality: an ability to evade responsibility for things he had done. Doing it wasn't wrong. Getting caught was.

By his junior and senior years at Central, Andy enjoyed the athlete's status of wearing a letter sweater, which increased his popularity with girls. But he also branched out and, loving the attention it brought, went out for debate and dramatics. He did well on the debate team (unless he came upon a deeper thinking, more logical opponent), and he was given a major role in the school play each year. He traded on his popularity to run successfully for senior class vice-president, already realizing that the position was all honor and no work. His grades at Central were good but never stellar. As early as junior high, his teachers were telling his parents that Andrew was certainly smart enough to excel in any subject he chose, but he just didn't apply himself more than it took to get a 'B'. The unspoken conclusion: he was lazy.

He also cheated regularly. The cheat sheets he carefully constructed and slipped under his sleeves took only a little less work than cramming for the exam would have. And the system wasn't foolproof, since some teachers, suspecting their students cheated, devised their own impromptu questions. Hence, 'B's, not 'A's.

It could be argued that Andy lacked (in the stuffy phrasing of social workers) a good role model. Mort was distant, both physically and emotionally. And he had little interest in sports. David, his stepfather, certainly shared

Andy's love of sports, drove him to practices and games and attended games as often as he could get away. They at least had that in common. But Andy sensed that David was always on the edge of trouble. Many times, he'd heard his mother berating David for his gambling and the no-goods he hung out with when he wasn't working. Many evenings David was gone, and until his mother resumed her work as a secretary, the family barely scraped by. When David was arrested in December 1942, the whole family knew and was ashamed. Meanwhile, his mother's time was taken up by her new job, leaving Andy and Sarah alone in the afternoons.

In his senior year at Central, 1941-42, the Draft loomed like a thundercloud; but Andrew got lucky and drew a high draft number. They might not get me until next year, he concluded. In the meantime, he considered a career in baseball. Michigan State College had offered him a small baseball scholarship, which he rejected out of hand. Who wanted to play for a cow college? Fortunately, one of the scouts who watched him play in the All-City Championship game was from the Detroit Tigers, his favorite team, of course. He invited Andy for spring tryouts in 1943. Ordinarily, this would have been in Florida, but the war curtailed civilian travel, so the Tigers' spring training was held in chilly Evansville, Indiana.

During that winter, he worked with weights to build up his strength and waited anxiously until March, meanwhile dreading the draft notice that might arrive any day. Because he was invited and not just crashing the tryouts, the Tigers paid his way and put him up at an Evansville hotel (there were only three; regulars got the best one, rookies and hopefuls the second best). Bosse

Field was cold in March, dreary and lacking good base paths. Rather than working out the kinks in warm weather, the players developed new muscle sprains, sore arms and chapped hands. Still, Andy wasn't discouraged; he was in good shape from his winter workouts.

Wearing a Tigers uniform with its Old English '𝔇', even the worn ones given to the newcomers, was a thrill. To sort out the candidates for infield positions, the infield coach had them line up behind each other; third base had four candidates including Andy. Then, they'd take turns fielding ground balls and throwing them to first base, where candidates for first took turns catching them. Initially, the grounders were easy to warm up the players. Gradually, they became harder, and some caused flubs or got through for singles. Andy was in his element, however, and fielded every grounder, no matter how hard it was hit. His throws were on target, too, though a few were one-hoppers when he had to turn and throw from a back-handed catch.

At bat, though, Andy barely held his own. The pitching was better than he'd experienced in high school. He managed to get several hits that would have been clean singles, but he hit no long balls for extra bases. And he had yet to face the starting Tiger pitchers, throwing their best stuff for the inter-squad games.

It was clear by the end of three days, that the competition for third base was down to two newbies including Andy and the current starter, Mike MacGinnis. MacGinnis was no ball of fire; he had come up from the Double-A farm team last fall and batted a weak .215. If it weren't for the player shortage caused by the war, he wouldn't have been brought up at all. Andy's other competitor was Al Jenkins, a farm boy who had played at Ohio State for three years. He was considerably bigger than Andy, and when he connected at bat, the ball sometimes sailed over the fence or came close. But he was noticeably less agile at third base and missed several hard shots down the third base line. So, it became a question of what the Tigers wanted most: a power-hitter and mediocre fielder or a singles hitter and solid third baseman.

Though both Andy and Al knew they were competitors, they were friendly to each other. Al was good-natured and easygoing; he told Andy about his farm and family. If he didn't make the cut, he said, he'd go back to farming but use his Animal Husbandry degree to farm scientifically. Andy was uncharacteristically reticent to talk about himself. He had half-expected to run into anti-Semitism at the tryouts, but so far no one had said anything, and Al was about the last person to express any prejudice. As they dressed for practice, Andy noticed that Al's shoes were worn, flat-soled sneakers rather than spikes. He commented on it (tactfully, he thought).

"Yeah, I've outgrown my old spikes," Al said. "Couldn't find a new pair anywhere, what with shoes being rationed now." Andy commiserated but wondered if that's what caused Al to flub those grounders at third.

Before the first cuts were announced at the end of the first week, the Tigers held an inter-squad game, evenly distributing the wannabes. Al had been hitting well the last few days, launching several balls over the left field fence. Andy knew that with Hank Greenberg serving in the Army, the Tigers needed long-ball hitters. They'd almost surely give Al the nod and try to improve his fielding. That's what decided him.

An hour before they were to suit up for the game, he slipped into the changing room, a trailer, and found Al's uniform and sneakers. Slipping a small bottle of Wildroot Cream Oil from his pocket, he quickly greased the soles of Al's shoes and left before anyone else entered. During the game, the first time Al batted, he hit a long fly ball between the outfielders, a double for sure, maybe even a triple. As he took off for first base on the slick grass of Bosse Field, Al slipped and fell. Scrambling to his feet, he barely made it to first base ahead of the relayed throw from the outfield. Assuming he hit a slick spot on the grass, he never bothered to look at his shoes. But the same thing happened the next time he batted. This time, between innings, he examined his shoes closely and found traces of the hair oil. He looked over at Andy, who was watching the game intently, shouting encouragement at his teammates. Andy had hit well that day, going two for three and had made some nice fielding plays at third, once turning a 5-4-3 double play that began with a diving catch.

Al's two falls were enough to decide the coaches. At the end of the week, he was gone and Andy kept on. Al had never confronted Andy with his findings. He really couldn't believe someone else would be capable of doing him dirt, especially someone as friendly as Andy. But someone obviously had.

That someone felt guilty about it — for a few days. *But it was really a question of ends and means*, Andy reasoned. *If you want the end, then any means to it were acceptable. It was really no different from cheating on a test.*

At the end of spring training — an abbreviated two weeks before the exhibition games — the final cuts were made and positions assigned and posted. Andy had expected to see his name by the third base slot — he was certainly better than MacGinnis and had even gotten some hits against the starting pitchers throwing heat. But his name wasn't on the starting lineup against the Yankees. Instead, the Manager, Steve O'Neill, told him that the General Manager wanted to see him.

The G.M. was direct. "Stein, we like what we saw out there. But we feel you need more experience against big league pitching. So, we're offering you a contract, but it requires you play for our Double-A farm team, the Buffalo Bisons. Then, if you do well this season and next, we'll move you up to the Tigers."

"How much is the contract for?" Andy asked, crestfallen.

"Two thousand, with a one hundred dollar signing bonus. It's our standard contract for rookies." He presented the contract already filled out. "You just need to sign here if you accept it."

"I have two questions," Andy said.

"Shoot."

"What happens if I'm drafted?"

"Then the contract is null and void as soon as you go in. It says so here," the G.M. said, pointing to the clause. "Then, you're Uncle Sam's responsibility." Andy noted that the pointing finger sported a large gold ring.

"Who's going to play third base for you now?"

"MacGinnis, but we're hoping to do better in a trade."

"I see."

Andy signed.

Sarah Stein, August 1944

By the time Sarah Stein graduated Central High in June 1940, she had had extensive experience as a violinist in orchestras and in solo recitals. She had risen to concertmaster in the Michigan Youth Orchestra, had played in the prestigious Interlochen summer orchestra and was first chair in the Central High orchestra. Encouraged by her violin teacher, Richard Neubauer, concertmaster of the Detroit Symphony, Sarah gave recitals both solo and accompanied by a pianist. Even as challenging a work as Beethoven's *Kreutzer Sonata* fell under her hands smoothly if not easily. Her audiences, comprised of family and fellow students, were enthusiastic in their applause, and she felt encouraged. Neubauer had written her a glowing recommendation for Indiana, Oberlin and Julliard. The last was obviously a long shot, but Neubauer urged her to try: "Why not? Shoot for the moon!"

As expected, Julliard said no, but Indiana and Oberlin accepted her. Money was an issue, of course. Oberlin was private and expensive, and at IU she'd be paying the much higher out-of-state tuition. Plus, there was room and board to consider. Miriam made it plain to her daughter that she'd have to apply for scholarships, not only from the school but from outside agencies like the Jewish Federation. Both colleges eventually offered modest scholarships, essentially reduced tuition. But Sarah found no support elsewhere. Fortunately, Mort had long ago put aside money for his children's college education, should they go that route. Since neither Edward nor Andrew were interested, a sizable chunk was left for Sarah.

"She's my daughter, after all," he said to Deborah, "and she obviously has talent, in fact, a career ahead of her. We should do what we can to further it." Deborah agreed. Secretly, Mort had hoped the support might bring him closer to Sarah, who had always seemed distant to him. Distant from the whole family.

Had he been present at one family squabble, he would have understood one source of that distance. Typically, it was Andrew who grasped it first. He and Sarah were arguing about who got to use the family car that Saturday night.

"You just want it to park with one of your girlfriends," Sarah accused.

"And you just want it to park with *your* girlfriend," Andy shot back.

"Bastard!"

"Lesbo!"

It was out in the open at last. Miriam had long suspected it. Sarah's disinterest in boys and vice versa. Her intense friendships with first one girl, then another. Even her appearance, which avoided all feminine touches, such as makeup, styled hair and dresses (except at recitals). Instead, jeans, sneakers and loose-fitting shirts with the sleeves rolled up, her blonde hair pulled back into a ponytail, was her constant outfit. "All ready for chores, but never does any," Andy cracked.

The Bloomington, Indiana campus was beautiful in fall. Among the tall maple trees with their leaves already changing and manicured lawns were majestic limestone buildings. The limestone was quarried nearby, but the workers — 'stonies' the students called them derisively — felt entirely remote from the college. In fact, the tension between town and gown was such that there were certain bars the college kids avoided unless they were looking for a fight. The most impressive of the campus limestone buildings was the auditorium, a recently completed WPA project with murals painted above the lobby doors by Thomas Hart Benton. The building had a large stage and good acoustics, perfect for the frequent concerts of the thriving music school.

Sarah was enchanted with the campus. Except for her summer at Interlochen, this was her first time away from home. And except for the absence of a good deli in Bloomington, nearly everything she saw compared favorably to the urban Jewish environment of Detroit's Dexter-Davison neighborhood. She settled into campus life quickly, making friends with her dorm roommate and throwing herself into her music and liberal arts courses. There was one Jewish sorority on campus, but she ignored it during 'rush' week. She had no use for the silly sorority rituals; she despised the conformity it enforced on its members, the girls all dressing alike; and she didn't need the shelter of a Jewish environment because she didn't feel particularly Jewish. First and always, she was a musician.

Her four years at Indiana were an unbroken pleasure that she often looked back on fondly. She did well in her courses, and she socialized easily, developing friendships of both genders and both 'queer' and straight. She had a few serious love affairs, easy to consummate with the connivance of roommates in the all-girls dorm. Though she didn't have a car, she always found a ride to Detroit from the ride board during school holidays, and most important, her musical career advanced steadily in an improving technique and regularly scheduled recitals. Her violin repertoire expanded from romantic showpieces back to Beethoven and Mozart and even to Bach's magnificent sonatas and partitas for solo violin, and forward to the Impressionists and a few modernists like Prokofiev. She even organized a student string quartet, with herself as first violin, so that she could learn some of the chamber music repertoire. She was nothing if not ambitious.

During her junior year in 1943, she was chosen to perform the Beethoven *Violin Concerto* at the culminating June concert of the student orchestra. It was conducted by Hendrik Van Loos, who had retired as Music Director of the Philadelphia Orchestra. Ironically, Sarah didn't particularly care for the Beethoven; it was atypical for that composer: a consistently lyrical piece with no fireworks, and a final movement of almost intolerable repetition. Still, she worked at it diligently for months and performed it well, receiving the predictable standing ovation. One more achievement to list on her *curriculum vitae*.

In 1944, Prokofiev's ineffably lovely *Second Violin Sonata* made it to the States, and Sarah was given the honor of performing it during the June recitals. Her instructor and mentor, Franz Lukacs, gave the American debut in New York. (The contextual politics was perfect, since any music from our Russian ally during the war was greeted with hoopla.) The sonata was difficult, and Sarah worked assiduously with her accompanist, Cecilia Jordan, to shape a moving performance. It gave her more satisfaction than anything she had previously achieved.

About the time Sarah graduated, she received a note from Richard Neubauer that the Detroit Symphony would be holding auditions in August to fill two violin positions; the Draft had taken the two men. Though he had retired as concertmaster, Neubauer said he'd put in a good word for her and urged her to try out. Immediately, she asked Franz Lukacs to write her a recommendation. Van Loos didn't write recommendations, he informed her, but then softened and said he might call Karl Krueger, Detroit's new music director. Sarah wondered how Krueger felt about hiring a woman.

Krueger had considerably more to worry about that year than whether he should hire women. The previous year, 1943, he was charged with rebuilding the entire symphony, which had disbanded in 1942. By the beginning of the 1943-44 season, he had cobbled together a symphony made up of former players who lived in the Detroit area and several new ones recruited from music schools. *Old-timers and youngsters*, he thought sardonically. A popular song put it best — *They're either too young or too old*. The war made recruitment difficult — men were increasingly scarce; musicians were here today, gone tomorrow; some were playing with a I-A draft category and could be called up at any time. Krueger wasn't a trailblazer regarding the hiring of women — almost no major American conductor was in 1944. But facts were facts. So, when Sarah Stein applied for one of the vacant violin positions that summer, Krueger did not reject her application out of hand but gave her an audition.

With him at the auditions was Stevenson, his new concertmaster, a dour man whom Krueger didn't particularly like, but he could hit the notes all right and seemed able to get the strings to play together, no small feat. There were several candidates for the two positions, once again older men beyond draft age and a few music school graduates with the dew still on them. Krueger had hoped he could get through them all in a day by assigning them the same piece: the Paganini *Caprice No. 24*, the famous one for which so many composers had written variations. He and Stevenson made notes on each performance, thanked the player and moved on.

338

Sarah was third from last. Sitting in the wings, she could hear the Paganini being ground out over and over again. *They must be sick of hearing it*, she surmised. *I certainly am.* The performances varied, but none was so good that she felt crushed. She had a decent chance *if* her gender didn't disqualify her. But if that were so, why would they have even invited her in the first place?

Finally, her name was called. As she reached center stage of the Music Hall, she took a deep breath and spoke up.

"Maestro, I was wondering if I could play something else, such as one of the Bach partitas? I don't particularly like the Paganini."

The concertmaster started to object, but Krueger hushed him.

"You realize, Miss Stein," Krueger said, "that if you were hired, there'll be many times you would have to play works you don't particularly like."

"Oh yes, I understand that, Maestro. That's fine."

"Which partita did you wish to play?"

"The first movement of the *D minor*, the *Second Partita*."

"Very well. Please proceed."

Sarah knew the entire *Partita* by heart. It was famous for its concluding *Chaconne*, which lasted almost as long as all the other movements combined.

She put her heart into playing the *Allemande*, but was careful not to make it romantic, as some violinists did by using rubato. While she played, Krueger listened with his eyes closed, deeply enjoying the music and relieved not to hear the Paganini again.

When she finished, in a few minutes, he said, "Please continue."

"But Maestro," the concertmaster objected. "It's late and we still have two more to hear."

"We can hear them tomorrow. Please continue."

Sarah played the next three short movements — the *Courant*, the *Saraband* and the *Gigue* — with the same intensity. Again, Krueger listened intently with his eyes closed; he seemed transported by the music. When she finished the *Saraband*, Sarah paused briefly, expecting to be stopped before embarking on the *Chaconne*, which alone lasted almost fifteen minutes. Hearing nothing from the two men, she launched into the magnificent work. *This is it*, she thought. *Everything. Give it everything.*

When she had finished, she felt exhausted and not just from the piece's difficulty. Emotionally spent. She looked up and thought she saw tears in Karl Krueger's eyes.

"That was fine, Miss Stein," Krueger said, clearing his throat. "Just fine."

He turned to the concertmaster. "No more auditions today, James. Please tell the last two candidates to report tomorrow at ten, with our apologies."

But he knew, and Stevenson knew, and even Sarah knew that those last two auditions would make no difference. She had nailed it.

Edward Stein, December 1944

Once he completed his V-12 course in meteorology using radar, Edward Stein's progress in the Navy was swift. He entered active service in summer 1942 as a Petty Officer 1st Class (the equivalent of a Staff Sergeant), and in November 1942, he was assigned to the radar plot of the heavy cruiser *USS Indianapolis*, the flagship of Vice Admiral Raymond Spruance. The 'plot' was the brain of the ship; a small room that squeezed in several radar screens, sonar detection, a small drafting table in the center to plot the ship's course, sea charts, and telephones connecting to the bridge. The flagship plot had the luxury of a radar devoted to the weather; Edward thus had his own station next to the radars searching for enemy planes and ships. That was where the main action was, especially once the kamikazes appeared in 1944. Finding and tracking those planes was a matter of life and death, compared to which, Edward's search for storms and squalls was a sideshow. Still, he took his job seriously.

By summer 1944, Edward had been promoted to Ensign (2nd Lieutenant) and was now assigned to the plot of the battleship *USS New Jersey*, the flagship for Admiral William 'Bull' Halsey, commander of Task Force 38.

The trouble began at a distance. Early on the morning of December 16th, while the fleet was positioning itself for the complicated and cumbersome task of refueling at sea the following day, Edward had spotted on his weather radar what appeared to be a fast-growing tropical storm southeast of the fleet. Waiting until he was certain and for an upper-level conference to end, he reported his finding to his immediate superior, Commander George Condon, the chief meteorologist for the fleet.

"Nothing to worry about, Ensign," Condon assured him. "We received a weather warning from Pearl today that that storm is — and I quote — 'very weak', a 'tropical storm' at least 450 miles distant and likely to curve away from us on a northwest-north arc. We ought to be able to refuel and head back with no problem if we can do it efficiently. Don't forget, some of our destroyers are very low on fuel, and that lack of ballast makes them vulnerable in a storm. We need to tank them up ASAP. I've already alerted Carney and Halsey about Pearl's assessment. Ulithi confirms it, by the way."

Edward knew it wasn't his place to question his superior's judgment. Condon struck him as competent if not especially brilliant. But he often tailored his reports to Halsey and Carney, Halsey's chief of staff, by taking their wishes into account.

Throwing caution to the winds, Edward spoke up.

"With all due respect, Commander, it doesn't look that way to me. I've been tracking this storm for a few hours, and it's growing rapidly. By now, I'd say it qualifies as a typhoon. It looks to me like it's heading straight for us. And, given its speed and expansion, I really doubt it's as far away as 450 miles. I'd estimate half that distance and closing fast."

Condon studied Edward's radar screen as Edward pointed out the indicators leading to his estimate of the storm's dimensions.

"Hmm. How sure are you of your estimates, Ensign? It's not every day we tell Pearl they're dead wrong."

"Very sure, sir. Or I wouldn't have spoken up."

Condon knew Edward's meteorological training and that he was a radar specialist, who had even managed to intensify the *New Jersey*'s weather radar on his own.

"All right, Ensign. I'll convey your report to the Admirals. They certainly won't be happy to hear it."

"No sir. I don't think they will."

"I'll say they won't," Sam Ellis said from the next screen after Condon left. "Halsey wants that refueling pronto so we can haul ass back for the Mindoro invasion. That's the scuttlebutt, anyhow."

'Pretty hard to refuel in a typhoon," Edward observed.

"No shit. But the old man doesn't want to be caught out of position again. Not after that Samar SNAFU when the Japs deked him." Ellis had the annoying trait of being a know-it-all who was usually right.

"That was bad, all right," Edward said. "He must have taken a lot of heat for that one."

"The gods are never wrong," Ellis muttered, turning back to his screen.

A half hour later, Admirals Halsey and Carney and Commander Condon entered the crowded plot. Everyone immediately stood to attention, which Halsey waved away. The three went directly to Edward's station. He had seen Halsey many times standing at the bridge, but was struck once again by his size. *Barely five feet eight*, Edward guessed. *But the man does exude authority and not just because of the stripes on his sleeve or the stars on his collar.*

"So, young man," Halsey began without introductions, "Commander Condon tells me you disagree with his assessment and with Pearl Harbor's assessment and with Ulithi's assessment of the storm. According to you, we're in danger and better hightail it back where we came from at top speed."

"Yes, sir," was all Edward was able to respond.

"So why are you right and Pearl wrong? Pearl says the storm will miss us by 200 miles."

Edward explained, patiently pointing out the indicators on his screen, which he was able to adjust for distance, and showing how he made the calculations. He sensed that

Halsey was only half listening as he concluded, "So, you see, sir, the expansion rate over the past few hours tells me that the storm is growing rapidly and moving in our direction, closer to 270-280 degrees than to 340-360. And the size of it on the radar screen is not consistent with 450 miles, but much closer. 250 miles at most. I think it's going to be a whopper sir, and it's heading this way fast, I'd estimate at about 45 knots."

"You realize, Ensign, the pickle we're in if we turn back unfueled."

"Yes, sir. Commander Condon explained it to me."

"And if we took an extra day just to steer out of the storm's way before refueling, we'd never make it back in time to assist General MacArthur's landing at Mindoro."

"Yes, sir."

Admiral Carney spoke up. "Admiral, there's another factor to consider. If Ensign Stein is correct, the conditions may be too rough here for refueling tomorrow. The lines might snap. And if so, we wouldn't be any better off than if we turned back now."

"That's true, Bob — *if* Ensign Stein is correct." He turned to Edward. "You studied meteorology in the V-12 program, I understand."

"Yes, sir. At Beloit College. For 12 weeks."

"That's a pretty short course."

"Yes, sir, it is. Before that, I specialized in developing radar for ships at General Electric."

"I see."

Halsey turned to Condon. "What do you think, George?"

Condon's eyes darted briefly between the two admirals. "I'll stick with my earlier assessment, sir — Pearl's assessment. I think it's a tropical storm curving north and is at least 450 miles distant." Edward sighed

344

silently at his failure to convince Condon.

Halsey turned to the other two men standing behind Edward's station. All of them had already noticed that, for all its huge size, the *New Jersey* was now rocking more vigorously than it had just an hour ago. The conditions were worsening. Dirty weather ahead.

"Well, gentlemen," Halsey began. "We're between a rock and a hard place. We absolutely must complete this refueling by the 17th — I repeat *must* — and get to Mindoro at top speed. That is my highest priority, and for that reason, and that alone, I'm going with Pearl's assessment and George's assessment of the storm's size and direction. No offense to you, Ensign."

"None taken, sir," Edward replied, saluting, as the three men left. *Shit, we're really in for it now,* he thought.

He glanced over at the others in the plot. They'd all been listening, of course, and now Ellis gave him a thumbs down.

"SNAFU time," Sam muttered. "You know what Halsey's problem is? He leads with his heart not his head. He's emotional."

"I hear you," Edward responded. "But he can do no wrong so far as the press and the folks back home are concerned."

"Yeah, but they're not on this ship. Kind of wish they were."

The weather steadily worsened that day, the seas regularly breaking over the *New Jersey*'s sleek bow, the ship heavily listing in the troughs of waves. Movements topside were restricted, as the winds howled and steadily increased. The night was even worse. *This ship can take it*, Edward thought in his rocking hammock. *But what about the tin cans, especially those with little ballast? How can they avoid being swamped even with the best seamanship?*

The next morning, the 17th, it was certain from Edward's radar that he'd been right. The storm was moving west-northwest, and its western edge looked to be right on top of them. Wind gusts were clocked as high as 90 knots (103 miles per hour) on the ships furthest east, and the barometer was falling rapidly. Just as Admiral Carney had predicted, the ships found it impossible to refuel in even 20-30 knot winds and heaving seas. Fuel lines snapped, and some ships collided. Still, Commander Condon refused to change his assessment from the previous day. Though the storm was certainly getting worse, he believed it would merge with a weak cold front and veer off to the north.

While Edward stayed glued to his radar screens, Sam Ellis said he was going to the radio shack nearby to hear what was coming in. Edward glanced at his watch. It was about 10:00. A few minutes later, Ellis came back with shocking news.

"Several destroyers are sending SOS's for help," he announced grimly. We've heard from *Spence* and *Hull*. They're rolling in the troughs of the big waves, rolling 50 degrees, 70 in one case. Some ships have lost control of their steering, and some reported failing electrical systems — their last report. A few are taking water down their stacks."

"70 degrees? They'll capsize!" another plotter exclaimed.

"Sure looks that way. And in these seas, you can forget about rescue."

Edward said nothing. He was trying to fight seasickness. He'd been in rough seas before, but nothing like this.

Everything loose on their desks — pencils, compasses, protractors, coffee cups, bigger gear — had been stowed.

At 11:40, Halsey gave the order to 'take the most comfortable course', freeing ships from trying to maintain predetermined rendezvous courses, and at 12:51, he called Condon and Carney into conference in the officers' mess. Condon hurriedly brought his weather charts. He still maintained the storm's center was 400 miles away. In fact, its center was just over a hundred miles distant, and the task force was already within the typhoon's sweeping arms. Reluctantly, Halsey postponed refueling until 06:00 on the 18th and ordered the task force to change course to the northwest. Later, believing the task force was clear of the storm, he would change course again to the south. Both changes were too little, too late, and the second was disastrous. The northwest course should have been enough to escape an ordinary storm, but the size of this one was simply too big, its proximity too close. And the southern course steered the task force *toward* the storm.

Now, the whole task force absorbed the brunt of the storm. Waves swelled as high as sixty feet, sometimes a hundred feet, breaking over the radar and radio towers atop the ships, sometimes smashing them. Wind speeds topped 100 mph and reached a peak of 150. Even the tall aircraft carriers were keeling dangerously at thirty and forty-five degree angles. The howling winds ripped equipment, ammunition, and even entire aircraft loose from their moorings and swept them into the ocean. Combat Air Patrol planes weren't allowed to land on the sloping decks of the carriers and were forced to ditch into the sea.

The next day, the 18th, the storm reached its peak. Between 11:00 and 14:00, winds had risen to 122 mph, with gusts to 150; seventy-foot waves were now typical. At times, it was impossible on some ships to distinguish between the sea and sky. By 08:30, Halsey, perhaps hoping that the task force could duck below the typhoon's west-northwesterly course, ordered it to continue on its southerly course (180 degrees), An hour later, he changed course to 220 degrees.

Astonishingly, what Halsey didn't yet know was that three of his destroyers — *Hull, Spence* and *Monaghan* — had already foundered in the storm at about 11:00. 790 sailors would be lost.

Finally, at 14:00, Halsey issued a Typhoon Warning to the fleet . Meanwhile, he finally accepted the inevitable, informing General MacArthur that TF-38 would not be able to support him on the 19th.

Edward stayed at his radar screen, and, amid the chaos, nausea, destruction and, yes, fear wrought by the storm, he saw something remarkable on the screen: the eye of typhoon close by. Some carriers reported seeing it with the naked eye.

The aftermath of this typhoon taught Edward several important lessons. In the Court of Inquiry that the Navy conducted, attended by Admiral Chester Nimitz himself, Admiral Halsey was let off with a wrist slap. Instead of finding him guilty of incompetence or criminal negligence, the Court softened it to 'errors of judgment committed under the stress of war operations'. It further helped exonerate him by stating that he had 'insufficient information' about the typhoon's locale. Essentially, Halsey was too popular with the American public to blame for those 790 deaths and remove from command. Nimitz wasn't about to see this happen to one of his friends. Edward wasn't asked to testify at the Inquiry; only Commander Condon was. For having provided Admiral Halsey with accurate information in sufficient time to avoid the disaster, Ensign Edward Stein was rewarded by being transferred to a minor ship in a different task force, a demotion, though not of rank. Obviously, Commander Condon didn't want him around as a constant reminder of the Commander's culpability.

Part VI: Outcomes

Mort and Deborah Stein

Mort and Deborah moved to New York City in the early summer of 1943. After much searching, they found a comfortable two-bedroom rent-controlled apartment in the East Sixties of Manhattan. When Mort soon realized he needed help in keeping track of incoming donations and correspondence, he obtained permission from Menachem Shulman to hire Deborah as his assistant.

That was the easy part. But dealing with the domestic responses to revelations of the mass murders, especially the Jewish responses, was like wading into a swamp. Mort had discovered when he started fundraising in 1936 that Jewish agencies and groups quarreled among themselves about the best way to oppose Nazi persecution. Now, incredibly, with the situation so dire, they were still quarreling. The pro-Zionist American Jewish Congress favored direct action — protest marches, rallies, boycotts, and the like. In March 1943, for example, it organized a large 'Stop Hitler Now!' rally at Madison Square Garden. The non-Zionist American Jewish Committee, however, opposed direct action as potentially counter-productive. This group favored using prominent Jews to influence government leaders. There were close to a dozen groups, each committed to its own approach. Getting them to agree on and promote *one* approach seemed nearly impossible. *While they're haggling*, Mort realized, *millions of Jews are being murdered. Thank God the JRO is committed to direct action and operates mostly in Europe, free of this impotent squabbling.*

It was not free, however, of the State Department's continual recalcitrance and harassment. Not only did the Department refuse to loosen immigration restrictions, it delayed granting the JRO a license to send money overseas, a requirement that the Department itself had created.

"Fortunately, we have a way of dealing with that stupidity," Shulman winked at Mort. "We just ignore it."

When the various Jewish groups finally agreed upon an action, it led to a dead end.

In the spring of 1943, an 'Emergency Committee on European Jewish Affairs' urged President Roosevelt to call for an international conference to deal with rescue and resettlement of European Jews. Roosevelt did so, and the resulting Bermuda Conference between the United States and England was a complete failure. Neither country was willing to enact any new rescue policy or change its restrictive immigration quotas.

Finally, the domestic logjam was broken by the appearance of a new group, 'The Emergency Committee to Save the Jewish People of Europe'. Opposed by the other Jewish groups as being too militant, the Emergency Committee placed full-page newspaper ads with provocative headlines, staged the widely attended pageant 'We Will Not Die' in several cities, and even organized in October 1943 a march on the Capitol by hundreds of American rabbis and cantors. Its aim was to pressure Congress to pass a resolution calling on the President to enact a plan to save the surviving European Jews from the gas chambers. Strongly opposed by Breckinridge Long of the State Department, the 'Rescue Resolution' stalled in Congress.

"Did you know that that son-of-a-bitch Long testified for four hours against the Resolution?" Shulman exclaimed. "Four hours!"

But Roosevelt did act on his own at the behest of friend and neighbor, Treasury Secretary Henry Morgenthau, after Morgenthau's staff documented how the State Department had suppressed evidence of the mass murders and resisted all efforts to permit refugees into the country. The War Refugee Board that Roosevelt created by executive order in January 1944 now had government money and privately raised funds to funnel into Europe for the express purpose of rescuing refugees.

"Why, they're doing exactly what we do!" Mort said with astonishment to Shulman.

"Of course," Shulman nodded. "But they're doing it legally. Well, semi-legally. At least they don't need a State Department license to send the money. Now, we can help them get that money to people who can make a difference, legally or not."

Handling the JRO portion of money provided by the War Refugee Board became Mort's chief duty. He quickly became expert in money transfers to banks in Basel, Zurich, Barcelona and Lisbon. From these banks, the money trail grew murky. Certain people, including Arno Steelbach, were given access to the accounts with the understanding that they would use the money primarily as bribes to smuggle Jews across the Spanish and Swiss borders. The Board also paid for the transit of Jews to Portugal, Turkey, even to Palestine and the United States. Most important, it conveyed money to people like Raoul Wallenberg, Carl Lutz, Chiune Sugihara, Giorgio Perlasca and Harry Bingham, who all used their diplomatic cover to protect Jews with phony documents and safe houses or get them transit visas to cross borders. Wallenberg alone was credited with protecting 200,000 Hungarian Jews from the Nazis.

Mort was also loaned to the War Relocation Authority to help supervise the only refugee camp in America. It was created at Fort Ontario in Oswego, New York and held nearly 1,000 refugees from several countries. They had come by boat from Allied-occupied Italy and were officially considered 'guests' of the United States, required to return to Europe after the war, though President Truman later made them eligible for immigration visas.

Mort made several trips to Oswego to make sure things were running smoothly. He met with Oswego officials who were initially hostile to the camp's existence and assuaged their concerns. Similarly, the townspeople of Oswego overcame their distrust of the refugee children they had allowed into their schools. The townspeople, as well as many others from around the world, donated parcels of food, clothing and even toys for the children. Mort took especial pleasure in knowing that the camp's existence was a thumb in the eye of the anti-Semitic bureaucrats in the State Department, people like Breckenridge Long, who had worked so tirelessly to bar Jewish refugees and immigrants from entering the country. During and after the war in Europe, Mort worked closely with John Pehle, the first director of the War Refugee Board.

After Germany's defeat, Mort made several trips for the JRO to Displaced Persons camps across Europe operated by the Allied authorities and the U.N. Relief and Rehabilitation Administration. About 250,000 survivors of the Holocaust, as well as 600,000 others, were placed in these camps from 1945 to 1952, as the Allies debated among themselves where to send them. One thing was clear — Holocaust survivors refused to return to their former homes in Germany, Austria, Poland and Russia. Britain blocked them from going to Palestine, though many thousands evaded the British Navy and arrived there illegally. Few countries were willing to welcome more than a handful before 1948. At several camps in Germany, Austria and Italy, Mort recorded conditions and what items were immediately needed to make life in the camps more tolerable. Such things as more blankets, winter clothing and shoes, more pot-bellied stoves and coal to better heat the barracks, books (in various languages) and sports equipment were some of the items he listed, subsequently bought with JRO funds and distributed among these camps. On the trains, German locals stared at his better clothing and well-fed appearance. Now, he wasn't hesitant to stare back. Finally, in 1948, when the State of Israel was created, the flood gates to Jewish immigration there opened, and two-thirds of Displaced Jews emigrated there. 1948 also witnessed, at President Truman's urging, 'The Displaced Persons Act', authorizing 200,000 DPs to enter the United States. By 1952, over 80,000 Jewish DPs had immigrated to the U.S. with the help of Jewish agencies. In these years Mort was busier than ever, helping to arrange these massive transfers. It was a huge undertaking involving the chartering of buses, trains and even ships, and securing care for the immigrants once they arrived in the U.S. In 1952, Mort became the New York director of the JRO and remained in that position until he retired in 1966. In addition to personally rescuing two Jewish children and helping escort eleven more to Cuba, he had the satisfaction of knowing that his work with the JRO in raising and transferring funds and in aiding the DPs helped thousands of Jewish survivors of the Holocaust.

Knowing he had helped was gratifying. *But why did so many Jews have to die,* Mort kept asking himself and writing down his thoughts, *for the survivors to learn an irrefutable lesson?*

The State of Israel was founded on that lesson: If you want respect in this world, you have to fight for it, with your fists if necessary, especially if you're a Jew.

Fight back!' should be the commandment that every Jew memorizes, that every Jewish parent teaches his child — and provides the training to do it — second in importance only to the Shema prayer.

But is that what you taught Edward and Sarah and Andrew? his conscience needled him. *Did you enroll them in boxing classes or — what's it called? — judo? No, you did not. But I would if I had it to do over again. Do you even know yourself how to box, you who have studied so many subjects? No, I do not.*

But suppose, just suppose, that once the Jews in Europe realized the Nazis had targeted them for extermination — they collectively chose to stop being 'the people of the book' — passive and obedient — and started fighting back. Even earlier, would German Storm Troopers have beaten up Jews with impunity? Would the Nazis have been able to round them up and deport them to the death camps so efficiently? Would the Nazis have even tried to do so if they knew that every Jew carried a gun or a knife to defend their families? That every threatening knock on a Jewish door would result in a dead Nazi? (Yes, many Jews would have been executed for this defiance, thousands no doubt, but millions?) And wouldn't the Nazis have finally tired of losing their own men in these roundups?

No, that's impossible, he thought, crossing out what he had written. *It could never have happened. Where would they have gotten the guns — and, more important, the will to use them? Even the certainty of what the Nazis intended for them took a long time — much too long! — to finally sink into the ghetto's collective understanding. And until it did, who in the ghetto would trade the uncertain fate that awaited them in the boxcars for certain death — and the deaths of their loved ones — if they resisted?*

Getting guns wasn't the real problem. The young Jews of the Warsaw Ghetto Uprising got hold of them, and look how long they held off the Germans, Jews armed with just handguns and pistols. Pistols against automatic weapons and tanks! Yes, the Warsaw Ghetto Uprising was the way to go; not just individuals fighting back and facing certain death, but <u>organized</u> resistance. Like the partisans in the Eastern forests — with rifles and grenades. Some Jews did this. Why couldn't all?

But it would have taken an opposite mindset for Jews to arrive at this armed militance, a rejection of centuries of being law-abiding, of rejecting violence, of believing that God would protect them, despite *repeated evidence to the contrary. It would have taken thousands of rabbis preaching from thousands of pulpits that the Lord is <u>not</u> our shepherd, and we should not be sheep.*

It was Jewish cooperation with the Nazis that sickened Mort most — obedience to orders to assemble and get into the boxcars, obedience furthered by the criminally misguided actions of the *Judenrat*, the Jewish governing group for each ghetto, which fatuously believed that by cooperating with the Germans, even facilitating their roundups by providing lists of names, they could somehow mitigate the horror — and, some of them believed, save their own skins. All delusions.

The Zionists had the right idea all along, Mort concluded, *in advocating militant resistance to any anti-Semitic attack, in realizing that they could count on <u>no one but themselves</u> in a scrap or a war.*

The Israeli War of Independence threatened annihilation with five Arab countries attacking Israel at once. But despite the good wishes of President Truman, America would not sell Israel any of its superb P-51 fighter planes, which were just rusting in the desert. Ironically, it was German planes that the Israelis finally found — obsolete Messerschmitts from Czechoslovakia — and these, armed and repainted with Jewish stars, made a difference.

No, Mort was no pacifist. He donated money to Israel and hoped it would go for buying weapons. Jew-hating hadn't abated after the Holocaust, especially among Israel's Arab neighbors.

Armed self-defense will never make Israel loved, but it might make it respected. It might enable it to survive in a hostile world.

That, for Mort, was the bitter lesson of the Holocaust.

And yet, he thought, *I am the world's biggest hypocrite to advocate this militance — I, to whom a gun seems a foreign object; I, who am truly a 'man of the book', even if the books are secular.*

In fact, once Mort had retired from the JRO, he returned full-time to his first love: learning. He applied and was admitted to Columbia University and double-majored in history and English, with a specialization in Shakespeare. He became Columbia's oldest member of the Class of 1970 and graduated *magna cum laude*. Applauding in the audience were Deborah, Edward, Sarah and some of Edward's children. Shortly after, Mort converted his honors thesis on *Hamlet* into an article, which a Shakespeare journal accepted for publication. Ms. Ryan would have been proud.

When they became grandparents, Mort and Deborah visited Edward's family often, took some vacations with them, and regularly invited the family to New York. The couple doubted that there would be more grandchildren from Mort's other children.

Chava and Anna Stein

Mort's sisters stayed in the Detroit area. Chava continued giving violin lessons until she retired; Anna, having mastered English, worked for Jewish welfare agencies and the Jewish Community Center. The two sisters never married and remained devoted to each other.

They did have one bad scare, however. In the early morning hours of Sunday, July 23rd, 1967, a nearby neighborhood exploded into a full-scale riot. It began when Detroit police raided an after-hours club and arrested numerous patrons. An angry crowd formed, and bottles were thrown at the police. One story claimed that police had thrown a man down a flight of stairs. It was a hot night; people were on the street, and there had already been riots in other cities: L.A. in 1966 and Newark just a week earlier. With all that tinder, it didn't take much of a spark to ignite it. Crowds were soon breaking windows of nearby stores, looting them, and, worst of all, setting buildings on fire. It quickly grew beyond the capacity of the Detroit Police to contain it, as building after building, block after block, went up in flames.

On Sunday night, Mort called his sisters long distance, and Chava answered.

"I've been watching the riot on the *News*," Mort said excitedly. "Are you two all right? Is it near you? It looked pretty bad on the news, and the police don't seem able to stop it. The important thing is, are you and Anna safe?"

"We think so," Chava replied. "We're a few miles from where it started, on Twelfth Street and Clairmount. But you can smell the smoke when you step outside. Anna thought she could even see flames in the distance from the upper porch. And fire trucks are racing every which way. It's scary. Sarah and Miriam also called."

Smoke and fires — with a shudder Mort recalled the night in Frankfurt when he had stood on his hotel balcony and witnessed *Kristallnacht*.

"While we were outside," Chava continued, "we talked to Mr. Pettigrew, our downstairs neighbor. His family was outside too."

"What does he think?" Mort asked, vaguely remembering Pettigrew as an ideal tenant: a quiet family man who paid his rent on time, made no trouble and even mowed the lawn.

"He thought we should leave as soon as possible. He said it isn't safe for White people, especially two old ladies, to be in this neighborhood right now. He said he would stay at the house and guard it from looters or mischief-makers. He has a rifle, I think."

"That sounds like good advice," Mort said. "But where will you go? You're welcome to come here, of course, but that's an all-day trip."

"Well, Sarah and Miriam said we could stay with them for a few days, until things settle down. I'll stay with Miriam, and Anna with Sarah."

"That's fine. And the sooner the better."

"We'll leave tomorrow evening after they're home from work."

"In the meantime, don't go out unless it's absolutely necessary. And lock your doors."

"We already do. You don't need to tell us, Mort."

Mort realized that it was absurd to play the role of big brother. They had lived on their own for decades. But the hugeness of the disaster stunned him — and it was so close to their home.

The riot worsened on Monday, spreading to other neighborhoods. Numerous fires were burning all over the Near North Side. Governor Romney had called up and deployed the National Guard, but even that drastic move proved insufficient. The Guardsmen were inexperienced, young and predominantly White. In hostile Black neighborhoods with snipers on some rooftops, they were scared and trigger-happy. Patrolling dark streets, they shot at such things as a match being struck in an upstairs window. Many people were killed. As it turned out, not until President Johnson ordered in the 82nd Airborne — experienced and cool-headed troops — did the riot dissipate several days later.

But when Chava and Anna piled their suitcases into their car Monday evening, the riot was still growing. And to make matters worse, Chava, flustered about driving in these tense, smoky conditions, got lost.

To avoid a National Guard roadblock on Linwood Avenue, she turned onto a side street which dead-ended, then turned again to find another avenue west or north. Instead of heading west to Livernois, the sisters were now headed east. Avoiding another barricade and taking a side street, they ended up on Twelfth Street, where National Guard troops were stationed on every corner, and buildings were still burning.

"We're going the wrong way!" Anna cried. But before Chava could find a major street to turn on that wasn't barricaded, the sisters got an eyeful of the riot. Twelfth Street looked as if it had been bombed from above — numerous buildings had been gutted by fire; others were still burning or smoking; the ones still standing had all their windows shattered. On one rare remaining window, they saw in a white smear of paint the words 'SOUL BROTHER — PLEASE!'

Finally, they found a place to turn — Fenkell Avenue. They headed west towards Livernois, a fashionable shopping avenue which now also had burned-out buildings and patrolling troops. From there, they reached Eight Mile Road, a major east-west thoroughfare and the border of the city. They headed west for Sarah's apartment in Oak

Park and Miriam's in Southfield.

A few months after the experience, Chava and Anna sold their flat in the Dexter-Davison neighborhood for a pittance and moved to an apartment near Sarah. Detroit, meanwhile, had been shattered by the riot. Not even winning the World Series the following year would revive the city or stanch the hemorrhage of tax dollars caused by White flight to the suburbs. A city that had been thriving as recently as the 1950s was now impoverished and rapidly emptying.

Uncle Yitzhak

Uncle Yitzhak lived a long, full life with his wife Minna. When she died in her seventies, Yitzhak's natural ebullience dimmed, and it took him years to get over her death. Mort had always considered their marriage a mismatch: the outgoing, cheerful Yitzhak checked by the dour, pessimistic Minna. So, he was somewhat surprised by the depth and length of Yitzhak's grieving. Love is a mystery, he reflected. Being the patriarch of his own family helped Yitzhak cope with his loss. There were grandchildren and great-grandchildren to attend to.

Miriam Reubner

In 1943, Miriam divorced her second husband, David Riskin, and resumed her single name. With her evenings free and assisted by the law firm she worked for, she began taking law classes at Wayne University at night and passed the Bar in 1948. She became a successful attorney, practicing in Southfield, Michigan. Having some experience in the subject, she specialized in divorce law and was eventually earning more than her two ex-husbands. She never remarried.

Edward Stein

After the war, Edward returned to the R&D departments of General Electric. Just as he had predicted to his father back in high school, his professional interest turned to television, to developing ever more powerful transmitters and eventually their ability to broadcast in color (Mort later said that he'd never known anyone who was so certain of his future interests so early as Edward was). Edward inherited Mort's stability, his sense of responsibility and perhaps also his prosaic nature. Eventually, he became Vice President in charge of Television R&D. In the late 1950s, however, he shifted his focus back to his original interest in radar, helping to develop phased array radars on ships for detecting incoming missiles and planes. When Mort asked him about this change, Edward simply said that developing ever-better color TVs wasn't very exciting and that radar technology for the military posed more interesting problems — and sometimes provided testing cruises on Navy ships.

Edward married a local girl; they had four children (Jimmy, Jeffrey, Janice, and Jamey) and remained in Schenectady, New York. To live well in Schenectady, Edward said, you needed to do two things: learn to spell the city's name and learn to ski. He did both.

Sarah Stein

Sarah Stein played in the first violin section of The Detroit Symphony for many years, eventually rising to Concertmaster. When the Symphony hired Paul Paray as its music director in 1951, it entered its golden years. A specialist in French music, Paray was a fine conductor and made many highly regarded recordings with the DSO. He was aided by the superb acoustics of Orchestra Hall and by a recording company, Mercury Records, which had developed new recording techniques using 35mm tape. One can hear Sarah playing the solo violin parts in symphonies such as Brahms *First*. Once, when a soloist cancelled at the last minute, Sarah was asked to substitute. She didn't feel comfortable playing the scheduled *Tchaikovsky Violin Concerto*, so she substituted Mozart's *'Turkish' Concerto* and made a hit. She could feel the orchestra and the audience pulling for her as she played, and it was gratifying. Applauding enthusiastically in the front row were Chava and Anna Stein.

Remembering how much she enjoyed the string quartet she'd organized in Bloomington, Sarah organized another from DSO players. At first, she'd hoped to create an all-woman quartet; none such existed, and its marketing appeal would be considerable, she believed. But she couldn't pass up the first-chair cellist, a young man who wanted very much to join them. Rejecting such prosaic names as 'The Detroit Quartet', the group came up with 'The Euphony Quartet' and met regularly to rehearse and develop a repertoire, beginning, of course, with Beethoven. In a few years, they had added quartets by Haydn, Mozart, and Schubert. Then, the cellist suggested something daring — why not add the quartets of Bartok, which were hardly known and almost never performed in the U.S.? That would give them the inside track on those works and spice up their concerts. By now, the early Fifties, they felt ready to give concerts and began with one at Wayne University. It went well and had an unforeseen benefit: the music director of WJR, a major Detroit radio station, was in the audience and liked what he'd heard. He had contacts with Columbia Records and suggested an audition. The group discussed it among themselves but decided they needed more concerts and more works before they were ready to record. No further offers came their way.

The state of the DSO declined in the 1960s for several reasons. First, in the mid-1950s, Detroit built a grand new hall, Ford Auditorium, to replace the more compact and rundown Orchestra Hall and other unsatisfactory venues. Ford Auditorium was an improvement in every way but one — it had terrible acoustics. Paul Paray retired, and the DSO hired the Swedish conductor, Sixten Ehrling. He was a thoroughly competent professional but lacked Paray's charm and spark. Possibly both of these factors caused Mercury Records to let its contract with the DSO lapse. The symphony made no new recordings in the Ehrling years. Sarah stayed with the symphony into the Sixties and retired in 1968.

When Sarah first started with the DSO in 1944, apartments were scarce in Detroit. In these war years, the city was teeming with migrants who had flocked there for the high-paying defense jobs, forcing Sarah to return to Miriam's flat. When she developed a serious relationship with another member of the symphony, they lived together at the flat. With Andrew and David gone, there was plenty of room, but tensions arose between Miriam and the couple. Eventually, Sarah and her mate found an apartment of their own, and Miriam sold the flat and moved to an apartment in Southfield.

Andrew Stein

Andy played for the Buffalo Bisons for only a few weeks before he was drafted. Near the end of basic training, he had a remarkable stroke of luck. On leave in Detroit, he ran into his former drama teacher, who was now an officer in Army Public Relations. Captain Burton was part of the team that handled USO Shows in Europe. He remembered Andy's participation in the school plays and encouraged him to apply for his unit. Perhaps he could even pull some strings and get Andy assigned there. He did.

Andy's job was to scout locations for USO programs in liberated territory, but not too far behind the front lines. The idea was that the frontline troops were the guys who needed entertaining most, not the rear echelon softies. Andy was given the rank of sergeant, a jeep and a driver. He was to find places for the shows — typically the basements of cafés — since there was no time to construct stages during the rapid advances of summer and fall, 1944. He was also to find billets for the performers and the accompanying crew. Since few hotels survived the onslaught, he placed them in private homes and ignored the objections of the owners. The job was easy, but there was just enough proximity to danger to give it a tang of excitement. Once, in late fall, his driver had taken a wrong turn, and they found themselves headed directly toward two

German tanks in the distance. One fired at Andy's jeep, but the shell exploded twenty yards in front of it. Simultaneously, his driver jammed on the brakes, wheeled around and was hightailing it out of there when a second shell exploded where they had been. *Close call*, Andy thought. *Well, now I've been in combat.*

The job had special perks. Often, the young women performers were scared to be so close to the front where not only the booms but the vibrations of American artillery could be heard and felt. (The male performers were scared too, but they didn't matter). Sergeant Stein took it upon himself to comfort these girls. He also provided alcohol-drenched parties in his room after the shows. His unit slept warm, seldom alone, and had plenty to eat, even if it was Army food. When no USO girls were available, there were plenty of hungry Frauen and Fräuleins in 1945 who were most obliging for the K-ration meals Andy could provide.

After the war, Andy returned to the Bisons and for the next few years knocked around in the Minor Leagues, playing AA and AAA ball. His batting was fairly good — .260-.270 usually — but not good enough to overcome the 'good field, no hit' label he was stuck with and not good enough to get that all-important call to get his tail to Briggs Stadium (or wherever) pronto. Once again, he made the best of a bad situation and was adept at finding girls in the towns his current team played in.

One incident always stayed with Andy. During a game with the Toledo Mudhens, he thought he recognized the large fellow coming to bat for Toledo. He looked like Al Jenkins from their tryouts with the Tigers in '43. When he hit a long double and was standing on second, it *was*

Al. Andy waved at him from third base, but Al didn't respond, concentrating on taking a big lead. The next batter hit a long single to right field, and Al took off. Rounding third, he intentionally tromped down hard on Andy's foot with his spikes. After the game, Andy's teammates never understood why he didn't go after Jenkins.

Finally, in 1949, Andy got fed up with the shabby hotels, mediocre meals, and lack of prospects and decided to quit the game. With financial help from his mother — a loan, she emphasized, knowing him — he took a bus to Florida with his belongings stuffed into two suitcases. No more Buffalo cold. Before Miriam's money ran out, he settled into a furnished apartment in Lakeland (not coincidentally where the Tigers held Spring Training) and took a course in real estate at the junior college there.

He did well in real estate, aided by his good looks, glib tongue and façade of self-assurance. He was also aided immeasurably by the post-war baby boom. Helped by the G.I. Bill and FHA loans, growing families in the Fifties were looking for houses. The sales seemed almost to fall into Andy's lap, and developers were building new suburbs and shopping centers around Lakeland as soon as they could get the funding.

For a time, Andy considered settling down. He had a steady girl who said she loved him and wanted to get married. But he knew he was just not cut out for monogamy. His easy successes with women, going back to his high school days, had spoiled him and made fidelity to one woman seem boring. And he knew he would hate lying and making excuses about where he had been, and why he hadn't called. He knew he wouldn't change and that married life would be a disaster. So, he decided to be honest for once and just tell her it was no-go.

After that, he remained just as he was, the promiscuous bachelor, always on the prowl for a bored housewife (there were many) in the houses he had sold. He had only to drive up a week or two after the sale (after hubby had left for work, of course), ask in his most sincere agent's voice if everything was okay with the house, to be invited in. After that, he had only one rule: they must come to his place, a modest ranch house with a few palm trees in front. He wanted no confrontations with irate husbands who had handled weapons in World War II or Korea. And so he passed his years. He repaid his mother but seldom visited her. He saw nothing of Mort, David, Edward or Sarah. In the spring, he never missed a Tigers game in Lakeland.

David Riskin

After Miriam divorced him, David's life went steadily downhill. He lost his gas stations from nonpayment of rent. Desperate, he tried to hook up again with his old Purple Gang cronies. But those not already dead (usually murdered) were in jail. For a time, he became a bagman in the numbers racket in Detroit, but he found the returns too small for his ambitions. When heroin became available in large amounts after World War II, he thought of it as the alcohol once banned by Prohibition, providing a socially harmless high. In the 1950s he became a distributor.

In 1959, David's body was discovered in an alley near the Detroit Race Course in Livonia. The murder went unsolved but was assumed to be a gangland killing for unpaid debts. It made page five of the *Detroit News*. After Mort learned of it from Miriam, he was the only one of his family to attend the funeral.

Schmuel Stein

July 14, 1947
Mr. Morton Stein
423 E. 61st Street
New York, New York

Re: Schmuel Stein

Dear Mr. Stein:

In regard to your inquiry about your father, Schmuel Stein, Yad Vashem *has definite proof that he was murdered by the Nazis, along with nearly all the Jews of Motal, Belarus, on or about August 2, 1941. We are deeply sorry to inform you of this sad fact.*

There were, however, rather remarkable circumstances surrounding the death, which we would like to share with you, believing that you would like to know them.

In the first place, not all the Jews of Motal were murdered by the Einsatzgruppe. *One man, Abraham Rabinovitz, miraculously escaped. Literally, he pushed the dead bodies off of him and, after dark, crawled away.*

Later, he joined a Partisan group and actually survived the war. He provided an eyewitness account of how the Nazis marched all the Jews of Motal — men, women, and children — to a field outside of town, made them dig their burying ditch, and then shot them all down into the ditch.

Mr. Rabinowitz, however, had a remarkable addendum to this sadly familiar story: As the Jews were lined up at the edge of the ditch, one old Jew, whom Mr. Rabinowitz identified as Schmuel Stein, your father, dropped his pants, turned his backside to the Nazis and shouted 'Kush mein tuchus!' *('Kiss my ass!' in English), while he pointed to his backside. Outraged, the Nazis turned all their guns on Mr. Stein and literally blew him apart. But all the other Jews of Motal had this last defiance of the Nazis ringing in their ears.*

We thought you would like to know.

Sincerely,
Avram Leitner
Assistant for Russian territories
Yad Vashem

End

About the Author

Milton Cohen is Professor Emeritus of Literary Studies at The University of Texas at Dallas, where he inflicted his literary opinions on students from 1980 to 2020. Cohen has published seven scholarly books quietly moldering on the shelves of university libraries: two on E. E. Cummings, one on modernist groups before World War I, one on Hemingway's *in our time*, and three studying how writers and politics intersected in the 1930s and beyond.

Since retiring, Cohen has turned his hand to writing fiction. Besides *The Steins*, he has published the war novel, *Silverman, the Soldier* (Pocol Press, 2023). Previously, he published *American Glimpses*, a book of three original plays set in the 1930s and 1940s (KDP Press, 2021). One of these plays, *The Five Knob Radio*, won a playwriting competition and was performed by the Curtain Players of Columbus, Ohio (*very* far off-Broadway).

Besides writing, which is more an obsession than a hobby, Cohen enjoys playing softball, studying astronomy, reading history, watching old movies, and listening to classical music and swing jazz, as well as being an obsolete relic to his three children and two grandchildren. He is presently living in Richardson, Texas with his wife and best writing critic, Florence Chasey-Cohen.

www.blossomspringpublishing.com